Infidels & Insurgents

Dome City Investigations
Book 2

Milo James Fowler

Copyright © 2024 by Milo James Fowler

All rights reserved.

This book or any portion of it may not be reproduced or used in any manner whatsoever without the express written permission of the author—except for brief quotations in glowing, 4.5-star reviews. (Your reward will await you in Heaven.) The story contained within this book is a work of fiction. All material is either the product of the author's overactive imagination or is used in a fictitious manner. Any resemblance to actual persons (living or dead) or to actual events is entirely coincidental—and worthy of further investigation.

For Sara

Dome City Investigations:

Dust Freaks & Demigods

Infidels & Insurgents

Angels & Androids

I

I'm scared.

That's the only explanation for this. Pulse racing, razor-sharp pains stabbing at my abdomen—not to mention the perspiration prickling across my brow. I don't think I'm feverish or suffering a panic attack. There's no reason for either.

I'm standing in the hallway outside a door I've passed through countless times over the course of my life, but now I'm frozen in place. My legs have turned to stone, refusing to budge. My breathing is shallow.

I've gone toe to toe with drunk and disorderly curfew violators. Underworld kingpins and their ilk. A freakish AI intent on total domination. You'd think I could handle a measly dinner party.

Except this one promises to be anything but meager. Knowing my parents, they've rolled out the red carpet to welcome their guests, and as soon as I allow this door to read my neural implant and slide open, I'll have to face them all. My parents, Dr. Victor and Abigail Chen, as well as my biological parents, Luther and Daiyna.

No idea if they have last names. I should know that, right? A daughter should know, even if she's been estranged from her birth parents her entire life. Maybe that's the wrong word. *Estranged* implies that I used to know them, but we've drifted apart over the years, becoming strangers to one another. The problem is I've never known them. I met them for the first time just last year, and we've talked maybe half a dozen times since then. Mostly in passing, never for very long, due to my hectic work schedule.

Not like this: an evening devoted to nothing but conversation.

That door is going to slide open eventually. It's inevitable, no matter how long I stare at it. My two sets of parents will turn to look at me, their conversation interrupted, and I'll be standing there half an hour late, with a bottle of sparkling apple cider from *Paine Orchards* in one hand and no idea what to do with the other.

Investigator Sera Chen in a dress and heels instead of my tactical suit, so far out of my element it's not even funny. Dressing up my avatar this way is one thing; in a VR StoryLine, I can be somebody else. But this isn't me. I don't feel like myself at all.

Why should I be afraid of my parents meeting my birth parents? My parents love me and accept me for who I am. They always have. And my birth parents seem...friendly enough. If it wasn't for the invisible wall I've built between us, I'm sure they would be downright amiable. But I haven't made it easy for them. I've been too busy, my job too important to make space for social gatherings.

Tonight's about changing that, about us getting to know each other better.

Maybe that's what I'm most nervous about: that these larger-than-life superheroes who somehow managed to survive outside the Domes for *decades* might have an overblown idea of what I'm supposed to be like. Their biological daughter, created from their DNA without their permission. Carried across the North American Wastes in an incubation chamber. Born safely inside the blue-tinted plexicon walls of the Domes. Will they expect me to be like them?

How disappointed will they be when they find out I'm not?

For some reason I can't explain, I want them all to get along well. My two mothers, my two fathers. But I'm worried they won't. My dad's a doctor. He believes in science and rational explanations for things. My birth father is religious. He follows the Way, an ancient belief system that, until recently, was outlawed in the Ten Domes. He also believes in *spirits of the earth*, which I really hope doesn't come up in conversation but have a feeling it just might. Because things won't be awkward enough, otherwise. As for my mothers, Mrs. Chen is an educator and a woman of peace while Daiyna is...not so much. I've seen her in action, and she's a real force to be reckoned with.

Worst-case scenario? This dinner party will be such a fantastic disaster that we'll never have to do anything like it again.

On second thought, maybe that's best-case.

The cognitive dissonance is killing me. I want tonight to be a success as much as I want it to be a failure. I want to get to know my birth parents, and I wish I'd never met them. I know things will never go back to the way they were, yet I want them to.

Life was simpler when I didn't know Daiyna and Luther

existed.

I don't look much like my mom and dad, but they're Mom and Dad. I share a connection with them that defies DNA. Now when I look in the mirror, I see Luther's piercing eyes and Daiyna's olive skin. And every time I turn off my augments and allow my weird night-vision ability to assert itself, I remember that Daiyna has the same gift. But the telepathy is all mine. I never asked for these strange abilities, yet they make my job a hell of a lot easier. And it's thanks to my birth parents that I have them.

I'd rather be on a case right now. Anything to avoid going through that door. And, at the same time, I want to see them on the other side. Smiling. Getting along. Happy to see me dressed up like Vivian Andromeda from my favorite Future Noir StoryLine. Telling me I look nice.

I think I just might puke.

Cursing under my breath instead, I allow the cube's door sensors to read my neuro and slide open, revealing the warm, inviting interior of the spacious apartment.

"Sera!" my parents cheer in unison, beaming at me.

They're standing in the middle of the living room on the sandy-colored area rug with ancient geometric designs around the edges. Egyptian, maybe? They've each got a wine glass in hand, and they're both dressed up. Dad's wearing one of his navy wool suits without a tie, and Mom's gown is even fancier than mine. The shimmery black matches her shoulder-length hair, a striking contrast to her porcelain complexion. Dad's hair is a similar shade except for at the temples, where he's gone a bit grey.

Facing them, each with a matching wine glass, are Daiyna and Luther. Either they didn't get the message on dress code, or this is the best they could do. He's in baggy trousers and a cable knit sweater, both in earth tones, and she's wearing something similar but more form-fitting. If they had boots on instead of sandals, they'd look like silver-haired paramilitary operatives. Not that they're ragged or unkempt. They're well put together in appearance. Just not dressed for a Dome 1 dinner party.

And I find myself instantly envying their disregard for the upper caste's unyielding conventions.

"I'm sorry we started without you," Mom apologizes, reaching for the bottle in my grasp with her free hand and admiring the flowing script on the label. "Oh, is this from Erik's farm?"

"Sorry I'm late," I mutter, averting my eyes from Daiyna and Luther's gaze.

They're smiling at me, too, just not as broadly. Nobody smiles like the Chens when their daughter shows up, tardiness be damned.

"Such a lovely dress. Is it new?" Mom always likes me in something floral, so I wore red satin with yellow orchids. One of the few colorful things I own.

"I've had it a while." But never worn it. Probably would have at Chancellor Hawthorne's *Revelation Banquet* for the Twenty, had the celebration not been indefinitely postponed due to an attempted coup and subsequent change in leadership.

"Didn't realize Paine Farms had expanded into vineyards." Dad takes the bottle from Mom and studies the label with an arched eyebrow.

"I believe they have." Luther's voice is commanding but calm. A leader with an aura of quiet confidence. "Samson and Erik have been doing quite a bit of expanding as of late. But if I'm not mistaken, that would be sparkling cider from their orchards. Another recent addition."

"So it is." Dad nods with a smile and holds up the bottle. "Shall we give it a taste test?"

Mom leans toward me. "I'll get you a glass."

"Thanks." They know I avoid alcohol when I'm on call, and they don't make a big deal of it. I notice that Daiyna hasn't touched her wine. Everyone else's glasses are half-empty.

Then I notice something else: She looks just as uncomfortable as I am right now.

Mom heads to the kitchen, and we naturally gravitate in that direction, following as if we're all somehow tethered to each other.

The cube is a quad—four times the size of mine. Registered married couples are assigned doubles, but since the Chens are members of one of the higher castes, and due to their careers in medicine and education, they're afforded a larger living space. Five people in here doesn't feel crowded at all. Helps that the design is very open-concept and free-flowing with the main space including a kitchen, living room, and dining room. Two bedrooms lie on the opposite side of the living room's far wall, and the restroom is located out of sight on the other side of the kitchen. Like my cube, a floor-to-ceiling windowall looks out on the domescrapers and other mirrored-glass buildings of Dome 1, their roof gardens overflowing with lush greenery. During the day, streams of aerocars would be gliding by in aerial traffic lanes, but at this time of night, after curfew, everyone's home, and all that soars through the Dome's air space are the intermittent red and blue lights of curfew enforcers' pilots making their rounds.

I'm sure Daiyna and Luther have been granted a special pass to travel anywhere they need to after dark, what with them being pals of Interim Chancellor James Bishop and all. After the horrors they endured together, it's the least he could do.

"So glad we're finally able to get together like this." Mom rounds the butcher block kitchen island and reaches for fresh wine glasses from the under-cabinet rack holding half a dozen upside-down. "I'm afraid I've been pestering Sera about it for months now." She glances back at me with an apologetic half-smile. "But we know how incredibly busy you've been. Particularly after that fiasco with the rogue artificial intelligence and all the damage done to your building."

Unlike Chancellor Persephone Hawthorne, her successor has no problem with telling Eurasia's citizens the ugly truth. While Hawthorne would have explained away the Prometheus incident as a series of unfortunate, unrelated accidents, James Bishop came on the Linkstream right away and explained exactly what happened. That a powerful AI sought to destroy the Ten Domes' way of life, that it succeeded in blowing up our police headquarters and causing a staggering amount of damage across Dome 1, but that it had been contained and was no longer a threat to public safety.

Which remains to be seen, of course. Last I knew, the Interim Chancellor's daughter—Commander Mara Bishop, who oversees all law enforcement activities in the Domes— had the AI imprisoned on an antique phone with a whole lot of memory, severed from any contact with the Link. Supposedly, we can breathe easier now, knowing Prometheus won't be able to mindjack any more victims and make them do its dirty work.

But I'd feel much better if it was completely destroyed.

"How soon until you're able to move back into HQ?" Dad asks, popping open the bottle and pouring the golden cider as Mom sets out the glasses, one at a time. Everything they do seems effortlessly synchronized, as if they're telepathically linked. Like dance partners for life who know each other as well as they know themselves. They've always been this way.

For some reason, being around them tends to calm me down. My pulse evens out. Those invisible knives stop jabbing my stomach. I think maybe, just maybe, tonight's going to be alright.

"Another month, probably." I take the glass Mom offers to me, and I watch the innumerable bubbles race each other up to the surface. "Until then, we're still crammed onto the third floor of Hawthorne Tower."

Daiyna exchanges her untouched wine for cider and takes a swig. She licks her lips and nods. Then she looks straight at me. "What am I thinking right now?"

Not sure how to respond to that. "It's good?"

"It is that, definitely." She smirks at the cider in her glass. Then she taps her temple. "Are you on or off?"

"Well, I'm on-call, so..." I shrug. Have to stay online so the boss-man can order me around at the drop of a hat. But then I realize what she's really asking. "I'm not reading your mind, if that's what you're worried about." I try to laugh it off, but I fail miserably and nearly choke. Because she's dead serious.

"Good." She looks away as she takes another drink.

Not hard to imagine: people don't like being around a telepath. It's the same at work. Avoiding me is a game everybody can play, and they're pretty good at it. But contrary to public opinion, I don't enjoy reading their thoughts. I save it for interrogations that are heading nowhere and emergency situations. That's it. Anything else just feels...wrong.

Have I ever peeked into my parents' minds? Never. I wouldn't even consider invading their most private space. And besides, I don't want to know what they're thinking. I want them to tell me. They know what I'm capable of, and they've never treated me weird because of it. They accept me as I am.

But this woman? My biological mother? It's her damn fault I have this bizarre ability, and she's the one giving me flak about it?

Calming down now. She just asked me a simple question. A fair question. One I might have asked myself, if I was standing in her sandals.

Dad clears his throat in the quiet awkwardness, interrupted only by the melodic background sounds of ancient woodwinds emanating from his antique stereo system, and samples his cider. "Ah yes, crisp and sweet. Very nice. My compliments to Paine Orchards." He turns toward Luther. "Do you see your friends Samson and Shechara often these days?"

"Not as much as I'd like, I'm afraid. The work in Dome 6 consumes most of our time." Luther glances at Daiyna. Is that a look of concern that passes through his clear-blue eyes? "We'll reconnect again at some point, I'm sure."

"After all that you went through, surviving the Wastes..." Dad shakes his head mutely. "You must feel as close as family. Closer, perhaps."

Luther nods with another glance at Daiyna. She's keeping her eyes on her glass. "Indeed we do. Sometimes it's hard to believe we're here. Safe inside the Domes. Protected from the outside world, which was all we knew for so many long years. It's strange not to see each other every day, after living elbow to elbow. Something you're dealing with now in your temporary offices, I'm sure." He gives me an understanding look. "Difficult to imagine a single floor with room enough for all of the lawkeeping that goes on across the Domes."

"We're packed in there pretty tight," I admit. "But thankfully I don't spend much time at HQ. My partner and I are usually out and about, investigating and stuff." So very eloquent. He must be proud.

"How is Dunn?" Mom asks. "He was injured badly, you said. Something to do with rampaging robots?"

Killbots, programmed by Prometheus. Not a fond memory.

"He's doing better. Both of the new arms are state-of-the-art prosthetics." Not sure what else to say about that. So I take a sip of cider. "This is good." I glance at Daiyna. She almost smiles at me but then looks away again. "Hope dinner didn't get cold because of me."

"Piping hot, actually." Dad gestures for us to take our seats at the rectangular table made of dark synthetic wood. "Hope you're hungry. We've prepared a veritable feast. No protein packs tonight. It's all the real deal, shipped fresh from our friends in Dome 9."

Only the best for the upper castes. Instead of synthesized

proteins in a variety of disguises, which is what everybody else eats in the Domes—even most of the farmers themselves—we're having actual foodstuffs. Vegetables. Noodles. Dumplings. Egg rolls.

"The orange chicken's a substitute, of course," Mom apologizes.

"Yes, until we can get those critters out of cryo in Futuro Tower, all of our meat will continue to be flavored tofu, I'm afraid." Dad chuckles.

Luther waits for Daiyna to choose her seat before he pulls out a chair beside her. "When will that be, do you think?" he asks with a curious frown. "I know there has been talk of constructing an eleventh Dome as a wildlife sanctuary. But after the Prometheus event, I'm sure those plans have been placed on the back burner, so to speak."

Dad nods grimly. "But it will happen. Only a matter of time. We'll crack open Wong's Ark and rescue all of those embryos, then bring them to term safely within the plexicon walls of Eurasia. Can you imagine? Seeing an elephant or a zebra in person?"

"Or even a chicken." Mom grins as she retrieves the first steaming platter from the oven.

"Why not wait until Wong's clones figure out how to terraform the planet?" Daiyna says. "Keep the embryos in cold storage until then. Let the animals live outside where they belong, once it's a suitable environment."

"That would be the ideal scenario, of course." Dad nods, assisting Mom without being asked to do so. "And if we're unable to build Dome 11 in our lifetime, that may be what our descendants decide to do. Keep the animals in cryo on the shores of North Africa, and wait for those clones in

Futuro Tower to discover the key to a better future."

"A new earth," Luther murmurs, half to himself. Daiyna looks at him and takes his hand. They've got their own version of unspoken communication, too. Maybe it's just a side effect of being married to someone for a long while.

"Have you seen Erik lately?" Daiyna asks me as I sit down.

Two for two. Is she going out of her way to make me feel uncomfortable? In my own childhood home? But I play it cool, keep things conversational. Because that's what we're going for here.

"He's busy on the farm. Growing apples." I raise my glass as *Exhibit A*. Pause for laughter, or even a chuckle. None. So I forge ahead, "He went through a lot. I figure he needs time to figure things out. Find himself again."

Daiyna stares at me without expression. "Being a monster's puppet will do that."

Spoken as if she knows what it was like for him. Or knows someone who went through something similar out in the Wastes. A chilling thought.

Mom and Dad have set out all the food, and the mingling aromas are incredible. I know they like to cook, but they've really outdone themselves tonight.

"Let's dig in," they say in unison and then laugh self-deprecatingly at the impromptu synchronicity. They take their seats at opposite ends of the table, bowing slightly to each other as they do so.

Luther holds up his hand, and in the warm light of the crystal chandelier, his scarred fingers are clear to see. The tips look like they were cut open once upon a time and stitched back together minus the fingernails, then left to heal badly on their own.

"If I may..." He smiles at each of us in turn. "...say grace?"
Three for three. Time to embrace the awkwardness.

2

"Certainly," Dad says, kind amusement shining in his eyes. He and Mom share a brief, knowing look before bowing their heads.

Luther clears his throat quietly and closes his eyes. He and Daiyna are still holding hands, but they don't expect the rest of us to. Thoughtful of them. "Heavenly Father, we thank you for the hospitality of our dear friends the Chens, and we praise you for this opportunity to share a meal together. Bless them for the hard work that went into preparing such a delicious feast for us, and bless our time of fellowship together. May we enjoy good food and good conversation, learning more about each other in the process. And may we be ever mindful of the needs of others, all across the Ten Domes. In the name of your precious Son, Jesus Christ our Savior, we pray. Amen."

Daiyna echoes the *amen* in a low tone. My parents and I just glance at each other, glad it's over. They're smiling, of course, friendly and accepting as ever. I have no idea what my face is doing.

"Have you always been followers of the Way?" Dad sounds genuinely curious as he passes the bowl of noodles.

"Ever since the bunker," Luther replies. "Speaking for

myself, of course." He glances at Daiyna. "Sectors 50 and 51 were very different."

She grunts in acknowledgement. There's a fierceness in her eyes I've seen before, in the heat of battle. We were inside Futuro Tower at the time, fighting Dr. Wong's trigger-happy scientist-clones, and she was a real warrior-woman. But I guess I kind of assumed she'd be able to set that demeanor aside at the dinner table.

"I can't imagine living underground for so many years, in seclusion like that." Mom frowns sympathetically as she passes the platter of spring rolls. "Only to be released onto the surface too early..."

Luther shakes his head. "The timing was right. It was far from easy, I assure you, but it was right. The Lord moves in mysterious ways, His wonders to perform. And the miracles He worked in us and among us made it possible for us to do His will." He arches an eyebrow at Dad. "Are you a man of faith, Victor?"

"I'm a man of science."

"You believe the two to be mutually exclusive?"

Oh boy. Here we go. Cue the cringe.

"Not necessarily. But in my experience, there are logical, rational explanations available to us without the need to reach for a higher power." Dad pauses, shrugging one shoulder. "And, of course, we have lived most of our lives in a society where such religions and cults were outlawed, due to what has been perceived as their divisive nature. Only recently have these belief systems been allowed to flourish once again."

Luther nods pensively. Then he offers half a smile. "Perhaps such is the case here, in Dome 1. But in Dome 6, we have encountered a vibrant community of believers, many of whom never forsook their faith, even when the government strictly outlawed it for the majority of their lives."

"Is that so?" Dad looks intrigued. "Do you enjoy the work you're doing there? Living among the—"

"*Sicks*?" Daiyna just about spits the word out. "Kind of tough to enjoy seeing people suffer every day, but we do what we can to help them." She hasn't touched her meal. "Resources are limited. Not something you're used to around here, I'm sure."

Dad blinks, his smile faltering. "I was not aware..."

"We make do." Luther tries to keep things upbeat, glancing at his wife. "We get by. The people we serve suffer from chronic mental illnesses and physical disabilities that require consistent treatment. Prayer helps." He pauses. "It helps them to know that we care. And it helps us make it through the difficult days, knowing we are not alone."

Daiyna nods silently, her eyes on her plate.

Dad watches her for a moment. "Chancellor Bishop has expressed an interest in reintegrating the disabled across the Domes. Do you think that is a reasonable goal?"

"Allow them out of the ghetto, you mean?" Daiyna looks him in the eye. "Are you sure anybody wants to see them? People disfigured by the Plague, wearing prosthetic limbs. Better to keep them all hidden away in Dome 6, don't you think? That way the upper castes can pretend they don't exist."

Should I start choking? Anything to interrupt the uneasy silence that has descended on the table, courtesy of my biological mother.

But then Mom reaches over and places her hand on

Daiyna's arm. "You're right. It has been this way for too long, and we have no excuse for our complacency. Things must change. And I have a feeling they will, with people like you working to make a difference, and Chancellor Bishop determined to undo the norms his predecessors put into place." She squeezes gently. "Tell us how we can help you."

For a moment, Daiyna just sits there, stunned. But then the fierceness melts in her eyes, replaced by eagerness, and she leans forward, speaking quickly as if Mom is the only other person at the table. "Medical equipment. Robodocs. Parts for repairs—upgrades. We're making do with outdated tech, so anything you can spare would be greatly appreciated. Basic medicine—antibiotics and antivirals, pain meds, mood stabilizers, you name it." She pauses to take a breath, glancing at Dad to find him nodding attentively. "You're welcome to visit anytime, to see for yourself what our needs are. As a doctor, you'd know better than most."

"Of course," he says without hesitation. "Let me check my schedule, and I will see what I can do." His eyes glaze over as he focuses on what his ocular lenses are showing him. *Check my schedule* wasn't a delay tactic. He's checking it at this very moment. "With MedTech offline at police headquarters, we've had to work double shifts at the MedCenter..."

Mom taps him lightly on the arm. "And there are always good excuses to keep us from doing the right thing. But not tonight."

His eyes clear, and he smiles at her. "No, not tonight." Then, to Daiyna, "I can take the train over tomorrow afternoon. Would around two work for you?"

Daiyna glances at Luther, and for the first time this evening, she's smiling. "That would be great. Thank you."

Then, as a quick afterthought, "I hope you don't think this is the only reason we came over. I don't mean to be rude." She glances at me. "It's just that our work can be all-consuming, and seeing how everyone in Dome 1 has so much..."

"An embarrassment of riches," I mutter.

She nods, holding my gaze. "Something like that."

"It's difficult not to make the work all there is, particularly when it is so important," Mom agrees. "But we need to take care of ourselves, so we can continue to take care of others. Which is why we must get enough rest. And we must eat." She withdraws her hand from Daiyna and gestures at her plate. "Please. Try something, won't you?"

"Right." Daiyna almost laughs as she digs in. Her shoulders have relaxed considerably, and I realize that mine have, too.

I should have realized why she was being so stand-offish. It had nothing to do with me. It had everything to do with visiting two members of the upper caste after spending the past months living among untouchables. The differences between Domes 1 and 6 are almost as stark as those separating Domes 1 and 10. Luxury living versus manual labor. Haves versus have-nots—in the extreme.

It wasn't that Daiyna felt uncomfortable meeting her biological daughter's parents. I didn't enter into the equation at all. This was just about getting the medical resources she and Luther need from a respected doctor—and his wife, who happens to be known for her philanthropic work. Daiyna didn't know what to expect. Would the Chens be shallow and frivolous like so many other rich people? Or could they open their hearts to the needy?

But the unnecessary rudeness was a weird way for her to

go about getting what she wanted from them. Which makes me think there might be more to it. Maybe I do make her uncomfortable, in the same way that mentioning her bunker in Sector 50 just about made her flinch. She doesn't like remembering the atrocities from her past, the things that were done to her. My presence makes that past—all that she's tried her best to forget—unavoidably real.

Would she rather not get to know me? If so, can I blame her? It's not like I've gone out of my way to meet any of my own offspring. The last thing I want to think about is those government doctors extracting my eggs after I reached puberty.

Of the one thousand children created from the Twenty's DNA, how many of them are even related to me? Their genes were spliced with those of their adoptive parents, mixed and matched to strengthen the gene pool of Eurasia's future generations. Can I really say with certainty that any of them are my direct descendants?

Does it matter?

I had no say in their creation. I have no attachment to any of them. In the same way, Daiyna had no choice about bringing me or any of my nine siblings into the world. It was done to her, without her permission. Not a reality anybody would want to be faced with. Yet it's something we share. Common ground. If we wanted to, if we were just masochistic enough, I bet we could really bond over it.

Luther nods sincere thanks to Mom and Dad, and then he looks at me. "As an investigator, you must travel across the Domes more than most. For the rest of us, it's natural to become fairly myopic, only able to see what is right in front of us. We seldom have any reason to leave whatever Dome we call home—or wherever we've been assigned. But you see what we have in common, and what has the potential to divide us. What, in your mind, is the single greatest threat against the precarious balance of these self-sustaining biospheres we've created for ourselves?"

Nothing like light dinner conversation to brighten the mood. Well, I'm up for the challenge. Try this on for size, Luther old chap:

"Someone told me once that the Domes have become a reflection of the United World, back in its heyday. They lived large while the Sectors of North America produced everything they needed. Now Dome 1 is that central authority, the hub of the wheel. The richest, the most powerful. The other nine Domes slave away to keep the citizens of Dome 1 living as comfortably as possible." Absently, I twirl my noodles around the bottom of my bowl with chopsticks. "What do I see, traveling out to the perimeter? People are discontent. They want to believe that Bishop will make things better, but they don't trust the Governors to upend the status-quo. The Patriots' concerns are becoming more mainstream, their rhetoric more insidious. And after the Prometheus incident, people are scared that our LawKeepers can't protect them from new threats—like getting mindjacked by a sentient AI."

Luther looks impressed, pleased even, by my response. Do I care? Is that what my nerves are all about? I want Luther and Daiyna to *like* me? What am I, a pathetic child?

"I still can't believe he's meeting with those terrorists." Mom shakes her head. "Chancellor Bishop. What is he thinking?"

"He hopes to avoid the mistakes of the past," Dad replies.

"What's that saying? Those who ignore history are doomed to repeat it? Well, we have been ignoring our history for decades here in the Domes. The credo itself: *We live only now, never looking back. For the common good.* It is incredibly shortsighted."

"The so-called Patriots have their own saying," I offer. "*The sun shines on Dome 1 while clouds cover everyone else.*"

Daiyna and Luther glance at each other. "We hear that one often," she says. "But not from wanna-be terrorists. Just your average citizens living outside the garden."

Dad scoffs, wiping his mouth on a napkin. "They seem to think Dome 1 is this majestic, opulent city favored by the Chancellor while those in the other Domes live only to serve. To provide for Eurasia's every need: agriculture, manufacturing, technology, oxygen generation, recycling, and waste management, to name a few. But it doesn't matter where you live or what your job assignment is. Our society would cease to function if anyone gave up his or her responsibilities. And that includes the work we're doing right here." He jabs the tabletop with his index finger. "Advancements in medicine, cybernetics—technology that bridges the gap between human and machine intelligence. It's all happening every day in Dome 1. We're building the future! And for visionaries to do the necessary work of planning for that future, we must of course have our basic needs met." He shrugs. "That's really all there is to it."

"Every Dome is vital," Mom agrees, looking at each of us seated around her. "As is every citizen."

Can't argue with that.

"And that population is growing." Luther glances at Dad and then me. "Once the Thousand reach an age when they are able to procreate, will that not put undue stress on the balance we strive so hard to maintain? Can the Domes continue to function with a sharp increase in mouths to feed?"

Mom nods slowly, her smile intact but dimmer than before. "Yes. There will be safeguards in place, of course, but projections indicate no major breaks in our current equilibrium. That is, as long as the Thousand limit themselves to one child per couple."

"Population control." Daiyna looks like she's tasted something foul. But it's definitely not the food. "You're seriously considering a one-child policy?"

Dad raises his hands, his smile unwavering. "This is new ground for us. Not that long ago, we expected the Terminal Generation to be our last. After the Plague rendered us sterile, we were prepared to witness the end of the human race." He pauses. "Now we have hope for the future. But we must be careful. Birth rates will have to be monitored closely along with oxygen and water usage, food production—the balancing act will continue in earnest."

"Have you met any of them?" Luther's looking at me again. "The children?"

He didn't say *your* children. I appreciate that.

"No." I shake my head, keep my eyes on my plate. Funny. I'm not hungry all of a sudden. "But I hear they're doing well. Keeping them safe from the Prometheus cult was a top priority."

Luther murmurs something under his breath that I don't catch. When I look up, he's still watching me. "To think...they would have been harvested for their DNA." He frowns. "Are any of them exhibiting special abilities as of yet?"

"Probably too soon to tell." Daiyna glances at me before returning to her meal.

"That's the prevailing thought. And once they get their neural implants, we won't know one way or another." Because as long as they're online, they won't even realize what they're capable of.

"Unless someone shows them," Luther adds. "Teaches them how to deactivate their augments in order to see what the Creator has blessed them with."

Just when I thought we could take a break from the awkward stuff.

"Like I said... We don't know yet if they'll show any signs of...certain talents." I drain my glass and seriously consider trading it in for something stronger.

"It's an incredible field of study," Dad interjects. "The extrasensory and telepathic abilities alone exhibited by certain members of the Twenty—"

"Milton can't fly anymore," Daiyna says without looking up. She glances at me again and shrugs, her shoulders moving the same way mine do. "I can't see in the dark, either. I noticed the night-vision fading a couple months ago. Now it's just...gone."

I frown and look at Luther. He nods, backing her up. But then he exhales, forces a smile, pats his wife's hand with affection. His scarred fingers are tough to look at. "The Creator blessed us with gifts we needed for a certain time. We don't need them anymore. What He gives, He can take away. It is not our place to question Him."

"There's more to it than that," she mutters.

"I haven't heard about this phenomenon..." Dad trails off,

brow creased as he glances at Mom. She shakes her head; she hasn't either. "Is it affecting all of the survivors from the North American Wastes?"

"Every single one of us," Daiyna says with a wink. "Cost of living indoors, I suppose. We weren't meant to be housebroken."

Dad's brow furrows further. "Why should living inside the Domes affect—?"

"Tell them." She nudges Luther. "Go on. They're dying to know."

He chuckles. "I'm not sure about that. And of course, I don't know for certain. But in our experience, if we spend extended periods away from God's creation, our abilities diminish. Here, in the Ten Domes of Eurasia, we are surrounded by human-made materials. Even the dirt is synthetic. We are separated from the dust of the earth."

"The dust..." Mom echoes, giving me a cautious look. "So...your abilities are due to..."

"We're not dust freaks." Daiyna's turn to laugh, and my parents join in, but it's forced.

I don't. Because I have a queasy feeling I know what's coming next.

"We don't snort the stuff," Daiyna adds. "But we have a connection to it."

Luther nods. "The spirits of the earth used it to change us. To make it possible for us to survive on the surface—in the Wastes, as you call them."

And there it is.

After a lengthy pause, Dad replies, "I see. So...after months without contact with the...dust of the earth...your lack of contact with these...spirits?...has caused you to lose your abilities." I've never heard him sound so unsure of a situation. Talk about a balancing act. He's trying very hard not to insult their beliefs while, at the same time, understand what the hell they're talking about. "But Sera, you and Erik have not experienced any such diminishing in your abilities, is that correct?"

"Right. No change." I smile at him. "You'd be the first to know, Dr. Chen."

His concerned look is replaced by a grin of approval.

"I would hope so!" Mom reaches over and rubs my arm. "You're such a private person, Sera. We want to know what's going on with you!"

"I know, Mom. I'll do better." I pat her hand.

Luther and Daiyna are watching me. They seem to like what they see. If they were hoping that I was raised by loving parents, then that hope was not misplaced.

"Feel free to stop by the lab anytime," Dad offers. "I'm curious what sort of genetic markers we're talking about here that would pass on specific abilities to your progeny and yet preclude you from carrying them indefinitely. Needless to say, there's no precedent for this! The entire realm of potential research is a fascinating new frontier."

Daiyna looks pale all of a sudden. Luther doesn't look much different.

"There are no markers," he manages hoarsely. "We have been tested before."

Not a fond memory, by all indications.

3

An alert flashes at the corner of my ocular lenses, and a wave of relief washes over me. It's an incoming hail from HQ, and it couldn't have come at a better time. I let my eyes glaze over and quickly check the message, hoping with everything in me that I've been assigned a new case, and I'll have to leave abruptly.

"You must forgive my husband." Mom's voice is quiet as she attempts to save face. "Sometimes he can be a bit...overzealous, shall we say?"

"Yes, of course. I didn't mean to dredge up any bad memories," Dad backpedals, chiding himself. "I should have remembered what you both went through decades ago. It was insensitive of me to think you'd ever be interested in visiting my lab."

The hail is from Chief Inspector Hudson: *Report to HQ at once. Your suit has been located.*

More good news. My exo's been MIA since the Prometheus uprising. I had to abandon it in Dome 10 when Drasko rescued us from a squad of killbots. There wasn't enough room for the motorized exoskeleton—halfway between light body armor and a full-on mech—in his muscle car. But when I went back for the suit later, after things settled down, it wasn't there. Stolen by local miscreants, I assumed. No way they'd ever be able to operate it without the command keycode, and I'm one of only two people who know it. The exo's probably been gathering dust in a grungy warehouse for the past few weeks.

I blink, restoring my vision of the dinner table.

"The past is never far from our minds, I'm afraid." Luther stares down at his scarred fingers. That's how close his reminders always are. "But our Lord has given us strength to forge ahead, despite the horrors that lie behind us."

Captivity. Torture. Human experimentation. Those are the horrors he and Daiyna survived at the hands of an evil megalomaniac named Arthur Willard and his underground cult determined never to set foot on the earth's contaminated surface.

Mom nods with sympathy shining in her eyes. "Time does not heal every wound."

"Got that right," Daiyna mutters. Then she exhales. "The wounds fade, though, given enough time. The ones on the inside take the longest. But maybe like our abilities, someday they'll vanish completely." She meets Luther's gaze, and he smiles faintly. "The Lord's mercy and grace are a real blessing. But it's good to have flesh-and-blood people to rely on as well during tough times." She looks at Mom and Dad but doesn't say anything for a beat. Then she adds, "I'm glad to have met you both."

Luther nods emphatically. "And I hope this is but the beginning of a long friendship."

Mom and Dad glance at each other, all smiles again. "We hope so as well."

Glad to see them playing so nicely together. It was touch

and go there for a second. I clear my throat as unobtrusively as possible and get to my feet, taking advantage of a rare moment with no awkwardness running rampant.

"Sorry to eat and run..."

"Oh no," Mom says, her expression crashing as she, too, rises. "You're not leaving already?"

"But we haven't even gotten to dessert!" Dad interjects. "I made steamed pears just the way you like them—with rock sugar and dates and everything."

Daiyna and Luther watch me without a hint of disappointment on their faces. Because they're glad to see me go? Because they don't care whether I'm there or not? Or because they accept the fact that duty calls, even when it's far from convenient?

"I wish I could stay." I try to sound sincere. I even wrinkle my forehead a little. Dessert would have been wonderful. "But when the boss-man calls..."

"Of course." Mom hugs my arm. "We know how important your job is. We will have to do this again sometime soon, perhaps when you are not on-call. If that's ever the case!"

She laughs, but I know she wishes I was able to spend more time with them. Part of me does, too. If only we could turn back the clock a few years to when I was still living at home and going to the academy, incapable of appreciating how good my life was at the time. There was so much I didn't know, so many of my own horrors that had yet to be revealed. Ignorance can really be bliss sometimes.

"Let me walk you out." Dad gets up and heads toward the door.

That's when Luther and Daiyna rise and approach me

self-consciously.

"It's been good to see you," he says, glancing at Daiyna. Undoubtedly noting our similarities in appearance. Except for the streaks of grey in her hair and a few wrinkles here and there on her face, she could be my sister. "I hope we can get together again."

Daiyna nods, not seeming to know what to do with her hands. Her eyes are glistening, and she looks down when I meet her gaze.

"We've all got our priorities." Not sure why I said that. A not-so-subtle jab at their request for resources, maybe?

Daiyna looks me in the eye then and takes a step toward me, her voice quiet. "This is new for us. For all of us. We'll have to figure it out as we go."

For some reason, I feel like a weight has dropped off my shoulders. The pressure squeezing my lungs evaporates. Because she wants to make an effort. That much is clear.

"With plenty of mistakes along the way?" I raise an eyebrow and almost smile. "That sounds good to me."

"Then it's settled." Mom clasps both Daiyna and me by the arm and sandwiches herself in between us. "We'll make this a monthly occurrence. Dinner with family. Yes?" She beams at each of us in turn.

I'm having some troubling feigning enthusiasm at the idea. Daiyna looks speechless.

"An excellent goal." Luther puts his arm around his wife's waist and smiles at me. Do my eyes sparkle like that? "And we'll do our best to make it happen, despite whatever obstacles life throws at us. This is important—breaking out of our bubble." He looks over at Dad. "Perhaps you would like to join us at our place sometime?"

In Dome 6. Dad's already agreed to visit the work they're doing at the local MedCenter, but to spend the evening in what's sure to be cramped quarters? That's asking a lot—

"Indeed we would! We could alternate every other month, if that works out." He's serious about this. And he's enthusiastic. He and Mom both are.

Luther and Daiyna brighten, probably just as surprised as I am. Not that I ever thought my parents were stuffy upper-caste types, but they're definitely creatures of habit. I've never known them to venture outside of Dome 1 for extended periods.

"No pressure, Sera." Luther holds up a hand. I try not to notice his scars. "But if you're available, we would love to have you over as well. And your partner—Dunn, is it? I would very much like to have a conversation with one of them."

I frown at that. "One of...them?"

"The clones. Dr. Wong's creations, made in his own image. I've seen plenty but never spoken to one before." Luther shrugs. "I am curious how well they're able to mimic the divine spark."

Daiyna nudges him and shakes her head. She must have picked up on my nonverbal cues. Arms crossed, brow furrowed. Annoyed as hell.

"I don't know about any *spark*, but Dunn's the best partner I could ask for. He's put his life on the line more than once in the line of duty. I wouldn't be standing here, if it wasn't for him." My muscles are tense. I try to relax. "I owe him my life."

Luther smiles warmly. "Greater love hath no man than this, that a man lay down his life for his friends. Or a copy of a man, in this case."

Dunn is no copy of Wong. "He's his own person. Trust me on that."

Dad steps in. "Sera has always been very protective of her pets. I remember a particular drone—"

"Dunn's not a pet!" I turn sharply to scowl at him.

"A pet project then," he rephrases. "The only one of his kind working in law enforcement, isn't that right?"

"He's not a project, either."

"Of course not, dear one," Mom consoles me with a side-squeeze.

They're treating me like a child. And what's worse, I'm feeling like one. Maybe even acting like it. Am I pouting? Outnumbered, the youngest one here. But while they might have the market cornered on life experience, I know my partner.

"He's not like other clones." I keep calm. "He's...evolving. Recognizing his humanity. Becoming more than he was originally intended to be."

Luther looks intrigued. "I meant no disrespect. My overweening curiosity sometimes gets the better of me. And I must confess a certain prejudice against science acting in roles reserved for God."

"Now there's a topic for our next dinner party!" Dad grins.

Another hail from Hudson blinks in the lower right corner of my lenses. The analysts have undoubtedly informed him that I'm not en route to HQ yet. The little tattletales.

At the same time, I receive a transmission via audiolink from Dunn: "I am on the roof, Investigator Chen. Ready to depart when you are."

I back away toward the door, reaching out for my parents and biological parents as if to gather them all in one warm embrace. "This has been great. We'll do it again. Sorry, I've got to go."

"Let me walk you down," Dad repeats. It's our usual routine. He still feels protective of me, even though I'm an adult and a trained LawKeeper, and he and Mom live in one of the safest neighborhoods in the safest Dome of Eurasia. It's just that father-daughter dynamic, I suppose. Tough to shake.

I give him a smile and point in the opposite direction. "My ride's on the roof."

He chuckles. "Bond. Sera Bond."

Everybody else seems to think that's quite amusing. But I have no idea what he's referring to.

"Goodnight. Love you." The door senses my presence and slides open. I'm out in the hallway before they have a chance to return the sentiment, and I half-run down the corridor to the speedlift, the thick carpet muffling every thump of my heels. "Need to make a quick stop at my place. Not dressed for work," I subvocalize to Dunn via my augments.

"Understood. Course laid in to your cube complex," he replies instantly.

The speedlift's polished plasteel doors open as I approach, and I step inside the vacant car, reaching for the control panel to enter my override code. Access to the roof gardens and landing pad is limited to the building's residents, but being an investigator comes with a perk or two.

As the doors close and the lift glides upward, I open the second message from Chief Inspector Hudson: *Report to*

HQ immediately, Investigator Chen. Reading between the lines, I get the feeling his patience might be wearing a little thin. And just when I thought we'd established a tolerable rapport.

All things considered, probably a better idea not to stop by my place and change. I'm sure the analysts would notify Hudson of any deviation in my route, no matter how slight. Part of the fun of living in a panopticon. The analysts see all and know all, hardwired into the Linkstream for twelve-hour surveillance shifts. More machine than human, shaved bald with thick cables plugged into cranial jacks on the back of their skulls, dilated eyes that never seem to focus. Impossible to converse with—not that I've tried. Their communication tends to be one-way: delivering information. Only Commander Bishop is authorized to issue them queries.

The speedlift doors slide open, and I jog out onto the garden pathway, lit with soft-glowing solar lights. It's a peaceful area up here with well-manicured lawns, geometrically shaped shrubbery, and healthy trees, not to mention all the varieties of flowers. A popular spot for residents to lay out in the sun, filtered through the Dome's translucent blue-tinted ceiling. Right now everything is vacant and still and dark, save for the subdued landscape lighting.

A black & white aerocar is waiting on the landing pad, its engines purring in idle mode. Dunn sits at the controls with the copilot door open.

"Change of plans." I hike my dress up around my knees and climb inside. The door drifts down behind me and locks itself into place as I strap in. "Straight to HQ."

Dunn looks my way for a moment, then seems to do a

double-take, the black faceplate on his white helmet hiding his expression. Without a word, he changes coordinates on the console in front of him, the fingers of his gauntlet tapping out a quick, precise rhythm across the touchscreen.

"I apologize for interrupting your dinner party, Investigator Chen."

"Not your fault, partner." I fail to mention how glad I am to be out of there.

He takes us aloft as the electromagnetic coils hum and the ionic thrusters kick in, sending us over the side of the complex and between two rows of gleaming domescrapers. Far below us, the street lies empty, proof that tonight's curfew enforcers are doing their job. It takes a concerted effort to conserve energy across the Ten Domes—each as big as an average-sized city in the Old World—and that means everybody staying in when it's dark out.

"Hudson said they've found my exo."

"That is good news. You have been wondering what became of it." He returns his attention to the neon green overlay on the windscreen with our trajectory mapped out in shades of blue. "Or is it not good news?" he adds with a quick glance at my face.

That's what I'm wondering. "I thought it was, at first. But now Hudson's urgency is making me nervous."

"You are thinking that perhaps the suit has been used for nefarious purposes?"

I smirk at him. "Thought I was the only mind reader here."

He dips his chin but doesn't say anymore. Is he smiling under that helmet?

I can't help thinking back to the brief interchange I had

with Luther. You'd think someone following an outdated religion that's all about loving others, particularly the less fortunate, would be more open-minded. But maybe the tenets of the Way don't apply to those its followers consider less than human. In his words, a clone is a *copy* of a human, lacking a divine spark. Or mimicking one. Not sure on that point.

Regardless, I probably shouldn't have gotten so irritated with him. He was only curious, asking to meet Dunn and find out what he's like. But I felt protective, for some reason. I didn't like the idea of my partner being scrutinized under a microscope. He's made so much progress since we started working together, seeming more like an individual, more *human*, with every week that passes. I don't want him to suffer any sort of setback.

I know I can't keep him from interacting with people who think he's no different from the other security clones in Eurasia. Human-shaped beings psychologically conditioned to obey orders, unable to think for themselves, without much in the way of personality. Hell, he has to deal with that brand of ignorance every day—most coming from fellow LawKeepers, the men and women we work alongside. But maybe it was more the idea of my biological father being unable to recognize Dunn's uniqueness that bothered me, that because Luther and I are related by blood, Dunn might wonder if I feel the same way. That because he's a clone, he's *less than*.

I don't want that doubt creeping into my partner's mind. I don't want it to damage our working relationship. Or his burgeoning sense of self.

Then again, maybe all it would take for Luther to change

his tune on the topic is to meet Dunn. Because nobody with an iota of sense would be able to interact with my partner without realizing how special he is.

"Did you enjoy the time you were able to spend with your two sets of parents?" he says at length, and I realize I've been quiet for a while.

I nod, watching the dark city pass by outside. Up ahead, looming over everything at the highest point of Dome 1, at the very center of Eurasia's central Dome, stands Hawthorne Tower. One hundred fifty floors of mirrored glass reflecting our approach.

Dunn glances at me. "That is a lovely dress, Investigator Chen."

"Thanks." I pluck at it. Not thrilled about reporting for duty in this thing. I used to keep a change of clothes in my locker, back when I had a locker. One of many things we're doing without now—until HQ gets rebuilt. "First time I've worn it."

First time he's seen me in anything but my tactical uniform or my bodysuit. I'm sure all the colors are quite a shock to the system.

"I do not consider Dr. Solomon Wong to be my father." The aerocar descends as he takes us toward the vacant street out front of the tower. "Yet he would be the closest analogue to a parent in my case, would he not?"

So that's what's really on his mind. Not surprising, I guess, considering where he picked me up tonight. "A parent is someone who loves you and raises you, prepares you for life. Not always someone you're related to by blood."

He nods slowly. "Then, in my case, there is no analogue. I was grown in a lab and psychologically conditioned to do my job. No one raised me or prepared me for life."

"I'd say you've done pretty well on your own. You're continuing to figure out your place in the world. All you need is the freedom to keep making progress."

Another nod. Another glance in my direction. "I have you to thank for that, Investigator Chen. Not many of your colleagues would have agreed to work with me."

None of them. Because they're bigots. "You impressed Commander Bishop, Dunn. You did that on your own." Credit where credit is due.

The aerocar descends vertically, jet wash billowing outward as Dunn parks us right out front of Hawthorne Tower. Without any ground traffic tonight, he's got his pick of parking spots. My door drifts upward, and I unbuckle my harness with a glance at the building's third floor. Impossible to tell from the outside that every light is on in there while the night shift goes about their regular duties.

"Would you like me to accompany you?" Dunn offers.

I shake my head and smooth down my dress self-consciously as I step out. "Keep the motor running. I've got a feeling this won't take long."

4

The transparent entry doors of Hawthorne Tower slide shut with barely a whisper as I step into the high-vaulted atrium and pass through the dark foyer, my clopping heels following a path of dim circular lights set into the floor tiles. The lone security clone on duty stands like a statue behind the main desk, accents shining from its pristine white armor. Identical to Dunn's except for the neon-blue line down the middle of its faceplate, along both its shoulders, and down the sides of its legs, glowing in the dark. Real fancy.

During the day, a human guard holds that post. His name is Karl. We're on a first-name basis and greet each other with the usual pleasantries-in-passing. But I don't even know this clone's designated alphanumerics.

Memory flash: Fort lying dead in a filthy Dome 10 street. A clone like this one, not like Dunn. Yet I'd seen glimmers of what Fort could have become, if given the chance. If allowed to evolve.

I'd already started thinking of him as a *him*, not an *it*.

Maybe that's the trick. Interact with them like human beings, and they'll respond in like manner. Treat them the way you'd want to be treated, and something will click in their brains, allowing them to act beyond their conditioning.

Could it be that simple?

"Investigator Sera Chen," the clone greets me in a voice without much in the way of inflection. No idea if we've ever met before, but it can scan my neuro easily enough to establish my identity. "Chief Inspector Hudson is expecting you on the third floor."

"Right. I bet he's chomping at the bit." I slow my pace as I approach the front desk. "Quiet night?"

No response.

"Place looks nice." I take a moment to look over the impressive interior. "Then again, most domescrapers do. Assuming they haven't been bombed to hell."

The glowing face shield is set straight ahead, hiding whatever expression lies beneath. Something neutral, probably. The clone doesn't carry a weapon out in the open, which would be too threatening for the general public, but there's a concealed holster built into the armor on its right leg. All it takes is a split-second maneuver, and that holster will pop out, launching a pistol with projectile rounds into the clone's gauntleted hand.

"Not one for small talk, I take it?" I give the guard a chance to respond, but the silence is deafening. So I shatter it with my noisy heels, heading straight for the hallway where two pairs of speedlift doors face each other in the staring contest of the century. Punching the up arrow on the panel, I cross my arms and shake my head at my foolishness.

Dunn is one of a kind. Fort might have been, too, if he'd survived long enough to find out. We'll never know. But I can't assume that every security clone in the Domes has the same potential. That's just as ignorant as assuming they're all mindless automatons. If I truly believe they are capable of being individuals, then I should treat them that way: individually. Just like any other person.

Doing my best to set aside any other pesky existential ponderings, I take the speedlift up two floors and step out into the crowded, frenetic energy of our temporary police headquarters, nearly stumbling back inside the car to avoid being run over by a surly looking, bushy-bearded technician grumbling to himself. His name's Hector, and judging from the direction he's going, there's been another glitch with the analysts' array. Or *cage*, as most of my colleagues refer to it.

Monitoring the movement and actions of every citizen in the Ten Domes takes a whole lot of processing power, and this floor wasn't built for that. Hawthorne Tower is a government building, designed for government business. Law-making, not LawKeeping. But we've done relatively well, considering how we weren't allowed to reenter our structural unsafe building to collect anything we needed. Good thing most of the important stuff is stored online. As far as everything else goes, like lockers and desks and a fully functional command center, we've had to make do the best we can.

And we've learned to deal with power outages from time to time.

Groans and curses by the hundreds echo from one end of the open floor to the other as amber emergency lights kick in around the perimeter, painting everybody in a coat of waxy sallow. But that's not the worst of it. With every outage, the cage has to reboot. And during the five minutes it takes to do that—no more, no less—the analysts are blind to whatever happens to be going on in the Domes. Lucky for us, curfew is in effect right now, so there shouldn't be anybody out and about looking to start some trouble.

But that's never stopped them before.

"Chen." Hudson beckons me over to the door of his closet-sized office. Judging from his grim expression, the news regarding my exo-suit isn't good. Either that, or he's got other bad news to share.

If it was just a matter of sending me the coordinates to my exo's location, that could have been done via Link. For some reason, he felt the need for us to meet in person. Which usually means he's going to put me on a new case.

I glance halfway across the expansive floor to where the analysts' array—an egg-shaped, floor-to-ceiling gold wire-mesh shield that protects them from electromagnetic interference—sits in the middle of our makeshift command center, flickering as it automatically reboots itself. Commander Bishop is undoubtedly standing nearby, overseeing the proceedings, but I don't catch sight of her. Probably for the best.

Not sure what she'd think of me showing up in this dress.

Hudson doesn't even seem to notice as he leaves the door to slide shut behind him. By the time I manage to wade through the bustling mass of humanity to reach his office, enduring a few catcalls and wolf whistles along the way courtesy of my coworkers, each of whom receives an ice-cold stare for their juvenile efforts, the chief inspector is already seated behind his desk. Looks like Hector's crew of technicians/wizards was able to replace the one he had in his old office with an identical model. But this space is about a sixteenth the size of what he's used to, and the desk wasn't shrunk down at all. So it runs from one wall to the other with no room whatsoever to walk around it. Which means he has to scramble over it in order to sit on the other side, every single time.

So undignified. No wonder he let the door close. He didn't want me to catch him in the act.

"I would ask you to have a seat, but..." He trails off, passing his hand palm-down over the glass surface of his desk and activating the holo projectors.

"Not a problem, sir." He likes it when I call him that—and when I stand at attention. So that's what I do as the door slides shut behind me, even though I'm way out of uniform. He's got the only chair in the closet—I mean *office*—so my high heels will have to support me for the duration of this meeting. I can handle a few minutes of pinched toes and sore arches. Sure I can.

"Take a look." He wipes his face with one hand and gestures at his deskscreen.

The bluish-white hologram projected upward from the flat, horizontal surface shows a three-dimensional scene of a local storefront. A jewelry store with its front window smashed and plenty of merchandise missing. Not to mention a message spray-painted in lettering over a meter high across the inside wall:

DEATH TO ALL INFIDELS - PROMETHEUS WILL RISE AGAIN

My insides sink at the sight. "Thought that cult had disbanded."

"As did I." He looks exhausted. Dark circles under his eyes. Sandy-colored hair and beard usually so well-kempt now frayed around the edges. Even his suit looks rumpled. Clambering over his desk multiple times throughout the day could be to blame for that. "And there's more."

Of course there is.

I watch him rewind the footage. There's a gap five minutes long, right when the break-in occurred. Followed by a split-second image of my exo-suit. It's blurry, but I'd recognize it anywhere. The person wearing it, however? Not so much. No distinguishable features. Hudson pauses playback and scowls at the poor quality.

"That can't be right," I murmur, half to myself.

"The security cameras went offline, and the system had to reboot. We assume the thieves used a localized EMP to knock them out. Then they broke in wearing your suit."

"But it can't be—sir. My exo was out of commission. In Dome 10. Whoever stole it would've needed the command keycode to get it running again." Not to mention how challenging it would have been to transport a motorized exoskeleton to Dome 1 without anybody noticing along the way.

Hudson nods wearily and slides his hand through the air a few centimeters above the deskscreen. The footage advances and then pauses just as a matte-black groundcar rolls into view. A vintage muscle car, to be exact. The gas-guzzling variety not allowed anywhere else but Dome 10, due to the exhaust.

My insides sink again, dropping even further.

"Recognize it?" He looks up and frowns as if seeing me for the first time tonight. "What the hell are you wearing, Chen?"

I avoid the question by asking one of my own, "You don't think he had something to do with this—a smash and grab? It's a little beneath his station."

Hudson exhales, shaking his head. "King of the underworld is about as low as you can go. But this?" He nods toward the holo. "It's more than a robbery. Coming here, doing something like this in the middle of the evening? Attention-seeking behavior, to say the least."

At most, a big statement. Worst-case: a trial run.

Hudson pauses before adding, "He's the only individual I know of who could have gotten your suit up and running again."

No doubt about that. Drasko's the one who upgraded the exo, mounting a minigun on the shoulder brace. And besides me, he's the only person in the Domes who knows the command keycode. Because he designed the damn thing.

"But he was never one of them—the *Children of Tomorrow* cult," I argue. "The Prometheus AI wanted to give everybody special abilities, take them outside the walls of Eurasia to live free under the sun. That has nothing to do with organized crime here in the Domes. Their goals don't overlap, not even a little."

Not many lucrative opportunities to be had beyond our walls, that I know of.

Hudson hunches up one shoulder. "He could be branching out. Plague survivor, isn't he? His family didn't fare so well. Dome 6 residents, if I'm not mistaken. Perhaps he wants a better life for them—something only Prometheus could have provided."

I frown at the holo-image. My exo. Drasko's groundcar. Both at the scene of a crime. No, more than a crime: a message to the citizens of Dome 1 after the destruction and mayhem we already endured. *You'll never be safe again.*

"What about other cameras in the vicinity?" I point out the holograms of shops on either side, as well as the ones across the street.

Hudson curses under his breath and nods toward the opposite side of his office door. "The break-in coincided with another glitch in our power. The analysts didn't see a thing."

I raise my chin. "Almost like it was planned."

He nods, his eyes cold.

"Curfew enforcers? Any aerocars passing overhead at the time?"

"None. The incident was somehow synchronized perfectly with our asynchronous flight patterns. And who would have access to that type of information?" He points at the muscle car. "Other than an undercover operative who used to fly for us?"

That doesn't ring true. "I don't know, sir…"

"Is your friendship with Drasko going to be an asset or hindrance here? Tell me now. If I need to assign another investigator—"

"If that's my exo," and I'm pretty sure it is, "and if that's Drasko's car," and I'm equally sure of that, "then I'm probably too close to this case to be on it."

He looks surprised for a moment. But then his gaze narrows, his hawkish features regarding me with what could be contempt. Or guarded appreciation. Tough to tell with this guy. "But now comes the part where you try to convince me there is no conflict of interest, that you are the perfect woman for the job, and that I would be a fool not to assign this case to you, considering how familiar you are with the prime suspect."

"I'd never say you were a fool, sir." Definitely not to his face. I glance back at the door, as if I can see through it. Which I can't. My freakish abilities haven't extended that far—yet. "When was the last time he checked in with

Commander Bishop?"

"Three days ago."

Long enough for Drasko to go rogue? I bite my lip, shaking my head as I study the holo. "Everything here is circumstantial." The exo, the car. There's no footage of Drasko himself. "Could be one of his lieutenants flexing, jockeying for position. Looking to take the throne for himself. Or herself."

"That's for you to find out. Assuming I've picked the right investigator for the job." He raises an eyebrow that was fairly manicured, last time I saw him. Now it's a bit wonky, like he's been rubbing it or twisting it. Stress can do that to the best of us.

"Thank you, sir." I nod. "I'll start with the neighboring shops, see if their cameras were working at the time of the incident." I check the timestamp at the bottom left corner of the holo-image: 20:38. While I was arriving late at my parents' cube, this robbery was going down just a few blocks away. "And I'll try to contact Drasko at the usual spot."

"Online." Hudson frowns with approval. "Right. Stick to your routine. Less chance of spooking him that way." His attention drifts toward my dress again. He seems confused by it. "You may want to change."

That was the original plan.

"The proprietor is on her way to the shop. You will interview her, of course." He seems distracted by something. But it's not my dress.

"Will there be anything else, sir?"

He leans forward onto his elbows, and the holo collapses like a sand castle as the projectors switch off. "Your partner. D1-436. I heard the nightly visits to Level 5 have been postponed for the time being."

"That's right." What with Level 5 no longer being operational, along with every other level of our old building, and MedTech currently operating out of MedCenter 1 but with limited resources. Apparently they haven't had the time or personnel to study Dunn since the bombing. Priorities tend to change following a terrorist attack. "But as long as he gets his four hours of sleep, he's good to go."

"Make sure of that." Hudson's look is pointed. "In your daily report, you will need to begin making notes on the clone's behavior. Keep an eye out for any abnormalities, no matter how seemingly insignificant. From here on out, it will be up to you to ensure that your probationary partnership is a success. Understood?"

Reading between the lines? Sure. If I want to keep Dunn as my partner, I have to treat him like a science experiment. Study him. Report on him. And if Hudson doesn't like what he reads, he'll terminate our partnership. Then who knows where Dunn will end up? Maybe recycled.

The alternative: ignore any *abnormalities* and give my partner a glowing report each and every day. Then what? He suffers some kind of psychotic break, ends up hurting somebody, and I'm to blame for pretending there weren't any warning signs?

I'm clenching my fists down at my sides. I've really got to stop doing that.

Taking a breath to steady my nerves and clasping my hands behind my back, I ask, "These...abnormalities I'm looking out for. Anything in particular, sir?"

He leans back in his squeaky chair. The squeak obviously annoys the hell out of him, but he keeps his cool. "You know

D1-436 better than anyone. Should his behavior change even in the slightest, you will be the first to notice."

That much is true. "Was behavior modification part of his nightly regimen on Level 5?" If so, this is news to me. I thought the powers-that-be were adopting a more hands-off approach with Dunn. Studying his uniqueness, analyzing his progress. Not keeping him under their thumb like every other clone in the Domes.

"Classified information, I'm afraid." Hudson rises to his feet to tower over me, even with the slight stoop to his shoulders. There's a guarded look in his eyes as he says, "Good luck out there, Chen. Dismissed."

5

The aerocar's engines are still humming as I exit the front vestibule of Hawthorne Tower and make my way to the open passenger door. I didn't bother small-talking with the guard this time. No point to it.

"You were right." Dunn glances my way as I tug the dress up over my knees and get in. "That meeting did not take long at all." He pauses a moment. "Were you also right about your exo-suit?"

"Nefarious purposes," I confirm, buckling on the harness as the door drifts shut and locks itself. "You up for chauffeuring me around? Or do you need to catch a few winks tonight?"

He takes us upward smoothly, like he's been flying all his life. Which may very well be the case. "I have not had my requisite four hours of sleep, but there will be time for that later." Another glance my way. "I assume you need to stop by your cube before we go anywhere else."

"You assume correctly." Hoping that's the last time I ever walk through headquarters wearing something like this. "I'll get changed, then we'll head over to these coordinates." I send him the holo-image that my ocular lenses captured off Hudson's desk. "Got a smash-and-grab to look into. Jewelry store. Members of the Prometheus cult might be involved."

Dunn remains quiet, either focused on piloting us between the soaring domescrapers, or pensive at the sight of both my exo and Drasko's vehicle at the same crime scene. Assuming that's what they are. Who's to say some industrious criminals didn't design an exoskeleton similar to mine or retrofit a groundcar to look like a certain underworld kingpin's vintage vehicle?

"Infidels," Dunn murmurs, focusing instead on that portion of the image. The spray-painted message. "That would refer to anyone who did not believe in Prometheus and its endgame?"

"The majority of the populace, if I remember correctly."

Dunn's helmet tilts to one side. "The outspoken majority, perhaps. Those who took action against Prometheus. I do not believe the AI's cult members would wish to kill everyone in the Domes, Investigator Chen. Then who would receive those special abilities and be taken outside the walls of Eurasia to live as humans of old?"

Good point. "So *DEATH TO ALL INFIDELS* might not be all-inclusive, you're saying."

His armored, mechanical shoulders shrug just a centimeter or so. A very human mannerism. "If the cult members are thinking rationally, then yes. But if they are not, then it is likely they will make an attempt on the lives of multiple citizens at once, perhaps in a public place." He pauses, pensive again. "The jewelry heist may have been merely a trial run."

That's the worst-case scenario, alright. "They could be planning something bigger, something worse, and this was just to gauge our response time. How fast they'd have to move in order to clear out before LawKeepers arrive on the scene."

Dunn nods. Grimly, I'd say, but that could be just the look of his dark face shield. "Do we know their point of origin? Or which Dome they escaped to?"

I curse under my breath. "The analysts were offline when the incident occurred. Another power outage. Coincidence, right?"

"Doubtful, Investigator Chen."

"I was being sarcastic."

He pauses. "Then in that case, you are correct."

I almost smile. I can see my report now: *At this time, on this date, Unit D1-436 engaged in witty banter.* Does that count as an abnormality? Luther might think so. His ilk expects every clone to act like that one guarding the foyer of Hawthorne Tower. Devoid of personality. Little more than a bot. Programmed to do its job.

Why did Luther's comment annoy the hell out of me? I mean, it must have really struck a nerve, because I'm still thinking about it when I should be focused on my investigation. Was it because he disappointed me? I expected more from him, and his ignorance let me down. I was worried about disappointing him and Daiyna, and instead the opposite happened. They didn't live up to my expectations.

And now I'm left feeling irritated with myself.

Focus, Chen. A little positive self-talk never hurt anybody. *The job is first.*

Dunn sets us down on the landing pad adjacent to my cube complex's roof garden. The trees and shrubbery sway with the mild jet wash flowing outward from the engines as they idle.

"I'll just be a minute." I duck out under the door as it floats open and take off as fast as I can go in these stupid heels.

"It will undoubtedly be longer than a minute, Investigator Chen," Dunn calls after me. "But I will remain here with the motor running."

I glance over my shoulder to find his dark faceplate watching me go. Any chance he looks as confused as Hudson did, seeing me in this getup? I give him a wave and head for the door to the speedlift that'll take me into the heart of the building.

The place is quiet this time of night, as should be expected, and the hallway running the perimeter of my floor lies vacant. Reaching my cube, I let the door scanner read my neural implant, and it slides open with barely a whisper.

The space inside is small, but just enough for me. Probably helps that I'm seldom home for extended periods. Usually just to catch some sleep or a little rec time in VR. The bathroom is sectioned-off on one side, and the bed, kitchen, dining nook and living room are all in one area. You could call it *open-concept* if you were feeling generous. The entire space is about as big as one of my parents' bedrooms.

I waste no time getting out of this dress and kicking off my heels. The door just shut behind me, and I'm already stripping. Then I pull on my tactical uniform—slim black trousers with button-down pockets, an equally form-fitting medium grey tunic, and a dark, charcoal grey zip-up jacket. The outerwear is designed to be impervious to your average projectile rounds, but it'll collapse under heavy artillery—the kind my drones and exo can fire, or anything more substantial. It will protect me against most blades used up close in a knife fight, but probably not against something like Dad's *miao dao* I have mounted up on the wall in its carved redwood scabbard.

My gaze lingers on the two-handed saber. I've been taking lessons online and, so far, have managed not to inadvertently slice up anything other than my bedspread.

Think I'll leave the blade here tonight.

Strapping on my shocker in its drop leg holster, I take a seat in the only chair at the dinner table—probably more suitable for a bistro—and drag over my pair of black, faux-leather boots. You'd think we would have self-lacing shoes by this point in time, but no, we've still got to tie the things ourselves. Which I do, nice and tight without cutting off my circulation.

Ready to go. But instead I hesitate, staring at that sword on the wall. Remembering the last time I used it outside of a practice session, when Dunn, Erik, and I went up against killer robots programmed by the Prometheus AI and built by its human acolytes. Apparently, it was naive of us to assume the Children of Tomorrow would die out once their venerable AI was no longer allowed to frequent the Link, once it could no longer mindjack anyone to do its bidding. Judging from the jewelry store break-in, members of that cult are now as fervent as ever, even without the AI messing with their heads anymore. Because the mental damage has already been done.

Either that, or the AI actually succeeded in cloning itself before Erik trapped it on that antique phone, cut off from the Linkstream. The copy of Prometheus could have been biding its time until now, waiting for the opportune moment to strike. To start infecting its followers with nanotech and hijacking their free will.

Maybe I'm still being naive. There could be people in Eurasia who actually believe in Prometheus's goals, even without an AI currently influencing them. Citizens who crave the supernatural abilities of so-called *demigods* and want to live free outside the Ten Domes, beneath the scorching sun. Never mind the fact that no human being would survive long in the Wastes without protective gear and a robust breathing apparatus.

But could they, if their DNA was spliced like Trezon's? The guy could make himself invisible at will. Who's to say Prometheus wouldn't have made it possible for its followers to live outside the Domes? Like Luther and Daiyna did, and their friend Milton and his wife and kids, and Erik's parents. None of them carried O_2 tanks or wore breathers out there. Yet somehow, they managed to live for decades in the Wastes.

Would I be able to survive outside the blue-tinted walls of the Domes? Would Erik? What about the children those government doctors created from our genes? The way Prometheus told it, we would. But seeing how the artificial intelligence was modeled after the mind of a delusional egomaniac, it's tough to say how strong a grip Prometheus had on reality.

And the same would go for its followers.

My fists clench at the chilling memory of going toe-to-toe with that AI. For a moment, I thought it had me trapped in VR. That I would never escape to the real world with my mind intact. Its power and intelligence were undeniable. As was its fury when I refused to accept the reality it showed me.

I don't want to face anything like it again. Give me psychotic cult members. Or jewelry thieves. Or some combination of the two. Just let them be human. Somebody my shocker can take down with a charged round that sends them into convulsions.

Close to ten minutes longer than predicted, I make it up to the rooftop and climb into the aerocar beside my partner. "You were right." I reach back to tap each of my drones on its disc-shaped chassis, waking them where they sit in the cargo compartment. "Longer than a minute."

Wink and Blink light up and give a little shudder as their systems come online, quadcopter rotors twitching clockwise, then counter, warming up.

"I have found that to be the case, Investigator Chen, whenever people say they will only be a minute," Dunn replies. "Often unexpected events prolong the time frame."

In my case: staring at a decorative sword and reminiscing.

"The ride down the speedlift, followed by the walk to your cube, would have taken an estimated thirty seconds in itself," he continues, fixated on this idea. Does that count as an *abnormality*? When does a quirky obsession become abnormal? When it harms someone else or impedes one's ability to function normally. Not the case here, as my door drifts shut, and he takes us aloft with a controlled burst of the ionic thrusters, heading on a direct route to the crime scene. "But I understand the purpose of the phrase's idiomatic usage: to put listeners at ease, to assure them that they are not being abandoned."

I raise an eyebrow at him. "Is this how you spend your free time, now that you don't have to report to Level 5? Analyzing colloquial speech patterns?"

His helmet tilts to one side just a smidge. "If it annoys you, I can keep my musings to myself."

"Not at all." I get comfortable in my seat—as much as I can in a harness's snug embrace—and fold my arms. "I'm intrigued by your musings."

He nods slightly. "Do you ponder such things yourself, Investigator Chen?"

Never *Sera*. Always so formal, no matter how many times I've reminded him that he's welcome to address me by my given name. "Sure, I'm a real ponderer." I watch the reflection of our aerocar soaring past the reflective surface of another towering domescraper, our alternating red and blue lights shining in the darkness. "I've been thinking about Prometheus. Hoping it hasn't escaped from wherever Commander Bishop has it locked down. That it hasn't somehow managed to get onto the Link. Or that there isn't another version of it on the loose, stirring up trouble."

"You are referring to the graffiti at the jewelry store robbery." He glances over in time to catch my nod. "Would it be acceptable for me to propose a theory?"

I've been hoping he'd take this kind of initiative on an investigation. "Go ahead."

He pauses, keeping his focus on the console in front of him as well as the windscreen with our route's trajectory a glowing overlay. "Could it be that the perpetrators are not involved with the Prometheus cult at all, and that they only painted that message on the wall as a diversion?"

Honestly, the thought hadn't occurred to me. "A diversion from what?"

"Their true purpose." Another pause, as if he's waiting for me to respond. When I don't, he adds, "Ensuring that they have your attention, Investigator Chen."

"My attention..." I echo. "What's a jewelry store have to do with me?"

Another shrug of his shoulders. "Perhaps nothing. It is just a theory."

And not a bad attempt, at that. "I like it better than Hudson's. He thinks Drasko is involved."

"Yes. I considered that possibility as well. But I avoided sharing it because he is your friend, and the prospect of his involvement might upset you."

"It does," I admit. "But if he is involved, then I have to believe he's working some kind of angle. Undercover."

Dunn gives a slow nod. "In alignment with the role he is playing, assigned by Commander Bishop herself." He pauses again, weighing his words. "Yet it is not unheard of for an undercover operative to go rogue when personal objectives outweigh the importance of following orders."

Unfortunately, that thought did occur to me. Because nothing matters more to Drasko than his family. He'd do anything to make their lives better. That's why he smuggled them out of Dome 6 during the Prometheus uprising and has had them living on Erik's farm ever since. But was that move sanctioned by the government? As a rule, Dome 6 residents aren't allowed to live elsewhere without official approval. There are certain hoops to jump through, proving that the citizens in question are healthy enough to rejoin society. If the authorities are pressuring Drasko to return them to their original residence, would that motivate him to buck the system? To fully embrace what has been only a role he's played up to now?

As we approach the crime scene, Dunn takes the aerocar

down in a gentle, vertical descent. Even from our current height, the smashed-in storefront is clearly visible, a dark cave with jagged teeth where remnants of the broken plastiglass remain. Some of the shattered pieces glint on the sidewalk out front, but most of the mess will be inside, courtesy of the exo-suit's minigun.

Maybe I'm in denial, but I can't believe it's mine. Not until I see overwhelming evidence that the criminal or criminals involved didn't just reverse-engineer my exo to build one of their own.

Dunn sets us down on the vacant street, close to the curb. A lone curfew enforcer holds his position, standing at the shop door. He wears slate-blue powered armor—lightweight and motorized, intended to give him an advantage when pursuing violators—but no helmet. A step down from my exo, with less in the way of bulk. Easier for someone his age to handle.

"Evening, Raul," I greet him as I step out of the aerocar. Dunn's door floats open as well, and he unfastens his harness. Reaching back for my drones, I tuck one under each arm. "All quiet?"

"Now, yeah." Raul grunts unhappily. "Can't believe I missed all the excitement."

"Not like you can be everywhere at once."

Raul and I used to work the same shift. He covered the southwest quadrant while I patrolled the northeast. The stories we could share...

"Still. You'd think I would've heard something." His permanent scowl lines, cultivated over fifty years, are furrowed deeper than usual. He'd be crossing his arms if his suit allowed it. "I wasn't that far away."

Neither was I. Too busy worrying about feeling awkward at dinner while this crime was going down.

I toss Wink and Blink into the air, and they hover above me, rotors whining as they spin up. "Sync with any cameras in range," I tell them. "Collect all video footage shot at the time of the incident and share it with my lenses."

"Yes, Investigator Chen," they reply in unison in their customary monotone, veering off in opposite directions to follow orders.

"The boys are doing well, I see." Raul almost smiles at the familiar sight, head angled back as he watches them fly off.

"They've been through more than their share of action. But they keep on ticking."

"Lucky you got to keep them after your promotion..." Raul takes a sudden step back as Dunn rounds the rear of the aerocar and moves toward us.

"Don't I know it." I glance at my partner. "Raul, this is—"

"Unit D1-436." Raul nods grimly and averts his gaze.

Dunn nods his helmet in return. "Enforcer Ortega."

And that's all they say to each other. I have no record of them ever meeting before, but I suppose it's common knowledge that Dunn is my partner. And it's likely that he would've scanned Raul's neuro as we landed. He always likes to be prepared in social situations, no matter how brief they may be.

Before the silence has a chance to wander into uncomfortable territory, I clear my throat and gesture toward the shop. "Let's take a look inside, shall we?"

6

Leaving Raul to secure the scene, regardless of the absent foot traffic this time of night, Dunn and I step through broken plastiglass that crunches beneath our boots as we enter the jewelry shop.

"Let us know when the proprietor arrives." I glance back at Raul.

He keeps his eyes trained on the silent street, his vigilance on high alert. This break-in wasn't his fault, but sometimes the truth takes a while to catch up with us. "You got it, Chen."

I double-tap my temple to disengage the augments courtesy of my neural implant and allow my weird night-vision ability to assert itself. Instantly, the shadows filling the shop's intentionally austere interior are washed away in a bluish-white glow—almost a negative image. The rows of display cases, or, rather, what's left of them, are the first thing I notice, their metal frames more or less intact. But the plastiglass shelves and exteriors are little more than piles of shards scattered across the tile floor. The far wall is peppered with holes from projectile rounds fired in great quantity. Something a minigun can do in a matter of seconds. Shell casings litter the floor.

"They stood there in the exo." I point outside at the sidewalk. "Fired the gun to smash through the front window." I trace my index finger through the air, gesturing at the back wall. "Then proceeded to shatter all of the display cases, but not with projectiles." No holes in the floor. They wouldn't have wanted to damage the jewelry. "This was done by hand, either with the exo's arm-braces or a club of some kind."

"Or perhaps a sonic weapon, Investigator Chen." Dunn faces me, his white armor shining angelic in my special sight. "In the interest of time, a single blast could have destroyed these cases all at once."

I nod, pausing before I cut his theory off at the knees. "Then again, if they had a sonic weapon, why shoot up the place?"

He turns to survey the bullet holes in the back wall. "Good point." He steps toward the nearest hole and reaches for it. As he does so, one of the fingers on his gauntlet twists and turns, transforming itself into a scalpel of sorts, which he proceeds to put to work extricating the round buried inside the wall. It doesn't take him long. "Does this look familiar?" He holds it up between an armored thumb and index finger.

Sure does. Like any other 7.62x51mm round. But not necessarily from my exo's minigun. "We'll have the techheads take a look at it." Forensic ballistics technicians is what they prefer to be called, of course.

He places it into a small hatch built into the side of his armored suit, just for carrying evidence. Then, turning to face the message left by the burglars, Dunn takes a moment to scan it with his helmet sensors, slowly panning his head from one side to the other. "The red pigment is inorganic,

Investigator Chen. In case you were wondering whether blood was used."

"The thought had crossed my mind." I frown at a smudge on the right side, next to the word *INFIDELS*. "Any fingerprints show up on scans?"

"None." He sounds apologetic.

"Guess that would make our job too easy." My frown deepens. "Wait a minute. No fingerprints anywhere—on anything? Not even the proprietor's?"

"That is correct. It appears that she wore gloves while handling the items for sale, and she required all customers to do the same."

He nods toward a sign near the entrance stating as much, alongside a glove-dispensing machine. Of course it's been knocked over and smashed to pieces. But like everything else in here, the components, along with the disposable gloves and the countless shards of plastiglass covering the floor, are all recyclable and will, most likely, be reconstituted in order to make the place good as new at some point in the near future.

Here's hoping HQ is ahead in line on the Governor's priority list, but who's to say? Leaving this place in its current state would probably be worse for the public morale. Dome 1's citizens love their fancy little shops.

"What sort of jewelry did this place sell?" I'd look it up myself, but I have to stay offline for my night-vision to work. Guess I'm not up to date on the best places to purchase fashion accessories.

It takes Dunn only a matter of seconds to find the information. He doesn't have full access to the Link—no clones are allowed that privilege—but he can locate just about anything of interest on the LawKeeper database.

"Artifacts from the Old World, Investigator Chen."

Not what I was expecting to hear. Diamonds, maybe. Precious gems. Something dust freaks suffering withdrawal might be able to trade for a hit. Dust smuggling is no longer allowed inside the Domes, not that it ever was. Not officially, anyway. Chancellor Hawthorne let it slide because she herself was an addict. But James Bishop has cut off the supply, which has, in turn, driven up the price on whatever milligrams of the stuff remain available in Eurasia. No idea how much it costs now, or how much some people would be willing to spend. Maybe the contents of this shop would just about cover it.

Lights flash outside, sweeping over us, and I tap my temple to re-engage my augments. Assuming the analysts are back online, they'll be keeping track of every time I toggle my neuro on and off, and now Hudson is requiring a strict accounting of my actions whenever I'm offline. Writing up those reports has been eating into my evening rec time. It's been over a week since I've been able to play the role of Vivian Andromeda, Book Smuggler, in a VR StoryLine. Woe is me.

"What kind of artifacts?"

"Unknown. No record of the shop's inventory is included in the database." Dunn turns with me to face the storefront. "Perhaps Ms. Edwards will be able to divulge that information."

I step out through the nonexistent front window, holding up a hand to shield my eyes against the bright-as-day floodlight of a curfew enforcement aerocar. Jet wash billows outward, sending bits of plastiglass skittering across the sidewalk as the pilot sets down right next to our vehicle. Raul raises his blue armored arm in greeting.

The sight brings back fond memories of working the night shift with Drasko as my pilot. I'd catch the curfew violators, and he'd transport them to a holding cell while I went after my next quarry. Then he'd circle back, keeping an eye on things from overhead while I patrolled the streets in our quadrant. We made quite a team.

The good old days. Before I had to worry about him going rogue.

Nevah Edwards steps out as the door drifts upward, her chartreuse long-sleeve tunic and fuchsia ankle-length skirt flowing about her. She's a white-haired senior citizen, easily a decade or few older than my parents without looking it, thanks to Dr. Solomon Wong's gene therapy—available to every member of the upper castes. Probably a member of Eurasia's earliest generation to boot, the first to live inside the Domes. With perfect posture and confidence in every step, she approaches me, her jaw clenched tightly to keep her emotions in check. Judging from the look in her hazel eyes, they'd be a mix of fury and sorrow.

"You're the officer in charge?" She says it to me but glances at Raul. Because he's older than I am and, presumably, more experienced.

"Yes, ma'am. Investigator Sera Chen. My drones are currently gathering video footage from the surrounding area—"

"What about my cameras?" She hoists her narrow chin upward just so she can look down her nose at me. Whatever makes her happy.

"Non-functional at the time of the burglary," Dunn

reports.

Ms. Edwards gasps and lurches back a step as if he uttered a foul epithet. Or questioned the legitimacy of her birth. "I did not give that *thing* permission to address me. Put it out of my sight, at once!"

Now I'm the one clenching my jaw. "This is my partner—"

"I don't care what you call it." She tugs her high collar tight around her throat in a peculiar attempt at self-preservation. "I don't want it near me."

I know exactly how she feels. But not about Dunn. It's probably a good thing I'm not wearing my exo right now, or I'd be tempted to punt this woman across the street.

"I will assist Enforcer Ortega in securing the scene." Dunn steps past me, giving Ms. Edwards a wide berth.

Raul doesn't look thrilled by the idea, but he has the good manners to keep his bigotry to himself. He gestures for Dunn to take the opposite side of the street, and my partner does so with a nod. And with more grace than most humans I know.

"What's this?" Edwards charges toward the remains of her shop only to pull up short, aghast, with one trembling hand over her mouth. She's staring at the graffiti, which, for some reason, looks even more ominous in the floodlight's harsh glare. "Oh, what have they done?"

Interesting. Spoken as if she knows who might have been responsible for this. File that away. Best not to pounce on it right out of the gate.

"Ms. Edwards, were you or any of your employees onsite at the time of the burglary?"

"Of course not," she snaps without looking my way.

DEATH TO ALL INFIDELS holds her captivated. "It was after curfew. And I don't have *employees*." Her chin rises a notch, which I wouldn't have thought possible. "I run the shop myself, as I have for decades. There has never been a need to hire additional staff." She pauses. Then she scoffs. "I would not call this a *burglary*, Investigator Whatever-Your-Name-Is."

"What would you call it, ma'am?" Asked in the most patient tone I can muster.

"An outrage! Nothing like this has ever occurred in Dome 1."

I nod, feigning sympathy. "Were you the last to leave the shop prior to curfew?"

She turns slowly to stare at me as if I just might be a complete idiot. "I said I run the shop myself. That means I open it every morning and I close it every night."

"And at about what time did you see your last customer of the evening?"

"Client."

"Excuse me?"

She rolls her eyes. "In my line of work, I serve a very specific clientele. A *customer* would refer to any random person walking in off the street, whereas my clients always have appointments." She sniffs, her gaze returning to the smashed front window. "I never accept walk-ins."

"I see. When was your last appointment with a client?"

She shrugs. "An hour before curfew."

"Did you see anyone loitering outside recently? Maybe a groundcar lingering at the curb?" She looks confused by the question, so I add, "The burglars may have been scoping things out ahead of time. Getting a good look at what you have for sale." I gesture at the smashed storefront. "Window shopping."

Her upper lip wrinkles in disdain. "No, detective. I did not see anyone *scoping* things out. People do not do such things around here. Everyone knows the quality of the items I offer, and they can check new arrivals online before making their appointment."

"What items were taken?"

"Everything!" She extends her hands to encompass the entire shop. "Can't you see that?"

"You deal in artifacts from the Wastes, is that correct?"

She obviously doesn't like the way I phrased that. "This is a jewelry shop. I offer priceless pieces from the Old World, many of them worth more than your annual stipend."

"I have no doubt." I point out her defunct security camera. "Anybody service your system over the past few weeks?" Maybe get a good look at the merchandise for sale while installing a secret means of deactivating the entire system?

"No." She folds her arms and scowls at me. At least her eyes do. The young, supple flesh of her forehead barely wrinkles. "There was no need. It has been working perfectly. Until tonight, that is."

I nod toward the message painted on the wall. "Does this have any special significance to you?"

Her jaw drops open a smidge. "Why would it?"

"Do you know anyone who might want to make a statement like this?"

"Trust me, detective, I do not associate with members of any cult or religion. And I do not approve of Interim Chancellor Bishop giving them free reign in the Domes. We have done perfectly fine since the very beginning without their ilk polluting the minds of Eurasia's citizens."

I give her an impassive, noncommittal look. "Thank you for your time, Ms. Edwards. We'll be in touch when we have more information for you."

Another scoff. "That's it? I am dragged out of my home in the middle of curfew for...*this*?" She gestures at me like I'm the most despicable thing she's seen all day. Besides my partner. "Couldn't you have conducted this interview online and saved me the inconvenience?"

I could have probed her thoughts telepathically and gotten all the information I needed. That would have avoided a whole truckload of inconvenience. But, unfortunately, Chief Inspector Hudson has forbidden me from using my ability in such a manner, except in situations where someone's life is at stake—or the safety of the Domes is in jeopardy.

"One last thing." I take a step toward her, and she looks instantly uncomfortable with my proximity. "I'll need your most recent inventory list. Along with the names of all your clients and suppliers."

Another jaw drop. Yet another scoff. "That is privileged information!"

"Or I can let the chief inspector know that you're unwilling to comply with a simple request. And by impeding this investigation, you'll be designated as a person of interest."

"You can't honestly believe that I would have anything to do with this!" she splutters. "Why would I? It will set me back millions of credits if the pieces are not recovered, not to mention what it will cost to make repairs—"

"Help me, or not. Your choice. But as to why we wanted you to come down here, Ms. Edwards, there are some things that only come to light in person. When someone reacts to graffiti painted on her wall, for example." I narrow my gaze as her lips work mutely. She stares at the painted message again. "Maybe you know who might have done this. Maybe not. But by holding back information that we'll get our hands on eventually, you're not doing yourself any favors."

"You mean...you would need a warrant," she clarifies.

I nod. "That's how we do things now." Back in her good old days, LawKeepers were under no such stipulation. "Just another change Bishop's made. So you can wait twelve hours or so, and we'll meet again when I have a warrant compelling you to hand over your client and supplier lists. Or you can send me a copy now, and we'll be that much closer to finding the criminals who did this." I take another step closer, well within her personal space bubble, and lower my voice. "We both know how much reputation matters in this Dome. Having your name associated with the Prometheus cult in any way? Not great for business. Best if we get this cleaned up sooner rather than later, don't you think?"

She narrows her gaze at me. "Can't you just read my mind to get what you want?" I must look a little startled by that, because she smirks. "Yes, I know who you are. Your *reputation*. It was all over the Linkstream when you foiled the plans of that Prometheus entity. An artificially intelligent *god* dethroned by a *demigod*." She scoffs, looking me up and down with disdain before turning away and crossing her arms.

"I had help." My shoulders shrug without really knowing why. Maybe to say that I'm no threat. That I won't dig through her thoughts without permission. I should probably say something to that effect to put her at ease. Not that I'm a skilled psychologist or anything, but her sour demeanor is obviously a self-defense mechanism.

Either that, or she was born this way. I shudder at the thought.

"I never asked for my abilities. But I use them when the situation calls for it—when the lives of our citizens are at stake. Linking telepathically with someone against their will under any other circumstance would be immoral."

She graces me with a sidelong glance. Untrusting. Obviously worried. But gradually a reluctant nod emerges. "I'll give you what you want, detective. If only to prove to you and your superiors, and whoever else is watching this—" She gives me a pointed look, knowing my ocular lenses are recording everything. "—that I am the victim here. I have no idea who would have done something like this, or even could have. Where was that curfew enforcer?" She jabs an accusatory index finger at Raul, who wisely keeps his focus elsewhere at the moment. "Don't we pay them to keep our streets clear at night? How could someone have gotten away with breaking everything, stealing everything, shooting up the place, and vandalizing my wall? I have always been a woman of peace, and I surround myself with people who share the same worldview. You will find no one among my clients or suppliers with a violent bone in their bodies, detective!"

That remains to be seen. But I give her a nod anyway. "Thank you for your assistance." I don't step away from her. Not until I get what I want.

She grinds her teeth for a moment before exhaling with

exasperation. "Oh, very well." Her eyes lose focus as she hops online to transfer the three lists via Link: inventory, clients, suppliers. "There. Are you happy now?"

I nod, taking a step back. "We'll be in touch."

She shoulders her way past me and shouts at the aerocar pilot, "Take me home immediately!" But she pauses before climbing inside, and she fixes me with a furious look. "Governor Raniero will be hearing about this, detective. He is a personal friend of mine. Your unseemly insinuations will not go unpunished!"

"Have a good evening." I raise my hand in farewell.

This serves only to stoke her fury, which she takes out on the unsuspecting harness once she's seated inside the vehicle.

"What sort of archaic contraption is this?" she screams at the pilot as her door glides shut and locks her inside. He leans over and tries to politely show her how to fasten the buckle, but she slaps his hands away from her bust line and hollers something at the top of her lungs about sexual harassment. I don't envy him.

Once they're airborne, and their floodlight no longer blinds us, Dunn returns.

"Sorry about that," I mutter. I shouldn't have allowed him to leave the crime scene. He should have been standing right there beside me, Ms. Nevah Edwards' prejudiced wishes be damned.

"You have nothing to apologize for, Investigator Chen." His faceplate turns to regard Raul, who keeps his own counsel, eyes to himself. He's making a habit of that tonight. "What is our next step?"

I shrug. "We wait for Wink and Blink to finish sweet-talking the local security systems, then we head back to HQ and sort through the puzzle pieces." Regardless of whether someone like Edwards deserved what happened to her. Because that's the job: solving crimes. We don't have to necessarily like the citizens we help.

As if on cue, the buzzing whine of my drones' rotors angle toward us, sailing through the night. I look up at them with a smile as they approach and settle into a holding pattern, hovering overhead.

"Mission accomplished, boys?"

"Mission accomplished, Investigator Chen," they reply in unison. "All eight security cameras on neighboring buildings with a line of sight on this establishment cooperated with our request for video surveillance."

I raise an eyebrow. "None of them asked to see a warrant?"

"The topic did not arise," they reply without skipping a beat.

Just like the good old days.

"Carry on." I salute Raul as Dunn and I board our vehicle. Wink and Blink swoop into the cargo compartment and power down while the doors drift shut.

"Be safe," the world-weary curfew enforcer replies. Then he steps forward. "Hey, Chen. You think she's really friends with the Governor?"

I can tell he's worried about Edwards issuing a complaint. As close as he is to retirement, it's the last thing he needs right now.

"What's that line you always used to give me? *Do it by the book, Chen, so nothing can bite your ass,*" I call out before my door shuts.

"Right," he chuckles, saluting me as Dunn takes us aloft.

But the laughter doesn't reach his eyes.

Something is seriously troubling him. I don't have to be a telepath to know that.

7

On our way back to Hawthorne Tower, while Dunn expertly pilots our aerocar through the night, I leave the usual note on a Link messageboard for VR StoryLine enthusiasts: *D - We need to meet up - Usual spot - S*

Not sure when I'll be able to hang out with Drasko at Howard's Tavern, or if he'll make the time to virtually see me. Even if he isn't involved with the jewelry heist, he's a busy guy. There's no rest for the wicked—or for those working undercover as such. But I've got to ask. I've got to know if that was really his vehicle at the crime scene.

I'm putting off reviewing the footage Wink and Blink picked up from the neighboring security systems. I realize that. I could sort through it right now while we're en route and see if any cameras in the surrounding area caught Drasko behind the wheel of his hulking groundcar. Not to mention whoever was wearing the exo-suit. But part of me wants to hear it straight from Drasko.

I've got to give him a chance. Even if it's only until we reach HQ.

Then I bite the proverbial bullet and hail Erik, audio only.

"Hey, how's the dinner party going?" He sounds as cheerful and energetic as always. Like one of those talking

Golden Retriever puppies in a VR advertisement.

"The cider was a big hit."

He catches something in my tone. Hate it when he does that. "Don't tell me. You left early."

"Working a case." I shift in my seat.

"Did you at least give them all a chance to shower you with affection?"

I don't dignify that with a response. "Have you seen Drasko?"

"Today? No." I can hear the smirk in his voice. "Just because his loved ones are living on the farm doesn't mean he can abandon his duties in Dome 10—y'know, crime and whatnot—to visit them anytime he wants. Man's gotta have his priorities straight."

So Drasko's wife and kids are still in Dome 9. "Has there been any pushback about them relocating?"

Erik doesn't answer right away. "From who? Are we talking government types?"

"Correct."

Another pause. "Not that I'm aware of. I mean, I don't know what sort of red tape Drasko had to cut through to move them here, but nobody's given Mom or me any trouble about it. Could be they know Samson would have something to say, if they did."

Not many bureaucrats have the intestinal fortitude to go up against a cyborg Samson's size. "He can be real imposing."

"That he can." Erik's pride in his biological father comes through loud and clear. The two of them are close. Much closer than you'd expect, having only met for the first time last year.

My thoughts, along with a whole mess of conflicted

feelings, start drifting back to Luther and Daiyna, but I can't let them. I've got to focus on the case. "I left Drasko a note to meet online. But if you happen to see him..."

"Something up?"

"Could be. Not sure." I shouldn't go into much detail with a civilian. Because it's not professional. But after everything he's been through, and everything we've survived together, I know I can trust him. For the most part. "Somebody knocked over a jewelry shop down the street from my parents' cube."

"In Dome 1," he confirms, just because it's unheard of.

I nod, even though he can't see me. "The burglars took everything. But they left something behind."

"A riddle, perchance?"

"A message." I hesitate. "Looks like they might be part of the Prometheus cult."

He exhales. Loudly. "Thought we broke up that band."

So did I. "Has there been any chatter about them getting back together?"

"I haven't been invited on a reunion tour, if that's what you mean." All levity has dropped from his tone. Which is to be expected, considering the mindjacking he endured, courtesy of Prometheus, and what he was forced to do while under the influence. "What did the message say?"

I recite it for him, word for word. He exhales again.

"Could be a red herring. Or..." He clears his throat. "How sure are we that the AI is still right where we left it?"

"As sure as we can be." I haven't asked Commander Bishop about it. I probably should, considering this latest development: *PROMETHEUS WILL RISE AGAIN*. But I'm not sure how to broach the subject. Hey-uh,

Commander? You know that powerful AI we trapped on an old phone a few weeks ago? Any chance it might have gotten loose?

"Well, if it's not a distraction tactic, and there really is a misguided cult of jewelry thieves roaming about, then I know of only one investigator for the job. And her handsome *consultant*, of course." I can almost hear him grin. So obnoxious. "Then again, if the AI has somehow escaped or managed to clone itself online, and it's collecting followers to do its bidding, then we might have to brace ourselves for another major crapfest. The sequel."

"No thanks. We haven't fully recovered from the last uprising." Case in point: Dunn flying to Hawthorne Tower instead of our own building, which remains unsafe to enter. The structural repairs are going slowly but steadily. Even so, the damaged edifice continues to stand as a lopsided monument to the worst day in Eurasia's recent history.

Erik adds a pensive afterthought, "Could be somebody's trying to take advantage of that. Kick us while we're down. They won't get a better opportunity than this."

They'd be right, whoever *they* are. With the debilitating power outages plaguing our makeshift HQ, the analysts are blinded for extended periods of time. Minutes might not seem like much, but they can make all the difference in collecting video evidence while a crime is taking place. Particularly when the burglars somehow seem to know they have exactly five minutes to get the job done.

"I've gotta go." I glance over at Dunn as he begins our descent, and the street rises up to meet us. Right about where we parked before.

"I could swing by later," Erik offers. "Bring over another

bottle of cider, fresh from the orchards?"

I can't let him get used to visiting my cube. That was a one-time thing. He knew I was a little nervous about having dinner with my two sets of parents, and he decided to offer some moral support. He doesn't make a habit of stopping by. We don't have that kind of relationship. I don't know what we have exactly, but it's not that.

"Got a feeling I'll be living at Hawthorne Tower until I make some headway on this case. Give Drasko's family my best. And your folks." I can't think of anything else to say, and I don't want to give him a chance to make things even more cringeworthy between us, so I end the call.

"Erik Paine's rehabilitation is going well?" Dunn keeps his focus on the controls as the aerocar touches down gently, and the engines power down with a low thrum. We unbuckle our harnesses in unison.

"He seems more like himself lately." By which I mean impetuous and annoying.

"I read about the Ship of Theseus, from Greek mythology, earlier today." The side doors swing upward, but his non sequitur keeps me in my seat. "Now that Interim Chancellor Bishop has allowed a broad range of previously banned books to circulate across the Domes, and now that I am allowed to read such materials, I am taking full advantage of the opportunity."

"The time you used to spend in Level 5?"

His helmet nods once. "I am finding other uses for that time. While I do not have access to the Link, I have nevertheless found much of interest on the LawKeeper database: a virtual library of ancient texts. The Ship of Theseus stood out to me."

I'm going to need a refresher on that one. "How so?"

"The Athenians preserved the ship by replacing every old plank as it decayed, putting fresh, strong timber in its place, until, eventually, there were no parts of the original ship that remained. Due to the passage of time and the diligence of the preservers, every piece of the ship was swapped out. So the question is, did the Ship of Theseus still exist? Or did it become an entirely new vessel? And if the latter, when did that occur? When more than half of its essence had been replaced? Or when every last vestige of its former self no longer had a place on board?"

Deep thoughts with Dunn. "Can it be neither? And both at the same time?"

His helmet tilts to one side. "Perhaps. I am thinking about Erik Paine and the ordeal he suffered under the influence of Prometheus. He was not himself at the time, and yet he will forever carry memories of what happened while his mind was hijacked by that AI. Thus, he will never be the same. And yet he remains Erik Paine."

"The one and only," I mutter, leaning toward exiting the vehicle. "Identity over the passage of time. Is that what we're talking about?"

"Humans evolve as individuals, often changing dramatically in the ways you think and feel about the world around you, based on life experiences." He pauses, holding out his arms, bent at the elbows, as if they don't belong to him. "I was not created with these arms, or this leg, or multiple organs inside me. I am now equal parts biological, synthetic, and mechanical, due to the physical trauma I have survived."

Being shot in the head. Thrown through a cube complex

windowall. Set upon by multiple killbots. Put back together by the best medical technicians in Dome 1.

But that's the question: Was he put back together, or made into something new?

"I am more like the Ship of Theseus than a human being. And I am left wondering whether I am still Unit D1-436...or if I am now something else. If I can be more than the sum of my parts, even though I am a human's clone. Or if, due to my conditioning, I will never be anything else, no matter how much of my body is replaced."

I knock on the plasteel armor covering his forearm. "Our bodies don't make us who we are. Biological or synthetic, they're just machines that carry our..." Soul? Spirit? Is that what I believe? I know Luther and other followers of the Way do, along with just about every religious cult springing up across the Domes these days. "Consciousness." I land on that one with a shrug. "So the ship analogy doesn't really work. Not for us. Because we're more than meets the eye." Damn. I was trying so hard to avoid clichés.

"You believe that applies to me as well?"

Can't help smiling at him. "I said *we*, didn't I?"

Leaving my drones in standby mode on the backseat as the doors shut behind us, Dunn and I enter the atrium of Hawthorne Tower with our boots striking a purposeful staccato across the polished tiles. The place is just as dark and empty as before, except for its lone occupant at the front desk, armor glowing neon-blue along the edges and down that vertical line on the front of its faceplate. For some reason, Dunn didn't qualify for the fancy upgrade.

"Investigator Sera Chen and Unit D1-436," the clone welcomes us with about as much enthusiasm as a funeral dirge. "Chief Inspector Hudson was not expecting you back so soon."

"What can I say? We get the job done." I nudge Dunn with an elbow. "Expedient, that's what we are. Right, partner?"

He doesn't always seem to know what to do with himself around other clones. Because they have clearly defined duties, and his are more free-flowing? Because he recognizes that he's different from them, but he doesn't know how exactly to quantify his own uniqueness? Or is that just me transferring my thoughts and feelings onto him?

He doesn't say anything as we head toward the speedlifts, and I don't try to get him to loosen up. After our discussion earlier, he's probably still pondering his identity issues. Seeing that security clone had to remind him of the stark contrast between who he was before and who he is now.

Or maybe I'm reading too much into his silence. Again.

The third floor is even more hectic than before. Power's been restored, but that hasn't done anything to take the frantic energy in the air down a notch. If I didn't know better, I might think we have another full-scale emergency situation on our hands.

Dunn drops the minigun round off at the ballistics station before joining me. Together we head toward Chief Inspector's Hudson's office. He's scowling outside his door, and judging from the look on his face, something bad is going down somewhere in the Domes. He beckons sharply in a swift, chopping motion, and disappears behind the sliding door. Probably to clamber over his desk again.

By the time Dunn and I make it across the crowded bullpen, Hudson is already seated, and his deskscreen is projecting a holo-image of the Dome 10 docks.

"Something up, sir?" I cram inside with Dunn, shoulder-to-shoulder, as the closet door shuts behind us.

"They picked a hell of a time to make a statement." Hudson curses under his breath and shakes his head, glaring at the holo display as if it can be intimidated by a sour expression.

"They, sir?" I glance up at Dunn, but the gleaming faceplate on his helmet is unreadable.

"Insurgents. *Patriots.*" Hudson scoffs. "They've decided to organize a riot. Tonight. Blocking water shipments from the desalination plant. No fresh H_2O for the Ten Domes until their grievances are addressed. Bunch of entitled children throwing a tantrum, that's all this is. Security clones are onsite containing the situation, but things have already escalated." He glances at me and then my partner. "There have been reports of explosives going off in the vicinity of the maglev tunnel."

If the patriots cut off Dome 10 from the rest of Eurasia, they will be the only Dome with access to the outside world. To the Mediterranean, and to the scavengers who collect raw materials from the Wastes to be repurposed inside our walls.

"I don't understand..." This doesn't make sense. Why now? "Chancellor Bishop has agreed to meet with them, to address the issues—"

"That was before." Hudson nods in the direction of the stampeding feet and raised voices outside. "Since the Prometheus incident, priorities have shifted to rebuilding, to repairing the damage done to Dome 1 and elsewhere. The solar arrays, the factories, our own headquarters. Listening to those extremists whine about how bad they've got it? Not on the Chancellor's to-do list as of late."

"So it is a cry for attention." Dunn's helmet tilts forward as he regards the hologram closely, and he points with the index finger on his right gauntlet. "If these insurgents are rioting at the docks, then it would follow that our security forces would gather there, leaving the maglev tunnel relatively unguarded. Blowing the tunnel and sealing off Dome 10 would be a radical move, but these so-called Patriots may feel they have no other choice, that this is the only way for them to be taken seriously."

I nod, watching him. Can't help feeling proud. Not that long ago, he wouldn't have spoken up in a meeting like this.

Hudson sniffs, unimpressed. "Standard guerrilla tactics. If their goal is to be viewed as terrorists, then I would say they are on the right track."

"Do you want us to head over and lend a hand?" I offer.

"No. Curfew enforcers are en route. We will have this uprising quelled within the hour, I'm sure." He leans back in his squeaky chair and rubs between his eyes. "You're already on a case, Chen. And I doubt you've had a chance to comb through all the video surveillance you've gathered."

"I was planning to do that in a quiet corner..." No chance of that tonight.

"You can use my office." He stands, looking past me at the door. "I should be out there anyway, in the thick of it. All hands on deck." Then he looks irritated by something and lowers his gaze toward nothing in particular. "You'll need to—That is, I will need to—"

"Right." I take Dunn's arm and backpedal us both through the door as it slides open. "We'll give you a minute." Trying not to get run over by the hustle and bustle around us, we stand outside and wait for him to make his exit from the cramped workspace.

Ignoring our hasty departure, Dunn asks, "Do you think there is a connection between the burglary this evening and the disturbance in Dome 10?"

"Only one way to tell." I give him a wink. "We follow the evidence."

8

So that's what we do, as soon as Hudson vacates his office. Via my ocular lenses, I cast all of the footage from those eight different cameras onto his deskscreen, and together they form a three-dimensional composite holo-image that we can rotate to view from various angles, zooming in and out as necessary with hand movements the projectors recognize.

"This is the first time I have accompanied you during the evidence-reviewing phase of a case," Dunn remarks, sounding intrigued by the process. Usually he'd be under scrutiny in Level 5 this time of night, his alpha and theta brain waves studied by a very intense team of scientists and technicians.

"Don't mind a little drudgery?" I raise an eyebrow at him. Then I frown slightly. "You can take off your helmet." We'll be in these close quarters for a while, and he should make himself as comfortable as he can.

His black faceplate reflects my mirror-image as he asks, "It will not disturb you...to see his face?"

Not that long ago, it would have. But those nightmares haven't returned whenever I grab a few hours of shuteye. The ghost of the man I killed no longer haunts me. I might even be able to sleep through the night, should the opportunity arise.

"That's your face under there." Not Solomon Wong's, nor any other clone's. "It belongs to you. Just you." I climb over Hudson's desk, passing through the holo-feed as I do. The projectors play the scene across me as if my body is a screen.

Dunn's armored shoulders rise and fall a centimeter or so. Then with a certain measure of hesitation, he removes his helmet and tucks it under one arm. He doesn't look at me right away, but when he does, I smile up at him.

"There he is." The scars are healing, but he still has a web of pink lines that intersect across his face, forming a wide grid of sorts where the laser sutures did their work. Given time, they'll eventually fade. "You're looking more like yourself."

"Thank you, Investigator Chen." He focuses on the holo-display before us. "Would you like me to peruse the client and supplier lists from Ms. Edwards while you review the video footage?"

"Good idea." I send him copies of the lists via my augments, and he nods once they're received.

Then we settle in. I sync up the video feeds and play them from start to finish over and over again, rotating the holo first one direction, then the other, to give me a better vantage point. A clearer view of who was in that exo-suit and who was behind the wheel of that groundcar. Meanwhile, Dunn stands at attention and stares at nothing in particular, his eyes unfocused as he scans the names I sent him across his ocular lenses. The LawKeeper database will have information on any persons of interest he comes across—the sort of people an entitled, first-generation Dome 1 citizen such as Nevah Edwards should have no business doing business with.

I'd hoped the footage would give me an answer, one way

or the other. That I would know without a doubt whether Drasko was in the car. But unfortunately the two burglars involved were no dummies. Even though they knocked out the shop's cameras with what appears to be some kind of EMP gun, they knew they were being recorded by neighboring security systems. So they wore masks: weird, light-absorbing things that made their faces look like whirlpools of dark matter.

Cursing under my breath, I advance the video feed to their grand exit. The guy in the exo grabs a duffel bag stuffed with merchandise and takes off running. In an exo, that's loping along with long strides, boot-struts punching into the pavement. The other guy grabs an identical bag and tosses it into the backseat of the groundcar, then climbs in and floors it, following his partner in crime.

But that's when things get weird.

They just vanish.

One second, they're heading down the middle of the street full-tilt. The next second, they're no longer there. Nowhere in sight.

I replay the scene, forward and back, again and again. It's not that they moved out of range of the cameras. They would have needed to proceed another hundred meters on their current heading or take a sharp turn around a corner going the opposite direction in order to do that. No, they should have still been here, right here in front of me. The cameras were still rolling long after the burglars disappeared. Wink and Blink knew to request plenty of footage, both before and after the incident. So the feed keeps running now, showing nothing but an empty street and a smashed storefront in the burglars' wake.

No sign of curfew enforcer Raul Ortega. Not for another twenty minutes, which I advance at ten times the playback speed, just to get through it. There he is, hustling onto the scene in his motorized armor, staring in disbelief.

I curse under my breath and shake my head. I've been so focused on the duo's getaway that I've neglected to take a look at how they arrived in the first place. So I swipe the footage back to the beginning and go from there, skipping through the boring part prior to the burglars' arrival.

Then I curse again, unable to believe my eyes.

Dunn focuses on me with a frown. "Did you find something?"

"I'll say." I point at the holo of the vacant street. "Watch the exit." I replay the moment the groundcar and exo-suit cease to exist following the robbery. "Some trick, right? And here's the kicker: They arrived at the exact same spot."

He nods, staring intently as I replay the scene a few more times for good measure. "Is there any chance they could be dust addicts? And that their ability is invisibility?"

"If they were on foot, maybe so. But I've never heard of a dust freak being able to make a vehicle disappear." And I've only known two individuals capable of making themselves invisible: Trezon, whose DNA was spliced with genes from the Twenty's children, courtesy of doctors mindjacked by the Prometheus AI; and a fellow by the name of Tucker who carried Erik and me in incubation chambers across the North American Wastes before either of us were born. Obviously I don't have clear memories of Tucker. He's more like someone I met in a dream, once upon a time.

"Holo-shielding, then?" Dunn suggests. "Perhaps it only appears that they disappeared, when in fact they were merely cloaked by a hologram."

I nod. "But how would that explain this?" I turn up the volume, and the sound of the exo bounding across the pavement is nearly drowned out by the thunderous engine of the muscle car, which only increases in volume as the driver guns it, tires squealing against the pavement. But at the exact second when both of them disappear halfway down the street, the noise does as well. As if they suddenly ceased to exist. "I've never heard of holo-cloaking tech with a built-in silencer."

Dunn's eyebrows arch upward. "Nor have I, Investigator Chen."

"Now try this on for size." I replay the arrival of the groundcar and exo-suit.

Dunn blinks. "It is as though...they materialized out of the air."

I nod. "My thought exactly. If they were using holo-cloaks, they wouldn't have turned off the tech long enough to smash the shop and grab everything of value. They would have remained invisible for the duration. This..." I extend a hand toward the holo-image, which I've paused at the instant the exo-suit and groundcar appear on the scene. "This looks like some kind of transportation technology I'm not familiar with."

"A portal generator, perhaps?"

"Wasn't going to say that." With a groan, I sink into Hudson's squeaky desk chair and rub my eyes with the palms of my hands. "Because something like that doesn't exist. It's like saying they used magic."

"Based on the evidence..." Dunn tilts his head slightly to one side as he studies the holo. "They were able to enter

Dome 1 undetected, rob the jewelry shop, and then make their getaway without aerial curfew enforcers detecting them. That is, indeed, some magic trick, Investigator Chen."

I can't think about this right now. I need a distraction. "Tell me what you found."

"Ms. Nevah Edwards' suppliers are the typical individuals who work as intermediaries between scavengers and proprietors of establishments who sell anything that isn't needed for the Domes' infrastructure: jewelry, baubles, and the like."

They're opportunists. Scavengers are paid by the Governors to collect reusable resources outside the Domes, but certain sparkly things like gold coins and diamond rings always seem to end up in every haul. So these intermediaries pay the scavengers a finder's fee and then hand over the valuables to their preferred proprietor with the understanding that should a sale be made, the profits will be split. So in Ms. Edwards' case, whoever supplied her shop full of *artifacts* is going to be very unhappy that everything is gone, and nobody paid a single credit for it.

"Any of these suppliers have a record?"

"No, Investigator Chen. They tend to navigate a fine line between what is legal and illegal in the Domes, but the six intermediaries that have done business with Ms. Edwards over the years do not have a history of criminal activity in their files."

"What a relief. We don't have to worry about them killing her." I don't allow my sarcasm to hang in the air too long. "Tell me about her clientele."

"There are forty-seven names on the list. Each citizen is a member of the upper castes and resides here in Dome 1.

Twelve of them live in the same cube complex as your parents." His way of saying they're doing well for themselves, but not the highest on the totem pole. "The other thirty-five are first-generation citizens of Eurasia. Based on my preliminary findings, they are well-acquainted with Nevah Edwards and likely have been friends for decades."

I'm sure they're all great at defying their age, too. "Any link between them and the Children of Tomorrow?"

Dunn shakes his head. "According to our records, none of the suppliers or clients were mindjacked during the uprising, and none had any known relations involved."

Known relations. That gets me thinking. "How about Edwards? What can you tell me about her family?"

Dunn's gaze loses focus for a few seconds as he trawls the LawKeeper database. Something I could have done myself, but I much prefer having conversations like this with my partner. Or maybe I just like how fast he's able to do the requisite research.

"Nevah Edwards is a widow. Her husband, Stephan Edwards, passed away three years ago from congenital heart disease. He could have opted for a synthetic heart but did not. She has one daughter, Mirela Edwards, an engineer specializing in solar technology who lives and works in Dome 8," Dunn reads the information displayed on his lenses.

"The husband chose to die," I muse aloud. Not a big surprise, considering the wife. "How far would the artificial heart have extended his life?"

"Unknown." Dunn's eyes focus on me. "Would you like me to research that topic, Investigator Chen?"

I shake my head. "Find out more about the daughter. See what she's into. Known associates. Anybody who might have an ax to grind with the mother." My attention returns to the holo-display. I advance the feed incrementally until the footage shows the groundcar driver with a can of spray paint, going at the wall with a vengeance. "They've got everything ready to go in those two duffel bags, and he takes time out for this."

Dunn raises an eyebrow. "If they utilized a portal generator, then perhaps time was no object."

I can't be sure, but there might be a twinkle in my partner's eye. Like he's teasing me just a bit. "Fine. Research portal generators while you're at it."

"Yes, Investigator Chen."

My gaze lingers on the holo projected upward from the deskscreen. "Interesting how they waited until the very end to make their statement. It wasn't the priority. Smashing and grabbing everything in sight was the first thing on their minds."

Dunn doesn't respond right away, but when he does, he sounds pensive. "This observation would support the theory that they were not actual cult members."

"Unless that's what they wanted us to think." Exhaling, I get to my feet and allow the holo to collapse. The deskscreen's black surface reflects Dunn and me standing over it, the mirror-images of our heads almost seeming to touch each other. I take a step back and bump into the chair. "I'm going to hail Raul, have him take a look at the burglars' arrival and departure point. See if there's anything out of the ordinary."

I might also take a quick dive into VR, just in case Drasko shows up at Howard's Tavern. Maybe check in with Hector or one of our other tech-heads and see if we can do anything about the masks those burglars were wearing. XR scans might be able to give us a match with dental records on file.

"And I have research to do." Dunn half-turns toward the door. "Should we...?"

"Hudson gave us the run of the place, so I say we take full advantage of it. Make yourself at home." Except there's no chair for my partner.

Dunn dips his chin. "I was wondering if perhaps we should check on the situation at the docks."

Hudson was pretty clear on that. He wants us focused on our case. But then again, how can we maintain our focus if we're worried about where our next glass of water is coming from? Not that we don't have an emergency backup supply, but it's only intended to last us a couple weeks. Plenty of time to get the rioters settled down.

Except that's not how we do things. Something like this has to be nipped in the bud. Otherwise, other rabble-rousers get the idea they can throw the government over a barrel until they get what they want.

"I think that's a good idea." Calling up the same live feed the analysts are viewing, I cast it across the deskscreen, and the holo-projectors bring it to three-dimensional life. "Just in case there's any overlap between our portal-jumping magical burglars and a full-fledged Patriot insurrection." I give Dunn a wink.

He doesn't respond. Probably because this isn't the time for joviality.

"Well damn..." I trail off, staring at the feed.

Dome 10 should be dark this time of night. Second shift crews are still hard at work after curfew—waste management, water recycling, and desalination aren't things that can be neglected for eight hours at a time in self-sustained biospheres—but there shouldn't be anybody out and about. And there shouldn't be landscape lights glowing as bright as day, gobbling up electricity. But the docks are crawling with people right now. Hundreds, by the looks of things.

A wall of angry, shouting, fist-raising people in stained coveralls squirm shoulder to shoulder, blocking the gates to the desalination plant and impeding the exit of two driverless tanker trucks. Facing off against them is a line of twenty security clones in the middle of the street, standing like a row of statues with non-lethal shockers aimed down at the pavement. If this were a serious situation, they'd be armed with assault rifles carrying lethal ordnance. Up above, a trio of curfew aerocars swoop to and fro with floodlights glaring while one of the pilots issues an ultimatum on loudspeaker:

"Disperse at once, or you will be gassed."

The crowd roars, boiling with fury and shaking their fists—along with plenty of rude gestures—up at the pilot.

"This could get very ugly." Dunn looks ready to put his helmet back on and head right over.

I hold up a hand to slow his roll. "They've got things under control." I hope.

Then I see something that makes me do a double take. At the same time, my stomach plunges a bit.

The rioters look like they might be dispersing. But no, they're just moving off to the sides, making room for a certain somebody among them who's wearing my exo-suit. That's what it looks like, at any rate.

The security clones raise their shockers as the exo lumbers toward them, its minigun pivoting into ready position and spinning up.

"Investigator Chen..." Dunn trails off in disbelief.

I don't know what to say to him. I can't believe this is happening either.

The rioters are cheering and chanting something I can't make out. The pilot is repeating himself, sounding desperate now. But it's too late. Tear gas won't stop this from happening. This atrocity playing out before our eyes.

The exo's minigun opens fire, its blazing salvo mowing down the security clones as if they're nothing more than tin soldiers.

9

So that's what a massacre looks like.

Except these aren't people. They're not human. And they're not like Dunn. They're more robot than—

I look at my partner as he stares at the holo-display, the blue-white light shining across his face. He's frozen in place. His eyes glisten with tears.

"They will be recycled." He catches me watching him, and he puts his helmet back on before a single tear has a chance to fall.

This is my fault. I can't shake the feeling, even though I don't know for sure that's my exo-suit. It only looks like it, has the same one-of-a-kind minigun upgrade.

Who am I kidding? It might as well have been my finger on the trigger. Leaving it behind the way I did was beyond negligent. Whether this one's actually mine or just an impressive copy, I'm responsible for what happened here.

I can't look away. Those clones weren't robots. They were flesh and blood. Like me. Like Dunn. Maybe with the right amount of encouragement and attention, they might have become as self-aware as he is.

Twenty bodies fell to the ground, gunned down, limbs twisting, helmeted heads snapping back. White armor cracked open, bursts of blood rupturing as shockers fired blindly. Blasts glanced off the exo-suit's frame like bursts of electric-blue fireworks, useless against inorganic matter, missing the operator underneath.

The horrible scene plays over and over again, emblazoned in my mind. Dunn's too, I have no doubt.

But now things are quiet at the docks. The rioters have stopped chanting. The pilot has stopped issuing orders. The aerocars now hover in place overhead, floodlights shining on the gruesome aftermath. The crowd doesn't seem to know what to do with itself. Did all that blood stun them into silence? Didn't they know that clones bleed like the rest of us?

The figure in the exo-suit staggers back from the carnage, looming over the broken bodies. The shoulder-mounted minigun retracts into standby mode. I zoom in on the face of the figure wearing the exo. The same person who smashed into the jewelry store earlier tonight? If so, they really get around.

No mask this time. Her face is clear to see. Jaw tight. Eyes glaring with singular focus. Older than Terminal age, in her mid-fifties. No gene therapy to hide the years.

She looks like she could be Nevah Edwards' sister.

"Identify," I subvocalize via audiolink, and a split-second later my ocular lenses populate with the citizen's government record. "Well, hello there, Mirela."

Not Ms. Edwards' sister. Her daughter, the solar engineer. She's obviously taken up some interesting hobbies on the side.

"You have three seconds to begin dispersing," the pilot reiterates.

Mirela scowls at the aerocar. Then she leans back, and the minigun lurches into ready position again, barrel rotating with menace.

"Don't do it." My fists clench down at my sides.

Dunn's face shield reflects the holo-image of automatic fire lighting up the night, a heavy salvo fired upward, right at the police aerocar. The pilot swerves in midair, avoiding a barrage that would have smashed through his windscreen and perforated everything inside, including himself. But the rounds tear across the hull, and smoke issues forth in black gusts. The other two aerocars relocate immediately, moving out of range as the damaged one limps after them, wobbling unsteadily in the night.

Mirela Edwards lets them go, watching their retreat with a steely eye. Then she turns in the exo to face the rioters, who stare at her, wide-eyed and mute, until she thrusts an armored fist into the air. That's when they all erupt in a cacophony of wild shouts and cheers, dispersing but not disbanding, some climbing the gate behind them while others charge straight for the airlock—a giant circular structure made of plasticon and thick panes of plastiglass, large enough to allow two tanks to pass through riding piggyback—on the other side of the desalination plant.

The hundred or so who scaled the gate begin attacking the first tanker truck with a vengeance, leaping onto one side in a misguided effort to tip it over. Good luck with that. The thing's a heavy beast. The rest of the mob, more than a couple hundred strong, take up their position in front of the barricades leading to the airlock—our only way in or out of the Ten Domes—in the same way they did at the gate. Their goal is unclear.

Unless they hope to block scavenging teams from entering or exiting Eurasia.

The port security personnel hunker down behind plasticon barricades and brandish their assault rifles. As a rule, citizens aren't allowed to carry guns that fire lethal projectiles, but these guards are tasked with protecting every citizen in the Domes from what's outside: deadly airborne toxins. Scavengers garbed in protective gear and working in teams of six are required to cycle through three separate chambers before reaching the Wastes beyond our walls. So these protesters, or whatever they think they are, won't be able to get out easily, if that's what's on their addled minds.

Mirela stomps forward in the exo, and rioters part for her like curtains on a stage, just like they did before.

"Go home!" she shouts at the port security. "You're not needed here anymore!"

The guards glance at each other, unsure of the situation. Even more so now that their air support has high-tailed it in the opposite direction.

"The airlock is ours!" she announces, and the crowd cheers. "The water is ours!" Another cheer. "And until things start changing around here, it's going to stay that way!"

As if to punctuate her statement, a massive crash fills the night. Somehow, those overzealous rioters managed to knock the tanker truck over onto its side, big chunky tires rotating uselessly like a clumsy, oversized creature unable to maintain its footing.

"Alert," the automated voice of the onboard computer announces. "Alert. Contact with the pavement has been lost. Alert."

With renewed vigor, the mob moves on to the second

driverless truck.

"Disperse at once!" Mirela aims the minigun at the guards and savors their anxious looks. She's got them cowed. "Or I will be forced to fire on you."

One of the security personnel links up to request backup. I have access to the feed: He's told to hold his position, that help is on the way. The other guards glance at him. He nods reassuringly and gestures for them to stay put. The holo can't show me enough detail to see the look in his eyes, but he's got to be wondering if his team will be able to hold out until backup arrives. More security clones, but armed with assault rifles this time? More curfew enforcers packing the same lethal ordnance?

For now, the guards keep their heads down and their guns ready. If ordered to return fire, they will. But as a rule, they don't shoot civilians.

My attention returns to the rioters. "They're not Patriots," I murmur, pointing at the ones at the front of the pack. "None of them wear the stars and stripes." An outdated insignia going back hundreds of years. Or so I'm told. "Hudson's intel is wrong."

"The Prometheus cult, then?" Dunn doesn't sound convinced. But then his helmet tilts to one side as if viewing the scene from a different angle. "This Mirela Edwards is quite a leader. It could be that she has taken Trezon's place in a more militant capacity."

My brow wrinkles. "If that was her at her mother's shop earlier, why wear a mask?" I gesture at the holo. "But not bother with one now?"

"Perhaps Mirela Edwards is not concerned about her mother's opinion of these actions. Because Nevah Edwards secretly supports them. Or Mirela Edwards may have lost her mask in-transit, assuming she was one of the burglars in question." He pauses. "It is equally likely that she may not have been. The evidence is inconclusive."

Right. And the exo-suit is just a bizarre coincidence.

"Either way, I'd say interviewing Nevah Edwards again might be a good idea," I mutter.

"You do not sound like you think it is a good idea." He still has a little trouble deciphering tonal contradictions, even though he's doing much better at grasping irony and sarcasm. Hanging around with me, that's a necessity.

"Probably because I'd be fine never interacting with that woman again for the rest of my life." Exhaling, I climb over Hudson's desk and head toward the door. Dunn takes a step back to make room for me. "Find out everything you can on Mirela. She's the key to this." Along with Drasko, somehow. I curse under my breath as the holo-display collapses behind me. "Whatever this is."

The door senses my neuro and slides open as I turn toward it. Hudson is waiting on the other side, along with a pair of LawKeepers in uniform. At the same moment that I make eye contact with the chief inspector, I receive the ballistics report—flashing in the lower right corner of my lenses. I open it immediately.

"Sir?" I ask, skimming over the report. The 7.62x51mm round is a match to the rifle ammo I regularly feed my minigun. And what's more, it has my fingerprints on it.

"There has been a development." Hudson keeps his hawk-like face stoic.

I try to do the same. Is he referring to the incident at the Dome 10 airlock or ballistics from the burglary?

"Your exo-suit has made another appearance." He's furious. I can tell that much without prying into his mind. But he's holding it together. For now. "Assuming that was your suit at the jewelry store earlier this evening?"

"Yes, sir. Ballistics confirmed as much." I didn't want to believe it. But now I have no choice. "And the proprietor's daughter is the one shooting up the docks."

His surprise lasts only a millisecond. "Of course. You were watching."

"There's a connection, sir. There's gotta be. I don't know how the stolen artifacts fit in, or why this is all happening tonight, but I'll find out." I take a step toward him. "Let me go there. Dunn and I can help de-escalate the situation."

"D1-436 was watching as well?"

I nod as the horrific bloodshed makes another appearance in my mind's eye.

"Twenty of them, blasted to pieces." Hudson curses under and looks away. The two officers with him keep their expressions neutral. "Can D1-436 remain objective?"

I'll never forget how Dunn hid his tears from me.

"Of course, sir." I raise my chin. "He wants to help. We both do. And I can conduct interviews en route. The burglary case won't be neglected. I have a feeling it's somehow integral to this situation at the airlock."

"Right now, that burglary is the last thing on my mind." Hudson watches me for a moment. Then he gives me a pensive nod. "Very well. Take Matthews and Shariq with you." He extends a hand toward the officers behind him.

I know them both. They're trackers, tasked with chasing down and apprehending criminals. Good at their job, but like most of my coworkers, they don't share my affection for

Dunn. Matthews is tall and blond with a clean-shaven face and hazel eyes. Athletic build without bulging muscles, in his mid-thirties. Shariq is also Terminal age with a similar physique, albeit more curvy due to her gender. Her olive-toned skin is a shade or two darker than mine, her eyes nearly black, the same color as the hair she keeps close-cropped above her ears.

I exchange nods with each of them in turn, noting their aloof expressions. I'm not thrilled with the prospect of Dunn and me being assigned an escort, but I'm not going to complain about it. The last thing I want is to be sidelined tonight. "Do we have confirmation on whether the maglev tunnel was bombed?"

"Not yet. Cameras are out at the Dome 10 train station, and the guards there are not answering our hails." Hudson's grim tone suits the situation. "If the tunnel is impassable, then you will need to find another way through, even if that means blowing your way out. Matthews and Shariq are both trained in the use of semtex and are carrying the necessary components."

My thoughts drift back to the burglars' escape. How had they managed that magic trick? And if Mirela in the exo had gone straight to the docks to stir up trouble afterward, where had the groundcar gone with the other bag of loot? Assuming that it was Drasko behind the wheel, had they already agreed to part company after he'd done his share of the deal—activating the exo—and received his payment? But if so, why had he paused to paint that message on the wall before making his getaway? Had he known I'd see it, and was it meant to point me in the right direction? That Mirela is a card-carrying member of the Prometheus cult, even if she's keeping that card close to the vest?

"Chen." Of course Hudson catches my attention wavering. "If you are unsuccessful at disabling the exo-suit, then Matthews and Shariq have orders to slag it. With or without the operator still inside. Is that understood?"

Cut the head off the snake, and the rioters will disperse. Great plan. Except for the life of Mirela Edwards, of course. As well as my poor exo—assuming it really is mine.

Maybe I ought to just go with that assumption. Without a doubt, it was my exo-suit at the burglary. Hard to argue with a ballistics report. And more than likely, it was my exo that gunned down those twenty security clones as well. My fingerprints are all over the—

Wait a minute.

A minigun fires six thousand rounds a minute. Six thousand. There's no way in hell that my prints would be on every single one of them. Loading the ammo pack, I might have touched a dozen casings at most. So what are the odds that the one round Dunn picked out of the wall just happened to carry my fingerprint? Not great.

"D1-436, you will accompany Investigator Chen," Hudson orders Dunn as he emerges from the closet behind me.

"Yes, Chief Inspector Hudson." He sounds eager to depart. Or maybe he only sounds that way to me because I know him so well.

Matthews and Shariq glance at each other, but they don't say anything. They continue doing a standup job keeping their expressions unreadable. Their posture isn't too shabby, either.

"Very well. We will be watching—assuming there isn't another power outage." Hudson nods at no one in particular and storms into his office, thrusting his hands into the pockets of his coat. "Dismissed."

Without a word, the two trackers head for the speedlift in the outer hall. Shrugging at Dunn, I follow them, and he's right beside me.

We keep our own counsel on the ride down, which I don't mind, but once we reach the aerocar parked outside and Dunn moves to assume his position at the controls, Matthews holds up a hand to halt us in our tracks.

"To avoid any confusion, let me make this clear from the get-go: Shariq and I are running point on this operation. I don't care how special you think you are, Chen, but you and your pet project are tagging along for one reason only: Hudson's orders. He wants you to disable your runaway exo. Other than that, you're welcome to continue working your case along the way. A jewelry heist, isn't it?" He smirks. Shariq almost does as well but thinks better of it. Smart woman. "Just stay the hell out of our way."

He climbs into the pilot's seat, and Shariq gets in beside him. They buckle their harnesses on simultaneously like it's part of some choreography they memorized long ago and settle in. Matthews goes through the preflight sequence, tapping screens in front of him and overhead while Shariq pulls up a live feed of the airlock and displays it on her side of the console for all of us to see.

"Right." I give Dunn a look that says I'm biting my tongue as hard as I can, and I gesture toward the cargo compartment.

Taking a literal backseat role for the time being, we buckle up as the doors drift shut and lock themselves into place. Dunn sits as still as a statue, holding Wink and Blink in his lap. Both drones remain powered down for now. No idea if Matthews will give me any flack about using them once we land in Dome 10, but I'd like to see him try to stop me. Not that I'm itching to fight him or anything. Now that I'm sleeping through the night more often, I've set aside that particular pastime.

But a sparring contest might be fun.

Time to focus. As the aerocar rises into the air and slowly pivots to take us in the direction of the train station—the ride not nearly as smooth as I'm used to when Dunn's at the controls—I take a quick dive into VR to check on my regular booth at Howard's Tavern.

10

It's raining acid in the Future Noir StoryLine, and the sky is dark as midnight. But since this retro-futuristic city never sleeps, garish lights and neon signs shine incessantly into the murk, and there's plenty of activity on the streets. Everything here is monochrome—black, white, shades of grey—from the heavy, curvaceous groundcars splashing through pothole puddles to the people moving to and fro with purpose along the congested sidewalks, their hats, coats, and umbrellas shielding them from the dangerous downpour. Some sort of ecological catastrophe due to past warmongering is the culprit, so you've got to keep your avatar protected. Otherwise, it's game over before any of the fun starts. And replacement avatars don't come cheap.

If I'd selected mystery mode for my interactive, clues would be glowing in primary or secondary colors for my eyes only. Some of the people I see may be players in the role of private investigator, femme fatale, gangster, or beat cop. The rest are AI characters with limited vocabularies and attention spans. Best to avoid both tonight.

I've got to see a man about an exo-suit.

My destination lies across a busy street: Howard's Tavern, dive bar extraordinaire. Plenty of booths in dark corners for people who value their privacy. Drasko and I chose it a while back as our preferred virtual meeting place, and we haven't felt the need to change venues since.

Making my way across the street, I dodge vehicular traffic as well as pockets of acid rain, my high-heels clopping across the wet pavement. Vivian Andromeda dresses to impress, and everything my avatar wears, from the long coat to the flared dress to the black stockings, is designed to repel the dangerous precipitation. Even my umbrella is more than meets the eye, charged with an electrostatic shield that protects Vivian's platinum-blonde locks and ivory complexion. Book smugglers tend to rake in pretty good money in this reality, so she can afford better than average accoutrements.

Once I reach the tavern and step inside, the contrast to the busy street behind me is like a slap in the face. Dim, quiet, warm and dry. Julian, the lanky, one-eyed barkeep, stands behind the bar drying a shot glass, and he gives me a slow nod as the door thumps shut on my heels.

I deactivate my umbrella and collapse it, keeping it down at my side as I make my way straight over to him.

"Quiet night." I nod toward the half dozen or so patrons who keep their eyes to themselves, two of whom sit slouched at the bar nursing their drinks.

"Never too quiet for me." White dish towel over one shoulder and a friendly smile on his narrow face, Julian plants both hands on the bar and winks with his good eye. "So, what'll it be?"

As with other AI characters in this StoryLine, conversations only go so far before he starts repeating himself. But even with his limitations, he tends to be more helpful than not.

"Information." I lean forward and glance over my shoulder surreptitiously before asking, "Madison been around?"

Drasko always goes for the world-weary private eye Charlie Madison when he picks an avatar. Similar backstory as Julian's: war vet who's been around the block more than a few times. Honorable-among-thieves type.

"Tonight?" Julian screws up his face as though that'll help him remember. "Nope, can't say I've seen 'im. Sorry, Viv. Wish I had better news for you."

"No worries." I nod toward my usual spot in a shadow-enshrouded back corner. "That booth taken?"

"It's got your name on it." Julian grins. "Gimme a holler if you need anything."

I salute him, and he returns the gesture with a chuckle as he goes back to wiping his shot glass. Probably the cleanest one to be found in this joint.

Sliding into the booth, I keep the left side of my ocular lenses focused on my surroundings, just in case Drasko decides to make an appearance, and I hail Raul on the right side. Not that Vivian Andromeda wears lenses or has Link access, but Sera Chen does, and she's currently in two places at once.

About to be three.

Raul answers right away, video and audio. "Miss me already, Chen?" From the way he's bobbing in the feed, he's on the move. Probably making his rounds while keeping Edwards' jewelry shop under drone surveillance. That's what I would have done, at any rate. Raul's drones are no Wink or Blink, but they do the job.

"Need a favor." I transmit a holo of myself to his lenses. From his perspective, now I'm walking right beside him. "Can you take a look at these coordinates?" I send him the location where the burglars arrived and exited.

He frowns as he reads them. "Sure thing. I'm heading back that way. Scene of the crime, right?" He sniffs. "Anything in particular I should be looking for?"

"Something...off."

"Can you be more specific?"

I've got a feeling he'll know it when he sees it. *If* there's anything there. "Our burglars appeared and then disappeared at that exact location. Which leads me to believe something weird might be going on."

"I'll say. We talkin' teleportation? Or a rift in the space-time continuum?"

At least he didn't mention a portal. "You've been reading too much sci-fi."

"Hey, now that it's legal, why not?" He chuckles. "Maybe it's my age, but I've never been a big fan of that virtual crap. Give me a book any day over the immersive stuff. Lemme imagine what everything looks like for myself!"

"Steady, old-timer." I don't mention that I'm currently in VR having this conversation with him. "Let me know what you find."

"Right. Lookin' for something weird." He slows to a halt and scowls at the space in front of him. I can picture him standing with his arms akimbo, shoulders hunched, really concentrating. He must have reached the coordinates. After a few seconds of turning his head this way and that, reaching out his hand and waving it side to side, he grunts to himself. "Don't know what to tell you, Chen. I don't see any—"

That's when he falls. Straight down. And my hologram goes right along with him.

"Raul!" I shout.

His feed has gone dark, but I can hear him grunt in pain as he makes contact with an unyielding surface below. Then he curses.

"What the hell?" he groans, his armor shifting and scraping against something that sounds like plasticon. He switches on his shoulder-mounted flashlight, and his perplexed face is washed in white.

"Where are you?"

"Dropped down a maintenance shaft, looks like." Another curse. "But the hatch wasn't open. Least it didn't look open when I stepped on it." He cranes his neck back, shining his light overhead. "Now it's shut. No reason it should've opened like that, right underneath me!"

He's angry, which is understandable. "Are you injured?"

"Don't think so. Would've broken something if I wasn't wearing this damn suit." Another grunt. "Should be able to climb up. There's a ladder running along the side here..." He trails off with a sudden scowl, his attention shifting as his head turns sharply to the right.

"What is it?"

"Thought I heard something." He lowers his voice. "There might be somebody down here." He squints. "There's a tunnel running under the street. Pipes along one side, looks like. Above and below, maybe freshwater and wastewater. Branches off this shaft here. Wide enough for maybe two or three to walk abreast. Plasteel grate floor...red lighting farther down. Can't tell where it's coming from."

"How big is that shaft?"

"Well, I've got room to spare."

"Big enough for my exo?"

He doesn't answer right away. Then he frowns. "I'd say." He clears his throat quietly. "You thinkin' the burglars came into Dome 1 this way? From Dome 10?"

Mirela in the exo-suit could have. But Drasko's muscle car? Not a chance.

Unless the groundcar was never really there.

Just some kind of holo-illusion, maybe? A weird thought, but based on the evidence, I don't know what else to think. Mirela might have had a holo-projector rigged up above the maintenance hatch, complete with sound effects, then pulled it in after herself as she made her exit. But that masked figure who spray-painted the shop's interior had been no hologram. The accomplice was flesh and blood.

"Can you climb up and get that hatch to reopen?" I don't want him down there any longer than necessary. Not if somebody else is lurking around the vicinity.

"I can climb." He squints, angling his shoulder-light upward again. "But I don't know about the hatch. Those things are keycoded. Authorized personnel only. I could probably hack it with a data spike, if I had one on me."

The hatch opened once without a code. Maybe it'll open again. "I need you to check the street for tire marks. As in burned rubber."

With a grunt and a grimace, he starts up the ladder rungs. "Don't remember seeing anything like that. But I'll take a look. Assuming I can get the hell outta here."

A crackling sound echoes below him. Not electric. It sounded like movement.

Raul freezes in place and turns to look down. "There it is

again," he mutters, eyes unblinking.

Another crackle. Closer to him this time.

He clenches his jaw and reaches for his shocker. I can hear the weapon's barrel slip free of its holster. "Who's down there?" he demands, sounding cocksure of himself as every curfew enforcer should. Half the job is intimidation. "Show yourself!"

Silence.

"Raul, get out of there. You don't know how many there are. They could be armed—"

"So am I." He drops down one rung. "I said show yourself!" he shouts, his voice echoing along the tunnel nearby.

This time the crackling noise is accompanied by shuffling footsteps that grow louder as they approach Raul's position, along with a strange chuffing sound. Like labored breathing.

"What the hell?" he murmurs, scowling as he peers into shadows his light can't touch.

"What are you seeing?" My avatar's fists clench on the table at Howard's Tavern. I'm sure my own do the same where I'm sitting in the back of the aerocar, soaring toward the train station.

"Yellow eyes?" Raul doesn't sound like he believes the words that just fell out of his mouth. "Chen, I don't know what to say," he whispers, his jaw trembling now. "They've got big yellow eyes, glowing in the dark. And they're staring right at me."

Nothing about this is right.

"Get the hell out of there." There could be some kind of noxious fumes making him hallucinate. Maybe Mirela cracked one of the wastewater pipes while she was hauling ass through there in my exo. "Did you hear me? I said climb out. Right now."

Raul tries to swallow, but it takes some effort. He's doing his best to exude all the bravado he's known for. "They're big as golf balls, Chen. And they're not blinking. You...ever play golf in VR?"

"Listen to me. There's something down there messing with your mind. Some kind of gas." There's no other explanation. "You need to get out. Climb up and see if you can get that hatch open. Do you hear me, Enforcer Ortega?"

He almost smiles in a strange, dreamy way. "Is that an order, Chen?"

"Yes!" I've just about lost all patience with the man.

And that's when Charlie Madison, private investigator, slides into the booth across from me. Unshaven with a crooked smile, he removes his black fedora and sets it on the table between us. His grizzled hair is slicked back, his eyes alight with a hidden knowledge. As if he knows more than I ever will. About everything.

"Heard you wanted to see me," he says.

Sure I did. Before one of our curfew enforcers fell down a hole and started seeing yellow-eyed monsters.

I try to focus on both sides of my lenses simultaneously. "Have you had your aerocar fumigated recently?" my avatar asks. The secret question only Drasko will know the answer to. Because I have to be sure it's really him.

"Don't do much flying these days."

Wrong. "Try again."

He squints up at the ceiling for a moment as if he's struggling to remember. It's been a while since our last virtual meeting, so maybe I should forgive the misstep. But if it's

Drasko under those shabby threads, he'll know it. He's always had a good memory.

He nods and closes his eyes briefly, realizing his mistake. "Don't fly much anymore," he says at length.

Bingo. "How's the family?"

"Enjoying farm life." A hint of a smile, there and then gone.

"Seen them lately?"

He shakes his head. "Wish I could, but..."

"Duty calls." I shift forward in my seat. "That heap of yours still running?"

"You want to borrow it?" he says with a smirk.

Raul cries out—something I've never heard him do. He falls off the ladder, straight down like he was tugged by the ankle, and he lands hard with a crunch of his armor against the unforgiving floor. But he doesn't stop there.

Something drags him away on his back.

"It's got me, Chen!" he screams, firing his shocker, pulling the trigger again and again. The feed lights up with splashes of electric-blue bursts. "It's got my leg!"

"Raul!" I shout as the call drops. No video, no audio. I hail him, but he doesn't pick up. "Damn it..."

I get up from the booth.

"Friend of yours?" Drasko says, keeping his eye on me.

I glance at the other patrons in Howard's Tavern, then at Julian. They're all staring at me in silence, not used to such outbursts from Vivian Andromeda. Neither am I. For a second there, my realities overlapped.

"He's in trouble." I step back from the table. "Sorry. I've got to cut this short."

Drasko reaches for his hat but remains seated. "Not a

problem." Easygoing as ever.

But I have to know if he was involved in that burglary. And there's no telling when we'll be able to meet again like this. So I send him a couple images of his groundcar outside Edwards' jewelry shop. And when I say *send*, I mean that I hand him a manila envelope. Because that's how such things are done in this StoryLine.

He gives the envelope a curious frown as he tears open one end and two photos slide out. Then he takes a moment to study the black & white images.

"Look familiar?" I watch his reaction, wondering how much of Drasko will filter through Charlie Madison's expression.

The avatar's face remains neutral. "Looks like my car." He meets my gaze. "But it wasn't in Dome 1 tonight. As far as I know, those wheels haven't left my garage since yesterday."

"As far as you know?"

He shrugs. "I'll check into it. Send you the security footage, if you don't believe me. As for this..." He taps the photo of my exo. "Looks a lot like the one you left behind."

"Because it is. But I didn't reactivate it."

"You think I did."

"You're the only other person who could have."

He nods slowly, keeping Charlie Madison's attention on the two photographs. "Don't know what to tell you, Andromeda. Other than to check out Heller's *Catch-22*. I hear satire is really making a comeback."

I shouldn't have any reason to doubt him. He's never lied to me before. But he's obviously holding back information. If only I had more time—

"Thanks for meeting." I backtrack down the aisle, high-heels thumping. "And sorry about bailing like this."

"Hope your friend's okay." He gives me a grim nod.

I hope so, too.

By the time I reach the door, the tavern's low murmur is back to normal, everyone's attention on their drinks and quiet conversation. Julian returns my wave like he always does as I make my exit. Then it's a quick jog through the downpour with my umbrella up until I reach the portal tucked away in a dark alley where other players won't notice my vanishing act. Less chance of interrupting the verisimilitude of the StoryLine that way.

"We have to go back." I lurch forward in my seat and unfasten my harness. "Enforcer Ortega has been attacked."

Matthews and Shariq keep their attention on the windscreen in front of them and their respective consoles. Neither one so much as glances my way as I grab onto the back of their headrests and stand between them.

"Call it in." Matthews couldn't sound less interested. "We've got bigger fish to fry tonight."

"And buckle up," Shariq adds as the aerocar's nose angles downward. The train station—a central hub, with tunnels like spokes on a wheel branching outward toward the other nine domes—appears below us. "We're making our descent."

Cursing under my breath, I hail HQ. Chief Inspector Hudson answers right away, audio only.

"What is it, Chen?" Curt as ever.

"Enforcer Ortega is in need of immediate assistance." I rattle off his coordinates as I enter my override keycode and palm the emergency release button on the side door. "Last I saw him, he was being dragged away by an unknown assailant. Down a maintenance tunnel under the street."

That's everything I know.

"What the hell do you think you're doing?" Matthews barks, struggling to keep the aerocar level as the door to the cargo compartment jerks open mid-flight. There are safeguards against such things, but my keycode overruled them all.

Dunn hands me Wink without being asked, like he knows what I'm planning to do. The drone wakes up as soon as it senses my neuro, red and blue lights blinking across the disc-shaped chassis.

"Answer me, Chen!" Matthews is losing his cool.

"You won't fly me back?" I confirm.

"There's no time!" he growls.

"Then drop me off right here." If I run as fast as I can, I should be able to reach the hatch Raul fell through in ten minutes. But even that feels like an eternity as my mind's eye replays his screaming face.

Shariq half-turns to glare at me. "We need you, Chen. You've got to disable that exo before it wreaks more havoc at the airlock."

Right. That.

I toss Wink out into the night with the subvocalized command, "Find Enforcer Ortega. Use whatever force is necessary to subdue his attacker. Transmit video once you reach the maintenance hatch." I share the coordinates.

Wink hovers in the air beside us, its quadcopter rotors spinning full-tilt to keep pace with the aerocar. "Understood, Investigator Chen."

It waits, seeming to wonder if Blink will be joining it as per always. But I need Blink for whatever we have in store for us at the docks.

"You're on your own this time, buddy."

With a slight dip forward like a nod of acknowledgment, Wink veers away, heading back toward Raul's last-known location.

II

"Sending trackers to Enforcer Ortega's position," Hudson reports. I almost forgot he was still on the line. "His pilot is also en route. They'll get this sorted in short order."

"Thank you, sir." I sound calm and detached as I strap into my seat, and the door closes beside me. But my heart is galloping a mile a minute. "Chen out," I end the transmission and focus on the task at hand: gritting my teeth and bearing Matthews' rocky landing.

I can't help feeling responsible for what happened to Raul. If I hadn't sent him to those coordinates, he wouldn't have fallen through that faulty maintenance hatch. How often does something like that happen? Or was it rigged like some kind of booby trap?

Dunn leans toward me as the aerocar touches down in front of the train station without breaking anything or anyone, surprisingly.

"Did you get a look at Enforcer Ortega's attacker, Investigator Chen?" he asks quietly.

I shake my head. *Yellow eyes*, Raul said. I thought he was hallucinating. But then somebody grabbed him by the leg and hauled him into that tunnel? What the hell?

"Yellow eyes," I murmur, the look on Raul's face frozen in

my mind. I've never seen anyone so afraid.

"Like an animal?" Dunn doesn't sound incredulous, but he should.

I scoff. "There aren't any animals in Eurasia." Or the Wastes outside, for that matter. Humankind did our damnedest to make them all extinct. Nuking a planet and bombarding it with bioweapons really isn't great for the fauna or flora, come to find out.

"Some sort of mutation, then?"

I glance at my reflection in my partner's faceplate. I look like I've tasted something off. "A yellow-eyed mutant living in the sewers. Is that what you're saying?"

"The Ten Domes do not have sewers as such, Investigator Chen," Dunn gently corrects me. "There are sewage pipes running through maintenance tunnels five meters below the streets. Those tunnels carry freshwater conduits as well."

Just the sort of tunnel Raul mentioned.

"Cut the chatter back there." Shariq peers up at the gate in front of us, a three-meter-tall plasteel monstrosity that shines in the aerocar's lights like every other polished surface in Dome 1.

It's closed and locked by the looks of things, and a trio of guards in khaki uniforms stand on the other side. They look tense. They've got every right to be, based on what we saw going down at the airlock.

At a gesture from Shariq, one of the guards nods and unlocks the gate, but it takes all three of them to heave it open.

"Lemme guess." The oldest of the guards, a woman named Jeffers who's been on the job as long as Raul, speaks into the radio clipped to her shoulder. Her voice comes through the speaker on Shariq's console. "You're flying right into the thick of it."

If Eurasia's a wheel, then the Dome 1 train station is the hub. Each of the maglev tunnels from Domes 2 through 10 end up right here. There's no way to get from one Dome to another without passing through this central station. The Governors planned it that way, long ago. I'm sure they had their own reasons for it, but nowadays, it seems like just another way for Dome 1 to maintain its superiority over the outlying Domes.

The only way for an aerocar to pass into another Dome is to take one of the nine maglev tunnels from here—preferably when no trains are running. Otherwise, the pilot has to time things just right to avoid a catastrophic underground collision. But at this time of night with no trains on the move, that's obviously not an issue.

And for a pilot as bad as Matthews, that's just as well.

"Dome 10," Shariq confirms. "We heard there might have been an explosion on the other side of the tunnel. Can you confirm?"

Jeffers shakes her head, sandy-grey locks bobbing. "Rumor has it you're right, but we've been ordered to stay put. No word from our counterparts at the terminal." She rests one hand on the shocker holstered at her side. "Guess you drew the short straw?"

Not one for small talk, Matthews curses under his breath and gestures for the guards to clear a path. Then he guns the accelerator, and the aerocar's jet wash blasts outward in all directions. Jeffers and the other guards hold up their hands to shield their eyes and squint, scurrying to get out of the way.

"Stay safe," Jeffers says to Shariq with a nod. Shariq nods back. "And tell Matthews to get himself an enema."

I choke back a laugh as Shariq shuts off the comm and keeps her eyes set straight ahead. She looks a little nervous. Probably because she's flown with Matthews before.

Clenching his jaw, he takes us up a few meters and through the gate. He could have flown us right over it; that's what Drasko would have done when he was my pilot. Then again, Drasko's flight skills seemed like second nature while Matthews looks as stiff as a corpse at the controls. I clutch my harness, tempted to close my eyes as he takes us down into the dark tunnel—wide enough for an aerocar to pass through, but just barely. Thanks to an overweening case of morbid curiosity, I watch the proceedings, too tense to even blink.

A floodlight mounted on the front of the vehicle white-washes the tunnel's plasticon interior. Matthews keeps our speed steady—a tolerable thirty kilometers per hour—but that's about all. The aerocar wobbles port to starboard, and more than once we hear a sudden shriek of plasteel against the walls. Hope he can afford the credits for a fresh coat of paint after this is through, because it'll be coming right out of his paycheck.

I realize I'm holding my breath, and I doubt I'm the only one. Except for Blink, sitting in Dunn's lap with its lights off. Maybe the drone has the right idea.

"Approaching Dome 10 terminal," Shariq announces in a calm, quiet voice, so as not to startle our pilot. "Two minutes."

I try hailing Raul again. Nothing. His pilot has landed at the maintenance shaft coordinates, and the pair of trackers

Hudson sent are currently five minutes out. Wink is a minute away. Everything is happening too damn slow. Or maybe it only seems that way because I'm trapped inside this vehicle, watching everything happen from the outside-in via the analysts' feed. If I was like Luther, I'd be praying right now that the power doesn't go out again at HQ.

Not until Raul is found. Alive.

Dunn sends me a message, text-only so as not to irritate our escorts: *It is understandable that you would rather be assisting Enforcer Ortega at the moment. But there are multiple lives at stake where we are headed, and only you can stop Mirela Edwards from firing on port security.*

That old argument: the good of the many versus the one. Maybe he's right, but it doesn't make me feel any better.

Drasko could shut down the exo. I text back, gritting my teeth with frustration as the words scroll across my lenses straight from my neuro. I think them, and they appear. *But for some reason, he's letting this play out.*

You met with him in VR, I take it. Dunn pauses. *But he did not admit to anything.*

Perceptive. Probably helps that he's never been a big fan of the guy. Having Drasko shoot him in the head wasn't a great start to their relationship.

Am I too close to the situation? Are Drasko and Mirela Edwards working together for some reason that completely escapes me—because I can't believe Drasko would ally himself with such a loose cannon?

Matthews curses as the aerocar decelerates and wobbles toward the tunnel floor. The floodlight shines across a wall of rubble completely impeding our route.

The insurgents did exactly what we thought. They blew

up their end of the tunnel.

"Shouldn't take long to clear." Shariq rummages through her pack.

"Every minute we waste, those guards are without backup." Matthews sets us down with a reverberating crunch that doesn't sound good at all.

There's no room on either side of the aerocar for the doors to swing open, so he gets to work dismantling the windscreen. Shariq lends a hand, and between the two of them, they release all eight of the tension-levers and have the plastiglass panel removed in a matter of seconds. Setting it down between their seats, they slide out feet-first into the floodlight's glare and start setting the semtex bricks into position. If it's done correctly, they'll pulverize the rubble into dust, completely obliterating our obstacle.

But we'll want to be at least a hundred meters back from our current position, if we want to avoid damage from the blast in this confined space.

"Get ready to fly us out of here if things go south," I mutter to Dunn.

"Do you have reason to doubt Trackers Matthews' and Shariq's expertise with heavy explosives, Investigator Chen?"

"Not necessarily." I give my forehead a one-handed squeeze and exhale. "But after the night we've had, I think it's best to prepare for every eventuality, don't you?"

He gives me a tentative nod, his faceplate directed toward the front of the vehicle. "I have concluded my research on Mirela Edwards. Would you like to hear what I discovered, or is now not a suitable time?"

I could use the distraction. "Go ahead."

"It appears that Mirela Edwards has been leading a double

life. On the one hand, she is the daughter of respectable upper-caste Dome 1 citizens, Nevah and Stephan Edwards. She lives and works in Dome 8, where she is a solar technology engineer."

None of this is new information. "By day, a tech-head. By night, a revolutionary?"

"She has spent the majority of her free time online, studying anything even remotely related to Prometheus and what the AI intended to accomplish." He pauses. "She has also devoted a substantial portion of her research...to you, Investigator Chen."

"Me?" Can't help frowning at that.

Dunn's helmet inclines slightly to the left. "Considering that you are the one credited with bringing an end to Prometheus and its grand scheme—"

"I did my part. Erik did his. Together, we brought that psycho AI down."

Dunn nods. "But the official record only includes your name."

"So she's definitely a member of that cult." And she blames me for castrating their exalted leader.

"It would seem so. However, there is nothing on file linking Mirela Edwards to any of the activities that occurred during the uprising. If she is a member of the Children of Tomorrow, then she may be a posthumous one, so to speak."

"Assuming the cult ever died out. It could be stronger now than ever. And even more dangerous." The sight of so many insurgents at the docks supports that much. They're rioting without the AI mindjacking them.

"If you are referring to the situation at the airlock, perhaps it would be best to wait until we have more information. For all we know, most of the rioters could be Patriots thinking they are participating in a political demonstration. They may not realize that the woman in the exo-suit is a cultist." He pauses again. "And we do not even know that for certain."

True. Something could have happened after the Prometheus uprising, something in Mirela's personal life that got her interested in what the AI promised. Maybe she was diagnosed with a serious illness and assigned to Dome 6 for her care, but she refused, instead looking into the gene-splicing that Prometheus had planned. Mixing every citizen's DNA with donations from the thousand children growing up in the Domes, offspring of the Twenty. Giving us superhuman abilities—among them, lungs that can somehow breathe the air outside Eurasia's walls. Like Luther and Daiyna and the others who were able to do so for years without any scientific explanation for it.

That's what the AI claimed, at any rate. I never saw the evidence, other than Trezon's bizarre *invisible man* trick. As far as I know, he never went into the Wastes to test his lungs. And I don't plan to step outside the airlock and take a big gulp of air to prove things, one way or the other. Even if I'm somehow able to survive out there due to a supernatural ability I'm not aware of, my life is here, inside the Domes. I have no desire to spread my wings in a barren wasteland.

The right side of my vision abruptly changes as Wink sends me a live video feed. The drone is hovering inside the maintenance shaft, its headlight shining halfway down the adjacent tunnel. At the limit of its range, I can make out Raul's armored form, lying on his back.

He's not moving.

"Report." I notice another light bobbing in the

background. Wink isn't alone. "Who's that with you?"

"Pilot Adair, ma'am," a woman says off-camera. Close to Raul's age, she's been his pilot as long as he's been patrolling curfew. From the tone of her voice, I can already tell the news isn't good. And since she's there on the scene, Wink refrains from reporting on the situation. Humans always have seniority. "I'm afraid Raul's gone. It's..." She clears her throat, doing her best to keep her emotions in check. "It's real bad."

"Give me eyes." I brace myself for what I'm about to see.

"Go on," Adair tells my drone, and Wink glides slowly into the tunnel, rotors spinning with a low whine that echoes off the plasticon walls. "I'll hold position right here, if you don't mind." She'll have to see him again when she loads his body into her aerocar. Soon enough.

"That's fine," I tell her absently, focused on what Wink's showing me—and wishing I could look away.

Raul had his face chewed off. There's no other way to describe it. Something tried to eat him but couldn't crack open his blue armor, so the monster settled with devouring the only part of him that was left unprotected.

Except I don't believe in monsters. Unless they're the human variety.

"Any sign of his attacker?"

"No, Investigator Chen," Wink replies.

"The only thermal signatures showing up on scans are my own," Adair adds, her voice echoing along the tunnel. "Wouldn't be down here, otherwise."

"And we're sure that's Raul." Other than the armor, there's nothing else to identify him at present.

"Yes, Investigator Chen. XR scans match dental records

on file," Wink says in its monotone. "The deceased is Enforcer Raul Ortega."

"Scan the rest of him." Just in case the killer left any trace evidence. "Prints, fluids, fibers. Anything that will lead us to the perpetrator."

"Understood." Wink sweeps the armored curfew enforcer with multiple scans simultaneously. "Other than an unidentifiable object located in an interior pocket, there is nothing to report."

"Unidentifiable...?" I murmur. "Send me an image."

Instantly, I receive a three-dimensional rendering of the object in question. I don't recognize it, and I have no frame of reference for comparison. Except maybe one of those obsolete phones Dome 6 residents use to access the Link, since they don't have neural implants. This is the same rectangular shape but slimmer and smaller in size.

On a whim, I run the image against Nevah Edwards' inventory list. Maybe because this strange object looks like the definition of an *artifact*. And maybe because a corner of my mind hasn't been able to understand why Raul in his motorized suit took so long to reach the crime scene.

I don't want to believe that he was paid off to look the other way.

But the unidentifiable object is definitely a match.

12

According to Ms. Edwards' inventory, the thing in Raul's pocket was categorized as an *MP3 Player* in the Old World. Since people back then weren't augmented, they had to play their music on peripheral devices. This was apparently before those antique phones were invented, which could do just about everything our augments can—except allow you to function without staring at a device in the palm of your hand all day.

One thousand credits. That's how much this relic is apparently worth to some people. Members of the upper castes, no doubt, with plenty to spend on their weird collections. But why would Raul have wanted it? Did he plan to sell it to the highest bidder? Take care of some languishing debts?

When had the item changed hands? Not before the break-in; Nevah Edwards hadn't logged it as missing. It's right here on her list of stolen items. Mirela and her accomplice vanished after the burglary. There was no way either one of them could have transferred the device to Raul—unless they met him off-camera on their way out of Dome 1, maybe at another maintenance hatch half a klick away by underground tunnel, to hand over the artifact and tell him it was a good time for him to arrive at the crime scene. For appearances' sake, if nothing else.

But this is conjecture. Nothing more. All I know for certain is that Raul had one of Ms. Edwards' stolen items on his person when he died. Is that why he was killed? Did his assailant try and fail to get inside Raul's armor to retrieve the device? But why would this useless relic be worth a man's life?

Matthews and Shariq are climbing back into the aerocar, their movements quick but sure. Neither one seems nervous about the explosion they've set to go off behind them.

I focus on the feed from my drone. "Hold position until Enforcer Ortega's body is loaded for transport." The incoming trackers will have to help Adair with that. I don't think she's up for doing it herself. "Then rendezvous at my coordinates."

"Yes, Investigator Chen," Wink replies.

"Something else down here you might want to see," Adair says. "There, drone. Show her that."

Wink pivots to focus on what looks like a crumpled tripod connected to a holo projector, smashed to pieces and lying across the tunnel floor where it branches off from the maintenance shaft. Strange that Raul didn't mention it.

"No idea what it's doing here. Thought you'd want to know."

"Thanks, Adair." Another piece of the puzzle. If that groundcar leaving the scene of the crime had in actuality been nothing more than a hologram, then Mirela's accomplice could be the one who stayed behind to kill Raul. Assuming she was in the exo, and both of them made their exit via the underground tunnel. "Chen out." I end the transmission.

Dunn faces me as our escorts drop into their seats and strap in.

"New developments?"

"You could say that." I send the images of Raul's remains and the artifact hidden in his pocket.

Dunn nods. "Enforcer Ortega and Nevah Edwards may have known one another." He pauses. "Or perhaps it was Mirela Edwards who gave Enforcer Ortega that artifact in order to secure his services. Namely, not being in the vicinity when she broke into her mother's shop and stole everything."

"Just what I was thinking."

Matthews curses under his breath, fingers flying across the consoles in front of him and above. Shariq doesn't look much calmer as she goes through the same motions on the copilot side of things.

"Engines are not responding," she mutters.

"Something wrong?" I lean forward as far as my harness will allow.

Matthews ignores me. "We've got two minutes to figure this out."

Shariq curses and shakes her head, movements becoming frantic now.

Two minutes until the semtex they planted is rigged to blow.

"The aerocar will not fly without its windscreen in place," Dunn offers. "It is a safety feature."

Shariq and Matthews pause a split-second to glance at each other. Then they scramble to reinsert the pane of plastiglass and seal it in place.

I give Dunn a nod of approval and try to hold back my

grin.

Once Matthews returns to the controls, he curses again. Apparently, the windscreen didn't do the trick. Shariq shakes her head and agrees. "Nothing."

"Got any more bright ideas, clone?" Matthews pounds the console with a fist.

"Thrusters may have been damaged during our rather rough landing." Dunn turns toward me. "But I might be able to get us out of here in time."

"Do it." I nod toward the cockpit as Matthews begrudgingly unfastens his harness and moves out of the way so Dunn can take over.

But once Dunn unbuckles his own straps, he hands Blink to me and heads in the opposite direction.

"What the hell are you doing?" Matthews shouts.

Because Dunn is plowing both of his mechanical fists into the back wall of the fuselage, punching through the plasteel and peeling large pieces of it out of the way. I get free of my harness and lend a hand, tucking Blink under one arm as I shove a stubborn piece flush with the cabin wall. It doesn't take my partner long to create a makeshift rear exit a meter wide, open to the dark tunnel behind the vehicle. More than enough room to dive through.

Dunn turns sideways and looks back at the trackers. "You may now—"

Matthews charges straight for us, looking ready to knock my partner senseless. I tense up, ready for a fight. Close quarters like this, it'll be ugly. But we'll make it work.

Despite the furious look on his face, Matthews doesn't throw a punch. Instead, he throws himself through the opening in the back of the aerocar and takes off running as fast as his boots can carry him. Without so much as a thank-you. Shariq follows suit, diving out and chasing after him like a shot.

I look up at Dunn. His faceplate reflects my worried expression.

"Go, Investigator Chen," he says.

"Promise you'll be right behind me."

He nods. "That is my intention."

I toss Blink out in front of me with a quick command, "Follow Tracker Shariq." The drone lights up in midair, and its rotors spin with a high-pitched whine as it plunges into the darkness. Then I jump after it, hitting the ground in a forward roll and lunging to my feet. Glancing over my shoulder as I run, making sure Dunn gets out in time. No idea how much we have left. Seconds?

Dunn's white armor flashes against the aerocar's cabin light as he slides headfirst through the hole and hits the ground with a clatter. Much less graceful than I. But he's twice as fast, and a split-second later, he's already overtaken me.

If I was wearing my exo, I'd be matching his speed.

"Go!" I shout and shove at him as he slows down to run alongside me.

"We go together, Investigator Chen."

Does he mean escape the blast or die in it?

There's little time to wonder. When the blast comes, it's as sudden and deafening as it is jarring, roaring across the tunnel walls around us, throwing us headlong off our feet. The aerocar is torn to shreds in the explosion, like tissue paper in a tornado, chunks and strips of jagged plasteel hurtling through the air over our heads. Dunn covers me with his armored body, and I curl fetal-like beneath him as flaming debris rains down around us.

An incoming hail lights up the corner of my ocular lenses. It's from Hudson. Audio-only, which I probably won't be able to hear, thanks to my ringing ears. So I switch over to text, and his message scrolls from left to right.

Investigator Chen, what the hell is going on there? He must have been notified that our vehicle was obliterated.

The tunnel is blocked by a wall of debris, sir. Trackers Matthews and Shariq rigged an explosion to clear it. The blast took out our aerocar as well. Thanks to somebody's poor landing.

Where are Matthews and Shariq?

Bad news. If they're not showing up on scans, then the shrapnel may have taken them down. *I don't have eyes on them.*

Get eyes on them. Then get your ass over to the airlock. The woman in your exo-suit has fired on the security personnel. They are holding their own for now, but the situation is escalating quickly.

I knock on Dunn's chestplate and nod that I'm okay. He rolls over and leaps to his feet, keeping an eye on the blazing wreckage. We'll have to pass through it in order to leave the tunnel—assuming the semtex cleared a path for us. Would've been nice if these tunnels had been built for two trains, one going each way. The designers must not have anticipated much traffic going to and from the outer Domes. I guess they were right.

What about the three patrols currently in Dome 1? The three pilots who decided to keep their distance from the docks after Mirela fired on one of them.

They will provide air support upon your arrival. Whether they like it or not, apparently.

I get to my feet and stumble in the direction Matthews and Shariq took. Digging into my hip pocket, I retrieve my flashlight and switch it on, then attach it to my shoulder clip. A spear of light slices through the dark, illuminating the maglev track ahead. I could switch off my augments and use my night-vision, but then I'd lose the transmission from Hudson. What a pity.

Maybe twenty meters away, Blink hovers over the forms of two uniformed bodies lying facedown on the ground. Motionless. I wince at the sight as I approach. No matter how many I've witnessed, it still hits me like a suckerpunch whenever I see someone with the life snuffed out of them. First Raul, and now these two. All in the same night.

Trackers Matthews and Shariq are deceased, sir. No response from Hudson. I can imagine him cursing to himself.

I crouch down and force myself to note the cause of death amidst all the blood. My light glints on plasteel shining through gore. Shrapnel from the blast.

A sharp piece the size of a dinner plate is half buried in the back of Matthews' head. It would have killed him instantly. Shariq must have been looking over her shoulder when the jagged piece hurtling toward her sliced deep across her throat, nearly severing her neck in the process. Scanning for vitals—as required in a situation like this, no matter how ridiculous it seems—I shake my head as the report populates across my lenses. Of course there are no life signs.

I will send a team to collect them, Hudson says.

Ortega as well, I add.

He doesn't respond right away. *Trackers are bringing him in now.* Another pause. *Twenty years in law enforcement, and I have never seen an assault this vicious. Do you have a lead on the perpetrator?*

No, sir. But I believe Mirela Edwards is involved. Or her mother, as Dunn suggested. *One of the stolen artifacts from Nevah Edwards' shop is in Enforcer Ortega's interior pocket.*

I will make a note of it. Keep me apprised of your situation. Hudson out.

"Looks like we're on our own now, partner." I rise as Dunn approaches.

He nods, flames reflected in his faceplate as he turns back toward the burning wreckage. "Can we afford to wait until the blaze dies down? I do not believe that you will be able to pass through safely." Whereas he should be fine in his armor.

"Hudson wants us at the airlock ASAP. The pilots already in Dome 10 are standing by, prepared to give us air support." I head back toward what's left of the aerocar. The good news: I can see a floodlight beam shining down from above on the other side, which means the Dome 10 end of the tunnel is now unobstructed. "Guess we could..." I trail off.

Dunn is still standing over Matthews and Shariq. "It does not seem right to leave them like this," he says in a quiet tone, his voice hanging in the stillness.

I return to his side. "Not much about tonight has been right. But we've got a job to do. And we have to leave them behind in order to do it."

His helmet nods. "Of course, Investigator Chen. Follow me. I will make a path for you through the wreckage."

And that's what he does—kicking smoldering and flaming debris aside as he forges through the remains of the aerocar, creating a narrow lane that I can walk along without melting my boots off or catching my attire on fire.

When we reach the end of the tunnel and enter the Dome 10 train terminal, washed in the light of a curfew patrol hovering overhead, it immediately becomes clear why the guards stationed here weren't responding to hails. All three of them lie dead on the ground, frozen in violent poses with their hands on their holstered sidearms. Gunned down fifty yards away from where explosives filled the tunnel's mouth with rubble. Assuming the same people were responsible, and that Mirela sent them to commit these unspeakable acts, then it's clear she's not squeamish about taking lives.

Unless she and the rest of them are working for someone else. A puppet master hiding in the shadows. Prometheus 2.0?

I hold up a hand in greeting, squinting against the blinding light, and the pilot—a man in his thirties named Nichols—hails me, audio-only.

"Investigator Chen, glad you could make it. We heard Matthews and Shariq would be with you."

"And I heard there were three of you. Where are the other two pilots?"

A brief pause. "Granger is holding position outside the minigun's range. Eklund had to set down. Her vehicle was badly damaged. We'll pick her up on the way."

I give him a nod, shielding my eyes. "Matthews and Shariq were lost in the blast. Our aerocar as well."

Nichols curses under his breath. "Quite a night."

"Only a couple hours until it's over." And here's hoping Mirela doesn't plan to extend her bizarre crusade into daylight. "How do you want to play this? Carry us as close to the docks as you can get, then we'll take it from there on foot?"

"You're the lead, Chen. You tell me."

Right. I have him land and pick us up, but I take a moment to send Blink ahead.

"Stay out of that minigun's range," I tell the drone before it flies off. "I want a live feed of the situation at the airlock. XR, IR, give me everything you've got. Stealth mode."

"Yes, Investigator Chen," it replies before zipping off into the dark. Stealth means no blinking status lights, so it disappears as soon as it's out of the floodlight's glow.

I climb into the backseat of Nichols' aerocar and slide in beside Dunn, who's already strapped in. The door drifts shut behind me as I fumble with my harness.

"Can't believe Raul's gone." Nichols doesn't sound choked up, but he will be when he's alone. We all will be. The curfew enforcement division is like a family, and we'll each mourn the loss in our own way. Even though I haven't been an enforcer for a while now, you never forget who your friends are. "They better find the monster who did it."

"Hudson said trackers are collecting his body. I'm sure they'll be on the trail of Raul's killer before dawn." Tracking the murderer through those tunnels under the streets. Undoubtedly the same route Mirela took in my exo when she made her getaway.

Which gives me an idea...

"Don't know how you can work for that clown." Nichols snorts. "A real step down after Commander Bishop."

"He's not that bad." Not as bad as I thought, anyway. But no comparison to Bishop, by any stretch. Having her as my superior officer was one of the best things about being a curfew enforcer. "The Prometheus uprising brought out his true colors. And they were solid."

"Some kind of metaphor there?" Nichols glances back at me with a smirk as he takes us into a gradual descent. Picking up Enforcer Eklund, I assume.

"Maybe." I look out the side porthole as we pass over a clump of rectangular, six-story brick buildings. The type Dome 10 is known for. Function over form. Could be an office full of flush counters, making sure citizens don't overuse our precious water resources. Or a factory assembling plumbing parts, the type that get corroded by all the salt water running through our pipes and need to be replaced on a regular basis.

Sitting in the middle of a vacant side street is the pilot and her grounded vehicle. Nichols' floodlight sweeps over her as we approach, and she waves, standing beside the aerocar. Tendrils of smoke drift upward from the engine. As we get closer, the rash of damage from those projectile rounds is clear to see, puncturing the hull.

Eklund and Nichols are close in age, and if the rumors are true, they might be sweet on each other. There's nothing in our policy and procedures against such things—as long as they're pursued off the job, and both officers are equal in rank. These two seem like a good match. Not that I'm an expert on such things, but they remind me of bookends in Vivian Andromeda's smuggler's lair. Similar skin tone, athletic physiques, blondish hair and bluish eyes. Wouldn't be surprised if they spent their free time together in a Hawaiian island StoryLine full of surfing and sunbathing. But no sunburning.

We touch down gently with Nichols' practiced hands at

the controls, and Eklund ducks her head under the copilot door as it rises to welcome her inside. She and Nichols barely acknowledge each other—probably another sign that they're an item during off hours. But she gives me a wink when she spots me in the backseat.

"Hey, Chen. Slumming it tonight?"

Not sure if she means spending my time with curfew enforcement or venturing into Dome 10. Either way, I appreciate the levity she brings to the moment.

I have a feeling it won't last.

13

Nichols keeps a low profile as we approach the docks, gliding through the night without the aerocar's floodlight or flashers on. Even the cabin is dark. He navigates via the infrared display on the windscreen, outlines of buildings showing up in neon green with our route delineated in blue. Visible only to those of us inside the vehicle.

"Set us down right there." I lean forward against the straps of my harness and point out a stop on the map. It shifts as we move.

"You're sure about this?" Eklund glances at me. "After what happened to Raul—"

"Because of it." I look her in the eye, and she nods grimly. "Hold position with Granger outside the minigun's range. As soon as I have control of the exo, you'll move in and disperse the crowd." With gas and stun grenades, annoyances that tend to send rioters packing.

"And if Raul's killer happens to be down there waiting for you?" Nichols keeps his attention on the display as we descend.

"He very well could be, Investigator Chen," Dunn adds, "if he is working with Mirela Edwards, and they agreed that he would meet her here. And if he is a *he*."

"Not a fan of the plan, partner?" I arch an eyebrow at him.

"Taking a tunnel under the street is one way to reach the airlock without being spotted," he allows. "And you will have me with you, whereas Enforcer Ortega was alone. But if the killer possesses some sort of superhuman abilities—"

"Dust freak? That's who you think killed Raul?" Eklund frowns at Dunn.

He dips his chin, and his helmet angles forward. "We do not have enough information to know for certain, Enforcer Eklund."

She watches him for a moment. Pensive. Then she looks at me. "Your partner might have something there, Chen. If you're dealing with a dust freak, trapped underground? There's no telling what you might be in for."

"The other option is going up against hundreds of rioters out in the open. We might be able to shock a few into submission before they overwhelm us." I shrug. "I'll take my chances in that tunnel."

Dunn gives a slow nod. He doesn't like the idea, but he's not about to let me go alone.

"How do you plan to disable your exo?" Nichols asks as the aerocar touches down with a negligible bump, engines humming on standby.

"No idea." I unbuckle my harness and step out under the rising door. "Never had to do this before."

Eklund and Nichols stare at me as I leave.

Dunn climbs out, and I lead the way over to the maintenance hatch in the middle of the street. Unlike the shaft Raul unfortunately fell into, this one doesn't slide open conveniently as we approach. So Dunn raises one hand, and a section of the white gauntlet covering his index finger seems to break in half, the finger curling while a spike-shaped data connector extends from the first knuckle. Flipping open the access port, he inserts the spike until we hear a click.

"Connection established." He nods as the air patrollers lift off behind us with a jet wash that whips my hair around. I smooth it back with both hands to keep the strands out of my face. "Entering the requisite keycode." Another item of note to be found in the LawKeeper database, undoubtedly. "Keycode accepted"

The hatch slides open, revealing a dark shaft below.

"Good work." I watch the data spike retract into Dunn's gauntlet. "There's really no way one of these could open by accident."

"No, Investigator Chen." He faces me. "You are thinking about Enforcer Ortega."

I nod. "He wouldn't have stepped into an open shaft. The guy was more observant than that." Had to be, on the job. "So someone must have rigged it to open right as he stepped on it."

"Equally impossible, I am afraid."

"As impossible as vanishing into thin air?" I glance at him. "There was a holo projector near where Raul was murdered."

Dunn doesn't reply right away. "To disguise the burglars' exit point?"

"And to make it look like one of them escaped in a groundcar identical to Drasko's."

His helmet tilts to one side. "So there was no groundcar."

"You're catching on." I wink at him. Then I climb down the cold plasteel ladder running along one side of the shaft. I keep my eyes on the rungs as each of my boots make contact, whitewashed in the glare of my shoulder-mounted flashlight.

"Shall I shut the hatch behind us?"

"Good idea." If Raul's killer is down here, I don't want to give the piece of crap an easy way out.

"Hello," Dunn says, apropos of nothing, as he steps onto the ladder.

Then I hear the whine of Wink's rotors approaching, and I look up. The drone is hovering above my partner, looking eager to join us. If I'd known we'd be taking this subterranean route when I ordered Wink to rendezvous at my coordinates, I would've had it take the tunnel route here, making a sweep of the entire section behind us.

Not too late for that, I suppose.

Beckoning for the drone to come toward me, I give it new orders. "Backtrack along this tunnel and ensure that it's clear. Any signs of life, you notify me at once. And keep your video feed on. I want to see what you're seeing." I pause. "You are permitted to use lethal ordnance if anyone tries to damage you. But aim for their feet."

"Yes, Investigator Chen." It descends the shaft behind me with an echoing whir, rotors adjusting to the change in direction, and proceeds through the tunnel, heading back toward Dome 1.

I keep Wink's live feed in the bottom corner of my lenses as it darts through the tunnel, its headlight turning the darkness into something brighter than daylight.

Stepping down from the ladder, I turn to face the silent section of tunnel before us. Not so silent with Dunn's boots clanking down the rungs behind me. Somewhere, either behind us or in front of us, Raul's killer is lurking. Dust addict with superhuman abilities? Or just your average human who's succumbed to their baser instincts? Greed.

Survival. Desperation. I'm not sure any of those would have induced someone to do what was done to Raul.

We've never had animals in the Domes, but we know what they are. We've seen them in just about every VR StoryLine available. And someday, when Solomon Wong's clones manage to figure out how to terraform the Earth, we'll have animals in our world again, thanks to all those frozen embryos stored in Futuro Tower on the North African coast. In the interim, some have proposed building an eleventh Dome for a few of the animals to live in. So the human species can learn how to coexist with them again.

I know what wolves and bears are. I know that certain animals can become extremely vicious when cornered. And the way Raul's face was torn apart, it looked like the work of claws or sharp talons. Not done by human hands. Something else.

Something that might be waiting for us up ahead.

Drawing my shocker, I glance back at Dunn. With a nod, he draws his as well. A pistol-shaped weapon that delivers a strong enough charge to knock out a person's daylights. And evacuate their bowels, if they've eaten recently.

We proceed at a fast clip down the tunnel. No need for a map overlay. There are no branches breaking off right or left. No risk of taking a wrong turn. This route is one-way: from Dome 1 to the docks.

The water pipes running along one side are just as Raul described them, as is the dull red light that glows, sensing our presence each time we approach a maintenance panel. Once we pass, the automatic lighting goes out to conserve energy.

Infrared scans show no signs of recent footprints, Dunn reports, text-only.

So Raul's killer hasn't made it this far. Either that, or one of multiple hatches along the way provided a quick escape to the surface. Assuming the murderer has a data spike and keycode handy. Maintenance worker, perhaps?

A holo of Chief Inspector Hudson's stern face appears without warning for my ocular lenses only. He doesn't look happy with me. What else is new?

"Status report." Something about his tone gives the impression he might already know what we're up to.

"On foot, sir," I subvocalize via audiolink, doing my best to keep my footfalls quiet. Dunn's managing to do the same. "En route—"

"Why aren't you taking surface streets, Chen? Are you trying to end up like Ortega?"

I shake my head. "We've seen no evidence that Enforcer Ortega's killer came this way. I sent one of my drones back to make sure no one is closing in on us from behind."

It's not always easy to catch nuances of expression in holograms, but I'm pretty sure Hudson relaxes a smidge. Was he actually *worried* about me?

"Fine. But pick up your pace. Mirela Edwards has gunned down two of our security officers, and she is threatening to kill the rest of them if they do not abandon their posts." He pauses, clenching his jaw. "Seeing their comrades killed in such a fashion, I cannot expect anyone's resolve to last much longer."

Such a fashion. Never far from my mind, images return of Solomon Wong bursting into bloody scraps of flesh when I turned my exo's minigun on him. The same weapon Mirela is now using to kill our men and women guarding the Dome 10 airlock.

More deaths I'm responsible for.

"We'll get there." I break into a run and gesture for Dunn to keep up. He does so effortlessly.

"Hudson out." His holo vanishes.

I bring up the airlock coordinates, as well as Mirela Edwards' current position, and sync the neon-green overlay to my lenses in augmented reality. Which makes everything around me look like it's part of a strategy VR game, complete with glowing arrows pointing in the right direction, a distance to target gauge counting down, and my rate of speed clocked in real time. Who said work can't be fun?

Too bad it's so damn annoying.

If we want to show up at the riot in the least conspicuous way possible and arrive as close to my exo-suit as we can, we'll have to take the next maintenance hatch, about fifty meters away. I share the updated overlay with Dunn, and he nods mid-stride.

Blame it on the endorphins from running, but I think we've got this.

Until the face of a monster appears full-frame on Wink's live feed.

Bulging, lidless yellow eyes. A gaping nasal cavity instead of a nose. Chapped, leather-like skin. And, of course, glistening fangs. Add some chuffing, growling sounds coming out of the gaping mouth, and you've got yourself a living nightmare.

Except it's only a guy in a mask. Because what else could it be?

"Detain suspect," I order Wink.

"Halt," the drone commands in its most menacing monotone.

The masked figure takes a swipe at Wınk before dashing away, and the drone wobbles in midair from the impact, its headlight swaying side to side in the dark tunnel.

"Pursuing suspect," Wınk reports, spinning up its rotors with a high-pitched whir.

"Did you sustain any damage?" I've reached the maintenance shaft. Stepping aside, I allow Dunn to proceed up the ladder with his data spike at the ready.

"Minimal exterior damage, Investigator Chen," Wınk replies. "The suspect's claws are sharp."

So he's got claws, too. That explains what happened to Raul's face. Must be wearing gloves with plasteel tips or something equally malevolent.

Dunn has the hatch open. I motion for him to proceed to the surface.

"Suspect has eluded detainment," Wınk reports. The feed shows a vacant tunnel as far as the drone's infrared scanners can scan.

"Check the nearest maintenance shaft." I climb up the ladder after Dunn.

"The suspect's footsteps end here." Wınk hovers over the footprints in question, lit up in shades of orange. They end abruptly in the middle of the tunnel. As if the suspect simply vanished.

Too bad I've already seen this trick tonight.

"Look for a holo-projector nearby." I keep my voice low, but there's really no need. The chanting rioters are making so much noise half a block away, they wouldn't hear me even if I shouted.

"There is no holo-projector in the vicinity, Investigator—" Wınk's feed lurches downward, as if the drone suddenly lost power and hit the ground.

Or something heavy landed on top of it, overpowering the lift of its rotors and sending it crashing against the plasticon floor. The chuffing and growling sounds are louder now, as are the violent grunts that echo with the impact of each leathery fist smashing into Wınk's chassis, again and again. The video feed glitches, alternately freezing up and displaying static.

"Get out of there!" I shout as pieces of my drone shatter, skittering in all directions. "Wınk!"

The suspect's footprints stopped showing up on IR because he's a dust freak. He launched himself straight up and hung from the ceiling, waiting for my drone to pass by underneath. Then he pounced.

And now he's punishing Wınk for finding him.

"Damn it." I clench my fists and contemplate dropping back down the shaft, running as fast as I can to intercept the freak and give him both barrels of my shocker.

But he's three klicks away. It would take me at least ten minutes to reach what's left of my drone. By then, the suspect will be long gone.

I curse again and leap clear of the maintenance hatch just as it slides shut, rigged not to remain open longer than necessary. Crouching beside my partner in the middle of the vacant street, I keep an eye on our surroundings as the drone's live feed goes dark. No video, no audio.

First Raul, and now Wınk. I sent them both to their deaths.

Dunn's watching me. "We must press forward, Investigator Chen."

He's right, of course. The security personnel at the airlock are depending on us. And it won't do anybody any good sitting here in the dark and allowing guilt to immobilize me. I have to keep moving.

So I head toward the sounds of the riot, shocker at the ready in a two-handed grip. Dunn's right beside me, his weapon held beside his helmet, muzzle directed at the grungy ceiling of Dome 10 high above us. I have a feeling we're both about to exhaust every charge in the power cells. Whatever it takes to get these rioters to disperse.

As we round the corner of a brick edifice, we have a clear view of the mob at the water processing plant. They've managed to tip both tanker trucks onto their sides. Now the self-proclaimed victors are jumping up and down on top of the slain beasts, chanting in unison: "Death to all infidels! Death to all infidels!"

Apparently, they want the rest of Eurasia's citizens to die of thirst. And they think knocking over a couple trucks full of fresh water will achieve that end.

Nobody ever said this bunch was encumbered by a surplus of education.

I pull up Blink's video feed and wonder if it's aware of what happened to its twin. The drone is holding position, hovering above a nondescript building across the street from the airlock and keeping out of sight as directed. Its vantage point provides a clear view of Mirela Edwards in my exo.

She's advanced twenty meters since her arrival, and the bodies of the three guards she's dispatched are proof that the territory she's gained was not yielded without a fight. The rioters with her hang back under the bright lights. Unlike her, they appear to be unarmed. But they're shaking their fists with great bravado and shouting the same churlish chant as the mob at the desalination center.

"Death to all infidels! Death to all infidels!"

Twenty clones. Three guards. Mirela has plenty of blood on her hands tonight. And she doesn't look ready to quit anytime soon.

Standing by, Nichols and Granger text me in unison. I can't hear the hum of their engines, but they must be keeping track of my position.

They can tell I'm ready to move in.

With a glance at my partner, I subvocalize via audiolink, "Straight to the airlock. Shoot anybody who tries to stop us."

Dunn nods. "Lead the way, Investigator Chen."

14

We have the element of surprise on our side. As well as the element of audacity. Who in their right mind would send an investigator and her partner to quell a riot? The insurgents sure as hell don't see us coming, and I plan to keep it that way as long as possible.

"Is it really worth your lives?" Mirela Edwards shouts at the airlock guards, and the chants behind her die down some.

As a woman of medium height, I can't see much past the crowd. But from Blink's perspective twenty meters in the air, I clearly spot the three remaining guards. Two men, one woman. All keeping their heads down and their assault rifles at the ready.

"I give you my word," Mirela says. "Lay down your weapons, and we'll let you walk away. There's no reason for you to die tonight."

Not exactly true. Guarding that airlock with their lives is their duty. Keeping wackadoodles like these rioters from doing something seriously stupid—attempting to exit the Domes, for instance—is an assignment none of them take lightly. If they did, they would have abandoned their posts at the first sign of trouble.

I'm ten meters away from the mob's backside and closing.

Nobody looks my way. Mirela has their complete attention. And since she scared off the air patrols, the rioters have no reason to keep an eye on their six.

Except for this one guy who must have heard either my footfalls or Dunn's. Because he glances over his shoulder at us. And then his eyes widen, and he points—

My shocker sends an electric-blue energy pulse slamming into his midsection, and he doubles over, convulsing before he hits the ground and lapses into unconsciousness. The woman next to him doesn't notice right away, but when she does, Dunn hits her with a pulse that sends her tipping over onto the first guy, her body wracked with spasms.

What follows is a ridiculous game of human dominoes as one after another, we hit the rioters with our shockers, taking them down and knocking them out. But the attention we're drawing has a ripple effect that expands exponentially, and it isn't long before Mirela takes notice.

"It appears we have some unexpected company," she says in a loud voice, and the chanting of her followers dies out as they make way for her. She stomps toward me in my own damn exo.

Via Blink's feed, I see the guards train their rifles on her back.

"Hold fire," I subvocalize via audiolink. I need Mirela Edwards alive.

"Can it be?" Mirela stares as if I'm the last person she expected to see. "Is that you, Queen of the Infidels?"

Not sure how to respond to that. "Pull the release and step out of the exo-suit." I aim my shocker at her face, the only part of her that's exposed enough for me to land a shot without the energy burst glancing off inorganic matter.

"She tried to kill Prometheus!" Mirela points at me, a stricken look in her eyes, and the mob lets out a collective gasp.

The cynic in me might say this feels a bit staged.

"Queen of the Unbelievers! That's what she is." A devilish smile spreads across Mirela's lips as her followers hang on every word. "And you know what must be done to—"

"You're the only one here with blood on their hands." My voice hangs in the stillness. Mirela looks startled by my interruption. The rioters glance at each other, appearing to understand the implications of what I said. Assuming they need a little more convincing, based on their less-than-intelligent behavior as of late, I add, "No one else killed those guards. No one else will be charged with murder."

A low murmur ripples through the mob. If I play my cards right here, they might disperse on their own before Nichols and Granger even show up. Assuming Mirela doesn't activate that minigun instead and turn my partner and me into bloody pulp.

"Interesting to note that your fingerprints are on every round this machine gun fires," Mirela continues, unintimidated.

"That's some trick," I acknowledge. No idea how she pulled it off. Honestly, I don't really care. "But your finger's on the trigger."

The minigun spins up, its rotating muzzle lurching into place as it locks on-target. Dunn steps in front of me without hesitation.

"Self-sacrifice?" Mirela raises an eyebrow. "Didn't know clones were programmed for that sort of thing."

"There's a lot you don't know about us." I tap my temple

to disengage my neuro and telepathically send the override keycode to the exo-suit.

No idea if this will work. I've communicated mind-to-AI with my drones before, and even with their limited level of artificial intelligence, they not only received my transmission but responded. But this is a motorized exoskeleton. As far as I know, it has no thinking center; it merely responds to muscle commands from the person wearing it.

Then again, my abilities tend to transcend what's impossible. They've surprised me before. At this point, just about anything is worth a shot in the dark.

"Perhaps I know more about you than you think," Mirela replies with a quiet chuckle. "*Demigod.* You enjoy having powers that set you apart from the average citizen. Yet you don't want anyone else to share the gifts you've been given."

I clench my jaw and try sending the keycode again. But for all I know, it's just floating out there in the telepathic ether with no receiver.

"Did you know that her biological parents lived outside our walls for *decades*?" Mirela turns toward her attentive rabble. "Proof that it can be done—but only for the select few. That's the way people like Sera Chen prefer it. She didn't want Prometheus giving every single one of us the ability to live and breathe out under the sun—"

"The Prometheus AI had no evidence to back up its claims," Dunn says. "The only human to undergo its gene-splice therapy—a man who called himself Trezon—never set foot outside the safety of Eurasia's walls."

This time, Mirela looks furious at the interruption. But the expression melts into something more sinister as she nods toward the line of dead security clones lying on the street in pools of their own blood. "Does it bother you, clone? What I did here?"

Dunn doesn't answer right away. The rioters stare at him, standing there in his pristine white armor, and wait to see what he'll do or say. Will he speak for the dead?

"They will be recycled," he says at length, without the slightest tremor in his voice. But I remember the tears I saw in his eyes.

"Wow." Mirela looks impressed. "Guess you weren't too attached to them. But I suppose emotional attachment is a human personality trait. Not something you're burdened with." She glances back at the broken bodies. "What were they to you, exactly? Siblings? Cousins? Or just identical copies of the same dead genius?"

She likes the sound of her own voice. And that's fine. As long as she's talking, she's not shooting anybody else, and I can make one more attempt at telepathically disabling my exo. But when I fail a third time, which I'm pretty sure I will, based on the lack of any response—not even a twitch—from the suit, I'm going to have to figure out a way to get close enough for it to recognize my neuro. Within a meter should do it. Then I'll be able to enter the keycode via Link, assuming she hasn't figured out a way to block proximal access.

And that's only if I can approach her without the minigun shredding my head.

"Prometheus is gone." I take a step forward, keeping my shocker out in the open in case any of her overzealous friends decide to play the hero and tackle me to the ground. "So is the gene-splicing miracle it promised."

Mirela laughs. "You can't honestly believe that! You, of all people, know the secrets our government has kept from us for decades. Their habit of lying to the people did not magically come to an end once James Bishop was named Interim Chancellor. The fact of the matter is that Prometheus hasn't *gone* anywhere but is only temporarily detained. And the gene-splicing regimen doctors performed on that Trezon fellow? It's a matter of record." She narrows her gaze. "A closely-guarded record."

How can she possibly know this? None of it has been made public.

Then I remember something her mother said about being a personal friend of Governor Raniero. Has the governor of Dome 1 been talking out of turn?

"Those doctors you mention were mindjacked." I take another step toward her. Less than three meters away from my exo now. Rioters flank me on both sides, but I'm counting on Dunn to shoot anybody who gets more than a little twitchy. "Is that what you want? Citizens' free will overwritten by a machine? Because that's what Prometheus was all about. It used human beings for its purposes, and when they were no longer useful, it killed them." I point at my head. "Fried the implants in their skulls." That wasn't made known to the public, either. "They dropped to the ground like discarded puppets."

A low murmur sweeps through the mob. People are glancing at each other, wondering if what I said was true. That's good. They're not looking at Mirela now.

She notices. And she doesn't like it.

"Cut off the head, and the rest will follow!" she cries, raising both arms encased in the plasteel exo-frame. "Death to all infidels!"

The overeager mob restarts the chant, shaking their fists at me and screaming until they're red in the face.

I have the shot, one of the guards sends me a text. On Blink's feed, he stands with his rifle aimed at the back of Mirela's head.

Standby, I message back. I can't let him kill her. She knows who murdered Raul. And she knows why the freak did it.

"This woman stands between you and a life of freedom in the Wastes!" Somehow, Mirela's voice rises above the rabble. "Sera Chen wants to keep you from the gifts Prometheus would have freely given you! The gifts that can still be yours, if the Governors stop holding us back!"

This is ludicrous. She thinks that by killing guards and security clones and commandeering the airlock, she'll force the government to turn over the details of Trezon's gene-splicing? And that doctors will, without being forced to do so by a powerful AI, perform the same operation that gave Trezon his invisibility-powers on any random person who wants to be turned into a *demigod*? Oh, and that the authorities as well as the medical community will be fine with the idea of harvesting DNA from a thousand children living throughout the Domes? Just on the off-chance that this Prometheus cult will be able to breathe outside our walls in an oxygen-deprived environment once their genes have been altered?

The truth dawns on me with a cold weight that lands in the pit of my stomach: Mirela Edwards is insane.

"Kill the queen!" She jabs an index finger in my direction, her eyes wild in the harsh light. "Death to all infidels!"

The mob echoes her sentiment in a sudden roar, surging

forward to answer the call with no shortage of enthusiasm. Dunn and I shoot as many of them as we can, rapid-fire, bursts of energy striking targets willy-nilly and dropping them to the ground in spasms, one on top of another—tripping hazards for the rioters behind them. But there are just too many closing in, with more running over from the desalination plant to join in the fun. Guess they realized where the real party was at.

Within seconds, we're completely overwhelmed.

Engage Mirela Edwards, I transmit telepathically as members of the mob take me down to the pavement, countless bodies landing on top of me with fists, elbows, and knees delivering punishing blows. I try in vain to block them all and manage to shield my face for the most part. I've lost hold of my shocker, and I've lost track of Dunn in the melee. Sure wish I had his armor right now. *Draw her fire.*

Yes, Investigator Chen, Blink replies via our telepathic channel. Glad I haven't lost my touch.

Hope I'm not sending my second drone to its doom.

Bodies go flying. One second, they're on top of me doing their damnedest to pound me into the ground; the next, they're flung aside like bags of garbage. Short cries of alarm are followed by groans as they slam into fellow revelers, toppling them over backward.

"Take my hand," Dunn says, and I look up to see him standing over me with his arm extended. His armor looks as spotless as ever. Weird thing to focus on.

The rioters fall back a step, having witnessed the ease with which he sent their ilk airborne. None seem eager to test their own flight skills.

I spot my shocker and scoop it up, then grab Dunn's

hand. He pulls me to my feet effortlessly and turns to face the rioters.

"Go home!" I shout, brandishing my weapon. "Leave now, and we'll forget this ever happened."

"I am afraid that's impossible, Sera Chen," Mirela says, stomping toward me in my exo. "We are Prometheus, and we have an excellent memory. We remember what you did to us. And we know what you will continue to do: withhold from us the special abilities demigods like you take for granted. Because you don't think people like us are *worthy*." She pauses to scowl at me in the silence, as the mob hangs on her words all over again. "Perhaps we should show you how worthy we are."

No idea what she has in mind, but that's when Blink shows up, buzzing through the air on an intercept course with her face. Mirela flinches, lurching backward in the exo, and my drone sweeps past, a mere centimeter from clipping her cheek with its rotors. Swooping upward in a steep arc, Blink comes around for a second pass.

Cursing furiously, Mirela plants her boot-struts and spins up the minigun, targeting the drone as it makes its approach.

Draw fire and evade, I clarify. But Blink's trajectory doesn't change. *Evade incoming fire!*

Yes, Investigator Chen, the drone replies. Then it adds something to the mix: its own lethal ordnance, a salvo of projectile rounds fired at the pavement, sparking on impact right in front of my exo.

The rioters yelp and scatter like startled children, giving Mirela a wide berth, but they don't follow my advice to head home. They want to see what happens next.

So do I.

She doesn't seem worried about getting shot. Maybe she's already called my bluff. If the airlock guards haven't gunned her down yet, it's because the lead investigator on the scene hasn't allowed it. The same LawKeeper armed with a nonlethal weapon, which she hasn't even fired at Mirela yet.

Right. On it.

I squeeze off a few rounds in quick succession as Blink's disc-shaped form hurtles toward the minigun's muzzle, and the energy bursts that go off around Mirela's head, smacking into the exo's frame, are disorienting enough to foul up her aim. The minigun spews its barrage up into the air, but my drone dodges easily, careening into a wide arc that takes it high over the heads of the security personnel.

That was just the distraction I needed. A meter away from the exo's backside now, I tap my temple to re-engage my augments. The instant the exoskeleton recognizes my neuro's signal with a blinking blue light along its plasteel spine, I transmit the override command keycode.

The exo-suit freezes up immediately. The minigun jerks backward into standby mode. And Mirela Edwards is ejected from the harness, stumbling forward as if somebody kicked her in the ass.

"Move in," I subvocalize via audiolink to the air patrollers and airlock security.

As the pair of aerocars sweep in with gas grenades and flashbangs at the ready, and the guards advance with their rifles trained on Mirela, the rioters suddenly look like they wish they were anywhere but here. Their fearless leader in her powerful weaponized suit was the center of attention. The exo gave her a real aura of gravitas. Without it, she's not much to look at.

Her stature is slender and small, birdlike for lack of a better term. There's a clear resemblance to her mother, except Mirela is older and more frail. She hasn't made use of the gene therapy that keeps Nevah Edwards looking decades younger than her actual age. Mirela seems lost, as though she woke up from a dream and can't decide whether the things she's seeing around her are actually happening.

I think about shooting her with a stun pulse just to see her collapse in spasms. But I don't. Because I'm feeling generous.

It's not every day one's glorious insurrection goes down in flames.

"Disperse at once," Granger orders, his voice loud and gravelly on the loudspeaker as his aerocar sways side to side in midair. "This is your last warning. Loading gas grenades."

"Flashbangs at the ready," Nichols adds, his aerocar adopting the same menacing posture on the other side of the rioters. I'm sure both pilots are relieved to no longer be on the sidelines.

The mob doesn't have to be told twice. Without so much as a backward glance at Mirela—who realizes the dispersal order wasn't meant for her, and stays put—the rioters disband, running as fast as they can in every direction other than the airlock or the desalination plant.

"Facial recognition active," Blink reports, flying over the revelers making their escape and identifying every one of them faster than humanly possible. Charges will be brought within twenty-four hours, and they'll have to report to the nearest police substation to pay a hefty fine. If they don't, and if we have to send trackers out to collect them, then they'll spend the next six months at a correctional center.

Their choice. "Scanning, scanning, scanning..."

"Good boy." I turn toward Mirela. She looks intimidated by me now, like she's afraid I'm going to deck her. I really should, all things considered. "Now, as for you—"

The roar of a groundcar's engine fills the night. Tires squeal around the corner across the street. I turn sharply in time to see Drasko's muscle car appear, drifting diagonally across the pavement yet somehow under complete control, heading straight for Mirela Edwards.

15

I've seen this trick before, too. There must be projectors nearby. Once again, Mirela is trying to use a holo of my friend's vehicle to confuse me. To make me think he would actually be part of this. The getaway driver, no less.

The groundcar's twin doors swing open while its tires skid sideways across the street. As if every move was choreographed ahead of time, Mirela makes a dash for the passenger side while the driver leans out, one hand on the wheel, a big gun in the other.

Which he aims right at me.

I instantly recognize the neutral expression on his face, the scarred neck, that large-caliber handgun with the armor-piercing rounds in his grip. I know it isn't really Drasko, but I can't wrap my mind around how Mirela managed this. It's wrong on so many levels, stealing someone's 3D image for criminal use. Not to mention delusional. Does she really think she can vanish into a hologram?

Unless there's another maintenance hatch underneath—

Dunn steps in front of me, obstructing my view. I try to shove him out of the way. "It's not real!"

That's when Drasko pulls the trigger, and it sounds like a bomb goes off. Dunn blocks the shot with a swing of his arm, and the all-too-real round cracks through his armor like it's mere plastiglass, sending white shards upward and outward. The mechanical forearm beneath sparks under the impact but doesn't hang limp. Dunn returns fire without hesitating, his shocker's energy bursts smacking against the groundcar's hood and fizzling out in lightning-like drizzles across the surface.

So. Not a holo.

The three security personnel open fire, full-auto, advancing in a wedge formation. Their rounds thud across the vehicle's rear before targeting the tires, and one blows out with a plume of smoke.

Mirela has already thrown herself inside, and the doors swing shut. Drasko guns it, and the groundcar falters, smoke whirling from the punctured tire. The guards concentrate their fire on the other rear tire as the vehicle fishtails, lurching side to side. Nichols lends a hand, swooping by to drop a flashbang onto the windshield. It's the best he can do, since our aerocars aren't outfitted with deadly ordnance. I hold up a hand to shield my eyes against the grenade's blinding light, accompanied by a jarring explosive sound, and hope it disorients Drasko long enough for the guards to take out the rest of his tires.

No such luck. He's already halfway down the street, out of range.

"Follow him," I subvocalize via audiolink, and both pilots veer off, Granger high—above the rooftops—and Nichols low—less than twenty meters behind the smoking groundcar.

"That is the second time Mr. Drasko has shot me," Dunn remarks, looking down at his arm. Between jagged cracks in the armor, his gleaming metal prosthetic shines through.

I stare after Drasko's retreat until the streaming cloud from his ruined tire dissipates into shadow. Guess there's no doubt about it now. He's working with Mirela Edwards. But he can't be part of her resurrected Prometheus cult, can he? She must have something on him, leverage of some type. Forcing him to act as her accomplice.

Hudson hails me. And, as expected, he's far from happy.

"Tell me I'm not seeing this," he growls, audio-only.

"The exo-suit is back in my possession, sir. And one of my drones is scanning the identities of the rioters as they disperse." Figure it's best to start with good news.

He curses under his breath. "So that wasn't your friend Drasko aiding Mirela Edwards in her escape?"

My shoulders slump. "I'm pretty sure it was."

"Pretty sure?" He scoffs.

"I've seen a few masks tonight." First the weird whirlpool variety worn by the pair of jewelry—*artifact*—heisters. Then the freakish leathery one worn by Raul's killer. "Could've been a really good mask, sir. Designed to look like Drasko."

"A mask. That's your prevailing theory."

"It was Mr. Drasko, Investigator Chen," Dunn says quietly, leaning toward me. "Scans confirmed his identity."

I glare at him, and he backs up a step.

"Chen, if you're too close to the situation..." Hudson leaves me a way out.

"No. It's fine." I take a moment to exhale. "I know a few places he might've gone."

"That is precisely the problem. You are well aware of his undercover work. And if you go in there like you own the place, that's going to raise more than a few red flags among his underworld associates." Hudson curses again. "It's a catch-22."

I frown. "What's that, sir?"

"Catch-22. An idiom referring to a problematic situation where—"

"He was trying to warn me..." I shake my head at the memory. I was standing next to our booth at Howard's Tavern in the Future Noir interactive. He was far from forthcoming. But then again, I had to leave. Maybe he would've opened up if I'd stuck around. Heller's *Catch-22*, he said. "Drasko is in a no-win situation."

"I don't give a damn what sort of situation he's gotten himself into! He has put *us* in an impossible position!" Hudson blusters.

"Almost as if she knew it would be," I murmur, half to myself.

Could Mirela have somehow discovered that Drasko was on a long-term, deep-cover assignment? Has she threatened to reveal that fact to his underworld lieutenants if he doesn't obey her every whim? Activate the exo. Be her getaway driver. What's next?

Or did she find out about his family living in Dome 9? Could she have threatened to alert the authorities—one of her mother's upper-caste friends in high places? Drasko would do absolutely anything to keep his loved ones safe and well cared for. But would he ally himself with a Prometheus cultist just so they could stay on Erik's farm?

"Mirela Edwards? How would she possibly know about Drasko's double life?" Hudson sounds incredulous. Because only he, Commander Bishop, and I are privy to that information. Not a solar engineer.

"She knew who I was," I mutter.

"Who doesn't? Every citizen in the Domes knows who the Twenty are."

"She's done her research, sir. She's aware of things that haven't been made known to the public." I pause. "Regarding the Prometheus AI."

He doesn't respond right away. Then he lowers his voice. "If you are about to suggest that we have a leak at HQ, let me stop you right there—"

"Is there any chance the AI has...escaped?" I don't know how else to phrase it. "That it might have activated sleeper agents mindjacked to do its bidding?"

"No. Absolutely not. We already lived through that. We are still recovering from it." He exhales loudly. "The Prometheus AI remains contained." He doesn't elaborate.

"What about a cloned version on the Link? Are we certain Prometheus didn't leave a backup of itself programmed to come online at a later date?"

"Our analysts have scoured the Link for any code that could be related to the AI. They have found nothing at all to support what you're suggesting."

I hesitate to ask, but I go for it anyway. "Are we sure they haven't been compromised, sir?"

"The analysts?" He curses in disbelief that I would even mention such a possibility.

"Do we know the power outages haven't...affected them? Left them vulnerable somehow?"

He's silent for a beat. Seething, no doubt. I often have that effect on him.

"One thing can be said for you, Chen," he manages, "and that is your ability to think outside of the box. For the moment, leave our cybersecurity issues to the experts, and the apprehension of both Mirela Edwards and her accomplice to the trackers assigned this case. I want you to narrow the focus of your investigation: Why would Nevah Edwards' daughter rob her own mother's shop—and what does this have to do with a resurgence of the Children of Tomorrow? Think you can do that?"

I nod to myself. "Yes, sir." But before he can end the call, I ask, "Trackers have been tasked with bringing Drasko in?"

"Obviously. He drove the getaway car for a murderer." He pauses, disgruntled. "Which will only serve to solidify his reputation among the underworld."

"So nobody's actually going to bring him in." If they do, they'll ruin his deep-cover assignment. And there's no way Commander Bishop would sign off on that.

"Not your concern, Chen. Hudson out."

Blink buzzes our way from a few blocks down and settles into a stationary orbit, hovering a meter above my head. "All rioters have returned to their domiciles," it reports. "Identities confirmed and recorded."

"Good work." I glance up, dreading the condition I'll find Wink in. Doubtful it will look anything like its twin. Then I turn to my partner. "Are you okay?"

Dunn nods, keeping the arm with the shattered armor down at his side. "I will need to replace this section of plating. According to self-diagnostics, the prosthetic underneath is undamaged."

I'll take whatever good news I can get.

Regardless of Drasko's situation, whatever it might be, I can't let go of the fury I'm feeling right now. Would he have shot me, if Dunn hadn't stepped into the way? Or was the shot just a centimeter or two off—enough to look convincing?

Jumping onto the StoryLine messageboard, I leave a quick note since I can't hail Drasko. For some reason, underworld kingpins aren't listed in the citizen registry.

D - What the hell? Charlie would never shoot at Vivian. -S

I don't expect a response. He's busy driving Mirela to safety, after all.

Instead, it's Nichols who hails me. "Chen, we've lost them. The car went under a bridge. When it appeared on the other side, it was driverless." He clears his throat. "We-uh didn't notice that right away. But from what we can tell, it's been programmed to lead us around surface streets until it runs out of gas."

"You and Granger can head back to the train terminal. We'll meet you there."

A short pause. "You're not going after them?"

"Not our job." I glance at Dunn. "We're not trackers."

Nichols curses quietly. "Alright, Chen. See you at the terminal."

He ends the transmission, and I step into my exo, tugging on the harness and adjusting the buckles. I'm not a big woman, but I'm bigger than Mirela. She had it sized for her smaller stature. Which makes this a weird feeling—encasing myself in an exoskeleton that, until now, no one else has ever used before. And the way it was used… To slaughter people and clones protecting Dome 10. Makes it feel like something alien and wrong, even as its familiarity brings back a flood of memories.

"Do you wish we were the ones pursuing Mr. Drasko and

Mirela Edwards instead?" Dunn asks, watching me.

"Not our job," I repeat, but with less gusto. "As investigators, we ask questions, put the puzzle pieces together. But we don't do all the work. Enforcers, trackers, and interrogators have their parts to play." A clearly defined division of labor. No idea what things were like in the Old World, but it's always been this way in the Domes. Nobody takes all the credit when things go right, and we all share the blame when they don't. "We've been told in no uncertain terms to focus on the artifacts heist. To find out why Mirela would steal everything from her mother's shop. So that's what we'll do." I shrug, and now that the exo is synced to my neuro, the plasteel frame curving over my shoulders makes a simultaneous approximation of a shrug.

Something about the tone of my voice causes Dunn to tilt his helmet to one side. "But we are going to do something else first?"

I nod and break into a jog in the direction of the Dome 1 train terminal, my boot-braces pounding the pavement as I increase speed, gobbling up the meters faster than I could ever imagine running on foot. Dunn has no trouble keeping up. Neither does Blink, buzzing over our heads.

"Gotta get Wink. That's the priority."

Dunn nods. "Because the murder suspect's fingerprints may be on its chassis."

"Right." Guess I can't expect him to share my sentimental attachment to the drones. "Wink mentioned claws on the suspect. So he might've been wearing gloves." Weird gloves, and a weird mask. Leave it to a dust freak to go completely off the rails. "But if we're lucky, Wink might've managed to scan the suspect's neuro before we lost contact."

"Do you believe the suspect to be at large?"

"Trackers have been assigned to apprehend him. But if the trail goes cold, as I have a feeling it will—" Based on Mirela's recent getaway, these people know how to disappear. Above and below the streets. "—we need to find out who the person behind the mask is."

"A maintenance worker?"

"They'd be familiar with accessing the hatches and shafts. Problem is, half the rioters we sent packing were maintenance workers." Based on Blink's ID scans. "We need to narrow it down."

Dunn's faceplate angles toward me as we lope along. "By *we* you mean that I will be doing the narrowing."

I give him a wink. "I'll have my hands full writing up the report for Hudson."

"And you still need to conduct a second interview with Nevah Edwards."

"Thanks for reminding me." I cast him a sidelong look. Not a very pleasant one.

We reach the train terminal just as Nichols and Granger touch down in their aerocars. The semtex from Matthews and Shariq cleared most of the debris covering the mouth of the maglev tunnel, but not enough for either vehicle to fly through. So Dunn and I volunteer to clear the rest of it. Thanks to my exo and Dunn's mechanical arms, we make short work of it, tossing sizeable chunks of plasticon off to the sides out of the way without even breaking a sweat.

Twenty minutes later, we're dusting ourselves off and climbing into the backseat of Nichols' vehicle—after stowing my exo-suit in the cargo compartment.

"Get a load of this." Eklund half-turns toward me in the

copilot seat, her brow furrowed as she activates the holo on her console. "It's all over the Linkstream."

A three-dimensional version of Governor Raniero composed of bluish-white light appears to hover in the center of the windscreen, almost like he's peering in at us from outside. Age indeterminate thanks to years of gene therapy. Dark features. Short, grizzled hair and manicured beard, intelligent eyes that lose none of their intensity in the holo-transmission. He looks sincere. And gravely serious.

The governor of Dome 1 is online before the crack of dawn, and he has something he wants every citizen of Eurasia to hear. By all appearances, he's been talking for a while already and is approaching the end of his diatribe.

"People of the Ten Domes, the time has come for a change in leadership. What we have witnessed over the past six hours defies description. Lives have been lost. Our very security threatened. Never before has any group of citizens within our walls sought to tamper with the airlock protecting us from those lethal toxins lurking outside. Yet that is exactly what Interim Chancellor James Bishop allowed to happen." Pause to nod dramatically. "He has permitted strange religious groups to flourish across the Domes, and this is the result. Say what you will about Chancellor Hawthorne, but at least under her leadership, we never had to concern ourselves with members of a bizarre cult forcing open the Dome 10 airlock and allowing the poisoned air outside to flood into our homes, ravaging our bodies, tearing us apart from the inside. Yet that is what nearly happened on James Bishop's watch." He pauses again to nod grimly. "I do not take this step lightly. Never in all my years as Governor could I have imagined reaching this point. But know that I have only the welfare of the citizens of Eurasia at the forefront of this difficult decision." One last pause. He raises his bearded chin and scowls as if it pains him to say what he's about to. "Let it be known on this day that I officially cast my vote of no confidence in the abilities of James Bishop to continue serving as Interim Chancellor, and I call upon my fellow Governors to join me in doing the same."

Shaking her head, Eklund mutes the holo. "What the hell?"

"It was only a matter of time," Nichols mutters, preparing to take us through the maglev tunnel back to Dome 1. "The Governors and Bishop never saw things eye to eye. They've just been waiting for him to screw things up royally. Now they pounce."

"But he had nothing to do with this." Eklund scoffs.

"Maybe that's the problem. His hands-off approach." Nichols lifts off, just a couple meters or so, engines humming and jet wash kicking up dust. He angles the aerocar's nose down a bit and steers us carefully into the tunnel with Granger following ten meters behind. Neither one's as fast as Drasko used to be, but they're much better pilots than Matthews was—may he rest in peace. "Bishop's had some lofty goals. But he's a military guy, not a politician. His way of doing things has alienated most of the Governors."

I lean forward against the straps of my harness. "By *his way*, you mean the opposite of an iron fist."

Nichols chuckles wryly. "Hey, don't get me wrong. I have no desire to go back to the draconian way things were." One of his shoulders hitches up. "But Raniero's got a point. What we saw here tonight? Never would've happened back when Hawthorne was in charge."

"Easy to say." I sit back in my seat and fold my arms. "Let's not forget how close the Domes came to imploding while she was busy snorting oodles of dust."

He grunts noncommittally. Eklund shuts off the holo and glances back at me.

"Weird to see Drasko again. Heard he'd turned to a life of crime after retiring. I mean, there were rumors he was always involved in dust smuggling, but..." She pauses with a curious frown. "Ever thought you'd see your old pilot driving a getaway car?"

I grace her with my most intimidating smirk, hoping to end this conversation before it has a chance to gather momentum. "Never in a million years."

Then I close my eyes and settle in for a slow, easy ride back to Dome 1.

16

Dawn is breaking by the time Dunn and I find ourselves dropped off out front of Hawthorne Tower, and as beams of blue-tinted sunlight filter through the plexicon wall on our eastern side, Dome 1 stirs to life. Boxy driverless cargo vehicles hit the streets, electric motors quietly humming, and orderly aerial traffic fills the sky. Now that curfew's over, people and goods have places to be.

As do Dunn and I. But it's not up to the third floor so I can start working on my report and he can do some research. That'll come later. Right now, we've got some underground work to do.

Returning to the scene of the crime—Edwards' jewelry shop and the maintenance shaft nearby—Dunn gets his data spike ready to open the hatch. Except it's already yawning wide open, and every transport vehicle on the street passing this way has to be careful to swerve around it. And us as well, while they're at it.

"The hatch must be damaged," Dunn says, kneeling down beside it.

"Intentionally," I mutter. "Which explains why Raul fell in. The freak was waiting for him down there."

Dunn's faceplate turns toward me, glinting with the

bright morning sun. "Do you have evidence that the suspect is in fact a dust addict?"

"He was able to hang from the tunnel ceiling." Right before dropping onto Wınk. "Only seen that trick once before: Trezon's flunky who called himself Krime."

"I remember him, one of the first of Prometheus's acolytes to have his neural implant fried. Or perhaps he was the very first..." Dunn's head twitches oddly. "Strange, that I am unable to recall that fact clearly from memory. But upon consulting the LawKeeper database, yes, he was in fact the Prometheus AI's first victim."

I give my exo's harness a final check as I get ready to hop down into the maintenance shaft, but my partner's demeanor gives me pause. "You didn't get your four hours last night."

"And you did not get your variable six-to-eight hours of sleep." He stands and faces me as the data spike retracts into his gauntlet. "That has proven problematic in the past."

When I wasn't sleeping at all, sure, it was bad. But those nightmares don't plague me anymore. "Maybe we should both schedule some rack time after I pick up Wınk."

"We go together, Investigator Chen," Dunn insists, the same way he did when I offered to take this trip alone. "As you said, the suspect remains at large. He or she may still be lurking in this maintenance tunnel."

More likely, we'll find the mask and gloves discarded near another maintenance hatch. But I appreciate the sentiment.

"Thanks for the backup, partner."

I drop into the shaft, ignoring the ladder running down one side, and the leg braces of my exo absorb the impact as I hit bottom. Landing in a crouch, I bring up the coordinates of Wink's last-known location. Fifty meters south of my current position.

But first is the blood.

"Enforcer Ortega was murdered there." Dunn drops beside me and points.

I switch on my exo's shoulder-mounted floodlight, and it blasts the tunnel stark white. Perfectly still. Eerie, really. Raul's remains have been transported to MedCenter 1, but no cleanup crew was dispatched to expunge the crimson aftermath from the plasticon floor. The only evidence of what happened here.

I keep my boot-braces from tracking through it and clunk ahead, one heavy step at a time, my shocker in both hands and trained on the empty space in front of me. Remembering what happened to Wink, I keep an eye on what's above as well. No freaky ceiling-clinger so far.

"Watch our six," I subvocalize to Blink as the drone descends the maintenance shaft behind Dunn, whirring rotors filling the tunnel with their low hum.

"Yes, Investigator Chen. Holding position."

On the off-chance the dust freak doubled back after smashing Wink and decided to lurk in the dark tunnel behind us, Blink will let us know if he comes creeping our way. IR scans aren't detecting any warm footprints or heat signatures nearby, so it's a safe bet our suspect hasn't been through here since he made his presence known.

My light reflects on pieces of plasteel scattered across the tunnel floor, maybe fifteen meters away. Too many broken parts.

"Here." My voice echoes, loud in the confined space, and I pick up the pace.

Reaching Wınk, I drop to one knee with a groan, my breath catching at the sight. I can't believe the extent of the damage. How will it ever be put back together again? Smashed and bent out of shape, the drone looks like it picked a fight with an industrial fan and lost miserably.

Holstering my shocker, I reach for the disc-shaped chassis. No blinking lights. No recognition of my presence. Rotors either broken off or twisted beyond recognition.

"The gouges and scrapes are consistent with the suspect wearing claws of some kind." Dunn leans over my shoulder brace. "But he or she was not content with knocking the drone down and putting it out of commission. The intent here was to utterly destroy it, due to a deep-seated malice."

"The freak was angry." I tuck the crumpled chassis under one arm and start scooping up all the broken parts. "He knew Wınk was recording him, and he really didn't like it."

"If I may?" Dunn holds out his gauntlet with the data spike at the ready.

"Knock yourself out." I hand him the chassis and focus on gathering the rest of my drone's pieces. "Doubt you'll find anything in there."

"The drone's memory core is shielded by a triple-layer of carbon fiber reinforced polymer. It would take more than the fists of a mere mortal to permanently damage—"

"The brain. You're saying Wınk's brain might still be intact."

"The memory core, yes." Dunn drives the data spike into the center of the chassis like he's impaling its heart, sliding into the port until it clicks.

"So what makes Wınk...Wınk—might be undamaged? We could transfer the memory core into a new body, and it'll be itself again?"

Dunn's faceplate tilts slightly to one side. "Unknown. But if the drone was able to identify the suspect's neuro before going offline, then we will know who is responsible for Enforcer Ortega's murder."

"Right." I glance at the debris I've scraped together into a pile. "So all we really need is the core."

"Correct." He pauses. "Your emotional attachment to the drone is to be commended, Investigator Chen. If the core can be salvaged, then yes, the drone and all of its recorded data, including its interactions with you, will remain, whether or not it is placed into a new chassis."

I squint up at him. "How's it looking so far?"

Another tilt of his helmet. "Data files appear to be uncompromised. Accessing scans made prior to offline status. Sending them to your lenses."

Immediately, footage of Wink's attack replays across my field of vision, the moment that dust freak pounced onto my drone and drove it to the tunnel floor. I don't flinch. I clench my fists instead.

"As you can see, Wink attempted to scan the suspect's neuro more than once," Dunn continues. "At such close range, it should have been instantaneous. The drone's scanners were not shattered until two seconds later."

"So either the suspect has some kind of blocker in place, or he has no neural implant."

Dunn nods. "Or the neuro has been damaged somehow, perhaps by snorting too much dust."

It's not unheard of, unfortunately. Dust addicts toggle off their augments, overdose on the stuff, and when they go to turn their implant back on, they find that it's no longer responsive. Along with their higher-order thinking skills and emotional stability." Might explain why he's a homicidal maniac."

"It would indeed, Investigator Chen."

"Alright." I stand, leaving Wɪnk's remains. "Get the memory core over to the tech-heads at HQ and see about replacing the exterior. Tell them I don't want a new drone. I want that drone in a new body." I point at the smashed chassis. "I'll be able to tell if they try to pull a fast one on me."

Dunn nods. "Where will you be?"

"Interviewing one of the most annoying people in Dome 1, of course." I turn around, boot-braces clanking, and gesture for him to lead the way out via the same maintenance shaft we entered. "This time, I think I'll show up at her door. That's sure to win me some points."

"I do not agree, Investigator Chen." He starts toward the shaft. But then he slows to a halt and glances back at me. "Unless you were being sarcastic."

"I was." I try not to smile.

"Very well. Then I am sure you will win a whole lot of points with Ms. Nevah Edwards." He continues onward, and I can't help chuckling. Then, out of the blue, he asks, "Do you think of me in the same way as your drones?"

I frown at that. "How do you mean?"

"You are emotionally attached to me as well, are you not?"

"I care about you, if that's what you're getting at. You're my partner." I shake my head. "You're nothing like them. You're a *person*. They're just machines."

"Yet you care about them." He raises what used to be Wɪnk in the palm of his right gauntlet. "In the Old World, humans had animals as pets. They cared for them and cared about them. Perhaps you would have as well, had you lived during that time. Now, in the absence of animals, do you think of your drones as pets?" A brief pause. "Am I your pet, Investigator Chen?"

"No," I reply quickly. Dad referred to Dunn that way, then rephrased it, saying he was my *pet project*. Neither was appropriate.

"Am I your equal?" There's something in my partner's tone that I haven't heard before. Not from him, anyway. Is he testing me? Where is this coming from?

As we approach the maintenance shaft, I do my best to steer clear of Raul's blood. Dunn stands at the foot of the ladder and turns toward me, awaiting my response.

Is he my equal? What does that even mean? "You're a person—"

"Yes, you said that."

Now he's getting snippy. "Maybe we should have this talk after you've gotten some sleep. We're both tired…"

He turns his back on me and climbs up the ladder with one arm, the other cradling Wink's remains to his armored chest. I watch him go and exhale, shaking my head, feeling like I've failed him somehow. Why couldn't I just tell him straight out that of course we're equals? We're both biological beings. We're both human, when you come right down to it.

I was grown in a test tube or a petri dish—not sure exactly how that came about. I was born from an incubation chamber. How is that any different from Dunn's emergence into the world? My DNA came from two unwilling donors, held captive deep beneath the North American Wastes. His DNA came from a genius who made hundreds of copies of himself. Equally abnormal.

Equally strange. Just in different ways. That's what we are.

"Dunn—" I'm about to tell him as much, launching upward once the shaft is clear, my exo landing on the street above with a heavy clunk. But his name dies in my throat.

"Investigator Sera Chen," says the man dressed in black, flanked by a pair of security clones. Behind the trio sits a large black van, unmarked with tinted windows, parked to divert ground traffic. Driverless cargo vehicles pass by on both sides instead, swerving around us without slowing down. "Step out of the exoskeleton and keep your hands where I can see them."

He's tall, well-built, his tactical suit tailored and form-fitting even with the armor plating. He has his sidearm in one hand, casually aimed at the pavement. Not a shocker. Projectile rounds. The kind of weapon Commander Bishop carries. Which means he's upper-echelon. The pair of clones he brought as backup support that assumption.

I give his neuro a cursory scan, and his government ID scrolls down my ocular lenses. "Agent Baatar, what's this about?"

"Please step out of the exo-suit, Investigator Chen. I was hoping we could have a short conversation." He gestures toward the van with an open hand. As if I'm going to get inside of my own free will.

Nothing in his file says who the hell he works for. *Government* could mean anything.

"I don't know you." I glance at the security clones. They're carrying assault rifles at rest. Also loaded with projectile rounds. And like the clone manning the front desk in

Hawthorne Tower, they sport the latest white armor with neon blue accents, a sharp contrast to the agent's colorless garb. "Who sent you?"

A meter to my right, Dunn's boots shift position, scraping across the pavement. He keeps Wink close against him, but his free hand hovers over the holster compartment in his armor. A split-second maneuver, and the shocker will launch into his gauntlet. He might be able to hit all three members of this trio before they're able to get off a single shot. He's just that good.

Seeming to realize as much, Baatar shakes his head at Dunn. "The clone can leave. We do not have any questions for it."

"You heard the man," I tell my partner without looking his way. Because the agent and I are in the middle of one helluva staring contest. "Get back to HQ. Have the drone repaired—your armor too, while you're at it."

"That drone is beyond repair," Baatar says.

I am not leaving you, Investigator Chen, Dunn messages me. He can be real stubborn like that. "Agent Baatar, you were asked a question. Who sent you?"

Baatar might have looked surprised if his face was capable of showing any sort of expression. Instead he clenches his jaw, and his grip tightens on the sidearm. Telltale signs of severe annoyance. Probably doesn't like having a clone speak to him that way. And he probably wouldn't think twice about shooting one. Right in the head.

"Unit D1-436, you are ordered to return to HQ at once." I raise my chin, hating the sound of my voice. Cold, commanding. I never order Dunn around like that.

But I have to keep him safe. And if there's one thing I can

already tell about this Baatar guy, nothing about him is safe.

Dunn's boots move again, backing away from me. "Yes, Investigator Chen." Without another word, he exits the scene, heading down the block toward Hawthorne Tower. No glance back. No further text messages. Following orders like every other clone in the Domes was conditioned to do.

My eyes sting, and I look away.

Baatar doesn't relax his posture any, now that Dunn's out of the picture. Probably because I'm still wearing this exo with the minigun poised like a viper on its shoulder. Wouldn't take much to spin it up and rip this trio to bloody shreds.

That's dark.

Can't let myself think that way. Unbecoming, if nothing else.

Moving slowly, I pull the release, and the exo frame folds back, allowing me to step down out of the harness and extricate my boots, one at a time. As soon as I do so, Baatar gestures sharply, and the two security clones advance, slipping their rifles into sheaths mounted on their backs. Then, between the two of them, they pick up my exo-suit and carry it to the back of the waiting van.

Baatar holsters his sidearm. "Now, Investigator Chen, we will have that little talk, during which I expect you to keep your neuro active the entire time. I am not interested in seeing your special abilities on display. Do I make myself clear?"

17

I fold my arms and plant my boots shoulder-width apart, sizing up the man. The hatch to the maintenance shaft yawns open between us. I could drop in, slide down the ladder, and make a run for it through the tunnel below. Considering his muscular bulk, I should have an advantage in the speed department. Or I could try to take him down right here. Kick his legs out from under him and chase after Dunn.

Option three: see how fast he is on the draw. If I beat him to it, I shock him into writhing spasms and give his clone pals the same treatment. But if he draws first and fires without a moment's hesitation, as I have a feeling he might, the projectile round will hit my center of mass and drop me flat onto my back. Unpleasant, not to mention the major bruising and fractured rib or few under my tactical suit's light armor.

If fight or flight are both off the table, then what's the alternative? Get inside that creepy-looking van for some chit-chat? Not happening.

Think. Who is this guy working for? Why would he want my exo? *Consider the timing.* Right after Governor Raniero makes public his lack of confidence in James Bishop as Chancellor, this government agent shows up. An agent who doesn't answer to local LawKeepers.

"Let's go for a ride." He nods toward the van and waits for me to make the first move in that direction. The clones have already gotten into the front seats like a pair of mute automatons.

"I'm not going anywhere." I nod toward the van as well. "You just took something that doesn't belong to you. I'll be pressing charges."

"No, you won't." Something related to a smirk flickers across his stone-like features. "You will thank me."

That's rich. I raise an eyebrow. "Really."

"I will explain everything. During our drive."

"Where to?"

He shrugs thick shoulders. "Nowhere in particular." He takes a step back as ground vehicles whizz by on both sides of us, the wind from their wake throwing my hair across my face. "Think of it as my mobile office."

I sweep my hair back and gesture at the maintenance hatch. "Can't leave this unattended. I'll need to stick around until the repair crew shows up." I give him a shrug in return, doing my best to maintain as casual a facade as possible, considering the circumstances. "Somebody might fall in and break their neck."

"Or be murdered." His turn to raise an eyebrow. "No one in their right mind would walk across this street." He has to raise his voice as another cargo truck speeds past. "As you can see, the onboard AI's are smart enough to keep their tires out of the hole. Your presence is not required. But I think you are going to want to hear what I have to say." Another step back. Without looking, he reaches toward the van, and the side door slides open automatically, sensing his presence.

"Last chance."

"You steal my personal property and expect me to believe you're doing me a favor?" I keep my feet rooted.

"Precisely. Except the exo-suit does not belong to you. It never has. And now it is evidence in what's sure to be the most important trial the Domes have ever seen." He stands beside the open door. Inside, a comfortable-looking bench seat awaits. "I would prefer that you assist me in my investigation, Chen. At this stage, you might still be able to salvage your career. But make no mistake. If you refuse, then when the time comes for us to make our case against you and your superiors, we will show you no leniency."

Can't help smirking at him. "You know, a threat like that might actually hold water if I knew who the hell you worked for. Is it Raniero?" I force a quiet chuckle. "Not even an hour since that big speech, and he's already got blackshirts in action?" I might be impressed if I wasn't so appalled. "How long has he been planning this little coup?"

Agent Baatar's gaze has gone cold, his expression neutral. "We could be of help to one another." He climbs into the van, keeping an eye on me. Probably making sure I don't go for my shocker and blast him in the back. "You have nothing to lose."

"Except my exo."

"Which was used to kill multiple security personnel in Dome 10 last night." He takes his seat but doesn't allow the door to slide shut. "Due to your negligence, and your association with a known criminal, this exoskeleton found its way into the hands of a dangerous individual rallying other misguided people to her cause. An exoskeleton which received an unsanctioned weapons upgrade courtesy of that same criminal. A man going by the mononym *Drasko*."

I'll say this much for Agent Baatar. He knows his stuff.

And it's a bit unsettling.

"You've got to give me something." Quickly I hail Chief Inspector Hudson and simultaneously send him the following message, words scrolling across my lenses at the speed of thought: *A government agent by the name of Baatar has confiscated my exo. He's in an unmarked van with two security clones. All three are well-armed. He wants me to go with him, but he's not forcing me at gunpoint. I'll try to stall him until you can send reinforcements to my location.* "How do I know you haven't been mindjacked by a dangerous AI? And that those clones with you aren't really killbots in disguise?"

Baatar blinks. "Considering what you went through recently, Investigator Chen, I can understand why you might ask such a thing. But rest assured that I have only the best interests of our citizens at heart. I serve the people of the Domes. That's the purpose of government work, is it not? The greater good."

"Depends on the government." Sidestepping the open maintenance hatch, I approach the van. "Whoever's in charge, that is."

Hudson replies almost immediately via audiolink, "Tell him nothing. Return to HQ at once."

Who does he work for, sir? Why is he taking my exo? I text, then I switch to transmitting audio so Hudson can hear what's going on.

"Absolute power corrupts absolutely." Baatar nods, holding my gaze. "A historian said that once, back in the Old World. Law enforcement used to have a division known as internal affairs designed to keep LawKeepers and their supervisors honest. IA agents would investigate suspicions of corruption and mismanagement. Criminal and professional misconduct would be punished. In this way, bad apples were not allowed to spoil the whole bunch."

"Is that a quote from another anonymous historian?"

He leans forward in his seat, brow furrowed. "You will be prosecuted for dereliction of duty, Chen. There's no way around it. You have blood on your exo."

Not literally, but of course I get what he means. I'd be lying if I said I didn't feel a measure of guilt for what happened at the airlock. It's been weighing heavy on me, but I've tried not to show it.

"You are not the only one to blame, however." The furrows relax. He's both good cop and bad. A split personality. "This goes all the way to the top."

"James Bishop."

"Father and daughter. Interim Chancellor and Police Commander. Nepotism at its finest."

I shake my head. "Get your facts straight. Commander Bishop was in charge of law enforcement long before her father returned from the Wastes."

"From the dead, was more like it."

"She earned her position of leadership. Nobody handed it to her."

He raises his chin, appraising my reaction. "You respect her."

"I owe her."

"For your promotion to investigator."

"For giving me a job in the first place."

He narrows his gaze. "Certainly as a member of the

Twenty, you could have had any job you wanted. And no one would have denied you." He almost smiles, but it's not a nice one. "Because you're so damn special."

"Chancellor Hawthorne didn't like the idea. But Mara Bishop promised her that I would be protected."

"Hence the exo-suit." He nods toward the van's cargo section behind him. "An advantage no other curfew enforcer has ever been afforded."

"Most enforcers wear motorized armor. The exo was just a step up from that."

"A giant leap, I'd say. And necessary. Because the Twenty were our only hope for the future, and they had to be kept safe." He pauses, never looking away from me. "Now it's your thousand children who carry that burden. Our future rests upon their shoulders. The Twenty can breathe a collective sigh of relief, for their work is done. You can spend the rest of your lives childless and alone, should you so choose, and no one will think less of you for it."

Hudson curses for my ears only. "Trackers have been dispatched. They should arrive at your location within five minutes. Keep him talking, Chen."

That's what I'm doing, in case he hasn't noticed. "If you've done your research, then you know we had no say in the matter."

Baatar offers another shrug. "Sacrifices must be made for the greater good."

"So I've heard." A stream of cargo vehicles whips by on both sides, and I pull my hair back to keep it in place. "What I'm sensing here is someone who thinks he's above the law. That you can take whatever you want with impunity."

He shakes his head. "Not above the law, Investigator

Chen. Adjacent to it."

"So you're not claiming that your jurisdiction supersedes law enforcement."

With a glance upward, he reaches for the side door. "Your backup has arrived, I see. Thought they would have gotten here sooner. But as I said, you're not as important as you used to be. Protecting you appears to be an afterthought these days." He gives me a pointed look as he says, "Do not be surprised if your superiors hang you out to dry."

The door slides shut with a solid thump, and the van accelerates into traffic, slipping into a gap between two haulers moving full speed ahead. At the same time, a police aerocar swoops down from above, red and blue flashers on as it follows the unmarked van.

"Target acquired," the tracker notifies me via audiolink. I don't recognize her voice. "We've been tasked with detaining a man identified as Agent Baatar and retrieving your exo, Chen. Anything else we can do for you this fine morning?"

"That about covers it." I watch the police chase until they veer around a towering domescraper, blocking them from view. "Be advised Baatar and the two clones with him are armed with projectile weapons. Lethal variety. Proceed with caution."

"Will do."

"I owe you one."

Blink rises from the maintenance shaft to hover beside me.

"About time you showed up," I mutter.

"Movement was detected farther down the tunnel."

I frown at that. "The murder suspect?"

"Scans proved inconclusive."

Blink didn't go investigate because I didn't give it orders to do so. Probably a good thing; otherwise, I'd be out two drones right now instead of one.

Strange for Raul's killer to remain underground. Like an animal returning to its den—what I've read about some den-dwelling animals, anyway. Tough to know if anything we read about them was actually true in the Old World.

I transfer the coordinates of that movement Blink detected to Hudson. "Raul's killer may not have gotten very far, sir." I glance at the dark maintenance shaft and briefly consider climbing down the ladder. Going after the murderer myself. But without my exo or my partner, it probably wouldn't be wise to go up against a clawed dust freak alone. And besides—

"Not your case, Chen," he's quick to remind me. Then he exhales. "I'll pass along your intel to the trackers tasked with apprehending the suspect."

And in other news, "Who's Agent Baatar? What do we have on him?"

"Very little." Hudson sounds disgusted. "Government field agent. Nothing in the database says who exactly he works for."

"My money's on Governor Raniero. He wants James Bishop out of the Chancellor's office, but he doesn't plan to stop there. He's going to use my negligence with the exo to oust Commander Bishop as well. To prove that my preferential treatment led to the deaths of three security personnel at the airlock."

Hudson curses. "I hope you're wrong. While I have made it clear that I do not approve of your exo-suit, I cannot deny what you have managed to accomplish with it on more than one occasion." He pauses. "That being said, perhaps now is a good time to consider retiring the damn thing. Video from the riot is all over the Linkstream. I have no idea how it went public so fast."

"Baatar would be my guess. Or whoever he's working with." The *trial* he mentioned will start in the court of public opinion.

"The optics are bad, Chen. We can't let you be seen wearing that exoskeleton again. Not after this. It will be retrieved, and then it will be locked away in evidence." As an afterthought, he adds, "We should have done that to begin with."

Yet they didn't. They let me keep it after it had been used to gun down three of our people and twenty of our clones. Further evidence of preferential treatment? I should have known better. It was a giant piece of evidence in a break-in and a killing spree, and it should have been treated as such. Instead, I was only too happy to throw the thing back on and put it to work.

Because it makes me feel strong. Almost invincible. And sometimes I need that.

Without the creepy van to block approaching traffic, I feel more than a little exposed now, standing here in the middle of the street. So I make a dash for the sidewalk the first chance I get, and then I pause to catch my breath, avoiding curious glances from well-dressed passersby.

I'm rather curious myself. Why didn't I draw on Baatar and demand that he return my exo? Was I worried he'd shoot me and take me against my will? Three against one are stiff odds, but not insurmountable. Did I just want to hear what he had to say?

Do I believe him? Will Hudson and Commander Bishop blame what happened at the airlock on my dereliction of duty—abandoning a heavily armed exoskeleton in the one Dome known for its robust criminal element? What the hell was I thinking?

Short answer: I really wasn't, at the time. I could blame it on the sleep deprivation or any number of bizarre things that were going on, but I won't. Because I'm the one who failed to do the right thing. And now people are dead because of it.

"It's my fault, sir. This never would've happened if I—"

The explosive sounds of a multi-vehicle crash echo from a few blocks away. I turn sharply as smoke billows around the side of a mirrored-glass domescraper. Driverless cargo trucks slow to half-speed but soon can do little more than crawl along as traffic congestion thickens in one direction.

The same direction Baatar took in his unmarked van.

"Sir—?"

"The aerocar following Agent Baatar is down. That's all we know." Hudson curses a foul streak. "Power's out again here. The analysts are blind."

Perfect timing.

I point Blink toward the smoke and subvocalize, "Give me eyes." It buzzes through the air at top speed, and I follow at a sprint, dodging citizens who've stopped on the sidewalk to gawk into the distance.

"Chen, don't even think about—"

"People may be hurt, sir."

"Officers have already been dispatched to the scene. You are to return to HQ—"

"I'm here. I have to help." Four blocks away now.

"Damn it, Chen! That's not your responsibility."

"I'm making it mine. Chen out." I tap my temple to disengage my augments. Because the last thing I need right now is a flashing light in my peripheral vision as Hudson hails me to offer a few castigating words.

Three blocks. It's humbling to discover how slow I run without my exo. And how winded I am.

Since I'm already offline, I send a telepathic transmission out into the ether, focusing all of my superhuman energy on one person in particular.

Dunn, I need my partner. Meet me at these coordinates. I send him an educated guess at where the crash occurred.

He doesn't respond.

18

I know he's not a big fan of telepathic communication, no matter how rarely I use it, but I hope to receive something back from him mind-to-mind. Even the standard *Yes, Investigator Chen* would be fine. Just to know we're okay. That I didn't ruin our working relationship, much less our friendship, by dismissing him out of hand the way I did.

The last thing I wanted to do was hurt his feelings or cause some kind of setback in his emotional growth. Not something I usually worry about. But in most cases, I'm not dealing with a burgeoning personality.

He has to realize I was only looking out for him. I had no idea what that government agent and his clones were prepared to do in order to seize my exo. For all I knew, they were authorized to use lethal force. Dunn's my partner, and part of my job is protecting him. Not just because he's one of a kind. I have to make him understand that.

But the silence inside my skull is deafening.

If I pay attention to how alone I'm feeling right now, I won't be able to keep running like this. Two blocks from the crash site and closing. There's no time to wallow in self-pity. My partner's ignoring me. My underworld ally has gone rogue. None of that matters at the moment. People could be hurt, and I might be the first responder on the scene. I'll have to assess the situation, determine who needs immediate care, do what I can to slow any bleeding. That's what I need to focus on.

Instead, I'm driven to my knees by an overwhelming wave of voices crashing into my head. Citizens along the sidewalk gasp and clear a path for me as I collapse, both hands to my temples, eyes squeezed shut. Groaning at the sheer agony impaling my brain like a javelin of fire.

My curled fingers won't cooperate at first. But when they do, I reactivate my augments, and the voices are muted in an instant. Then it takes a minute for the pain to subside. And another before the ground beneath me stops spinning.

"Are you alright?" An elderly citizen and her much younger escort, obviously out for a morning stroll, places her wrinkled hand on my shoulder with concern. "You look like you had a fit and fell into it!"

"Stupid mistake," I mutter, hardly able to believe what I did. Hoping Dunn's thoughts would eventually come through the telepathic link between us, I inadvertently left myself exposed to every thought from every citizen in a two-klick radius. And just about made my brain explode in the process. "I tripped. Sorry to startle you like that."

Heart racing, I get to my feet and start running again—a little off-kilter at first but picking up momentum. Needless to say, I don't have my abilities all figured out. They didn't arrive with an owner's manual. I think I know what works and what doesn't, but I've still got a lot to learn. And I need to be more careful.

Just a block away now.

The smoke from the crash is thicker, heavier here. Our air

recyclers will have to work double-time to filter it out. I hope they're up to the task. It's not like this sort of thing happens every day around here. The last time we had flaming wreckage in Dome 1, the Prometheus uprising was in full swing with killbots shooting down aerocars and smashing them into buildings.

I round the corner, and my pace slows.

It's the police vehicle that was chasing after Agent Baatar. The aerocar crashed into the middle of the street, taking out a pair of driverless haulers along the way and sending them plowing into a few others of their kind. The end result: a crumpled, fiery mess of mangled plasteel blocking the road.

Both trackers stand on the sidewalk, mad as hell and gesturing violently but apparently unharmed. A third figure—

"The smoke is interfering with my camera, Investigator Chen," Blink apologizes in its toneless voice as it descends, hovering beside me. "Visual clarity is negligible."

"Don't worry about it." My shoulders relax somewhat at the sight of the crash survivors. "Looks like everybody's okay."

The third figure is Dunn. He got the coordinates I sent. And he beat me here.

Well, of course he did. Because I wasn't wearing my exo.

My neuro identifies the trackers as Cirillo and Petrova. I've never worked with them, but they have a reputation for getting the job done regardless of obstacles—even if it means bending the rules a bit. Appearance-wise, they're the inverse of Matthews and Shariq. Petrova is the tall, slender blonde woman, and Cirillo is the short, stocky guy with dark features. Neither one looks very happy about Dunn questioning them.

"Hey Chen, call off your clone," Petrova grumbles as I approach, folding her arms and scowling at me. Soot streaks her otherwise goddess-like features—the type you might see in a shampoo ad on the Link.

"Yeah, what's with the third-degree, buddy?" Cirillo, looking just as sooty, throws his hands around as he talks, glaring up at Dunn. "You think we did this on purpose? Crash-landed on a few trucks just for the hell of it?"

Dunn half-turns to face me. "I merely asked what happened here, Investigator Chen."

I nod. Standard procedure. He's got the situation under control.

"Your clone's memory banks are screwy," Petrova sneers. "The analysts—"

"Are offline at the moment," I interrupt. "And were offline when you went down. Which means we have to ask you what happened, because nobody actually saw it take place." I shrug. "So indulge us, won't you?"

She glances at Dunn with contempt. "Guy shot us down."

I frown at that. "Agent Baatar?"

She nods.

"With what?" The gun he had on him wouldn't have packed enough punch to bring down an aerocar, even if he'd hit one of the electromagnetic coils with everything he had.

"EMP." Cirillo juts out his chin. "Looked like a shocker, only it fired a whole different kind of pulse."

"Hit us right on the nose," Petrova adds, shaking her head at the recent memory, "and everything went dark. Consoles unresponsive. Like that." She snaps her fingers.

"EMP," I murmur, remembering what happened at

Edwards' jewelry shop. I look at Dunn, wondering if he's mulling over the connection. The analysts were offline when that happened, too.

His faceplate remains angled toward the pair of trackers. Avoiding looking at me? Or merely attentive?

"So Baatar got away." I exhale and look past the wreckage. There's no sign of the black van.

Petrova and Cirillo glance at each other. Cirillo clears his throat. "Who the hell is this so-called *Agent*? Why isn't there anything on him in the database?"

"He might be a spook." I send Blink a text message to collect local video footage, and the drone buzzes away. If it wasn't a machine, I'm sure it would be experiencing a certain level of déjà vu at the moment. I know I am. "Alright. We'll collect what we can from cameras in the vicinity and go from there. Chief Inspector Hudson will undoubtedly be assigning another investigator to this case. My partner and I just happened to be in the neighborhood." Partially true.

As if on cue, a pair of aerocars swing into sight overhead, one black & white with its lights flashing, the other solid white with an encircled red cross emblem on both sides.

"Cavalry's here," Cirillo mutters, running a hand over his stubble-covered jaw. He looks like the type who might have to shave every few hours if he wants to look presentable. "Thanks for stopping by, Chen. Sure hope you catch that clown."

I give him a nod as an alert lights up in the corner of my lenses. Chief Inspector Hudson hailing me, as expected.

Turning away from the trackers, I answer the call, speaking fast to postpone the dressing-down he's sure to deliver. "No injuries to report, sir. Trackers Petrova and

Cirillo are unharmed. Wish I could say the same about their vehicle—and the ones they crashed into. Agent Baatar hit them with an electromagnetic pulse that knocked out their power. Same as the jewelry heist."

Dead air. Then, in his most authoritative tone, "You will report to HQ immediately."

"Sorry, sir. There's a lot of noise here." I hold back my hair with one hand as the two aerocars descend vertically, blasting us with their jet wash.

"You heard me! Get your ass back here on the double!" He's seriously losing his cool. "I want you filling out your report on the past twelve hours before you even think about—!"

"We're following a couple leads at the moment. We'll return to HQ as soon as we can. Chen out." I turn to Dunn and nod toward the opposite direction. Time for us to take our leave. I cross the street, keeping track of Blink's progress via my lenses. The drone has two more security systems to visit before it'll be heading back my way.

Dunn pauses to watch the four uniformed officers file out of the police aerocar, two moving to secure the scene while the other pair, carrying fire suppressive gear, tackle the burning wrecks. At the same time, three medical personnel garbed in white approach Petrova and Cirillo with handheld scanners, checking their vitals and ensuring they remain fit for duty.

I'm halfway down the block by the time Dunn catches up with me, his boots thumping across the sidewalk. Together we navigate a path that winds around citizens with nothing better to do than stand like statues, staring at the unsightly mess in the middle of their street.

"You dropped off Wink with the tech-heads?" I didn't need to ask. It's obvious that he did. He's not carrying the smashed drone anymore. And I never have to double-check whether he follows orders. Because he always does.

But I don't want to walk with him in silence. Which means we've got to talk about something.

"Yes, Investigator Chen."

"They give any timeframe on repairs?"

"No."

"Blink mentioned movement down in the tunnel. After you left. Could be Raul's killer."

Dunn nods pensively. "You want to check it out."

"Not our case." I exhale, shaking my head. "Hudson wants us back at HQ. I've got that report to write. And we both could use some rack time."

"Is that where we are headed, once the drone returns with surveillance footage of Agent Baatar's escape?"

I stop at the curb as we reach the end of the block and look up at him. "What do you think we should do?"

His helmet angles downward slightly to meet my gaze. "You outrank me, Investigator Chen. You always will. I can only offer suggestions, from time to time. But you must decide our next course of action."

"You asked me if I thought we were equals—"

"It was an irrelevant question." He shakes his head. "I should not have asked such a thing."

I wish I could see his face, his eyes. What is he feeling?

"This. Our working relationship." I gesture at the two of us. "You're right. I outrank you. But only because I have more experience." As much as any twenty-something could have. "So in that way, we're not equals. But in every other way that matters—"

"I am a clone. You are human. We will never be equals in any way, Investigator Chen."

My fists start clenching down at my sides, but I force them to relax. "Says who?"

His helmet tilts to one side, but he doesn't say anything. Maybe he's curious what I'll say next. Hell. I am, too.

"Things don't have to be the way they are. We've already seen change happen. Just because Solomon Wong or Persephone Hawthorne put certain things in place, and just because we're accustomed to them being a certain way, doesn't mean they'll always be that way." Not the most well-constructed argument I've ever made, but I think he'll get the point. "We don't have to settle for the status quo. We can strive for better." I place my hand on his forearm where Drasko cracked open his armor. "Our partnership shows everyone willing to notice what it would be like for us to live as equals."

He doesn't turn away. But he doesn't say anything, either.

Blink's rotors whir above us, and as it descends, it reports, "Video footage successfully retrieved from all six cameras in the area. Transmitting now, Investigator Chen."

I pull my hand away from Dunn as half a dozen video files appear in my lenses, organized by proximity to the black van's escape route. "We should probably head over to HQ and run these through Hudson's deskscreen..." Just like we did with footage from the artifacts heist.

"You do not appear enthusiastic about that idea," Dunn notes.

Guess I'm not. "Something Baatar said before he fled the scene. I don't know who the guy is, or who he's working for.

I have my suspicions. But he insinuated that my superiors might try to blame me for everything that happened at the airlock."

"The deaths of those three guards." Dunn nods slowly. "Did he happen to mention the twenty security clones that were also gunned down?"

I frown up at my partner. "Do you want to talk about that?"

"There is nothing to talk about. They are replaceable." A brief pause. "But now that your exo-suit has been stolen, your superiors will have no evidence tying you to the incident at the airlock last night."

"Not exactly. My negligence is the issue. Dereliction of duty." I shake my head. "I never should've left that thing in Dome 10."

"You could not have guessed that anyone would be able to activate it and use it the way Mirela Edwards did."

Or that she'd have Drasko's help. Still can't wrap my head around that.

"Baatar said he's prepping the way for a big trial. I assume it has something to do with Raniero's vote of no confidence in Chancellor Bishop. They're building a case against him. Saying I was given preferential treatment as a member of the Twenty."

"You believe Agent Baatar is working for Governor Raniero."

"Prevailing theory. But it's weird, right? The same kind of EMP gun used to knock out the jewelry shop cameras takes down Petrova and Cirillo. And both times, the analysts' cage loses power at HQ, blinding them to what's happening."

Dunn nods. "And both times, your drones have had to

collect video footage from security systems in the vicinity. Systems the perpetrators could have disabled with that EMP weapon as well, yet opted not to."

"You're right. We end up getting the same footage the analysts would have gotten, only instead of their usual real-time access, we get it after the fact. And we sort through it even later on. So it's not a matter of keeping us blind to the incident itself. That's not what the perpetrators are after."

"It is a delay tactic."

"Exactly. But why? What do they gain by postponing the inevitable? We're going to see what happened eventually. It's just a matter of time."

"Perhaps time is all they need. The burglary at Nevah Edwards' shop, for example. The delay allowed Mirela Edwards enough time to reach the airlock in Dome 10 via that underground tunnel."

I nod. "And now with Agent Baatar, instead of apprehending him, we've got to take time figuring out where he went. Meanwhile, who knows what he could be up to?"

"In which case, it would be best if we surveyed that video footage sooner rather than later, would it not?"

There's my partner.

"It would indeed." I send him half the video files, and I bring up my half in synchronous playback across the lower section of my lenses. It's nothing like casting the footage onto Hudson's deskscreen holo-projector, but time is of the essence here. And I'd prefer not to deal with Chief Inspector Hudson in person right now. Let him regain his composure a bit before I return to HQ. "This way." I start walking at a fast pace in the direction the van went. "Obtain video from all security cameras along this trajectory," I subvocalize to Blink, and the drone takes off ahead of me.

"Do you believe Agent Baatar and Mirela Edwards are working together?" Dunn is right on my heels as we weave through pedestrian traffic along the sidewalk. Most of the citizens out for a stroll don't seem intrigued in the slightest by our presence. Probably because their eyes are glazed over, watching some sort of augmented reality via their ocular lenses. "And if so, to what end?"

"I'd like to ask Baatar a few questions." I glance over my shoulder. "Having that EMP gun in common isn't much to go on. Same goes for the power outages at HQ." I pause a beat. "Unless Baatar and Edwards have someone on the inside."

"You mean someone may be intentionally sabotaging power to the analysts."

"Blinding them at opportune moments." I curse under my breath. "But what would a government agent and an unhinged solar technician have in common? Why the hell would they be working together?"

Not to mention Drasko. How does he fit into this? I quickly check the VR messageboard. No response to my note.

For a few seconds, only the steady thump of Dunn's boots answers me. But then he says, "Mirela Edwards may not be working with Agent Baatar—not knowingly."

An interesting idea. "Not if he's the one pulling strings behind the scenes, orchestrating events. Using her to get what he wants."

Footage shows the black van turning sharply at the end of the block and heading west. Dunn and I make the turn as well, picking up our pace as pedestrian traffic thins out.

"Change of trajectory," I update Blink.

"Synchronizing," the drone replies via audiolink, and I hear the buzz of its rotors high overhead as it overtakes us and maintains a lead of fifty meters, collecting video from cameras along the way. As it shares the files with me, one by one, I keep the most recent footage playing in my lenses and discard the rest.

"If so," Dunn says, "then the riot at the airlock may have actually been his doing. From what I have been able to gather, Mirela Edwards does not have a large social circle. Nor is she engaged in subversive online activity. It is therefore unlikely that she alone would have been able to draw such a large crowd of insurgents."

I clench my jaw. "So Baatar somehow provided the audience of Prometheus fans. He could have given her the exo as well."

Dunn nods slowly. "It is conceivable. However, we do not have all the facts."

Maybe not. But at this moment, an agent of unrest might be planning another riot. Stirring the pot, inspiring a lack of confidence in our current Chancellor.

And he's got my exo-suit.

Who's he going to hand-deliver it to this time?

19

Blink stops twenty meters ahead of us, hovering outside the entrance to a basement level parking garage located beneath a residential domescraper. As the video footage in my lenses catches up to the drone's position, I can see why it came to a sudden halt.

The unmarked van entered that garage, heading down the ramp in no hurry at all.

"Proceed into the parking structure," I tell my drone. "Collect video from the system on-site."

"Access restricted, Investigator Chen," Blink replies. If I didn't know better, I might think its monotone sounds apologetic. Maybe a little disappointed, too. "Unable to proceed without a warrant."

Right. Unlike the security systems we've encountered thus far, this building is a private residence. Or, rather, a towering mirrored edifice chock-full of private residences. Not as many as you'd find in a cube complex; I'm sure there are people in this domescraper who own entire floors. Rich people who value their privacy.

"Nevah Edwards resides in this building," Dunn says.

Something I would've known if I'd actually been focused on the case Hudson assigned to me.

"Well, what do you know? Another coincidence." Leaving Blink to hold position outside the garage, I head down into the cool, grey plasticon depths. One hand on my holstered shocker, eyes skimming over the two dozen sleek electric groundcars parked in their charging stalls. No black van among them.

"That was sarcasm." Dunn follows me inside, the clunks from his boots echoing through the underground structure. "And, as you are undoubtedly aware, we do not have a warrant, either."

I smile back at him. "Oh, I'm just here visiting my ol' pal Nevah."

Dunn nods. "More sarcasm."

I give him a wink. "If Agent Baatar's van makes a reappearance, follow it," I subvocalize to Blink.

"Yes, Investigator Chen," it replies from the sidewalk.

"A reappearance..." Dunn sounds intrigued. "Do you think the van is down here, but we cannot see it?"

I nod. "Wouldn't be surprised, after the night we've had. Scan for heat signatures. Even if they're hiding it under a hologram, the engine should still be warm."

"Scanning." Dunn halts to give the garage a good once-over, his faceplate slowly panning from left to right, the tube-lights along the low ceiling reflecting off its black surface. Halfway through, he raises his arm with the cracked armor to point. "There."

I draw my shocker and head for the far corner where a charging station sits vacant. Or so it seems. The holster compartment on Dunn's leg ejects his shocker, and he grasps it in both hands, held out in front of him. Together, we approach the parking stall.

"Get out of the van." I'm going for an authoritative tone, but ordering an invisible trio to exit an invisible vehicle is kind of ridiculous. So I fire a couple rounds at the empty space, just to be sure we're right.

The pulses slam into a solid surface and spread laterally as they fizzle out, revealing the general shape of the van's hood in jittery lines of electric-blue lightning. Shocker rounds won't do anything to inorganic matter, but they do a pretty good job of exposing things that would rather remain hidden.

"Agent Baatar, exit the vehicle. Or we're coming in." I lean toward Dunn and whisper, "Think you can rip the side door off?"

He nods without pause. "However, IR scans do not indicate heat signatures of anyone inside the van. Only the engine cooling down."

Well, damn. I glance at the security cameras—black half-domes set into the ceiling every fifty meters—and take a moment to resent the rich and powerful. They've taken full advantage of the changes James Bishop has made to life in the Domes. In the old days, investigators never needed warrants. They'd access any camera they damn well pleased. Must've been nice.

"Baatar and his security clones are in the building." Unless he's figured out a way to wear some kind of holo-cloak. Then they could have walked right outside after parking the van, and no cameras in the vicinity would have recorded them. But that sort of tech doesn't exist. Holograms require projectors, and as far as I know, there's no way to maintain the illusion of invisibility while in motion. "How much do you want to bet he's here to meet with Nevah Edwards?"

"I have nothing to bet, Investigator Chen." He shrugs. "But that would be quite the coincidence, would it not?"

"Indeed it would." I turn toward the polished-to-pristine speedlift doors midway across the sublevel and stop. "But we should probably be sure." I nod toward the invisible van. "Go ahead and rip that door off."

He hesitates only a split-second, and I like to think there's a smile under that helmet. Then he holsters his shocker and approaches the empty stall, reaching into the air as if he knows exactly where the side door is. His gauntleted fingers scrabble across the invisible surface until they find purchase. Then his mechanical arms tear the door off like it's a tarp covering some sort of hidden stash. It becomes visible the instant he detaches it from the vehicle, and he tosses it aside with a loud clatter.

The van's dark interior appears to hover half a meter above the parking stall while its exterior remains invisible under the holo-projectors, wherever they're located. A weird sight, to be sure.

"Confirmed," Dunn reports, peering inside. "All passengers have exited the vehicle, and they took your exo-suit with them."

"Glad that's settled." And I'm glad he could have a bit of fun. Not that I approve of him going around destroying things willy-nilly, but when you've got a pair of powerful robo-arm prosthetics, you might as well flex them from time to time. "Now let's see about crashing Nevah's party."

According to the citizen registry, Ms. Edwards resides on the one hundred twentieth floor. The penthouse level. Sensing my neuro, the speedlift doors glide open, and I step inside to enter my override code. Hoping I won't need a warrant to leave the basement level.

Dunn joins me, and the doors slide shut behind him. We're going up.

But not all the way to 120. We stop at ground level with a ding announcing our arrival.

"Get ready." I aim my shocker at the doors.

"For what?" Dunn draws his weapon.

As the mirrored doors part to reveal a lone security clone waiting for us, I mutter, "This."

"Investigator Chen," the armored clone greets me without enthusiasm. Behind it, the spacious lobby—all shiny marble floors and high ceilings and comfortable looking furniture surrounded by potted plants and mini-waterfalls, doused in natural-looking artificial light—extends from the speedlift to the concierge desk, fifty meters away. All quiet for the moment. "State your business here."

"Where's your boss?" I peer past its imposing form, but the lobby looks empty. "And your partner?"

"I alone am responsible for the security of the Edwards Estates."

"Named the place after herself? Well, that figures." Holstering my shocker, I elbow my way past the guard and head toward the concierge desk. "You see three people come through here? Tough to miss. Tall, dark, and muscular with a pair of security clones in tow, dressed just like you. And they would've been carrying an exo-suit."

"I beg your pardon." The clone hustles to follow me, boots thudding across the floor tiles.

"Like a suit of armor, only bigger, with more negative space and a harness inside." I pat my right shoulder. "Plus a minigun."

"Investigator Chen, this is highly irregular," the clone complains without sounding like it's complaining. Because that would require a shift in tone. "You cannot—"

"Do you man the front desk, too?" I glance back at the speedlift as Dunn steps out but decides to stay put as the polished plasteel doors shut behind him. His faceplate pans left to right as he scans the lobby for anything out of the ordinary. At least that's what I assume he's doing. "Or is beleaguering visitors strictly within your purview?"

"Beleaguer..." the clone trails off, undoubtedly hopping onto the diction database to define a word it hasn't heard bandied about much these days.

I pivot to face the guard, and it stutters to a stop in front of me. "Did you see them or not? Would've been within the last twenty minutes."

"No one entered these premises during that timeframe."

"How about the speedlift? Anybody take it up to the 120th floor?"

The clone's helmet twitches. Not exactly a shake of the head in the exasperated sense, but within spitting distance. "I am afraid I must ask you to leave. The Edwards Estates are very private domiciles. But if you were to return with a warrant—"

"Why should I need a warrant to visit an old friend? Sorry. A well-preserved friend."

"And who would this friend be?"

"The eponymous Nevah Edwards, of course. Or is it the building that's eponymous? Either way, she's expecting me." I gesture toward Dunn. "Us. Her shop was robbed last night, and we're hot on the trail of the miscreants who stole her fancy junk."

The clone half-turns to briefly regard Dunn. "Is this true, D1-436?"

"Which part?" Dunn says mildly.

"Call her up. Tell Ms. Edwards we were on our way to see her when we found ourselves rudely shanghaied by the draconian concierge." I fold my arms and glare up at the clone's faceplate. Like the one at Hawthorne Tower, it's got that new, improved armor with those fetching neon-blue accents. "Go on. I'll wait."

It gives me an uncertain nod. "Yes. Please wait here." Then it goes over to the front desk and activates the holo-phone. A pre-Link, nostalgic piece of tech the oldest generation tends to be fond of. After a few warbles, a life-size, three-dimensional projection of Nevah Edward's face appears, hovering above the projector pad. The clone stands at posture-perfect attention and waits for her to speak first.

"What do you want?" she demands, squinting suspiciously. Cordial as ever.

"There is an Investigator Sera Chen here to see you, ma'am. She says it has to do with a robbery at your shop."

"Actually, I have a few questions about your daughter." I sidle up next to the clone, nice and cozy, with a big smile. It grunts at my proximity and shuffles away a step. "And your friends in high places."

"My daughter." She clenches her jaw, just as happy to see me again as I am to see her. "What does this have to do with Mirela?"

"There have been a few developments."

"Have you found the criminals responsible or not?" She scowls.

"We should talk." I glance around the vacant lobby. "We

can either do this here, or..."

Her gaze flicks back to the clone. "Send her up, D1-502." Then the holo dissolves.

"This way, if you please." D1-502 extends an arm toward the speedlift and bows forward ever so slightly. I appreciate the sudden change in manners.

Dunn reenters the speedlift, and I follow him inside. D1-502 reaches in and taps a code into the panel that will send us straight to the 120th floor with no stops in between.

"There. That wasn't so hard, was it?" I give the clone a smirk.

It retreats without another word. The mirrored doors slide shut, and we're on our way, gliding upward at a leisurely pace. I guess that's something the rich can afford.

"You enjoyed antagonizing D1-502," Dunn observes.

Did I? "Maybe a little."

"It is only doing its job."

"Acting as gatekeeper. Do you think it saw Baatar come through here?"

"It would have indicated as much, had that been the case."

I glance up at my partner. "So it wouldn't have lied about that?"

"We are conditioned not to lie, Investigator Chen."

"But you can. Right? You can overcome your conditioning." He obviously has in other ways. "Should the situation call for it—or if you're ordered to do so?"

"That would take an incredible force of will." Dunn pauses. "Which is something most clones do not possess."

"Have you ever lied to me?" I raise an eyebrow.

"Not to my knowledge, Investigator Chen."

I nudge him with a smile. "Likewise."

An alert flashes in the corner of my lenses. Incoming hail, video and audio. I accept the call, and Erik Paine's too-handsome face appears for my eyes only.

"Hey, where were you last night? Thought we had a date." He looks hurt.

"What?"

"I was sitting on the floor outside your cube for hours..." His forlorn expression transforms into a grin, and he shakes his head, unable to keep up the facade.

"Funny," I mutter.

"Have you seen this?" The grin disappears—as a one-time wannabe actor, he's a master of facial expressions—replaced by a grim look. "It's all over the Link."

He shares footage of Governor Raniero pontificating. The *no-confidence* speech. "Quite the windbag. He's going after Bishop—"

"That was earlier. This is now." Erik turns up the volume. "Live."

Governor Raniero, looking just as serious and sincere as he did before the break of dawn, addresses the viewer directly. And in the upper right corner of the feed, he displays an image of...me. Wearing my exo.

"Investigator Sera Chen is no soldier. She has had no military training. Yet she is allowed to stomp around the Domes in this military-grade exoskeleton. With lethal upgrades, no less!" Raniero shakes his well-manicured head in disbelief. "As a former curfew enforcer, Sera Chen roamed the streets of Dome 1 after dark in this powered suit, making her faster and stronger than anyone else on duty. When she was promoted to the rank of investigator for reasons that completely elude me, she was allowed to continue wearing this monstrosity when the situation called for it. Again, the only investigator granted such a privilege." He raises his chin. "Why was Sera Chen afforded this preferential treatment? As a member of the Twenty, yes, of course, there were certain safeguards in place to protect her. At the time, it was reasonable. But why does she continue to benefit from such favoritism? The answer lies in the fact that her biological parents are friends of James Bishop. But not merely friends. Fellow survivors. The bond they forged while living in the Wastes—"

Erik cuts the audio. "He's gunning for you, Sera."

"Let me hear the rest." I glance up at the digits on the screen above the speedlift doors. We just passed the hundredth floor.

"—and obvious nepotism, with his own daughter filling the role of Commander. But that's not the worst of it." Raniero pauses dramatically. "It has come to my attention that Sera Chen is a close friend and ally of one of the worst underworld figures to blight the Ten Domes since their inception. A self-styled kingpin responsible for the dust smuggling, illegal weapons trade, and human trafficking that our venerable former Chancellor Persephone Hawthorne fought so hard to keep from festering within our walls. A man who goes by the name Drasko—"

"I've heard enough."

Erik cuts the audio again. "They're lies. All of it, every word."

"Not all of it."

He frowns. "Okay, sure, the Twenty had it pretty easy. We were the future. But now with all those kids they made from our DNA—"

"We're not as important as we used to be." Reminds me of something Agent Baatar said. "Have any of the other Governors fallen in line with Raniero?"

"You haven't heard?" Erik blinks.

"Been kind of busy."

"Almost half of them. The Governors of Domes 2, 3, 8, and 10 cast their vote of no confidence in James Bishop's leadership an hour ago."

I glance at the muted Governor as he displays images of my exo gunning down our airlock security personnel. No mention of Mirela Edwards, of course, and her face is indistinguishable in the scenes Raniero has decided to share. But the subtext is clear enough: a picture of me in my exo right next to a picture of the minigun blasting away, tearing three Dome 10 guards to bloody pulp in an instant.

Erik watches my reaction. Guess I'm not doing a great job of keeping my expression neutral right now.

"You can't blame yourself for this," he says in a low tone. "Sera, we had to get out of there when we did. We couldn't bring your exo with us. There wasn't room in the car."

"I should have gone back for it. Immediately." I curse under my breath. "You don't leave a loaded gun lying in the street."

"You do when robots are trying to kill you."

20

The speedlift dings pleasantly, announcing our arrival at the 120th floor, and the doors open. I draw my shocker, holding it out in front of me.

Do I expect Baatar to be lurking nearby? If he is, that could explain why Nevah allowed us up here. She knew her secret agent would be more than capable of handling a pair of interlopers

"Gotta go." I end the transmission, and Erik's confused face vanishes. With a nod to Dunn, I step out into the hallway.

Silent. Still Vacant. And very short. There's only one pair of ornate double doors a few meters away, flanked on either side by towering potted palms. Unsurprisingly, the building's entire top floor belongs to Nevah Edwards.

"Would you like me to request a warrant to access the security cameras, Investigator Chen?" Dunn has his shocker in hand, aimed at the tile floor.

"Might as well." I walk up to the solid wood doors, each one as tall as two of me, wider than three, and bearing carved floral relief patterns. "Don't be surprised if you're denied."

"Because we have not been tasked with tracking down Agent Baatar."

That's right. "Not our case," I sigh, looking for a doorbell or something to announce our arrival. So far, there's no indication that the scanner has recognized my neuro. Which means either the system wasn't told to expect us, or we're intentionally being made to wait. My money's on the second one.

"Do you think Agent Baatar is an associate of Nevah Edwards?"

"She said she's friends with the Governor." I shrug.

"Assuming Agent Baatar works for Governor Raniero, which we have not confirmed, do you believe that Ms. Edwards may be harboring Agent Baatar inside her domicile, along with your exo-suit?"

"Good chance." I glance up at him. "But without a warrant, we can't go searching the place. I'll ask her a few questions, see how far I get. Meanwhile, you scan for heat signatures."

Dunn nods. We've got a plan.

If Baatar's here, he won't be able to stay put forever. And when he makes his escape, Blink will be right outside the parking garage waiting for him. Who knows, maybe if I ask nicely, my drone will shoot out the black van's tires. Take that, spooky agent man.

The doors swing open slowly without a sound, and a dark plasteel robot as boxy as those robodocs in MedTech is there to greet us. It rolls forward on treads with its spindly metal arms extended outward in welcome, its head an oblong shape with a glowing white circle at eye level that undulates as it speaks in an oddly harmonic voice.

"Investigator Chen, you are expected. Please, follow me. Your clone, however, will need to wait here. Outside in the hall, per Ms. Edwards' instructions."

Well, that won't work. I don't have anything on me that will scan for body heat signatures. And I probably shouldn't wear Dunn's helmet. Too obvious. And weird.

"My partner goes where I go." As I enter Edwards' place, I can tell right away who was responsible for the lobby's interior design. Same marble tile, high ceilings, plants and water features, but up here on the penthouse level, all the blue-tinted light is natural thanks to windowalls on three sides. Outside, aerocars glide by in clearly defined aerial traffic lanes, and it almost feels like you could reach out and touch the Dome's plexicon ceiling—along with the white, puffy clouds beyond.

The robot rolls alongside me. "Ms. Edwards was very clear on this matter, Investigator Chen. Either the clone waits outside, or you will be asked to leave." It pauses, rolling around to face me. "Escorted off the premises, if necessary."

I glance down at the pincers it has instead of hands. Strong enough to crush bone, if I'm not mistaken.

"New plan." I look over my shoulder at Dunn and grit my teeth, furious at what this woman is, once again, making me do. "I'll meet you in the hallway once I'm through here."

Dunn doesn't nod or reply. Instead, he shakes his head very slowly in disgust as the pair of massive doors shut slowly of their own accord.

My stomach sinks. I've failed him again.

"This way, if you please." The robot extends one arm toward a semicircle of very comfortable-looking couches thirty meters away. A wall of bamboo with a sizeable screen mounted on it separates this slightly sunken receiving area from whatever lies beyond it. Two dozen bedrooms and half as many bathrooms? A bowling alley? Symphony hall? The possibilities are endless when you've got this much space to call your own.

Scans inconclusive, Dunn reports via text. So he wasn't shaking his head at me, after all. That's a relief. *I was not able to sweep the entire floor.*

As soon as the doors shut him out, the IR scanner in his helmet was useless. Infrared can't detect heat signatures on the other side of solid matter, only heat inside that matter. The bamboo wall would have proven problematic as well, even if Dunn had been permitted to stay.

I could have Blink run a few XR scans from outside the building, but if it was caught doing such a thing without a warrant, Hudson would probably confiscate it. And I'd be reprimanded. Again. Besides, I need Blink right where it is, in case Baatar tries to make a sneaky getaway.

"Make yourself comfortable, Investigator Chen. Ms. Edwards will join you shortly." The robot inclines itself forward in an approximation of a bow before rolling away, its treads noiseless across the tiles.

"Thanks." I take a seat in a cushy, earth-toned sofa and scratch casually at my temple before tapping it to disengage my augments. Then I close my eyes and focus all of my telepathic energy on seeking out other minds on this floor. Not to read their thoughts. Just a cursory sweep to see how many individuals I'm dealing with here.

Dunn's mind shows up first, since he's closest in proximity. The robot doesn't register at all. Which means that despite the intriguing voice and polished demeanor, its machine intelligence is even less sophisticated than Wink's or Blink's. Nevah Edwards is the next to cross my path, and she's moving in my direction from halfway across the penthouse level. Taking her sweet time.

That's fine. She can take all the time she wants.

I reach out with my nascent telepathy, searching for the presence of any other minds in the domicile but coming up short. I give the floor a couple passes, just to be sure, before reactivating my augments with a quick temple-tap.

So Baatar and his security clones aren't hiding out here. But they have to be somewhere in the building, on one of the other hundred and nineteen floors. If I wasn't in a rush, I'd sweep them all. And probably be tempted to dig through his brain, once I found him, just to find out who he is and who he's working for.

"Detective." Nevah Edwards rounds the corner of bamboo and fixes me with a cold stare. Arms folded, garbed in a silky, emerald green robe, she juts out her chin with regal defiance. "Thank you for keeping your neuro active."

"Of course. If I may?" I gesture toward the wallscreen.

"Be my guest."

I cast an image from the recent airlock riot to prove that my neural implant is online, and I won't be reading her thoughts. "Do you recognize this woman?"

She frowns, sitting very still as she coolly regards the larger-than-life image on the screen. "What is this supposed to be?"

"An incident that occurred last night at the Dome 10 airlock." I pause. "Is that your daughter—Mirela Edwards?"

"Of course not. Why would it be?"

"Look closer. Please."

Her nostrils flare—a physical reaction to being told what to do. But she does what I ask, shaking her head with an irritable sigh. "This sort of thing can be easily doctored, made to look like something it's not. I hear it happens online all the time. What do they call it? Deep-faking?" She scoffs and then scowls at me. "I thought you were here to update me on your investigation. How does this photo have anything to do with anything?"

"The exo-suit your daughter is wearing in this image was the same exo used to break into your shop." I wait a moment for that to sink in. "Is there any reason why your daughter would do such a thing?"

"No reason at all. That's how I know she didn't do it." Narrowing her gaze with obvious suspicion, she adds, "Isn't this contraption the same one Governor Raniero told us about just a few minutes ago? Something a soldier would wear, correct? And that you happen to own, yourself? Well, Detective, my daughter is not a soldier, nor is she in law enforcement. She is a solar engineer living and working in Dome 8. And, as is the way of things, we do not see much of each other these days. We are both so very busy, and we do not run in the same social circles."

"When was the last time you saw your daughter?"

Arranging the silk robe over her knees and wiping down wrinkles only her eyes can see, she says, "I don't know. It has been a while. New Year's Day, perhaps? What would that be—seven months or so?" She nods to herself. "About that long. But as I said, neither of us has much in the way of free time. Mirela has her career, and I have my shop..." She trails off, her gaze distant. Remembering how it looked the last time she saw it, no doubt.

I don't have to read her mind to know that she misses her daughter. What's unclear is whether the seven months apart were Nevah's idea or Mirela's.

"Is your daughter suffering from any health issues that you're aware of?" Anything serious enough to make her interested in what Prometheus promised its followers?

"That is a strange thing to ask."

"Covering all bases, ma'am."

She pshaws. "No. As far as I'm aware, she has always been the picture of health."

"Did she ever happen to mention a group called the Children of Tomorrow?"

Ms. Edwards looks baffled. "That cult? No, never. Why would she?"

"The graffiti in your shop indicated an interest in the Prometheus cult."

A shrug. "I don't have any idea what that was all about."

Yet I distinctly remember her reaction upon seeing it: *What have they done?* Not lamenting the messy paint on her wall. Expressing disappointment. Sorrow, even.

"Did you have an argument with your daughter the last time you saw her?"

"Mirela and I do not argue," she replies coolly, refocused on her imaginary robe wrinkles. "We never have. We would have nothing to argue about—except her taste in men," she adds with a sardonic smirk.

"A maintenance worker?"

Her eyes flash at me, surprised. But she's quick to hide it. "Truly, I wish you would not be so obtuse. What does any of this have to do with capturing the criminals who robbed me, and recovering my merchandise? My reputation is on the line here. I have clients expecting items that only I am known to deliver."

"Can you tell me the value of this item?" I cast an image onto the wallscreen of the antique device Raul had hidden under his armor, replacing the picture of Mirela.

Ms. Edwards' brow furrows with concentration. "Yes, I remember this piece well. Has it been recovered?"

"In a way. It was found on a murdered curfew enforcer." And it's got to be worth plenty for that dust freak to claw him to death, trying to get at it.

She stares at me. "Murdered..."

"What can you tell me about your daughter's significant other?"

"How is this relevant?"

"He may be a person of interest in this case."

Something behind her eyes relaxes infinitesimally. "Well, he's never been good enough for her. And if you're saying he may have had something to do with what happened to my shop, I would not be surprised." Her nose angles upward. She has to look down it now in order to meet my gaze. "He used to be a soldier, you know."

No, I didn't. Filing that tidbit away.

She exhales and shakes her head, looking up at the ceiling. "But that was a while ago, of course. Before Bishop cracked down on smuggling."

"Dust smuggling?"

She nods absently. "The way Mirela tells it, her *significant other*, as you call him, was quite a talent at foraging in the wastelands. But she's only had nice things to say about him, of course. Her way of telling her dear mother that I was wrong about him." She scoffs. "As if a certain skill set made him worthy of her. He was beneath her station! It wasn't bad enough that she'd already chosen to work in the service industry?" Another shake of the head at her progeny's tragic life choices. "I don't know why she insists on slumming it the way she does."

"Did he use dust?"

"Snort it, you mean? To give himself superpowers?" She laughs without much in the way of mirth. "Oh, I wouldn't know. But after that Bishop fellow made it impossible for the dust trade to continue, Jumaro was transferred to a raider detail, traversing the Wastes in search of salvageable materials."

"And the occasional artifact?"

She almost smiles, but there's a sneer in it. "He was earning a little extra on the side working with my suppliers. Then he got greedy, demanding more than his usual cut. Claimed he was due hazard pay or some such for his trouble." An insouciant shrug. "He threatened to take his treasure elsewhere, but my shop is the only one that matters in Dome 1, and my suppliers told him as much. Alas, the fool would not be dissuaded. But after his accident, the issue was moot. He had to take whatever job he could get. And thus...maintenance worker, as you already know."

I didn't. But now I have confirmation. "What sort of accident was it?" Had to be serious to result in his discharge.

I run a quick search on the citizen database for a former soldier/raider with given name Jumaro who currently works in Dome maintenance. One result: Jumaro Tanaka, Dome 8 resident. Mirela's home turf.

"You would have to ask him." Ms. Edwards sniffs dismissively. "The man is of no import to me."

"Why would he have raided your shop?"

She scowls. "I never said that he did."

"You said you wouldn't be surprised if he was involved."

She blows out an exasperated sigh. "You're using my words against me. Recording everything I say!" She jabs an accusatory index finger at my lenses.

"Could the burglary have been retaliatory in nature?"

Another sniff. Eyes ablaze with fury. "I will say this much. It would be just like Jumaro to try to get even with me. He has the mental acuity of a petulant child!"

"Why would he feel the need to get even? You weren't responsible for his discharge. Or for the suppliers refusing to increase his cut."

She blinks, surprised that I'm taking her side. Then she nods. "Of course not. But such logic matters little to a madman. Psychotic is the word for it, I believe. I saw all the signs and tried to warn Mirela, but by then he had already turned her against me."

I soften my tone. "Is that why you haven't spoken to her in seven months?"

Her eyes become glassy, and she looks away. "Mother-daughter relationships are complicated by nature. I don't have to tell you that." She glances at me, and I nod to show I'm listening. "Mirela has always had a good head on her shoulders. We have not seen eye to eye on everything, but that's alright. We are each our own person. It's healthier that way. Yet where Jumaro is concerned, she habitually blinds herself to the facts. And after his accident..." She shakes her head and inhales, sitting up straighter. Then she turns toward me as if she's come to a decision. "If he has continued to poison her mind against me over these past months, then yes, I can unfortunately imagine the two of them doing what was done to my shop last night." All the anger seems to have left her. Now she just looks sad. And a little lost, in her own home.

"Thank you for meeting with me." I get to my feet. "You've been very helpful."

She barely nods, her gaze fixed somewhere between the floor and the far wall.

"One last thing, before I leave. I noticed a few masks included in your inventory, but there weren't any details. Did one of them happen to look like this?" I bring up an image of the dust freak in the maintenance tunnel—bulging yellow eyes, gaping nasal cavity, leathery skin. That's what I expect to see. Instead, I get an error message on my ocular lenses: FILE CORRUPTED.

"Like what, Detective?" she snaps impatiently, glaring at me.

I try again. Same result: no freak. For some reason, I can't access any of the footage from the moments prior to Raul's murder. I switch over to Wink's feed, from when it was attacked. There were brief flashes showing the murderer's grotesque face. But now I can't access them, either. FILE CORRUPTED is all I get.

"My apologies. I thought I had—"

"These are the masks that were taken." She casts three images onto the wallscreen, and in each one, the mask is made of carved wood. Very tribal and menacing, but nothing like the horror from that tunnel. "Priceless, all of them."

Not exactly true, if she had clients lined up to pay good credits for them.

"Thank you, Ms. Edwards." I head toward the entrance.

The robot is stationed off to one side like a statue, awaiting orders. As I approach, the double doors swing open to reveal Dunn standing in the short hallway outside.

He's not alone.

Agent Baatar gives me a direct look. "Good morning, Investigator Chen. D1-436 and I were just getting acquainted."

21

I don't go for my shocker. Because Baatar hasn't gone for his concealed holster. And Dunn's weapon is back in its compartment. For the moment, the three of us are having a nice, if unexpected, conversation.

"Wondered when you'd show up." I offer the secret agent my best attempt at a confident smile as Nevah Edwards' doors swing shut on my heels. "Saw your van down in the parking garage. Where are your two buddies?"

"Here I thought my holo-projector was state of the art. I suppose very little escapes your superhuman eyesight."

Sure. Let him believe that. "Had a good talk with Ms. Edwards." I glance at Dunn. "We've got a new lead."

My partner doesn't respond. He stands facing Baatar with both arms down at his sides. If I didn't know better, I might think he'd turned to stone.

"Are you here to return my exo?"

Baatar shakes his head. "It was never yours to begin with. Are you a soldier? Do you have any military training? No, I thought not."

"Raniero mentioned that earlier today. Sounds like you're both reading off the same script."

His expression remains neutral. "Before we were so rudely

interrupted earlier, I asked for a moment of your time."

He wanted to talk. I fold my arms and make a valiant effort at staring him down. "So talk."

He angles his head back a micrometer, appraising me. "Change is coming. The people in power who have shown you such favoritism—their days are numbered. So my question is, Investigator Chen... Where do you want to be when the new regime arrives?"

"Right here." I shrug. "Doing my damn job."

"And if you no longer have this job? Because your superiors decide to save their own necks by blaming you for what happened at the airlock?"

"That's not how we do things. Nobody takes all the credit or all the blame."

A smirk touches the grim line of his mouth. "I didn't think you were so naive."

"Enlighten me."

"James Bishop will not be Interim Chancellor for much longer."

"That's debatable."

"And once he is out of the way, our next Chancellor will appoint a new Commander in charge of law enforcement. Mara Bishop will enjoy an early retirement." He pauses. "When that time comes, do you honestly think Chief Inspector Hudson will stand by you? Or will he, more likely, seek to distance himself from your dereliction of duty? Your negligence? Your insubordination? If I were him, I would relish the opportunity to be rid of you."

"You know, this ability of yours to foresee the future? It's superhuman."

My sarcasm doesn't have any effect on him.

"So you have a choice here, Chen. You can either assist us in the changing of the guard, or you can go down with the Bishops. But don't take too long making up your mind. Events are already in motion that will forever change life in the Domes."

Events. "So, who'd you give my exo to?"

"It is no longer your concern. You will never wear it again." Spoken as fact, not a threat. "What you need to focus on right now is your future. Where do you see yourself? Do you wish to continue working in law enforcement? Or perhaps something LawKeeper-adjacent? You would make a fine agent." A short pause. "On the other hand, you could find yourself locked away and forgotten in a correctional center, perhaps the one out in the Wastes that is rumored to exist. It all depends on the decision you make right now."

I raise my chin. "If I play my cards right, you'll make all my dreams come true. Because you're my bona fide genie in a bottle."

He clenches his jaw. Nice to get a reaction, no matter how small. "Sarcasm is the lowest form of wit, Investigator Chen."

"But the highest form of intelligence. People always seem to forget that part. Attributed to Oscar Wilde, if I'm not mistaken."

His stare is devoid of recognition. Guess he's not a book person.

"Last chance." He takes a step back toward the speedlift.

"You told me that once before. Yet here we are, having this delightful conversation." My hand inches closer to my drop leg holster. If he thinks he's going to flee the premises, he'd better think again.

I glance at Dunn, surprised he hasn't launched into action

to detain Baatar. Equally surprised he didn't send the agent into convulsions with a shocker round as soon as he arrived on the scene.

"Next time we meet, things won't be nearly as delightful, I'm afraid." Baatar reaches toward me, and something launches out of his sleeve into his grip. It looks an awful lot like—

I draw my shocker, the muzzle clearing just as Baatar fires his EMP gun. The electromagnetic pulse hits me squarely in the chest. But that's all it does. No convulsions, no blinding headache. Just buying himself time. A momentary distraction.

I pull my trigger again and again, lunging after him.

"I see you've made your choice." He ducks and rolls across the floor beneath the stream of pulse rounds I send hurtling his way. The speedlift doors slide open, sensing his presence, and he throws himself headlong inside. "Goodbye, Investigator Chen!"

He's not getting away that easy. I keep firing as I charge toward the speedlift, expecting to pin him to the interior wall with a few bursts that'll send him into undignified spasms. Instead, I find him standing there with a sidearm in his other hand, aimed at my chest. Expecting me.

He pulls the trigger, and it sounds like a bomb going off. The projectile round hits my center of mass like a 900-kilo sucker punch, knocking me flat on my back. The hallway ceiling spins above as the speedlift closes, carrying Agent Baatar safely away.

"Investigator Chen, are you alright?" Dunn asks, standing stock-still.

I think I know why.

I roll my head toward him with a grimace. "He hit you with an EMP?"

"Yes. My armor is locked. I cannot move to assist you."

"I'm fine." I curse and struggle to sit up, gingerly touching my abdomen where Baatar hit me. The armor plating in my tactical suit caught the brunt of it, but I'll have some serious bruising underneath. "Agent Baatar is on the move," I subvocalize to Blink before realizing my augments are offline. "Damn it." That electromagnetic pulse he shot me with knocked out my neuro. All I have now is biologic to rely on.

And my abilities.

Agent Baatar is attempting to escape. Move to intercept, I transmit telepathically to my drone. No, I'm not insane; this has actually worked before. Human mind to machine intelligence. Sounds like something from a Gibson novel. *His vehicle is located in the southwest corner of the parking garage, cloaked in a hologram.*

No response from Blink. Either it didn't receive my weird attempt at communication this time, or it's already en route, buzzing through that sublevel toward the secret agent's unmarked van. Assuming Baatar doesn't have another means of transport lined up. Aerocar on the roof, perhaps?

Wincing at a stab of pain from my sternum, I slowly get to my feet. "Let me guess. They still don't let you carry your own keycode for situations like this?"

"No, Investigator Chen," Dunn replies. "If by *they* you mean Commander Bishop."

"And those Level 5 tech-heads," I mutter, surveying his locked-up armor with a scowl. The only way to get him moving again is with an extra-long string of alphanumerics on a translucent card. First you read the letters and numbers aloud, then you tap the card against his chest plate. Like magic, the armor reboots, and he's able to move. But I have no way of contacting HQ right now, and I've never attempted telepathy with my superiors before. If the analysts are doing their job, they'll report to Hudson that I'm offline. Then again, he'll probably figure I'm just being difficult again, toggling off my augments after he told me in no uncertain terms to put an end to that bad habit. Because it causes brain damage, apparently. "We've got to break you out, partner."

"Impossible, I am afraid."

"Never say never." I return to Nevah Edwards' double doors and make my presence known. No neuro for the scanners to detect, so I pound with my fist until the doors float open.

The robot wheels out to face me.

"Investigator Chen, is there something else you require?" it says without a hint of annoyance.

"How strong are those pincers?" Before it can respond, I point at Dunn. "I need you to crack open my partner's armor without injuring him. Think you can do that?"

The robot stutters back a centimeter, as if in surprise. "I am not permitted to take orders from anyone but Ms. Nevah Edwards."

"This is a matter of Dome Security. A dangerous individual is attempting to escape—"

"Go without me," Dunn says.

I ignore him. "If you need permission from Ms. Edwards, then get it. Now."

Seeming to stare at me for a moment, the robot rocks

forward slightly. "Please wait here." Then it rolls away, and the doors shut behind it.

"Agent Baatar shot you, Investigator Chen. This makes him a criminal. He cannot be allowed to escape."

"He won't. We'll get him."

"Not if you wait for me," Dunn insists.

I clench my fists and glance at the speedlift, just as a red light flashes along the perimeter of the ceiling and an automated voice announces, "Lockdown. Lockdown. The Edwards Estates are now on lockdown. Shelter in place." Repeating itself on a loop.

Blink must have gotten my message after all. Somehow, the drone managed to trigger the building's security protocols, maybe by unleashing a burst of projectile rounds on Baatar's van. That would do it. And if Baatar hasn't already gotten out of the building, he'll be trapped inside with the rest of us. Because every door in the domescraper is now on auto-lock, and that includes the speedlift.

I like imagining him stuck in there.

"With the lockdown in effect, that robot will not return, Investigator Chen," Dunn says. "The doors will remain closed until any potential threats are neutralized."

Best laid plans. "LawKeepers will be dispatched to this location, and we'll have backup." I approach him. "But for now we're on our own. We can figure this out."

I reach for the broken section of armor where Drasko shot him in the arm and try to peel back the stubborn white plasteel, but it immediately becomes clear that this strategy won't work. I'd need the extra oomph of my exo to even think about removing these armored plates by hand.

Blink has a grappling claw that extends from its

underbelly. It might be able to grab onto the cracked armor and peel it off, one strip at a time. Except there's no way for the drone to reach us up here on the 120th floor during a lockdown.

Now I'm wondering if this was Baatar's doing, as well. Leave Dunn and me stranded up here, unable to contact HQ, and then set off the building's lockdown protocols after making his exit. Just the sort of thing a secret agent would do.

Intercepting vehicle, Investigator Chen, Blink reports, mind-to-mind.

That's my boy. *Did you set off the lockdown?*

No. Straight answer. So it must have been Baatar.

Give me a play-by-play.

Vehicle is attempting to exit the parking garage, Blink replies via our shared telepathic channel. Weird, I know. *Initiating automatic weapons fire, full salvo. Front tires punctured. Vehicle has crashed into a support pillar. Two security clones are exiting with projectile weapons drawn. They are firing—*

Get out of there! I shout telepathically.

No response.

"Is something wrong?" Dunn asks.

Guess my face is an open book. "I think I lost my other drone." Cursing under my breath, I tug at his damaged armor with all my strength.

"Were you able to connect telepathically with its machine intelligence?"

I nod, gritting my teeth and pulling with both hands.

"Did Agent Baatar shoot it down?"

"More or less," I mutter. With a frustrated grunt, I let go

of his arm and shake my head. "This is ridiculous. There has to be a way to get you out of that thing."

"The override keycode is the only method I am aware of."

A loud clatter rattles in the empty speedlift shaft, followed by a forceful collision, then another, and another. Moving upward, closer to our floor with every impact, reverberating through the walls like seismic tremors.

I glance at Dunn. "Something's climbing up."

"Heading toward us," he agrees.

I draw my shocker and grip it in both hands, aimed at the polished speedlift doors. Taking a step to my right, I stand between them and my partner, confined in his powerless armor.

A heavy blow slams against the doors from inside the shaft, strong enough to punch the plasteel outward in a large, fist-shaped lump. *What the hell is in there?*

"Whatever it is, I believe it intends to break through," Dunn observes.

"Our backup?" *We should be so lucky.*

Another strike, followed by a few more, rapid-fire, and the seam between the doors begins to crack open amidst a field of identical warped lumps.

"Do you believe your exoskeleton would be strong enough to accomplish this?"

It just might. But why would Baatar climb back up here in it?

"We're about to find out." I hold my shocker at the ready, prepared to send a pulse round into the face of whoever emerges from that shaft.

With a shriek of resistance, the speedlift doors shudder open, shoved aside by a pair of arm-braces I recognize at once. Because they belong to my exo.

But what's harnessed inside defies description. Or would have, if I hadn't already seen what Raul's murderer looked like.

"Death to all infidels!" the figure rasps, bulging yellow eyes locking onto me as soon as he stomps one boot-brace into the hallway and pivots my way. Almost as if he was expecting me to be there.

I fire three rounds in quick succession, blue pulses of frenetic energy sizzling as they streak through the air, all of them aimed at the guy's bald, leathery head. But he's quick and agile in my exo, and he bats them away with a plasteel arm bar, sending them smacking against the ceiling where they fizzle out with a flurry of sparks.

This isn't his first rodeo. He's worn an exoskeleton before.

"Sera Chen," he hisses through teeth sharpened to points. "You may think that you defeated Prometheus. But you will see him rise again—through us. The Children of Tomorrow!"

He lunges toward me, and that's when I realize he didn't come alone. A dozen men and women clad in grimy maintenance coveralls identical to his own scrabble out of the defunct speedlift with menacing shouts and angry looks on their maskless faces. They must have followed the dust freak up the shaft, climbing 120 floors on that extra-long ladder in there. Impressive. You'd think they would be exhausted by this point, but they charge full-tilt into the hallway, right behind the leather-headed weirdo like he's their fearless leader.

Doing my damnedest to shoot every target in sight, I retreat until my backside runs into Dunn's statuesque front side. Uncanny how the dust freak is able to knock away every one of my pulse-rounds as he advances, but a few end up hitting members of his entourage. They go into sudden convulsions and hit the floor, bodies wracked with uncontrollable spasms as they lapse into unconsciousness.

"You will not stop us!" the freak screams, one hand snatching away my shocker in a crushing grip while the other smacks me across the face.

The guy isn't muscle-bound by any stretch. But his hand is powered by my exo right now, so when it hits, it feels like a brick smashing into the side of my head at speed. Then I'm thrown against the wall where I struggle and fail to keep from collapsing to the floor.

Dunn is the next to be tossed aside. Unable to move, he topples over and skids against the opposite wall, lying there like a felled tree.

"You and others like you—ignorant *infidels*—will not stand in our way!" The freak holds up my shocker and crushes it to pieces as a demonstration, allowing shards of plasteel and other shattered components to rain down to the tiled floor. His leathery hands sport vicious, five-centimeter claws. I'll never forget what they did to Raul's face. "Once your kind are done away with, we will rescue Prometheus from his restraints. And when he is unbound, we will receive the gifts he promised to us!"

He looms over me, inhaling and exhaling convulsively through that hideous nasal cavity in his face. Or mask, rather—assuming that's what it is. But how could a mask have gruesome lidless eyes that quiver and pulsate in their sockets, staring with such palpable hate?

"Thanks for giving me a rundown of your game plan." I

offer my best attempt at a confident smirk. "Very villain-like."

"Silence!" shouts a husky, bearded member of the rabble clustered behind him. Looks like my shocker missed five of them, and they're all glaring at me. The rest lie on the floor in various states of repose. "You will show proper respect to your betters!"

I honestly have no response to that. I mean, it sounds like something from a Victorian-era novel. A mediocre one.

Instead, I force myself to look the freak right in his bulging yellow eyes. "You planning to kill me? Is that it?"

He snorts, and bile-colored mucus oozes out of his skullish nasal cavity. Then he leans toward me, and I have to fight my gag reflex at his rotten stench. Essence of corpse.

"No, Sera Chen. We cannot kill you," he rasps. "Not until you take us to Prometheus."

22

As bizarre as it sounds, I'm getting the feeling this guy isn't wearing a mask. But if not, then what the hell's wrong with him? I've seen plenty of Plague survivors, and they don't look like this. Did he suffer some kind of disfiguring accident?

That's when it hits me.

"Jumaro Tanaka." I wouldn't have thought it possible, but his hideous eyes seem to widen in surprise for just a second. "That's who you are."

He was a soldier, Nevah Edwards said, a raider out in the Wastes, scavenging and salvaging. So that's why he knows his way around an exo. And, according to her, he had some sort of serious mishap, which caused him to be discharged. But what could have turned him into...this?

"You don't look like yourself." Nothing like the handsome, clean-cut image that came up on the citizen search. "When did you decide to become a murderer?"

"Hold your tongue, or you will lose it!" Beardo shouts. "And get on your feet!"

Jumaro raises an arm-brace, and the bearded fellow falls silent. "We have taken the building," he whispers into a comm device attached to the collar of his coveralls. Then to me, he hisses, "I have never killed anyone outside the realm of combat."

"I know a curfew enforcer who would disagree with you. If he could."

Jumaro juts out his wrinkled chin. "Rise, Sera Chen. You will take us to police headquarters. And there you will show us where they have imprisoned Prometheus."

I shake my head as I get to my feet. "Not a chance."

He stares at me for a few seconds. Then, never breaking eye contact, he turns toward Dunn and stomps my partner's legs with a boot-brace. The armor crackles beneath the blow, fracturing in web-like patterns. Dunn doesn't move, not even a fraction of a centimeter. Nor does he make a sound.

"Lead the way, Sera Chen. Or this one dies." Jumaro bares his fangs in a mockery of a smile.

"Do you know who lives here?" I nod toward the ornate double doors.

Another snort from his hollow nasal cavity as his head rocks back. "Of course."

"It wasn't enough to smash up her shop and steal all her merchandise. You've got to commandeer her building as well?" I don't give him a chance to respond. "Is that Mirela on the line? Tell her Mommy misses her."

Jumaro grinds his fangs and stomps Dunn a second time, driving the boot-brace into his torso. Cracks in the armor shudder outward from the point of impact. Another blow like that will crush my partner underneath.

Once again, I'm forced to witness my own exo used in a criminal act of violence. Hudson was right. The thing should be retired. But with my neuro offline, I can't even deactivate it. Baatar thought of everything—assuming he's the one who handed the exo-suit over to Tanaka. The puppeteer at work, once again.

"How long have you been working with Agent Baatar?" I keep my tone casual while my fists clench down at my sides. I can't stand seeing Dunn lying there without a sound, unable to fight back. Everything in me wants to jump onto Jumaro and rip his eyes out. Maybe I will, if he goes after my partner again. "He's not a card-carrying member of your cult, is he?"

"The Children of Tomorrow are not a *cult*!" Beardo screams—apparently his preferred manner of speaking. "We are the *future*!"

Again, Jumaro raises one hand, and the bearded fellow snaps his mouth shut.

"Quite the hothead. Too bad I missed him earlier." I mime shooting Beardo between the eyes with my finger. The guy looks about ready to rip me apart.

"We are on our way up," Jumaro hisses into his comm. Then he reaches for me with a clawed hand, like he's going to carry me off, whether I like it or not, and there's nothing I can do about it.

Except I'm not going anywhere with this bunch.

Since actions speak louder than words, I grab onto his arm-brace for leverage and twist sideways, kicking him in the face with everything I've got. His leather-head rocks back, eyes goggling, snorting in surprise as he staggers a couple unsteady steps, boot-braces clanking against the floor. Disoriented for the moment.

Without being told to do so, his gang decides to intervene, charging forward to dole out their own brand of punishment. Beardo doesn't make it very far before getting an uppercut right in that hairy mess coming out of his chin.

His head snaps upward, eyes rolling in their sockets before he collapses, out cold. Had a feeling he was all talk. But the other four are another matter. They're younger, lighter on their feet, and from what I can tell, they've had practice fighting as a group.

They surround me, throwing punches and kicks—half of which are feints, designed to position me right where they want me. I'm able to block the blows that land, but sticking to defense isn't going to get me anywhere. I've got to take them down before Jumaro comes at me again.

"Subdue her," he rasps. Guess he's delegating now.

This isn't a kung fu interactive. I'm not going to take on all of them at once with gravity-ignoring flying side kicks. And they're not going to line up and politely take turns. Their goal is to get hold of me and overpower me.

I realize I'm in the worst-possible position, with opponents on four sides. The only option right now is to fight my way out before they close in. Focus on the weakest member of the band and take that one down like I did ol' Beardo. Then move on to the next. Facing them, preferably, with nobody flanking me and no one behind me.

That will involve a bit of circling on my part. Punish and turn, punish and turn. Deal a devastating blow and roll toward the next opponent, always moving. And, if I'm lucky, confusing them enough in the melee that they end up hitting one of their own.

I pick out the smallest of the bunch and move fast, evading her front kick by spinning to my right and throwing a punch at her temple. It should have knocked her out, but she only drops to one knee, stunned. That's enough to keep her out of the picture for the moment, so I turn toward my next opponent and deliver a debilitating inside kick to his knee. He stumbles sideways with a groan, breaking the circle, and I grab hold of him, dragging him in front of me as a human shield. His comrade on my right realizes his mistake too late: throwing a haymaker at me but hitting his pal instead. Right in the jaw. The guy's dead weight drops to the floor, and he lies still.

Two down, three to go.

But that's when I hear Dunn scream. A sound I've never heard before.

Jumaro is standing on him, the combined weight of the freak and the exoskeleton slowly crushing my partner inside his broken armor.

My turn to scream. "Get the hell off him!"

"Stop fighting the inevitable," Jumaro hisses, yellow eyes glaring. "You will go with us to your headquarters, and you will lead us to Prometheus."

Another scream from Dunn as the exo sinks, crumpling the cracked armor and mashing it into his body.

"Fine!" I've lost track of my opponents, and one of them kicks me from behind, sending me to my knees. I can only stare at Dunn's faceplate, wishing I could see his face. "Just leave him alone, or I swear—"

A fist plows into my temple, and I fall sideways.

"You are in no position to make threats, *demigod*," growls a voice in my ear.

The three left either standing or hobbling grab hold of me and yank me to my feet. The hallway looks blurry now, and it seems to be slowly capsizing. A bad knock to the noggin can do that.

Jumaro takes his sweet time stepping off Dunn. But as

soon as he does, he realizes that he's made a grave error.

He should have squashed my partner into the floor.

Dunn launches himself upward, breaking free of his compromised armor, white shards cascading down around him. Only his helmet remains intact. His black bodysuit leaves both mechanical arms and his prosthetic leg exposed, all three limbs cold metal and twitching servomotors. One hand clamps onto the back of the exo, and without preamble, Dunn effortlessly hurls Jumaro headlong toward the end of the hallway. The exo crashes into the wall with a deafening clatter, leaving an ugly indentation. Then he dashes after the freak and grabs hold of the minigun, tearing it free from its mount, the ammo belt trailing behind as the exo-suit falls over backward with a resounding clunk.

"Step away from Investigator Chen." Dunn aims the sizeable barrel at the trio standing around me. Without a word, they retreat toward the speedlift. He keeps the minigun trained on them. "Now halt," he says before they can even think about diving down the shaft in a risky escape maneuver.

They obey, freezing in place and failing to blink.

I have no idea if the gun will even fire, disconnected the way it is, but with his black faceplate and cyborg-commando appearance, I can't fault them for being intimidated. He strikes a very menacing figure.

Jumaro tries to lurch onto his boot-braces, but he's having some difficulty. He looks a bit like that turtle I once saw in VR that had been flipped onto its shell. Neck straining forward, limbs swinging to no avail.

"Are you alright, Investigator Chen?" Dunn asks, his faceplate still directed at the motionless trio.

"I should be asking you that. You sounded like you were dying."

"That was the effect I was hoping for."

I almost laugh. I guess I could be slaphappy after that blow to the head. "He was crushing you."

"Only my armor. Thank you for agreeing to his terms before he could do any serious damage. Now I am free."

Once again, my partner impresses me. "Nicely done."

His helmet dips forward in acknowledgment.

Despite the blinding headache and the ringing in my ears, I can still put one foot in front of the other. So that's what I do, moving toward Jumaro and keeping clear of his flailing claws.

"Thought you used to be a soldier." There's no reason why he should be having this much difficulty getting himself upright again. "Don't you know how to operate an exo?"

He growls at me like a vicious animal—or one I've seen in VR, rather. Maybe a rabid wolf, or a badger. Eyes bulging with hate, fangs flashing, seriously gruesome.

"Is Agent Baatar waiting on the roof with your girlfriend?" I arch an eyebrow. "C'mon, Jumaro. You're neck-deep in trouble. Murdering a curfew enforcer. Assaulting an investigator and her partner. You won't be seeing blue-tinted daylight for a very long time." I crouch down, doing my best to hold his wild gaze. "Tell me what I need to know, and I'll put it in my report that you were cooperative. That you aided in my investigation. Might decrease your time in a correctional center by a year or two."

He coughs. Or it could be a chuckle. "I will tell you *nothing*."

Alright then. Time for Plan B.

The situation calls for it. I have no idea what sort of mayhem these Children of Tomorrow are cooking up. I'm blind to what else could be going on in any of the floors below us. I need answers.

So I dive into Jumaro's mind.

And immediately regret it.

Underneath that not-so-handsome exterior is a howling cacophony of cognitive dissonance, a wailing maelstrom of conflicting emotions and desires. I'm no psychologist, but I'd venture to say he might be some sort of split personality.

There's Jumaro the soldier. Well-trained, disciplined, good at his job. A man who loves Mirela and would do anything for her.

Then there's this savage...creature. Overwhelmed by bloodlust and baser instincts, its fight-or-flight response kicked into high gear and flooding Jumaro's disfigured body with unhealthy levels of adrenaline.

The two of them refuse to coexist. Each one wants to dominate the other. That's the impression I'm getting, anyway. No clear thoughts or memories that I can access. I guess I'm not skilled enough to sort through the complete chaos going on inside his head. How can anyone function like this?

He lunges toward me, snapping his jaws, and I jerk back.

"Don't tell me you're a cannibal," I manage, trying to stay calm.

Then I remember Raul's face. I could've been wrong about claws slashing it to shreds. What if fangs had been the culprit? And the missing pieces of flesh...

Jumaro grins at me, and it's his most grotesque expression yet. But it's gone in an instant.

"The hunger," he whispers, "is strong. I can fight it...sometimes. Not always."

Okay. So he's a monster. But he's also a man, a soldier who can keep a lid on the creature's desires most of the time. He'd have to; otherwise, these Children of Tomorrow never would have agreed to join him on a climb up the speedlift shaft. They would have been too worried about becoming his next meal.

"When did it start?"

His eyes twitch away from me, staring at the ceiling now. "When I began to change. A few months after the...accident."

"Tell me what happened." Having witnessed firsthand his state of mind, it's a wonder he can compose a coherent sentence.

His leathery head jerks side to side. "I was out on a raid. There were six in my squad. We found a treasure trove in a blown-out sublevel. Salvageable materials among the debris." He pauses. His throat wriggles. "My protective gear was damaged during extraction."

So he was exposed to the elements. The contaminated air of the Wastes.

"I had no idea this could happen." I always assumed that if you breathed the bad air, you died. Not that you turned into a freak of nature.

"No one knows," he rasps. "It's...classified."

"Those two statements are incompatible," Dunn remarks.

I'm inclined to agree with him. Because someone would have to know about it in order to classify it. "You mean the public at large is unaware."

While authorities above my paygrade know this is what happens if you breathe the air outside. Hell, Chancellor

Bishop may have seen it happen firsthand, back when he was out roaming the Wastes, along with my biological parents and Erik's. But why'd they never tell us about this? Does Commander Bishop know? Hudson?

"I should not be alive," Jumaro adds, eyes quivering as they focus on me. "I would not be, if I had not escaped to the tunnels."

"What are you saying?" I frown.

"I showed no signs of contamination at first. Everything checked out. Screeners at the port said I should count myself lucky. It was not until later, when my body began to change...that I had to quit my maintenance job and go into hiding. Others were not so lucky." He stares up at me. "They were exterminated."

I find that hard to believe. "Other soldiers like you, who were accidentally exposed to the elements. You expect me to believe your superiors had them...killed?"

"Yes," he whispers.

This doesn't track. With Hawthorne no longer Chancellor, the Domes have been distancing themselves from the authoritarian ways of our past. We still have a long way to go, but executing the infected? It's barbaric. We don't do that. We find a place for the sick, usually in Dome 6.

"So you weren't discharged because of your accident."

Another head jerk in the negative. "My tour of duty was over, and I was honorably discharged. But I knew better than to re-up. I did not think my luck would hold out." He exhales through his fangs, returning his gaze to the ceiling. "Some part of me must have known...this is what I would become."

He took a maintenance job instead of another tour of

duty. Found the tunnels under our streets to his liking. Figured he'd hide out down there once his body started mutating. Ate the occasional curfew enforcer who wandered where he shouldn't have.

"You didn't care about the artifact Raul was carrying." I appraise the monster before me. "You didn't kill him to get to it, under his armor."

"Enforcer Ortega?" Jumaro snorts, and yellow bile streams from his nasal cavity. "We paid him off. He agreed to be elsewhere when we hit the jewelry shop."

I narrow my gaze. "Do you feel any remorse for murdering him?"

Jumaro stares at me longer than necessary. "I feel nothing, Sera Chen. Nothing but hunger."

23

Boots clomp onto the tile floor as a figure garbed in black swings out between the mangled speedlift doors on a rope. Not something you see every day.

"Time to go." He levels a large-caliber handgun on Dunn, a weapon both he and I recognize by now—along with the man wielding it. "Don't even think about it, clone."

Drasko. Not coming to our rescue. Working with Jumaro Tanaka.

This day couldn't get much weirder.

Dunn holds the minigun ready but doesn't fire. The three conscious members of Jumaro's crew dash past Drasko and dive into the shaft, clutching onto the rope and climbing up like skilled circus performers.

"Get on your feet," Drasko barks at Tanaka.

"What the hell is going on?" I take a step toward my old friend.

"We are." Drasko's expression remains neutral. "You're coming with us, Chen. The clone stays here."

Dunn shakes his head. "Do not think for a second that I—"

"Want me to shoot you again?" Drasko steps forward, handgun aimed at Dunn's faceplate. Not intimidated in the least by the minigun in his metal hands.

My partner doesn't flinch.

Grunting, Jumaro tries in vain to roll to his feet. I've fallen over a few times myself wearing that exo, and while it takes some abdominal fortitude to get up again, it's not that difficult. But something about the way his body's changed makes it impossible for him now. Which means he's not as strong as he looks.

So the sooner we can pry him out of that exoskeleton, the better.

I could lend a hand, but I don't. Because after what this monster did to Raul, I like seeing him struggle.

"I'd be more concerned with the damage that minigun could do." I take another step toward Drasko.

"Disconnected from the exo like that? It won't do diddly."

I suppose he should know; he installed the damn thing. Unless he's bluffing.

"How are you involved in all this?" I'm at a loss.

"I've got my reasons." He glances at Jumaro, not fazed in the least by the former soldier's appearance. "I said we're leaving."

Tanaka hisses a string of curses, rocking side to side but no closer to standing than he was a minute ago.

"Fang-face was too busy sharing his life story," Drasko mutters, and I notice a comm device identical to Jumaro's clipped to the collar of his tunic. He must have been listening in on our conversation earlier.

"You reactivated the exo for Mirela Edwards." My tone is flat. "Why?"

"No more questions. You—take five steps back." Drasko advances, shoving his handgun up against my partner's faceplate with a clink. Dunn remains rooted. "Chen, I'm gonna need you to climb up to the roof. Aerocar's waiting. You've got three seconds to get a move on, or I shoot your partner in the head. Again."

Cut him off at the knees, I think at Dunn, even as *This can't be happening* flashes through my mind.

Dunn pulls the trigger.

The minigun clicks. No rotating muzzle. No blaze of weapons fire.

A split-second before Drasko fires his weapon, I tackle my partner to the ground. The gunshot goes off like a bomb in the short hallway, the round burying itself in the far wall. I stare at him in disbelief. If I hadn't intervened, he would have shot Dunn in the head. At close range like that, it would have shattered his faceplate and punched its way straight through his skull, killing him instantly.

"Told you it wouldn't work." Drasko keeps his handgun trained on my partner, but his cold gaze is fixed on me. "Last warning, Chen." He nods toward the open doors of the speedlift, gaping like a mouth bent out of shape. "Go. Now."

My fear that he's gone rogue appears to be justified. This isn't the Drasko I know.

"*Catch-22*," I mutter, searching for any hint of recognition in his eyes. "A friend of mine told me to check it out. I'm thinking he might be in a no-win situation."

Drasko raises his chin. "I'm thinking you are, as well."

He's got a point. If I go with them, they'll expect me to lead the way to wherever the Prometheus AI is kept. Good luck with that, since I have no idea where it is. But if I refuse, Drasko will put a bullet in Dunn's head. I never would have thought such a thing possible until this moment.

I glance at my partner. It wouldn't take much for him to swing that minigun up into Drasko's jaw and send him flying the length of the hallway. After seeing Dunn in motion a few minutes ago, I have no doubt he'd be able to move faster than Drasko's trigger-pull. But my partner won't go after Drasko without permission. Because Drasko is supposed to be one of us. And clones are conditioned never to assault a LawKeeper, even an undercover one.

But I'm under no such restriction.

"Erik says your family's enjoying the good life on his farm." I notice a flicker of unease pass through Drasko's eyes. Target acquired: I've found the right nerve ending. Now all I do is press. "You know, you never told me how you managed to swing that. Moving them out of Dome 6. Must've cost you a small fortune to grease the right palms—or make certain eyes look the other way."

Drasko clenches his jaw.

"Maybe that little jewelry heist was the ticket. Priceless artifacts, right? Just the sort of thing to satisfy folks in high places. With your share, you could pay—"

"I had nothing to do with that," he grates out between his teeth.

For some reason, I believe him. "So it was Jumaro and Mirela. Guess that makes sense, considering their strained relationship with Mommy Dearest. But why'd they project a holo of your muscle car? What was that all about?" I pause in the silence, watching him for any sign that I'm right. But he's as cold as stone. "They were ensuring that I'd be put on this case." Not to mention cluing me in as to his involvement.

Drasko winces suddenly, as if someone might be shrieking at him on comms. "We're on our way," he says quietly into the device on his collar.

Then he faces me. And he lowers his gun. In his eyes, I see the man I know.

I slug him across the jaw as hard as I can, and he topples over like a pile of bricks.

"That was unexpected." Dunn sets the useless minigun down.

I snatch Drasko's handgun. "He gave me an opening. I took it." I take his comm device as well. Then I gesture at the eight unconscious bodies littering the tiled floor. "Grab some clothes. We're going to the roof."

Dunn doesn't hesitate. He goes straight to Drasko and strips him of his greatcoat, trousers, and boots with the bedside manner of a wrecking ball. In no time, he's covered up his mechanical parts as well as the skintight bodysuit that left little to the imagination. Not sure why he's still wearing the helmet. All of its scanning functions were knocked out when Baatar hit him with that EMP. Maybe he needs to wear something familiar to feel like himself. Or could he be self-conscious of those facial scars?

Instead of thrashing around, Jumaro lies flat on his back now. Taking a breather. Or waiting to see what I do next.

I try not to disappoint.

"Who's on the roof?" I aim Drasko's big gun between his bulging eyes. "Baatar and Mirela? Anybody else?" I need to know what Dunn and I will be walking into. "They've got an aerocar waiting. Drasko was the pilot." But either of Baatar's security clones would be able to fly the vehicle. "Start talking, or I start shooting."

Jumaro hisses up at me with nothing but spite in his unhuman expression. "You won't shoot—"

I lower my arm and pull the trigger. The handgun kicks like nobody's business, but I manage to hold onto it one-handed, and the blast is almost deafening. So is Jumaro's scream as the round plows into his leg with a burst of blood. Red blood, as one would expect to come out of a human.

"Damn you, Sera Chen!" he rasps, exo-braces clanking against the floor as he grabs hold of his wounded limb. "Damn you straight to hell!"

"Did you hear that, Mirela?" I speak into Drasko's comm device. "I've got your boyfriend. And I've taken out eight of your crew. So how about you come down here, and we have a little talk? Just you and me. No secret agents."

Silence—except for Jumaro's cursing.

Then a familiar voice comes on the line: "Mirela would very much like to repay you for the injury you have inflicted upon her loved one. But that will have to wait until another time." Baatar pauses dramatically. "We'll be seeing you, Investigator Chen."

I spin to face Dunn and break into a sprint. "The roof. They're taking off."

My partner's right behind me as I jam the handgun into my empty holster and climb into the speedlift shaft, illuminated only by dull amber emergency lights. Foregoing the rope, I opt for the maintenance ladder, clambering upward until I reach the roof access point. With my neuro offline until MedTech fixes it, there's no way to prove to the security system that I'm a LawKeeper and should be allowed entry to the roof gardens and landing pad outside. Even during a building-wide lockdown.

But Dunn has a workaround.

You wouldn't think two people could share the same

length of ladder, but we manage somehow, each of us clinging to a side rail as he reaches up and plows his mechanical fist against the hatch like a powerful battering ram. Once, twice, third time's the charm. The hatch flies open, swinging outward off broken hinges, and I pull myself into the blue-tinted morning light.

Just in time to see a sleek, black aerocar lift off and dive over the side of the domescraper. The sort of vehicle that government-types like to ride around in.

I draw Drasko's gun and charge across the well-manicured lawn, gripping the hand cannon out in front of me. But by the time I've reached the line of shrubbery along the roof's edge, the aerocar has already slipped into orderly aerial traffic lanes, and there's no way I'm firing a projectile weapon after it now. Even if I managed to hit Baatar's vehicle and throw it off-course, it could collide with another and then another, endangering innocent bystanders. The results could be catastrophic.

So I watch them go, and as a trio of police aerocars approach with red and blue lights flashing, I take solace in the fact that we've knocked a few members of the Prometheus cult out of play. Along with a co-leader, if that's Jumaro's role when he's not lurking underground, hunting for his next meal.

As for Drasko... I don't know what to think.

"His shot was off by three millimeters," Dunn says.

I turn to find him standing behind me in Drasko's clothes, seeming to read my mind again. Guess we're on the same wavelength. "So I didn't need to tackle you the way I did?"

"That is correct." His helmet's dark faceplate hides his

expression, but it sounds like there might be the makings of a smile under there.

"He intentionally missed." And he let me knock him out. That much was obvious. "He's in too deep, whatever this is. He's looking for a way out." I shake my head. "His family's involved, somehow."

I look at the comm device in my palm. It's just a little bigger than a corn kernel.

"Do you think they are listening?" Dunn keeps his hands behind his back as two of the black & white aerocars land on the roof. The third will be setting down at ground level. Standard procedure during a lockdown.

"Mirela and Baatar?" Assuming that's who was in the getaway vehicle.

He nods.

I raise my hand and speak to the device: "We have Jumaro on murder and assault charges. You'll never see him again, Mirela."

"Don't be so sure about that," Baatar replies.

Then the kernel threatens to burn a hole into my skin, and I drop it, stifling a yelp. On the ground, the comm device dissolves in a hissing puddle of smoke.

"Damn spy gear," I mutter, rubbing my sore palm along my hip.

"We should ensure that Jumaro Tanaka is where we left him, Investigator Chen." Dunn turns back toward the roof hatch.

"Why wouldn't he be? I shot him in the leg, for crying out loud." But I follow my partner anyway, and I gesture for the patrol officers stepping out of the two aerocars to tag along. "This way," I call back to the six of them, and they nod, hustling to catch up.

Dunn's about to take the ladder down the speedlift shaft, but I tug on his arm and nod toward the officers who head straight to the stairwell door instead. Each one is decked out in riot gear with a bulletproof shield and shock-prod. They came prepared for the worst, after what happened at the airlock last night.

The security system scans their neuros, and the door slides open instantly. But the officers hang back, waiting for me to lead the charge. Right. Because I'm lead investigator on the scene.

I step forward with Drasko's handgun down at my side. "One flight down. We left eight insurgents unconscious and one incapacitated. Be advised, the conscious one is wearing an exo-suit, and he's got a taste for fresh meat—of the human variety."

The officers glance at each other, faces blank, none of them sure whether I'm kidding. They'll soon find out.

Holding Drasko's gun out in front of me in both hands, I descend the stairwell at double-speed with seven pairs of boots echoing behind me. I hit the crash bar as I reach the door to the 120th floor and step out into the undersized hallway leading up to Nevah Edwards' home.

For the most part, things are just as Dunn and I left them. The Children of Tomorrow remain on the floor, some unconscious, others moaning as they begin to come to. Drasko's still out cold. And my exo is still lying on its back.

Except now it's empty.

A trail of blood across the floor tiles shows the route Jumaro took after extricating himself from the harness. He went straight for the speedlift shaft.

"He couldn't have gone far," I mutter, dashing to the mangled doors and peering down into the amber-hued darkness, too murky to see much of anything clearly. But allowing my night-vision to assert itself, the shaft transforms into a bluish-white chasm with a dark human-shaped figure descending the ladder a dozen floors below us. "There!"

Dunn and the officers gather around.

"I don't see anything." One of them shines a flashlight down the shaft, and the others murmur in agreement.

"I see him," Dunn says. I know he can't see squat, since his helmet sensors are offline, but I appreciate the vote of confidence. "Would you prefer to lead the way, Investigator Chen?"

I nod. "Prepare these miscreants for transport," I tell the patrol officers as I climb into the shaft and grab onto the ladder running along the plasticon-brick wall. "Notify the correctional center. Eight incoming."

They glance at each other. "You expect us to fly them—?"

"That's right." I start making my way down. "Good luck!" I call back.

Dunn follows, his metal hands clanking against the rungs above me. "How far ahead of us is Jumaro Tanaka?" he asks in a low tone once we're three levels below the penthouse, his voice echoing faintly around us.

I glance over my shoulder. "Maybe fifteen floors." Impressive, considering that wounded leg. "We'll have to pick up the pace."

He nods. Good thing neither of us is afraid of heights.

As we descend, doing our best not to slip and plummet four hundred meters to our deaths, I bring up a delicate topic. "You lied. When you said you saw him."

"Yes."

"I thought clones were conditioned to always tell the truth."

A short pause, punctuated by our quick, syncopated rhythm down the ladder. "We are."

"Have you ever lied before?"

"No."

Well, that's a relief.

"Have you ever lied to me, Investigator Chen?"

That gives me pause. He didn't ask if I've ever lied; I suppose it's a given, since I'm a living, breathing human being. What he wants to know is whether I've ever lied to *him*.

I wish I could reply *No* as quickly as he did. But I also want to be honest with him. And the truth is, "I try not to."

My voice hangs in the stale air.

A pained grunt echoes far below us. Despite his mutations and potential dust addiction, Tanaka isn't superhuman. Yet he soldiers on.

So do we, our pace steady. I could be wrong, but I think we're gaining on him.

24

"You know how this ends, Jumaro," I call down, almost sure he can hear me. "Once I get close enough not to miss, I'll shoot you again. If you're lucky, you'll somehow manage to hang onto the ladder."

No response.

"Now, if you need a break, my partner can force open the speedlift doors on any floor you like. He's got some major upper body strength. We can sit down, catch our breath. Maybe tend to that wound of yours." I wait, hoping to hear him slow down.

I don't. But now he's grunting with every rung, sounds like. That wounded leg has got to be smarting a bit.

"I get it, you know. Why you and Mirela would want to resurrect the Prometheus AI." I let him chew on that for a moment. "You think gene therapy will heal you. That somehow, DNA from those miracle kids running around the Domes will reverse what happened to you."

Only the sounds of our boots striking the ladder answer me.

"You're desperate. And scared. You didn't want to kill Enforcer Ortega. But that hunger you've been fighting overwhelmed you. Now you're afraid you won't be able to hold it in check. That you might even hurt Mirela without meaning to."

After a few beats, Dunn says quietly, "He may not be able to hear you."

I reach out telepathically and try not to flinch when I make contact with Jumaro's tortured mind. The human side of him, his original self, squirms within the confines of his leathery flesh, wrestling with doubts. Amidst the writhing chaos, I sense a slim ray of warmth. Of hope. Love, even. But it's slowly dying out, and I have to wonder if it's somehow connected to his relationship with Mirela.

As the monster asserts itself, taking over Jumaro, usurping every aspect of his being, is he despairing that he'll never be able to see his girlfriend again?

"He can hear me," I tell Dunn, loud enough for Tanaka to hear. "There's a battle raging inside him. And he's losing."

"Do you think the sort of gene therapy Trezon underwent would help someone suffering such abnormal mutations?"

No idea. "It's a long shot." Jumaro is grasping at straws.

Or maybe it was Mirela, equally desperate, worried about the man she loves, who discovered Trezon's successful gene therapy—if you call the ability to turn yourself invisible on command a success. That would explain why she was never counted among the Prometheus cult until now. She never had a reason to be.

But the AI didn't claim to cure physical maladies. It promised to bestow *demigod*-like abilities upon those who received the DNA of the Twenty's children. To make it possible for them to live outside the Ten Domes.

Why would Jumaro want that? It was outside our walls

where his protective gear was compromised and he came into contact with those fast-acting mutagens.

"Could he and Mirela Edwards have robbed her mother's jewelry shop in order to pay for Agent Baatar's services?" Dunn's mind is going a mile a minute, attempting to connect the disparate dots we've encountered over the last twelve hours.

"An agent moonlighting as a mercenary."

"Assuming his agent status is not a fabricated identity," Dunn replies, "designed to fool our neuro-scanners into believing he is truly a government agent."

More spy crap? I wouldn't put it past the guy. "I still can't shake the feeling he's working for Governor Raniero. Off the books, maybe." Setting events in motion that will culminate in James Bishop being voted out of office.

Dunn is silent for a minute or two. Then, "Should our pursuit of Jumaro Tanaka take us one hundred twenty floors to ground level—"

"Hell no. We'll catch him long before that." I hope.

"But in case you need to rest—"

"My arms aren't even feeling it yet. How about you?"

"My prosthetic arms do not feel anything, Investigator Chen."

Should've seen that one coming.

Sera...

The voice in my head is a familiar one, but that doesn't make it any less unexpected. My pace down the ladder slows momentarily.

Sera, it's me. Erik.

Figured as much, I reply mind-to-mind. *Where are you?* He must be somewhere nearby in Dome 1. He sounds like he's right beside me.

Are you still inside the Edwards Estates?

The speedlift shaft. Dunn and I are pursuing a suspect.

The daemon?

That gives me pause. *What?*

You're in trouble, Sera. Governor Raniero is all over the Link. He's got footage of a...daemon...wearing your exo, terrorizing residents of the Estates. He's saying you're part of some high-level cover-up. Crazy stuff, but it's gaining traction. People are believing it.

What the hell is he talking about? *Erik, I don't have time for political garbage right now. I've got to catch this guy—*

He's dangerous, Sera. If what Daiyna says is true, he's not even human anymore.

My pace slows again. *You've been talking to Daiyna?*

She's here with me. We're across the street. I tried hailing you earlier, but you're offline. I tracked your last-known coordinates to the Estates. He pauses. *The place is a zoo. Cops everywhere. They've got the parking level blocked off, no way in.* Another pause. *I can't locate your drones.*

They're out of commission. I frown. *Why is Daiyna with you?*

She saw the latest broadcast from Raniero. The security footage of your exo with a daemon inside it—

You keep using that word.

Daemon? Daiyna's term. Bishop would probably call it a muto or something.

So I was right. James Bishop and my biological mother are familiar with the bizarre transformation taking over Jumaro Tanaka's body. Because they witnessed it firsthand out in the Wastes.

"Investigator Chen?" Dunn notices that I've slowed down.

"It's Erik." I make up for lost time without being reckless, my boots and hands moving quickly down the rungs. "He's inside my head."

"Does Erik Paine have anything helpful to share?"

"Not really."

I heard that, Erik mutters telepathically.

This is a man we're chasing. He's a person, not a...thing.

Does he look like a person? I can picture Erik quirking an eyebrow at me. *Tell me if I'm close: buggy yellow eyes, no nose to speak of, freaky fangs? Skin like a faux-leather handbag that's been out in the sun too long?*

I can't deal with his level of obnoxious right now. *Erik—*

Raniero's saying Bishop knew about this. A Dome 1 citizen somehow became contaminated on the Chancellor's watch, and he kept it quiet. You don't have to tell me any top secret details, but I think there's more to it than that.

You'd be right, I admit. *Still putting the pieces together. Now stay out of my head so I can do my damn job.*

Right. Just...be careful, okay? Don't let that thing bite you. Daiyna says they're meat-eaters. Human meat. Gross, right? And don't exit at ground level. It's a real circus out here, and I have a feeling they're planning to arrest you on sight.

I choose to ignore that.

"How close are we to overtaking Jumaro Tanaka, Investigator Chen?" Dunn asks in a low tone, one of his boots a rung above my hands at all times.

I glance at the negative space below me glowing bluish-white in my night-vision. Jumaro's dark form continues to scramble ever downward, but he's lost some of his momentum. Maybe he's hungry again.

"Eight or nine floors now."

"I could slide down the side rails and intercept him in a matter of seconds," Dunn offers.

Out of the question. "He'll try to eat your face off."

"My helmet should impede his efforts. And my metal arms would not be much to his liking."

"He'd find something to chomp on. Like your throat."

Dunn doesn't reply to that. "At our current rate, and assuming Jumaro Tanaka does not increase or decrease the speed of his descent, we should overtake him within the next fifteen minutes. That is my best estimate."

"Good mathing, partner. Let me guess: two trains leave the station going the same direction, but one is ten minutes ahead of the other?"

"What does our situation have to do with trains, Investigator Chen?"

I shake my head. "Nothing. Just reminded me of the word problems our math teacher would give us when I was a kid. Back at Camp Hope, the boarding school where we..." I trail off. Those memories are blurry at best. Not something I usually think about.

"Where the Twenty were raised, prior to being placed in your adoptive families."

Right. Two sets of ten siblings, created from genetic material that Daiyna, Luther, Samson, and Shechara did not donate willingly. But because of the nightmare they endured, Erik and I and eighteen others like us are alive today. We were able to grow up and learn math and science while our biological parents fought for their survival on another continent, thousands of kilometers away.

Now here I am, pursuing a horror just like the kind they faced in the North American Wastes. Is history repeating itself? Is Jumaro the first to become contaminated—or only the first that we're aware of? Here's an even more terrifying thought: If his condition is contagious, will the Domes be overrun by mutants like him?

Once it's no longer safe for us within our walls, we'll have to go outside. There will be no other choice. Those thousand children born from the DNA of the Twenty will be forced to make genetic donations of their own. Then we'll see if the procedure Trezon received will be the ticket to breathing in the Wastes with no dire consequences, just as the Prometheus AI promised.

Did it somehow know this was where we were headed? A crazy thought.

Chancellor Bishop knew about Jumaro's mutation and kept it quiet—that's what Raniero is telling our citizens. A government cover-up at the highest level, designed to hide the truth. That any one of us at any time could turn into the monstrosity Jumaro has become. All it takes is a breath of contaminated air from the outside world.

FILE CORRUPTED—the error message I received when I tried to access two different images of Jumaro attacking Enforcer Ortega in that maintenance tunnel. The first was transmitted via videolink, straight to my lenses. The second was recorded by Wink. I should have been able to bring up both of them, but for some reason I couldn't. Almost as if someone in high places didn't want me to.

The Governor had no problem obtaining recent footage from the Edwards Estates' security system and splashing it all over the Linkstream. Is he responsible for blocking my access? Agent Baatar at work again, or someone else—an operative embedded within the ranks of LawKeepers, tasked with reporting to Baatar whenever the analysts are offline? That might explain why weird things are tending to go down when the power's out at HQ.

"Once we manage to reach Jumaro Tanaka, how do you intend to go about apprehending him—without having our faces eaten off?" Dunn asks.

"Figured I'd shoot him again." Not that a gunshot wound seems to slow the freak down much. "If we can't talk him nicely into exiting at the next floor."

I glance down at our quarry. Jumaro is trembling now as he descends. Once or twice, he nearly slips from the rungs.

"Careful there," I call to him. "How will Mirela take it if you end up a bloody puddle after all this?"

"Come any closer, Sera Chen," he hisses across the distance—five floors now, soon to be four, "and it will be *your* blood and bones decorating the bottom of this shaft."

"Police are waiting at ground level. You have nowhere to go." I pause to let that sink in. "What's your big plan here, Jumaro? Lead me on a stupid chase while your girlfriend and Baatar do the real work? Is that all you are in their grand scheme: infidel bait?"

"You will either join us or *die*!" he rasps. "Death to all unbelievers! Prometheus will rise again!"

At least I've got him talking. "What does Mirela see in you, anyway? Certainly not the man she fell in love with. Not anymore. Now, that Baatar guy, he just might be her type. Does she happen to like tall, dark, and muscles?"

Jumaro comes to a halt and throws back his head to growl—an unnatural, guttural sound dripping with menace.

Then he reverses course, climbing fast, his bulging eyes fixed on me as he closes the distance between us.

Unexpected.

I loop one arm around the side rail to brace myself and draw Drasko's gun with my free hand, training the muzzle on Jumaro's fanged face below me. "My father is a doctor. Right here in Dome 1. Best MedCenter in all of Eurasia." Time to play good cop. "He can help you. Stop the mutations—hell, maybe even reverse them."

Not sure he's listening anymore. The look on his messed-up face is nothing but raw hunger. He's the predator. I'm the prey.

"Investigator Chen." Dunn slides down the opposite side rail until we're face to face. "He is not interested in conversation."

"I'm getting that."

"You must shoot him."

I don't want to kill him. He didn't ask to become this monster, to be overwhelmed by this ravenous hunger. I wish there was some way to get him the help he needs. But clambering up a ladder above an eighty-floor drop, with a hand cannon staring him straight in the eye, there's little chance this is going to end well for him. Even if I don't send a projectile round through his head or chest, a nonlethal wound will do just as much damage if it causes him to lose his grip, and he goes plummeting to the shaft floor.

I have to try to keep him alive.

I pull the trigger, and in the confines of the shaft, the shot is a bomb blast. Jumaro snarls as the round hits him in the shoulder, throwing him back on that side and taking his right arm out of play. It hangs limp, yet he manages to hold on with his left, his upward momentum lost for the moment.

But not for long. He lurches up a rung, shoving off with his unwounded leg and clutching onto the side rail one-handed. His pulsating, lidless eyes never look away from me. His mouth hangs open, drooling, fangs glistening in the weird light of my night-vision.

By all appearances, Jumaro Tanaka has left the building. All that's left is a very hungry beast.

"Stop right there!" I shout, my voice echoing above and below us.

Unfazed, he lunges up another rung.

"I can subdue him." Dunn looks ready to slide down and intercept.

I shake my head. "Open those doors."

He drops to the next level and braces himself on the ladder with both legs. Then he reaches out and digs his metal fingers in between the plasteel doors, all the while keeping an eye on Jumaro—two floors away but steadily closing, blood oozing from his wounds and splattering across the rungs beneath him.

The doors are no match for my partner's mechanical arms, and they slide apart easily, revealing a vacant hallway twice the length of the one outside Nevah Edwards' penthouse. Warm, bright light spills into the shaft.

When Jumaro passes that floor, you grab hold of him, I think at Dunn. *Drag him inside and pin him down. I'll be right behind you.*

Dunn's helmet dips in the affirmative, and he steps into the hallway, out of sight. I have no idea if this will work, but what other options do we have? We can't intercept Jumaro without endangering him or ourselves. We've got to get him off this ladder. And if Dunn can keep Jumaro's fangs and claws at arms' length long enough, I should be able to come up behind him and crack Drasko's gun over the back of his leathery head.

Assuming all goes according to plan.

I keep the gun aimed at Jumaro's forehead as he ascends in herky-jerky fashion, and I hold position, even as every muscle in my body screams at me to climb out of harm's way. I've never been a fan of those survival horror VR StoryLines, but this feels like a scene torn from any one of them. The hungry creature just a few meters away looks like the sort of thing birthed by a game designer's deranged imagination.

Except this is a human being. Or he was, once. He's been fighting the monster while clinging to the remnants of his humanity. But now the monster is in complete control, and all it knows is its insatiable appetite.

"Jumaro, stop!" Can he even understand me anymore?

I fire a round over his head as he enters the patch of light thrown from the open doorway. The sound of the gunshot makes him flinch, disoriented for just a second—but that's all Dunn needs to reach out and grab hold of him, hauling him off the ladder and throwing him facedown onto the hallway floor. Jumaro squirms and thrashes, making strange gargling noises deep in his throat, but Dunn manages to stay on top of him, shoving his mechanical knee into Jumaro's back while pinning both arms to the floor tiles. Restraining the monster.

So, not such a bad plan, after all.

But as I climb down and step into the hallway, keeping Drasko's handgun trained on Jumaro, one question weighs on my mind.

What do we do with him now?

25

Thanks to my partner and I both being offline, there's no way to call in backup, and no way for any of the officers on site to locate us here on the eighty-seventh floor. After what Erik said, I'm not sure I'd even want them to. Not if somebody's feeding them bad intel about me. So we've got to figure this out for ourselves. Find a safe place, and contact our superiors. Let Hudson and Commander Bishop know what we've discovered so far, and that we have the creature formerly known as Jumaro Tanaka in custody.

Meanwhile, I can't expect Dunn to hold him down indefinitely.

I grip the big handgun by the barrel and swing it down hard, hitting the back of Tanaka's head. He collapses instantly, all the fight gone out of him, eyes staring without seeing.

"Restrain him." I holster the gun and fish through a button-down pocket in my trousers, coming up with a couple zip-tie cuffs. "Hands and feet."

Dunn takes one and cinches it around Jumaro's wrists while I take care of his ankles. "Shall I carry him to the roof, Investigator Chen? The patrol officers may still be on site."

"Someone corrupted the video files of Tanaka. Before

Baatar knocked out my augments, I couldn't bring up either image."

Dunn faces me. "Which would lead one to believe that Jumaro Tanaka's condition is a closely guarded secret."

"That's the line Raniero is spouting. He was able to procure video footage from security cameras on the 120th floor—of Jumaro wearing my exo. He's saying I'm involved with the cover-up."

"That footage was undoubtedly obtained by Agent Baatar before he left the building." Dunn pauses. "Am I correct in assuming you would rather avoid the patrol officers?"

"For the time being. Baatar gave Jumaro my exo just so the Governor could have that footage to share with the public. To build his case against Chancellor Bishop, his daughter, and her pet *demigod*." I curse under my breath. "What the hell does Raniero have against me?"

Dunn's helmet tilts to one side. "If you are correct, then you are merely a means to an end—a way for Governor Raniero to accomplish what he has wanted to do for some time now: remove James Bishop from office. He may have nothing personal against you at all."

"It feels personal," I mutter. "Someone didn't want me accessing those images of Tanaka attacking Raul and Wink."

"Could it be someone looking out for you?" Dunn shrugs. He's getting better at it. Or the absence of his armor allows his shoulders to move more naturally. "If there is no evidence that you were ever aware of Jumaro Tanaka's transformation, then you could not possibly be involved in any potential cover-up."

Can't argue with that logic. Could it be Commander Bishop keeping an eye out for me? Or maybe Chief Inspector

Hudson, despite our differences in the past? Hell, it might even be Erik for all I know, sticking his nose where it doesn't belong. He's proven on more than one occasion to be fairly adept when it comes to hacking into systems he has no business accessing.

Dunn turns toward the open doors to the speedlift shaft. "That appears to be our only way out. But there will be police officers waiting, whether we climb up to the roof or slide down to the parking garage."

He's really got his mind set on sliding down that ladder. Hate to disappoint.

"Can you carry him?" I nod toward Jumaro.

Dunn kneels down beside him and is about to sling his unconscious body over one shoulder in a firefighter's carry. But that's when Jumaro's fanged jaws start chomping.

"Drop him!" I lunge forward and give his limp body a shove, sending it to the floor with a thump and a groan. The freakish, lidless eyes remain wide open, making it difficult to tell if he's out cold or not, but his stillness would lead one to believe so. "He looked ready to take a chunk out of your throat."

"He is unconscious." Dunn nudges him with the toe of his boot. No response.

"Tell that to his teeth." Cursing under my breath, I slip out of my jacket and grab hold of the tunic sleeve underneath, tearing it free from the shoulder seam. "Here." I hand it to Dunn. "Gag him. And keep those fangs where you can see them."

"Some sort of autonomic response, perhaps?" Dunn muses, reaching toward Jumaro's gaping jaws without hesitation. The fangs don't look interested in the proximity of my partner's prosthetic hands.

"Could be. Even when he's unconscious, the hunger remains."

Dunn glances at me. "You pity him, in spite of the fact that he murdered your friend, Enforcer Ortega."

I guess I do. The man needs help—if there's still a man inside that horror. I try reaching out with my telepathy, but I can't sense Jumaro amidst the storm raging inside him. He's been swallowed up by it. Or devoured.

"We need to get him to my dad. He'll know what to do. Stop the mutation or whatever it is…" I trail off, shaking my head.

"It is unlikely the officers we encounter will be interested in escorting him to MedCenter 1, particularly if they have orders to apprehend you and shoot him on sight."

I have an idea. "What time do you think it is?"

Neither one of us has Link access, but if anybody's likely to be in tune with some sort of ethereal internal chronometer, it would be Dunn.

"It was nearing ten hundred hours when Agent Baatar hit me with that EMP gun on the 120th floor."

"And that had to be over an hour ago." Easy to lose track of time when you're climbing down a speedlift shaft.

"A reasonable estimate."

"My dad's meeting Luther in Dome 6 at fourteen hundred…" He's probably already on his way. "We'll take Jumaro there."

"To Dome 6?"

I nod.

"Past the officers waiting to apprehend us?"

"We'll have help." I'm about to reach out to Erik

telepathically, figuring if anybody can whip up a stupendous distraction on the fly it's him, but that's when a familiar buzzing whir echoes from the speedlift shaft, and Blink floats into the hallway to hover beside me. "Hello there." Not sure how else to respond to its unexpected appearance. "Thought you bit the dust earlier."

"No, Investigator Chen," the drone replies in its customary monotone. "I was able to evade the security clones' weapons fire."

"What have you been doing since?"

"Keeping a low profile. Searching for you."

I give it a wink. "Good job." Then I face Dunn. "Told you we'd have help."

"I am not sure how a single weaponized drone will be able to assist us in avoiding the attention of multiple patrol officers on site."

"Don't underestimate my drone." Turning to Blink, I ask, "Are you online?"

"Yes, Investigator Chen."

"Hail Chief Inspector Hudson."

"Hailing," Blink replies. Silence holds the moment.

Thirty seconds pass. It appears that Hudson may no longer be accepting my calls.

Then Blink's holo-projector switches on, and a three-dimensional rendering of Hudson's head appears in blue-white light before me.

I've never seen him so angry.

"What the *hell* is going on over there, Chen?" he demands, eyes blazing and teeth bared. "Why have you and your clone been offline for two *hours*?"

"Agent Baatar hit us with a localized EMP, sir. But we

managed to apprehend Jumaro Tanaka—Mirela Edwards' boyfriend. His disfigurements were caused by accidental exposure to the elements while scavenging in the Wastes." I gesture toward the motionless body on the floor, bound and gagged. "His associates, including Drasko, should now be in custody. We left them in the capable hands of patrol officers on—"

"Stand down, Investigator. You and your clone are to surrender yourselves to officers en route." He dips his chin and subvocalizes *End lockdown, but keep all residents sequestered in their units. Chen is on the eighty-seventh floor. Proceed with caution.*

Good thing I can read lips.

"The optics on this have gone from bad to worse, Chen. We cannot afford to give the Governor any more ammunition to use against our department."

"I can explain—"

"I am sure you can." His face is a mask now, devoid of expression. "And you will have ample opportunity to do so, once you're in custody and escorted to HQ. Trust me, your debriefing will be quite thorough."

The speedlift doors slide shut automatically as power is restored, and the automated voice returns to announce from the ceiling speakers, "Lockdown ended. Lockdown ended. The Edwards Estates are no longer on lockdown. However, all residents are to remain in their units until further notice, by order of the police. Thank you for your patience."

The officers Hudson is sending to apprehend me will arrive in less than a minute, now that the speedlift is operational again.

Without turning away from Hudson's hologram, I think

at Dunn, *We have to leave. Now.* He scoops up Jumaro and throws his unconscious form over one shoulder. Then he waits for me to lead the way out of here.

But I have a few things to tell Hudson first.

"Agent Baatar is working with Raniero, orchestrating events like a puppet master. They're taking advantage of Mirela Edwards and Jumaro Tanaka and the Children of Tomorrow, using them to serve their own purposes. Baatar stole my exo and gave it to Tanaka—"

"I have seen the footage. Twice, in less than twenty-four hours, criminals have used your powered exoskeleton against the people of Eurasia. Thankfully, we now have it in our possession, and it will be dismantled in short order." He gives me a pointed look. "While no one was killed at the Edwards Estates, seeing the monstrosity Tanaka has become will do more than enough damage to the status quo. With the support Governor Raniero is gathering, it is unlikely that James Bishop will serve as Interim Chancellor much longer, or that his daughter will be our Commander." He pauses to glare at me. "We have your carelessness and ineptitude to thank for that, Investigator Chen."

On that note, he ends the transmission, and the holo vanishes.

"That was harsh," Dunn comments.

"He's not wrong." But there's no time to dwell on the mistakes I've made. I have to make things right—somehow. "Stairs." I point out the emergency door at the end of the hall and lead the way. Dunn's right behind me, hauling Jumaro, and Blink keeps pace above us, rotors spinning with a quiet whir.

The speedlift dings, and the polished-to-perfection doors

slide open. But before a single officer has a chance to step out, I give Blınk a telepathic order to act as rear guard. *Do not allow anyone to follow—but do not injure the officers.*

I'm already halfway down to the next floor, boots skimming across steps in the grey plasticon stairwell illuminated by garish white tube-lights, when I hear Blınk unleash a salvo of projectile rounds. Hopefully straight into the floor as a deterrent. Fingers crossed the little drone will be able to evade whatever return fire the officers have in store for it.

"I have a feeling this will add to even worse optics," Dunn says in a low tone, his boots striking a steady rhythm behind me.

"Not a big fan of that term," I mutter.

"And the phrase *going rogue*?"

I exhale. "Guess Baatar was right. They're going to do their best to hang this mess around my neck. And once the Bishops and I are out of the picture, good ol' Hudson will probably enjoy a nice promotion."

Dunn is quiet for a beat. "Do you think he may be attempting to bring you in for your own protection?"

"I don't need protection. I need to figure out what the hell is going on." I glance over my shoulder at him. "Feel free to bail out anytime. You didn't sign up for this. No reason you should lose your career over it."

"The only reason I have been afforded this opportunity to serve as your partner is because of you, Investigator Chen. Your belief in me has made it possible. Furthermore, I believe we are taking the correct course of action. Surrendering ourselves to the authorities will not help anyone at this juncture—other than those who wish to upset the Domes' current power structure."

So I've got one ally. And maybe another, across the street.

You still there? I think at Erik, reaching out telepathically for his mind while taking the steps down as fast as I can. Dunn's having no problem keeping up, even with Jumaro's added weight.

What do you need? Erik replies instantly.

A getaway driver.

On it. A short pause. *Where shall we rendezvous, m'lady?*

Good question, despite its cringeworthy flavor. The front of the building is out. Probably the entire ground floor. LawKeepers will have it sewn up tight, now that I'm on the run.

Around back. How are your leaping abilities these days?

I keep in shape. Thought with a confident smirk, I'm sure. *What floor are you on?*

The placard on the wall says 82 as I round the corner and take the next flight down. *Out of your reach. But we're on our way down.* Not sure I should tell him this, but I suppose it's better that he prepares himself. *We have the suspect in custody—*

The daemon? He would've spluttered in disbelief if we were actually talking.

—and we're taking him to Dome 6. My dad's on his way there. He'll know what to do. I hope.

Erik doesn't have any thoughts on the subject. Other than, *Be careful, Sera.*

I will. See you soon. I end the telepathic transmission and strain to listen for any sounds of gunshots above us. Our fast footfalls echoing around us make it difficult to hear much else. But if those officers were descending the stairwell in pursuit, I'm sure I'd hear them.

I'm about to reach out to Blink for an update when the drone's machine intelligence reaches out to me, instead. Guess I kept the telepathic connection open between us without realizing it.

The officers have left this floor and are taking the speedlift down, Investigator Chen.

They're planning to head us off. Blink's fusillade must have been too hot to handle.

New plan, I think at the drone, my mind racing. Blink can't open the stairwell door, so it can't fly down here and take position ahead of us on a lower floor. Nor can it open the speedlift doors and fly down the shaft. Right now it's stuck on the 87th floor. Nowhere to go. Nothing to do. Except... *Set off another lockdown.*

No idea why the building didn't go back on lockdown as soon as Blink started firing its first salvo. You'd think the domescraper's security system would've recognized such a blatant threat and acted accordingly.

Unless officers on site disabled the protocols...because they just happen to be carrying projectile weapons and don't want their lawkeeping efforts impeded in any way. In which case, Blink could deplete its ammunition stores yet accomplish nothing. No lockdown. The speedlift continues moving right along, carrying that squad of officers on their way down to the 80th or 75th floor where they'll disembark and take the stairwell up to intercept us.

Please explain, Blink says—or thinks, rather.

I need you to create a credible threat to the building's security so that the lockdown protocols will reactivate and stall the speedlift in its shaft.

A short pause as its machine intelligence ponders for a moment. *I can shoot out the ceiling lights.*

Do that.

Dunn and I continue ever downward, passing the 80th floor placard on the way. Then the 79th. The 78th. Too far to hear my drone's automatic fire. No sound yet of officers rushing up the stairs toward us.

And no building-wide lockdown.

Projectile rounds expended, Blink reports. *Switching to flamethrower.*

Wait. *What?* Since when has it had a flamethrower in its arsenal?

"Fire alert. Fire alert," the same automated voice announces from a speaker mounted somewhere in the stairwell. "Fire detected on the eighty-seventh floor. All residents, please remain in your units. There is no need to evacuate. Your fire doors will protect you. Fire suppression systems activated." A short pause. "Speedlift override in effect. Passengers will disembark at ground level and not be allowed to reenter the building while fire alert is in effect. Speedlift will remain inoperational until fire alert has ended."

That'll work.

Blink gives me an update: *Suppression systems are putting out the conflagration. Flamethrower currently at twenty percent. Will continue firing at combustible surfaces until exhausted.*

Weird to imagine my drone hovering to and fro, blasting the hallway with a jet of flame, but I guess that's another one of the upgrades it received from Drasko a while back. It's just never had a chance to flex these particular muscles before.

The next ten minutes pass without incident, our boots

beating the same rhythm down every flight, floor placards passing by, decreasing in number. As we reach the seventeenth floor, I'm starting to think we might actually get out of here.

"Fire contained and subdued. Fire alert no longer in effect." If I didn't know better, I might think the security system sounds proud of itself.

Flamethrower at zero percent, Blink reports simultaneously.

Good work. It did its best and bought us some time. *Sit tight until we can come back for you.*

Acknowledged.

"Speedlift is now operational," the automated voice adds.

The officers will split their forces, half taking the speedlift, half the stairwell. Once the stairwell crew intercepts us, they'll notify their counterparts on the speedlift, who will disembark on the floor above our location and take the stairs down to block our retreat, trapping us in the middle. Standard procedure.

They'll know I'm aware of this. And they'll expect me to act accordingly.

So it would be in our best interest to try something...unpredictable.

26

Upon reaching the fifteenth floor, I shove open the door to the hallway beyond and head toward the opposite end where a windowall glows with warm afternoon light. Unlike those uppermost levels where a single resident like Nevah Edwards owns every square foot—or maybe half, in some cases—the closer you get to the ground, the more units there are. Here I pass three sets of ornate double doors on each side of the tiled hallway before reaching the end.

If any of the residents happen to glance at their security feeds, they'll be treated to a peculiar sight making its way past their domiciles: a clone in everyday clothing instead of armor—but with his helmet still on, of course—carrying a nightmare from the collective subconsciousness of humankind over one shoulder, bound and gagged, fanged jaws working half-heartedly in an unconscious stupor.

Maybe Jumaro's dreaming of eating us raw, one bloody limb at a time. I could take a peek at what's going on inside his head, but I think I'd rather not.

Dunn joins me at the windowall. Quietly, he says, "Please tell me you are not considering—"

"They'd never expect it."

"We would never survive it. Not a fall from this height."

"You did." I glance up at him. "Give or take a few floors."

He gestures self-deprecatingly at his body with a metal hand. "And now I am half the clone I used to be. Do you want that for yourself? To be as synthetic and biological as you are mechanical?"

"What I want is to get the hell out of here." Before we end up trapped and have to shoot our way through a squad of good patrol officers.

So I raise Drasko's handgun and aim it at the glass. Then I pull the trigger before my doubts have a chance to stop me.

The first round doesn't do much. I didn't really expect it to, the windowall being made of shatterproof material. But the second does more than create fractal patterns emanating outward from the point of impact. It punctures the glass. And a third shot sends a few shards raining outside. I take the gun by the barrel and smash my way through, and Dunn punches with his fist. Together, we break open a two-meter square—more than enough room to throw ourselves out.

I can't believe we're doing this.

No time to think about it.

"Alert. Alert," the security system announces. "Multiple gunshots fired on the fifteenth floor. Windowall has been breached. Police are en route."

You down there? I reach out to Erik as I peer outside the Domescraper. Fourteen floors of mirrored glass lie below us, reflecting blue-tinted sunlight, shadows from passing aerocars high above, and neighboring buildings equally reflective and pristine. Quiet. Peaceful. Nothing like my stampeding heartbeat.

The speedlift dings halfway down the hall, and the security clone from the lobby steps out with a shocker in its gauntlet. Without preamble, it strides toward us and fires, unleashing one round after another, electric-blue pulses sizzling through the air with one purpose: to knock Dunn and me flat on our asses.

Dunn turns to face the incoming shocker rounds, blocking each of them with a swipe of his arm. The pulses fizzle and spark, finding nothing but metal beneath the sleeve of his greatcoat. The security clone isn't discouraged. It shifts its aim, sending pulse rounds at Dunn's organic center of mass. Which he bats away easily.

"Investigator Chen!" shouts one of three patrol officers to come charging from the speedlift next, weapons drawn. "Stand down!"

Ready to go, Erik thinks at me.

I take another glance out the windowall. There's a clay-colored cargo vehicle parked on the street below. Otherwise, the area behind the Edwards Estates is vacant.

But it won't be that way for long.

"Go," Dunn tells me. "I will hold them off."

"She can't seriously be considering—" says one of the officers.

"You will not survive a fall from this height, Investigator Chen." The security clone continues to advance, firing its weapon with every step.

Dunn blocks each and every shot, his arm chopping side to side through the air like some kind of martial artist.

I reach around him with Drasko's gun and put a round in the security clone's shooting arm. It staggers sideways without a sound, dropping its shocker. Dunn moves quickly to retrieve the weapon and aim it at the clone's helmet.

"We're leaving." I step past my partner and level the

handgun at the three officers. Their eyes nearly pop out of their heads.

"But it's suicide, Chen!" one yelps.

"Shockers on the floor," I order them. "Now!"

Slowly they obey, disgruntled looks on their faces as they lay down their weapons. But they don't appear worried. Reinforcements moving up the stairwell should arrive any second.

I'm gonna need you to catch me, I tell Erik telepathically.

Had a feeling. He pauses. *Is that the fifteenth floor?*

Can you do it?

Another pause. *Nothing like the first time...*

I can sense his signature smirk, but his overconfidence does nothing to alleviate my fear. That's what I'm feeling right now: terror. Because I've never jumped from a considerable height without wearing my exo.

I grab one of the officer's shockers off the floor and tuck it into my waistband, holstering Drasko's handgun as I do so. Dunn keeps the security clone and three officers covered as I prepare to make my exit.

"You do not have to do this," Dunn suggests quietly. "We could take the speedlift down—"

"Where more of them will be waiting." I glare at the officer who yelped earlier. "Isn't that right?"

He shrugs and mutters something inaudible, avoiding eye contact.

"So that's a yes." I take a quick breath and pat my partner on the shoulder. "See you on the ground."

Then I dive outside headfirst.

The rush of air is expected, enough to take my breath away, as the building's reflective surface rushes past me.

There's no slow-motion freefall where seconds pass like minutes and I'm acutely aware of my surroundings as my life flashes before my eyes. None of that. This is a quick plunge to my death, already over before it even started.

I slam into Erik with a force that nearly knocks the wind out of me, and we both let out an involuntary groan as he catches me in his strong arms and holds me tight.

"Hey." He smiles, his face a centimeter or two from mine.

"Hey." I look at him and frown.

Time seems to stand still. And we seem to be floating.

In the middle of the air.

"What the hell?" I gasp.

"You fell. I jumped." He chuckles. "We met halfway. Guess this is what happens when upward momentum cancels out downward—"

The floating ends without warning, and we plummet to the street below. But he lands solid on both feet, and we slam against each other with another simultaneous groan.

"Out of your freaking minds, both of you." Daiyna's waiting for us, and she's far from happy, scowling as Erik sets me down. "You're letting that *demigod* crap get to your heads. You do realize you could have died, right? Hurling yourself out a damn window fifteen stories up?"

I realize most of her ire is directed toward me. But I don't have time to deal with it right now.

"Dunn is carrying Tanaka." I look up at the smashed windowall.

"The daemon?" Daiyna's scowl deepens. "What the hell are you thinking?"

I wasn't talking to her. "Can you catch both of them the way you caught me?"

Erik's confident demeanor falters. He glances at Daiyna. "We might be able to. Together." He nods to her, and she curses under her breath, reluctantly nodding back.

Both square their shoulders and spread their feet, eyes fixed on the breach in the domescraper's mirrored exterior high above us.

"Wait." I take a step toward Daiyna. "I thought you said you lost your abilities."

"Only the night-vision." She doesn't look at me, keeping her gaze set on her target. "I've still got hops."

"Hops?" I echo with a frown.

Erik shrugs. "Generational slang."

I'll take his word for it.

Dunn falls out of the building next, both arms clasping Jumaro's unconscious body. By the time the two of them plummet past the eighth floor, Erik and Daiyna are already in motion, leaping upward like a pair of rockets but without any sound or plumes of smoke, their vertical momentum carrying them straight to my partner. When they collide, they seem to float in midair for a moment—one of the weirdest, most amazing things I've ever seen—as Erik and Daiyna wrap their arms around Dunn's torso and hold on tight. Then they drop to the pavement like dead weight and land with a slight spring to their step.

"You should shoot that thing in the head." Daiyna storms past me to pull open the running van's side door. "You'd be doing it a favor."

"Jumaro Tanaka is wanted for murder." I nod to Dunn, and he places the bound and gagged body—still chomping against the gag—into the vehicle's cargo section. "As well as for his involvement in a robbery."

Daiyna scoffs. Then she points at Jumaro. "That daemon doesn't know how to steal anything but human lives."

"Can we discuss this en route?" Erik climbs behind the control panel of what should be a driverless cargo vehicle. "Assuming we have a route?"

I get into the passenger seat beside him, and Dunn and Daiyna hop into the rear section with Jumaro. Our doors slam shut in unison, just as half a dozen patrol officers round the end of the block and come sprinting toward us.

"Halt!" two shout at once, leveling their shockers on the van—not that they'll do much against a vehicle, but their postures strike the right threatening note.

Erik smiles and waves at them, and the van lurches forward, going from zero to sixty kilometers per hour in less than a second. I'm thrown back into my seat, and the officers dive out of the way as we head straight for them.

"So..." Erik winks at me. "Exit strategy?"

"Let's get away from here." I watch as he steers us into rushing ground traffic, our vehicle blending in well with others of its kind. Except ours has people sitting in the front and no cargo in the back. "As soon as you can tell we're not being pursued, find a quiet street with a maintenance hatch."

"You planning to take the long way to 6?" Erik frowns. "Those underground tunnels go straight to Dome 10. They channel water and wastewater to the port. They don't meet up with maintenance tunnels from other Domes."

"I know that." Didn't mean to snap at him. I glance his way and soften my tone. "We can't take the maglev tunnel to Dome 6 from here. Too many opportunities for law enforcement to head us off. They're probably already waiting for us at the train station."

"Impossible to blend into the crowd when you're carrying along a freak of nature, am I right?" He smirks at me.

I ignore the remark. "So we'll take the maintenance tunnel under the streets to Dome 10. And once we're there, we'll locate the tunnel from Dome 6 and—"

"This is insane." Daiyna exhales behind us, shaking her head.

What is she even doing here?

"The long way it is, then." Erik keeps his tone chipper.

We ride in silence for a few seconds.

"Anyone following?" I lean forward to glance up through the windscreen. No black & white aerocars with flashing blue and red lights, that I can see.

Erik's eyes glaze over briefly as he links up. "They've lost us. For the moment."

Let me guess. "You've managed to hack the LawKeeper network."

"Guilty." He grins. Then the expression fades. "It's how I knew you were in trouble. That, and the Governor's online diatribe. He really seems out to get you—not to mention the Bishops."

Father, daughter, and daughter's protégé. Yeah, right—I should be so lucky. She may have shown an interest in my training and looked out for me while I was a curfew enforcer, but it's not like Mara Bishop has ever taken me under her wing and offered any career advice, as much as I would have appreciated it. And now with Hudson separating us in the chain of command, I hardly get a chance to speak with her at all.

What would she think about my decision-making lately? Am I acting in the best interest of the Domes? Or am I just too stubborn and proud to admit defeat and turn myself in, as my commanding officer ordered me to?

"Thought these things were self-driving." I watch as Erik taps course adjustments into the console before him.

"Oh, they are. And they don't like interlopers. If I'm not careful, it'll pull off to the side of the road and shut itself down."

He glances at me with that ever-present twinkle in his eye. Might be endearing if it wasn't so obnoxious. But I guess I should be glad he seems more like himself again—at least on the surface—after what Prometheus put him through.

"You just have to speak its language is all." He mimes massaging the control panel. "Make it think it's still following its prescribed route while we send it elsewhere." His eyes lose focus again as he consults something online via his ocular lenses. Some type of map, perchance? "And there we are. An access hatch to a maintenance shaft, half a block away. We'll hang a right at the next side street."

I nod, already planning what will have to happen next. "That's where we'll part company."

"Us and the van? Right," Erik says. "It'll rejoin traffic and do its thing. Probably head back to the depot for a load-up."

Not what I meant. "You and Daiyna have done enough."

"Really?" He glances over his shoulder. "Does it seem that way to you?"

"Not yet," Daiyna replies in a dry tone.

"I believe they intend to join us, Investigator Chen," Dunn says.

That's what I'm gathering. I turn to face Daiyna in the backseat. "Why are you here?" I ask bluntly. "Erik just can't help himself. He's always getting tangled up in my cases. But you've got people who depend on you in Dome 6."

"And you are dealing with something you've never encountered before. Any of you." She sweeps her gaze across each of us before inclining her head toward Jumaro's unconscious form in the cargo area. "We did everything we could to rid the Wastes of those monsters. And now, somehow, one of them has gotten inside the Domes." She shakes her head slowly, the horror behind her eyes clear to see. A past life that haunts her to this day. "There is nothing to study, nothing to cure, Sera. Taking it to your father will do nothing for the man it once was. Best-case scenario, it breaks its own neck in a wild fit once it regains consciousness and starts thrashing around. Worst-case...it kills innocent citizens in an attempt to satiate its uncontrollable hunger."

Dunn raises the shocker in his hand. "I will not allow that to happen."

She exhales. "You'll see. The hunger will reach a point where no deterrent will be strong enough to subdue the daemon." Her shoulders lift and fall, and she glances at Drasko's gun in my holster. "You'll have to put a bullet in its head before you reach MedCenter 6."

"You could be wrong."

A faint smile plays across her lips, equal parts wry and hopeful. "Wouldn't be the first time."

"In your experience, does everyone exposed to the toxic air of the Wastes exhibit the same grotesque mutations?" Dunn asks.

She doesn't answer right away, and she doesn't seem to know how to interact with my partner, faced with her own reflection when she looks at his helmet. What Luther wouldn't give to be in her sandals, interacting with a real, live clone!

"I don't know what your religious beliefs are..." she begins.

"I have none," he replies, matter of fact. "I am a clone."

She stares at him. "Right. Well, by the time we'd crawled out of our bunkers and lived on the surface for a while, there were different theories as to where the daemons came from. My female-only enclave thought they were men, reduced to their most vile nature. It was men in power who'd brought about the end of our world, so the idea tracked. But then we met Luther and Samson and others from their bunker, good men who wanted to make a life with us, a future." She pauses. "Luther had his own ideas about the daemons and the strange abilities manifesting themselves among us. He believed spirits of the earth searched our souls, and based on what they found, they either blessed humankind with superhuman abilities or cursed us with ravenous hunger."

"And that caught on?" I try not to scoff. Not sure if I succeed.

"It did." She gives me a blank stare.

I look over at Jumaro's motionless form. "Tanaka was a scavenger. His protective gear failed him. He didn't meet any *spirits.*"

Daiyna tilts her head to one side. "That you know of. Regardless, the spirits promised us they wouldn't interfere with humankind's future. That going forward, we'd be on our own. So whatever happened to this man, it was not their doing."

"They...spoke to you?"

She nods. "Appearing as people from our past."

"We're here," Erik announces, and the van lurches to a halt in the middle of a vacant side street, shrouded in shadows from towering buildings on both sides. "Quick, everybody out before this thing changes its mind."

I throw open my door, appreciating the diversion from Crazy Time with Daiyna.

27

As the cargo van speeds off on its own, no doubt returning to the Dome 1 train depot to be restocked, Dunn sets Jumaro on the pavement beside him and kneels down to open the maintenance hatch. Fingers crossed that his data spike will work again, and the powers-that-be haven't changed the entry codes to prevent us from taking this route.

Then I remember: Dunn has no data spike at the moment. It was part of his right gauntlet, and he left both of those behind with his smashed armor. But he does have a backup plan. And that would be brute force.

Digging his metal fingers into the slight indentation around the circular hatch, he heaves with all the strength of his prosthetic arms and every muscle in his upper body, shoulders rounded, chin up, straining with the effort. Unstoppable force, meet immovable object.

Nothing doing. But he's not about to give up anytime soon.

Daiyna watches the main boulevard behind us, and Erik keeps his eye on the airspace above. No telling how much time we have before LawKeepers catch up with us. They can't track Dunn or me, since we're offline, so that's one small favor. But if they know Erik and Daiyna are aiding and abetting our efforts, or if the neuro inside Jumaro's deformed head is sporadically active, they'll be able to trace—

With a sudden screech of plasteel against its own kind, the hatch cover grudgingly pulls free, slightly bent out of shape in my partner's hands. Sparks fly from where it was attached via three thick cables, a last gasp of defeat as they snap apart like twine.

"Nicely done." I take the ladder down, keeping an ever-watchful eye on my surroundings. In the light of my night-vision, the plasticon maintenance shaft and tunnel beyond give me a brief sense of déjà vu. I can't help but be reminded of Raul's remains and Wınk's smashed chassis abandoned in identical locations. Both a result of encountering Jumaro Tanaka, the man I'm trying to help.

Why? What the hell am I doing? Do I really care whether he gets the medical attention he so obviously needs? Or am I only interested in clearing my name—making damn sure the truth comes out? That despite Governor Raniero's claims, I had nothing to do with any sort of cover-up.

As far as I know, neither did Commander Bishop or her father. What happened to Tanaka was a freak accident, one he did his best to hide. Only Mirela knew about it, and her hunt for a cure brought her to the brink of madness. To a point where her only answer lay in the promises of a dangerous AI intent on the Domes' destruction. The lives of anyone standing in her way became immaterial.

Dunn follows me with Jumaro slung over one shoulder. He remains unconscious, but you wouldn't know it by looking at him, what with the wide-open eyes and slowly chomping jaws. The stuff of nightmares.

"Water and wastewater systems have been restored,"

Dunn notes, pausing to listen to the rushing sound through rows of pipes mounted along the tunnel wall.

Whatever Mirela Edwards hoped to achieve last night was merely a temporary setback. The airlock in Dome 10 is secure, and water systems are flowing. What did she really expect to accomplish with that little riot? To prove that the Children of Tomorrow are still a force to be reckoned with, even without their artificially intelligent leader running amok? How could she not have known she was just being used by Baatar to incite unrest?

Footsteps rapidly descend the ladder. Daiyna—with Erik right behind her, struggling to drag the warped hatch cover back into place. They're determined to join us on this unsanctioned mission, whether or not I want them along.

"That's better." Erik grunts as the damaged cover shuts out most of the ambient light from above. "Might buy us a minute or two."

Once we're all out of the shaft and inside the tunnel, I turn to face them. The dull red light of a nearby maintenance panel glows to life, sensing our presence.

"We move fast, and we stay quiet," I say in a low tone.

Erik gives a cringeworthy pirate impression, "And them's that falls behind stays behind."

I shake my head. "Nobody falls behind."

"There isn't any way I can talk you out of this?" Daiyna averts her eyes from Tanaka. Tough to do with him dangling over Dunn's back right in front of her, but she manages.

"Any chance I can talk you into staying out of this?" I ask.

She shakes her head resolutely. So that's settled.

She's a brave woman. I've seen her in a fight, so I'm not worried about her ability to take care of herself. But the work she's doing with Luther in Dome 6 is important, and I don't want anything to jeopardize that. Assisting a rogue investigator could really throw a wrench in the works, particularly if we both end up tossed into the same correctional center.

"Erik, take the rearguard. Let me know the moment you notice anyone following us." I tap my temple, hoping he understands my attempt at sign language.

Got it, Boss, he replies telepathically. Message received.

"Let's move out." I lead the way at a steady clip, more than a fast walk but less than a sprint. Dunn's long strides have no trouble keeping up. Daiyna and Erik aren't far behind, their footfalls quiet for the most part.

Why'd you bring her along? I think at Erik.

Daiyna? She found me. He shrugs telepathically. Not sure if that's a thing, but it comes through somehow. *I think she might've been worried about you. She's had experience with daemons, up close and personal, you know.*

She's made that abundantly clear.

Maybe she wants to lend her expertise, he suggests.

By killing Tanaka?

Another telepathic shrug. *If it comes to that.* He waits a minute or two before asking, *You think they'll follow us down here?*

Might make more sense for them to wait for us at the other end. Them: Mirela, Baatar, and his pair of security clones? Or a squad of officers dispatched to our location? Could be all of the above.

Right. Bop us on the head as we pop out of another maintenance shaft.

If they're tracking Tanaka's neuro—or yours—we might

have some company sooner rather than later, I reply.

Turns out to be a whole lot sooner.

"Investigator Chen," a deep voice echoes from fifty meters ahead, and a muscular figure steps into the tunnel from an adjoining maintenance shaft. He claps slowly. "Bravo. You have played right into our hands."

He appears to be alone. But appearances can be deceiving.

Retreat is clear, Erik offers.

So nobody's behind us. For now. I reach out with my telepathy for any other minds in the vicinity and come up short. No idea why I didn't sense Baatar ahead of his grand entry. Maybe he's good at keeping his thoughts to himself. Or he's a brainless robot.

"Agent Baatar." I come to a halt. "Had a feeling we'd be running into each other again."

He walks toward me. Unhurried, his posture confident. "A dozen security clones are standing by on the street above, waiting for me to give the word to converge on this location. The Governor's very own troops. So feel free to go out in a blaze of glory, if you wish. I have a feeling it would be much more palatable for you than the alternative."

"Which is?" I slide one hand toward my holster. With the other, I gesture nonchalantly for Dunn to fall back.

He stays put. He can be real stubborn that way.

"Come now. I'm sure you have put all the pieces together." Baatar arches an unruly eyebrow and chuckles quietly as he approaches. "Show me how that impressive investigator's brain of yours works."

I suppose I might as well stall for time while my mind races for a way out of this trap I've led us into. Prolonging the inevitable? Maybe.

"Well, I'm pretty sure you don't work for Governor Raniero. But you don't *not* work for him, either. You're one of those off-the-books clandestine operatives a government official can disavow knowledge of, even as you go about doing their dirty work." I rest my hand on Drasko's gun. "You've had your eye on the Children of Tomorrow for a while—no doubt the Patriots, as well—thinking they might make the perfect agitators in a Domes-wide insurgency. But your superiors deemed the collateral damage to be too great, considering what we just went through with the Prometheus uprising. So instead, you focused on one unstable woman with an ax to grind. Since her mother is friends with Raniero, I'm figuring he steered you in that direction. Extra bonus: Mirela's boyfriend is a walking mutation." I pause. "When you discovered her obsession with me, your plan of attack became clear. And you've been pulling the puppet strings ever since."

"Have I? How so?"

Honestly, I have no idea. Spy crap isn't my area of expertise.

"Now's the fun part. For you, anyway," I go on, no closer to figuring out an escape. "You get to watch me take the fall. Along with the Bishops, of course—can't forget them. They've been the target all along. And then there's Drasko. At first I thought Mirela paid him to activate my exo, but now I'm thinking that was you, too. You blackmailed him into it, threatening to notify certain authorities regarding his family's unauthorized move to Dome 9—while at the same time informing Drasko which government paper-pushers could be paid off to look the other way. And once you owned him, you got him to work for you. Dome 10's underworld kingpin, bent to your will."

"Is he, though?" Baatar cocks his head to one side. "A kingpin? From what I've gathered, he's an undercover operative whose illegal activities are sanctioned by none other than Mara Bishop herself." He pauses to let that sink in for everyone present. "The criminal you know is better than the one you don't? Something like that? It makes no sense to me, nor will it to the public at large. Wouldn't a crime-free Eurasia be the goal? Or have the Bishops and their protégé given up on that ideal long ago?" He laughs quietly, but the sound is devoid of mirth. "If so, why would we want such people in positions of authority?"

So he knows about Drasko. And if he knows, then so does Raniero—who will, undoubtedly, add Drasko's undercover role to his ongoing litany of offenses against Commander Bishop whenever he feels the need to make another speech. Which will serve to blow Drasko's cover and throw the Domes' criminal underworld into a state of upheaval as lower-level crime bosses snap at each other, scrambling to become the next top dog. Undoing everything Drasko has accomplished during his tenure. Namely: a period of peace and order among the most disorderly elements of our society.

"Were things so much better under Chancellor Hawthorne?" I ask. "When you were a member of the secret police?"

The flicker of a smile across his chiseled features indicates my guess was correct.

"I know that many of the Governors haven't been big fans of James Bishop," I continue, "and I fully realize he's been *Interim* Chancellor. Nobody expected him to fill the position indefinitely. But we did assume the transition of power, when it eventually came, would be smooth. Civilized. Not a disorganized coup."

The faint smile vanishes. He clenches his jaw. So I've touched a nerve there.

He must pride himself on being methodical, systematic in his approach—his puppeteering. Every move deliberate, every detail planned well in advance.

"Your guerilla tactics have been all over the place. First the airlock. Then the Edwards Estates. What's next?" I'm genuinely curious. "Were you going to have the Children of Tomorrow hit a MedCenter? Or maybe knock over another jewelry store?"

Baatar is not amused. "The cult you mention acts on its own prerogatives, Investigator Chen." He slows to a stop a few meters away from me and folds his thick-muscled arms. "For a time, their objectives aligned with my own." He used them, in other words. "But such is no longer the case."

"So you don't know where Mirela Edwards is." I find that hard to believe.

"I did not say that." A sinister look passes through his dark eyes.

"Did you kill her?"

"I do not make a habit of murdering civilians."

But his proxies do. Mirela has plenty of blood on her hands after what went down at the airlock.

"You just discard them when you no longer find them useful. You set her up to fail."

"Hardly," he scoffs. "The woman is psychotic. Any failures were her own doing, trust me. And after the havoc she caused, she deserves to be punished to the fullest extent of the law."

"So the police have her in custody." Drasko, as well.

He gives me a slow nod. "Now all they have left to capture...is you. An investigator with a history of insubordination defying orders yet again. Transporting the Chancellor's dirty little secret through an underground tunnel to Dome 10. To flush it all away with the rest of our wastewater."

"This guy?" I hook a thumb at Tanaka. "He's no secret. Raniero splashed images of him in my exo all over the Link."

"Ah yes, but you've been offline, haven't you? You were not aware of the Governor's public announcement. All you know is what you have been trained to know: protect the Chancellor and his daughter, Commander Mara Bishop, at all costs." He pauses. "Even if it means the end of your career in law enforcement."

I see. "That's the spin you'll give it."

He smiles broadly. "I did try to warn you."

"And what will you do with him?"

"The creature will be disposed of." Baatar raises his block of a chin and regards Tanaka's unconscious form with mild disgust. "Such a thing cannot be allowed to exist inside the Domes."

"His name is Jumaro Tanaka. He's a person. Not trash to be tossed out."

"The man he was is irrelevant. That person no longer exists. Only the creature with its sordid appetite is here with us now."

"What I've been trying to tell her," Daiyna mutters.

"But if his condition can be reversed—" I argue.

"It can't," Daiyna and Baatar say in unison. Then he gives her a deferential nod and adds, "Your mother is well-acquainted with such things, of course."

"She's not my..." The words die on my lips. I clear my throat and whip out Drasko's gun, leveling it on the secret agent. Guess I am quicker than he is. "Tanaka made a bad decision. He should've sought medical attention as soon as he started noticing changes in himself. This was never a government cover-up."

"Why should that matter?" Baatar seems genuinely curious. "All that will concern our citizens is the fact that such a creature has been allowed to live among them."

"People care about the truth. They'll see through the lies you're spinning."

"A lie can travel around the world and back again while the truth is still lacing up its boots," he retorts. "Does Vivian Andromeda recognize that quote?"

I am so not comfortable with how much he knows about me. "Mark Twain," I reply. "He's also quoted as saying, 'Do the right thing. It will gratify some people and astonish the rest.'"

Baatar smirks. "You think you're in the right, do you?"

"Of course I do."

Then I shoot him.

28

Erik rushes forward as Baatar collapses, the shot plowing into the armor plating of his tactical vest and knocking him over backward.

"One helluva weapon..." the agent gasps in surprise as he hits the tunnel floor.

"I've got him." Erik stands over Baatar, one hand to his own temple and the other reaching out toward the fallen man's head.

Baatar's eyes lose focus, and he twitches—just one weird jerk—from head to toe before going completely still.

"What do you mean, you've *got him*?" I demand.

"I've commandeered his neuro."

My jaw drops. "What?" He can do that?

"Been waiting for an opening. That bullet to the diaphragm distracted him just long enough for me to—"

"Wait. Are you talking about mind control?" Daiyna asks.

Erik gives an involuntary shudder. Understandable, considering what he went through recently. "No. Not that. I'm just inside his head, controlling his Link access. I can send a hail to any of his subordinates, and they'll think he's the one making the call."

"A morally grey distinction, at best," Dunn says.

"Agreed." I fold my arms. "This is wrong, Erik."

"So wrong. But it's not like we've got a whole lot of options here." He squints as though he's reading an extra-small font displayed across his ocular lenses. "Twelve security clones are at his beck and call, just like he said. Standing by above us, cordoning off the street. Where shall we send them?" He raises an eyebrow at me. "How about Dome 8? They could polish the solar array. Or better yet: Dome 2. Do a little tree trimming, perchance?"

"Split them up." I'm not thrilled with his apparent ability to hijack a citizen's neuro, but at the moment, we have to make use of every advantage we're afforded. "Send half of them to act as our escort to Dome 6. We'll take the train straight there. And send the other half to collect Drasko and Mirela Edwards from police custody. We're bringing them with us."

Erik stares at me. Daiyna and Dunn do the same. Nobody says anything for a few moments.

"Gutsy." Erik blinks. Then he frowns. "But how will it work? The police have no reason to go along with this."

"Chain of command. Pecking order." I offer him a shrug. "The Governor's troops have jurisdiction once they're mobilized. LawKeepers won't like it, but they'll stand down." Or they should. I'm hoping they will.

"You want to take this daemon on a train." Daiyna shakes her head in disbelief. "You'll put the life of every passenger in jeopardy."

"No passengers." I nod to Erik. "Include that in Baatar's orders. The train to Dome 6 is to be cleared immediately."

Erik nods back. But it's obvious he has some misgivings about my plan.

Well, join the club, buddy.

"There's just one problem." He scrunches up his face. Wish I could say it's his most unattractive expression, but the guy is too handsome for his own good. "No Baatar. The clones will be more than a tad suspicious escorting us without their fearless leader present."

I hate asking Erik to do this. "Can you get him on his feet?"

"You mean...force him to..." He trails off, staring at a point midway down the tunnel wall. "I don't know. I've never done this before."

Daiyna curses under her breath. "We're wasting precious time. We have to make a move or stick to the original plan."

Leave Baatar here and continue onward to Dome 10? Or see if Erik can induce the agent to climb up to the surface with us?

"I'm getting a call," Erik says. And he doesn't sound happy about it. "I mean someone's hailing Baatar."

"Source?" I step toward him.

He gives me a look. "Police headquarters."

Hudson calling for an update? Has he been working with Agent Baatar all along? Or could it be the infiltrator embedded at HQ? I've had a feeling someone's been sabotaging our limited power supply, blinding the analysts at opportune moments. Not to mention the matter of that lost footage of Jumaro Tanaka that someone deleted at the source.

"Put it on holo. One-way glass." Assuming Erik can do that.

He nods warily. "They'll see Baatar's placeholder image, and we'll see them."

"But they won't see us?" Daiyna frowns. "Or hear us?"

"That is correct," Dunn replies. "Assuming Erik Paine is able to convince Agent Baatar's neural implant that he is, in fact, Agent Baatar and not Erik Paine."

Daiyna blinks up at my partner like he's an alien from another planet.

"I'm able," Erik mutters.

The holo-projector clipped to the lapel of Baatar's coat flares to life, and a three-dimensional image of a surly, bearded guy appears in the air before us.

Of course I recognize the face. It belongs to Hector, our head technician at HQ.

"Agent Baatar, report," he says quietly, glancing back over his shoulder like he's nervous someone might overhear him.

Now for the real test. Erik glances at me.

I put my hand on his arm and give it a squeeze. For luck.

He almost smiles. Then his eyes glaze over, and he's all business. "You're interrupting," he subvocalizes. "What have I told you about doing that?"

I clench my jaw, hoping Erik's interpretation of their working relationship is correct, that this is something Baatar would actually say to Hector.

Hector blinks. Then he stammers, "I-I'm doing everything I can on my end, sir. But I need an ETA on Chen's arrival. They're...getting suspicious around here. Starting to think the outages are an inside job."

So maybe Hudson did take seriously what I said earlier. Or Commander Bishop. Great minds think alike—or something like that.

"New plan," Erik says, channeling his words through Baatar's neuro. "I'm taking Chen to Dome 6. And I don't want the police involved."

"Dome 6? I don't understand. Governor Hahn has not sided with Raniero—"

"Precisely. We'll give her an up-close and personal experience with Tanaka and see if she changes her tune. Once she realizes what Bishop's policies are doing to our people, she will side with Governor Raniero, and we will have the majority vote." He pauses. "I'll need Mirela Edwards and the fellow called Drasko transferred into my custody. The Governor's troops will collect them shortly."

Assuming Erik can get the clones to follow new orders out of the blue.

Hector glances away again. "I'll do what I can, sir. But I'm going to need an extraction ASAP. It won't be safe for me here much longer."

"Of course it will." Erik smiles, and the expression comes through in his tone. "Once our plans come to fruition, you will be hailed as a hero."

"I will?" Hector looks unsure about that. Yet hopeful.

"Baatar out," Erik says, and the holo vanishes. Then he subvocalizes, "On your feet, soldier."

Baatar jerks again, full-body, and sits up. Face devoid of expression, he gets to his feet and stands there as if awaiting orders.

"Is he your puppet now?" Daiyna murmurs uneasily.

Erik shakes his head adamantly. "He's been conditioned to follow commands. I'm just sending them to his brain via his neural implant, the same way his superiors do." He pauses. "I think?"

It's new territory for him. For all of us. But we don't have time to analyze it. We just need it to work long enough to get to Dome 6.

"Let's see if he can climb." I head down the tunnel to the nearest adjacent maintenance shaft and take the ladder up. "Order one of his troops to open the hatch at this location," I call over my shoulder.

"Done." Erik and Baatar enter the shaft below me. The agent looks like he's in a dissociative fugue. Works for me.

Daiyna and Dunn are right behind them. Tanaka squirms in fits on my partner's shoulder, wriggling for a moment before going completely still. The shock must be wearing off. I'll have to hit him again before we get on that train.

The hatch slides open, allowing blue-tinged early afternoon light to flood the shaft. Six security clones are waiting for us, along with a pair of black, unmarked ground vehicles—the same type Baatar was in when he stole my exo. The Governor must have a fleet.

The clones step aside, and the vehicle doors drift open automatically. We're expected.

Erik, Baatar, and I get into the lead vehicle with three clones—two up front, one in the rear seat, us in the middle—while Dunn and Daiyna climb into the second vehicle with the other security clones, all of them wearing that fancy updated armor with the glowing, neon-blue lines. Tanaka goes into the cargo compartment.

Daiyna gives me a look before our doors shut, and it seems to express her hope that I know what the hell I'm doing. Right there with you, bio-mother.

No LawKeepers in sight, on foot or in the air above. Traffic makes way for us as our two vehicles speed up and enter the main boulevard. Driverless cargo carriers are programmed to recognize the Governor's troops moving in a hurry and hang back.

They didn't confiscate our weapons, I think at Erik.

Probably because Baatar told them we're working together. Like one big, happy family. He winks at me. *So long as you keep everything holstered, we should be fine.*

We'll see about that.

When we arrive at the train station—Dome 1's central hub with tunnels radiating toward each of the outlying Domes—Baatar's other six security clones are already waiting for us, standing like statues with their stunners held at rest. They have Mirela and Drasko with them, both wearing shapeless grey coveralls and manacles. She looks confused and anxious, wide-eyed and unable to stand still, while he stares straight ahead, his bruised, unshaven face neutral.

Until he sees me step out of the vehicle. Then he looks intrigued.

Erik dips his chin into his collar and subvocalizes Baatar's next command: to lead the procession. The agent does so, walking straight into the station as if he runs the place, heading for the maglev train waiting at the tunnel to Dome 6. The clones escorting Mirela and Drasko follow, as do Erik and Daiyna. Two clones drive the government vehicles up a ramp into the train's freight car. Orderly. Methodical. Seemingly well-rehearsed, if one didn't know better. Agent Baatar should be pleased.

The four guards on duty, dressed in khaki uniforms with their stunners holstered at their sides, glance at each other and don't engage, seeming to realize that whatever's going on right now is way above their pay grade. I avoid eye contact with them.

Without a word, one of the clones provides a black hood

to go over Tanaka's head, and Dunn tugs it down into place before removing him from the back of the second vehicle and slinging him over his shoulder once again. I walk with my partner, and the six security clones follow. Unhurried. Silent, save for the sound of our footsteps striking the pavement. Rhythmic, like an antique clock—or maybe a time bomb, counting down until this scheme of ours implodes all over itself.

The passenger car is vacant, as requested, all royal blue industrial carpet and white ergonomic seats made of cushy faux-leather. The security clones take up residence at the doors—six at one end, six at the other, standing at attention. Baatar seats himself smack-dab in the middle of the car, thirty rows down. Mirela and Drasko take the pair of seats facing him, watching him warily as if he holds the power of life and death over their heads.

Erik sits next to Baatar. Best to keep his telepathic influence as close as possible. Daiyna and I sit across the aisle from them, facing the same direction. Dunn sets Tanaka down a couple rows away and unnoticeably draws his shocker as he takes his seat, keeping the muzzle trained on the hooded, mostly unconscious mutant beside him.

Nobody says anything as the high-speed train glides out of the station, its movement negligible. There are no windows, since passengers wouldn't be interested in watching the grey tunnel walls pass by, and there is no change in light—just that steady artificial daylight from glow-tubes mounted along the ceiling. A wallscreen nearby shows our progress in real-time. We'll be underground for about five minutes.

"So. Dome 6." Drasko keeps his eye on Baatar, who

doesn't respond, who hasn't moved—not a millimeter—since he took his seat. Who stares back at him without expression. "The next stage for another bit of theater?"

"Can someone please tell me what's happening?" Mirela whispers, sounding like she's on the verge of a nervous breakdown. "I don't understand. You said you would protect us, that they'd never catch us. But now we're being taken away like this, and I don't know what's happened to Jumaro. Where is he?" Her words pour out in a rush, all of them directed at Baatar.

I lean forward in my seat and make eye contact with her. "We're getting Jumaro the help he needs, Ms. Edwards."

Her expression changes in an instant, from fear to intense loathing. "*You*," she grates out. "How dare you speak his name, Queen of the Infidels!"

That again. Can't say I've missed it.

"I should've known you were behind this," she hisses, teeth and eyes flashing with hate. "You who want to keep all the power for yourself, you who chained up Prometheus when he promised to make us *gods*!"

I take a breath and keep my voice low. "I'm not your enemy here. My father is a doctor. We're going to have him take a look at Jumaro—"

"Doctors," she spits the word. "What good are they? Offering guesses and bottles of drugs, throwing crap against the wall to see what sticks. Prometheus has the answer! The DNA of the Thousand will heal my Jumaro, and the Children of Tomorrow will live outside these walls—we will reclaim the Earth!"

I shake my head sympathetically. That's what I'm going for, anyway. "There's no proof that what the Prometheus AI promised could work. No proof at all." I pause while she seethes. "Jumaro should have sought medical attention as soon as he started to change. Why didn't he?"

She blinks. Her face falls. "He was frightened. We both were. We couldn't believe what was happening to him. He decided it would be best to hide under the streets where he worked, while I searched for a cure. Day and night. I never stopped, never did anything else, until I found it."

"Why didn't the analysts at police headquarters notice his transformation?" Erik asks.

"They weren't allowed to," Drasko says, still watching Baatar. Judging from the look in his eyes, he's realizing the shape of the situation. Had a feeling he might. "Secret Agent Man over here kept them blind to it. He didn't want anybody to know about the mutant until it served his purposes."

"He's not a *mutant*!" Mirela just about shrieks.

"You're right," Drasko replies calmly, and she groans, hanging her head. "He's a means to an end. We all are."

I tilt my head toward Baatar. "The master manipulator."

Drasko nods. "Had me over a barrel."

A real *Catch-22*. "Offered to pay off certain authorities to look the other way, so your family could stay at Erik's farm. In return, you activated my exo."

"He would've turned them in, otherwise. Sent them back to Dome 6. Being on that farm..." He glances at Erik. "It's been the best thing for them. Ever."

"We're glad to have them," Erik says quietly.

"What is this?" Mirela demands, cold suspicion flaring up in her eyes. "How do you all know each other?"

"Drasko and I used to work together. Erik and I are both

members of the Twenty. Daiyna's my biological mother. Dunn's my partner." I stare her down. "All caught up now?"

"Yeah, I guess..." She drops her gaze. Then she glares at Jumaro's hooded figure. "Who's that?"

"Prisoner transport," I answer without skipping a beat. Then I ask, "What did he want with your loot?"

"What?" She looks confused.

"Agent Baatar. He robbed your mom's shop with you. Set up the holo-projector to make me think Drasko was your getaway driver—before he actually was." I give Drasko a sardonic look. "What was in it for him?"

She glances at Baatar, as if he might advise her to keep quiet. When he doesn't, she clears her throat and in a voice barely above a whisper, asks, "Is he okay?"

"Resting." With his eyes open. "He's had a long day."

"Yeah..." She nods, her gaze distant. I doubt she's gotten any sleep since her murderous rampage at the airlock. Join the club. "Well, he kind of showed up last-minute, when Jumaro wasn't feeling well enough to break in with me. He offered me the exoskeleton-suit, and in return, he wanted half the take."

"Last minute." Let me guess. "He told you he was part of your cult."

"Movement," she snaps.

"The Children of Tomorrow."

She nods reluctantly. "I didn't know he worked for the government."

"I'm not sure the government knows it, either."

Drasko grunts in the affirmative. "Former secret police. Served under Hawthorne. All-around dangerous fellow."

So I've gathered. "And since you were a relatively new

recruit yourself, Mirela, you didn't question it."

She scowls at me. "He said he had a lead. That we were going to free Prometheus. But it would cost plenty. Not credits—too easy to trace."

I nod. "Artifacts were the way to go. Just the sort of thing the upper castes really go for. People with power and influence." I pause. "Like your mother."

"She had nothing to do with this."

"Friends with Governor Raniero, right? Over for cocktails every now and then?"

Mirela's jaw trembles, and she clenches it.

"I'm sure you came up in conversation. You, and the boyfriend you were slumming it with. Just the sort of patsies he was looking for." I shrug one shoulder. "Of course Nevah mentioned you. She probably does all the time. Because she misses you."

Daiyna shifts in her seat beside me.

"You don't know what you're talking about," Mirela says.

"More than you might think. I don't see my mom nearly enough. Of course I blame it on my job. It's so important, you know, working in law enforcement. Just as important as keeping our solar array functional."

"I don't care about that anymore. I haven't shown up for work in weeks. All that matters is freeing Prometheus—"

"It's not going to happen, Mirela. Ever. You need to realize that, along with every other Child of Tomorrow." I hold her gaze. Tough to do, the way her disturbed eyes twitch. "Teaming up with someone like Agent Baatar didn't get you anywhere close to your goal. Because he was never interested in setting that dangerous AI free. He was just using you to get rid of James Bishop—because that's all his superiors want."

Without warning, the overhead glow-tubes switch from white to red light, and EMERGENCY STOP flashes on the wallscreen. We're still underground, with a minute to go before reaching Dome 6, when the train screeches to a halt.

The six security clones at each end of the passenger car hold out their stunners and advance toward us.

"Is he doing this?" I glance at Baatar, still catatonic.

"No. The order didn't come from him." Erik's at a loss. "I can't get them to stand down. I don't know what's going on."

Drasko curses under his breath. "Cleanup." He gives me a direct look. "We're the only ones who know what Raniero's been up to lately. Nobody's leaving this train alive."

29

"What do you mean?" Mirela wails as the clones close in from both sides, oozing menace with every step.

Drasko's meaning becomes abundantly clear as the security clones holster their stunners mid-stride in compartments along the left side of their leg armor—and then draw a different type of sidearm from the compartments on their right. Like Drasko's hand cannon, they're the lethal variety.

"Get down!" I hit the floor as the clones fire without pause, sending a hail of projectile rounds our way. The barrage is a deafening roar followed by countless thuds as shots from each side pass over our seats—right where our heads were a second ago—and smack into the bulletproof armor of their comrades.

You don't have to do this, I try to telepathically communicate with them. *You're not killers. You're not robots. You have free will. You can choose not to murder us.* What else can I tell them? *Governor Raniero is wrong. He's just using you to clean up his mess. Don't let him.*

Another hail of automatic weapons fire shreds everything in sight. Message not received, I guess. Or their conditioning is too formidable a wall for me to break through.

Daiyna grabs the shocker from my waistband as I twist to return fire with Drasko's gun. I don't have time to tell her the pulse rounds won't do any good. I'm too busy aiming down the aisle at the first clone in sight and pulling the trigger.

The armor-piercing round blows a hole in the clone's faceplate, sending shards of white plasteel in all directions as its head jerks back and its body falls onto the clone behind it. They don't go down like dominos—that would be too cartoonish—but the next one in line struggles against its weight, pausing to heave the dead clone's armored body and throw it across the nearest row of seats so they can proceed.

Turning the other way, I take out the first clone coming from the opposite direction, and the scene repeats itself. I can't allow myself to think about what I'm doing. That I'm killing security clones tasked with protecting the Domes, just like Mirela Edwards did at the airlock last night. All that matters right now is protecting the people with me. And crazy enough, Mirela's one of them.

So. Two down, ten to go.

Too bad I've got only three more rounds.

Daiyna jumps to her feet and squeezes off a salvo of electric-blue pulses, pivoting one direction, then the other, but shockers don't do squat against armor. All she succeeds in doing is decorating their chest plates with short-lived splashes of liquid lightning that quickly fizzle out.

Dunn takes a different tack. He hurls his shocker through the air, and the weapon spins end over end before striking a clone's forearm and smacking it off-target—which would have been Daiyna's center of mass. She glances at my partner with gratitude before hitting the deck again.

"That's some partner you've got," she shouts over the roar

of the clones' next barrage, rounds tearing through the head support cushions of the seats on either side of us and sending clumps of stuffing bursting upward.

"Sorry you tagged along?" I ask her.

She holds my gaze, and her eyes are glassy. "I had to know you were alright."

I don't think she's telepathic. And I'm not reading her thoughts. Yet they come through, loud and clear: She cares about me.

"He loves you, you know." She nods across the aisle.

She just had to go and ruin the moment. Because I'm pretty sure she's not referring to Drasko or Agent Baatar cowering over there as their seats are shredded by the advancing security clones. She means Erik.

Sit tight, he thinks at me. *I've got an idea.*

But he's unarmed. *Don't do anything stupid—*

Too late. He's already put his bizarre leaping ability to use. Not vertically, breaking every bone in his body by smashing into the ceiling. No, he's jumping horizontally—seeming to fly like an oversized arrow shot from an extra-large bow. Straight at the line of clones approaching on one side as they try and fail to shoot him in midair.

Daiyna takes her cue and does the same insane thing, pouncing headlong at the security clones on the other side of us. A tumultuous crash of armored bodies fills the passenger car as they topple like lines of dominoes falling in opposite directions. I might think it's comical if I wasn't so angry at Erik and Daiyna. But there's no time to reprimand their reckless behavior. Because we're all too busy scrambling for the clones' weapons and wrestling them away from their grasping gauntlets.

Dunn charges across their prostrate forms like a high-speed train, slugging them with his mechanical arms. One punch to the helmet, and the security clones lie still on the aisle floor with a sizeable dent alongside their faceplates. In a matter of seconds, he's managed to take them all out of play without killing a single one.

"Good work." I give him a nod as he turns to face me.

He nods in return.

"Trade you." Manacled, Drasko holds one of the clone's sidearms. He has his eye on the gun in my hand.

"I was keeping it warm for you." Gracing him with half a smile, I make the trade.

"Anything you can do about these?" He raises his bound wrists.

I shrug. "Baatar probably has the keycode—"

Mirela screams her guts out.

All eyes turn toward her in time to see Jumaro Tanaka vault across the torn-up seats like a cheetah from a Wild Safari interactive. He's fully conscious now, and the restraints don't slow him down one bit. He's even managed to pull off his hood somehow. Jaws chomping, he hurls himself at Agent Baatar, and amidst subhuman growls of hunger and overwhelming desire, he rips into the man's throat like a powerful apex predator, sending great gouts of blood in all directions as he feasts.

Mirela can't stop screaming, her shackled hands shaking in front of her face. "No! Jumaro, no! Stop it! Stop it!"

Baatar doesn't fight back. He can't.

Erik is still in control of his neuro.

"Oh God..." Erik lurches forward, unable to look away from the horror taking place before us. No one can.

"Turn off his pain receptors." Drasko raises his gun.

Erik nods grimly. "I did." The only mercy he could provide at this point.

I put my hand on Drasko's arm and shake my head. He lowers his weapon. I keep mine trained on Tanaka as I step toward him, the sound of my approach drowned out by Mirela's wild screaming and the grunting noises coming from the mutant.

No longer a man. A man would never do what he's doing to Baatar. A hungry beast would. A creature without a soul.

Tanaka snarls and looks up sharply, his leathery face covered in blood, yellow eyes bulging at me with hate.

I pull the trigger and send a round through his forehead. His head snaps back, and his body goes limp. Then he collapses beside Agent Baatar and lies still.

"Is he alive?" Erik's right behind me. "I'm not getting anything from his neuro."

I shake my head and lower my sidearm. Like poor Raul, Baatar is missing most of his face and neck—portions of his body not covered by the armor-plated tactical suit. Blood spurts from his jugulars and carotids. He doesn't move, doesn't make a sound.

"He's gone." My voice sounds hollow, unable to believe what's happened. That in a matter of seconds, both Agent Baatar and Jumaro Tanaka are out of the picture.

Mirela lunges at me, her manacled hands grasping like claws. "You murderer!" she shrieks. "Queen Bitch of the Infidels! I could have gotten him help, but *you*—"

A pulse round smacks into her dead-center, and she drops to the floor with a whimper and a thud, out cold.

Daiyna lowers her shocker. "So it does work." She hands

me the weapon, and I slip it back into my waistband. "What now?" She surveys the fallen security clones before returning her gaze to the two dead bodies keeping Mirela company.

"Same plan. Dome 6." I frown at the end of the passenger car. "Assuming we can get this thing moving again."

Drasko shakes his head. "Once Raniero learns the kill order was a bust, he'll summon the train back to Dome 1. Then he'll try again."

"With more clones, Investigator Chen," Dunn adds. "Many more."

"So we don't let him find out," Erik says.

Easier said than done. I have a feeling the security clones' status relays are updating the Governor as we speak.

"Why continue on to Dome 6?" Daiyna asks me. "You wanted to see if your father could cure the daemon. Can't cure a corpse."

I realize that. "But he could study Tanaka's DNA. Find out how this happened to him."

"I told you how—"

"A scientific, medical explanation," I interrupt her. "So we can avoid this happening to anyone else, ever again. I think that's what Mirela has wanted from the start." My gaze drifts back to the unconscious woman. "There has to be a solution that doesn't involve turning people into *demigods*."

"She wanted to put an end to scavenging in the Wastes," Drasko says quietly. "She came to hate the line of work her mother's in. As a purveyor of so-called rare artifacts, Nevah Edwards and others like her have encouraged raiders to put themselves at risk in order to locate objects of greater value."

"She blamed her mother for what happened to Jumaro." That makes some sense, in a twisted sort of way.

"You believe that Dr. Chen may be able to devise some sort of treatment that raiders may take prior to venturing into the Wastes," Dunn suggests, "in order to offer protection against airborne toxins, should the protective gear fail them. So that what happened to Jumaro Tanaka will not happen to any other citizen of the Domes, ever again."

I nod, pointing at Tanaka's body. "That's why I'd still like to take him to Dome 6 as fast as possible."

"So we get the train running again." Erik shrugs like it's no big deal. Then he takes off, jogging toward the end of the passenger car.

"I'll go with him," Drasko offers, keeping his big gun at the ready as he follows Erik out.

Dunn stoops to pick up Tanaka and sling him over his right shoulder one more time. Blood drools from the mutant's fangs and dribbles down the back of Dunn's coat. I retrieve the black hood and pull it over the corpse's leathery head. No reason to frighten the locals when we arrive. With his other arm, Dunn picks up Mirela and drapes her over his left shoulder.

Ready to roll.

That's when a series of sizzling pops echo up and down the aisle, and the security clones jerk like they've each been hit simultaneously with a low-grade electric pulse.

"What the hell?" I lead the way at double-speed, careful to step over the clones' lurching limbs. Daiyna is right behind me.

"Their armor is shocking them awake," Dunn says, bringing up the rear of our little procession.

"Did your armor do that?"

"I never sleep on the job, Investigator Chen."

Once we reach the door and pass through, leaving it to slide shut behind us, I send a couple rounds into the control panel. Sparks erupt in a frenzy. Fingers crossed it's now out of commission.

We find ourselves in another vacant passenger car and hustle down the aisle to the door at the far end, which I disable as well. No reason to make the clones' job any easier, as long as they've been tasked with eliminating us.

By the time we make it to the lead car, Erik and Drasko are already hard at work hacking the controls. Everything is automated, so there's no engineer like in the Old West interactives, and no conductor. No engine, either, since every car hovers above the maglev rail, the magnetic field generated by electrified coils propelling the train forward.

"There we go." Erik exhales and leans back from the console, a big grin on his face as the EMERGENCY STOP warning vanishes and the train eases forward, quickly picking up speed. Here in the control car, there's a window the full width of the train that provides a scenic view of the grey plasticon tunnel ahead of us, lit only by white glowpads placed along the ceiling at regular intervals.

"Good job." I almost pat him on the back. Instead, I course-correct and use my hand to smooth back stray locks of my hair instead. "You wouldn't happen to have one of those ancient phones on you?"

"This thing?" Daiyna pulls one out of her pocket and hands it to me. None of the survivors from the Wastes have opted for a neuro, instead choosing to use outdated tech like this thin slab of plastic with a touchscreen to access the Link.

"I can hail anybody you like," Erik offers.

I shake my head. "I don't want you getting more involved

than you already are."

"Feeling protective, are we?" He arches an eyebrow.

I ignore him. "Is this device untraceable?"

Daiyna shrugs. "No idea. I hardly ever use it."

Erik takes the phone from me without asking and proceeds to tap and swipe the glowing screen a few times. "Now it is." He hands it back.

"Thanks." I hail Governor Raniero's office, audio-only—or *speakerphone*—as we hurtle along through the tunnel, less than a minute away from Dome 6 at our current speed. A polite and perky assistant answers, but I cut her off with, "This is Investigator Sera Chen. Please inform the Governor that Agent Baatar is dead. As is Jumaro Tanaka. You might want to let Raniero know that his plans for a coup are dead on arrival, while you're at it."

I end the call to smiles from Erik and Drasko, even a hint of one from Daiyna. Nothing from Dunn behind his helmet.

My next hail goes to Governor Hahn's office in Dome 6.

"This is Investigator Sera Chen. Please inform the Governor that I am inbound on a train from Dome 1, and I am seeking temporary asylum. Governor Raniero has issued a kill order and sent security clones after me, my partner, and three of my friends in order to suppress our threat to his coup. We remain loyal to Chancellor Bishop, and we require your protection for the time being. Please advise."

The assistant—equally chipper at first—is dead silent for a few beats. Then he manages hoarsely, "Please hold."

Probably not the sort of call he's used to fielding.

While I'm waiting for him to come back on the line, I grit my teeth and hail Chief Inspector Hudson. As expected, he's not happy to hear from me. But after a few minutes of heated bluster, topped off with threats of demotion and even termination, I'm able to get a few words in edgewise.

"Hector the tech-head is responsible for the power outages at HQ."

Hudson goes mute. Except for the panting. He really put a lot of energy into reaming me out. "What?" he manages at length.

"Hector was working with Agent Baatar, who is now deceased."

"What? Did you kill him?"

"No, sir. But Baatar was working for Governor Raniero, using Mirela Edwards and Jumaro Tanaka—and me as well—in order to bring down Chancellor Bishop."

"You have proof of this."

"Yes." I glance at Erik. "Recorded evidence."

Erik nods. His ocular lenses have caught everything, from the moment he picked us up in that cargo van.

"Which is why Raniero wants us dead," I add.

"What?"

Governor Hahn's assistant is back on the line.

"Please hold," I tell Hudson.

That doesn't go over real well. But I don't hear him cursing for long as I swipe the touchscreen and switch over.

"Investigator Chen? Governor Hahn would like to meet with you," the assistant says. "When you arrive at the train terminal, please proceed—"

"We have to go to the MedCenter first. I'm meeting my father there." Although he doesn't know it yet. "Dr. Victor Chen. He would have arrived on an earlier train from Dome 1."

"Is someone in your party injured?"

"In need of medical attention, yes." Close attention—studied and analyzed, with the hope that an anti-mutation treatment can be developed. "We also have Mirela Edwards in custody, the woman responsible for that airlock riot last night."

"I see…" He trails off. I half-expect him to put me on hold again, but he clears his throat quietly and says with more confidence than he's shown thus far, "Very well, Investigator Chen, we will have an ambulance and law enforcement personnel standing by at the terminal. They will see you shortly."

"Thank you." I hope I can trust him. That Governor Hahn hasn't decided to side with Raniero against Chancellor Bishop. Because if she has, then there won't be any ambulance or LawKeepers waiting for us. There will be more government troops instead. Security clones tasked with our extermination.

Good thing we're armed to the teeth. Well, a few teeth anyway.

I tap the touchscreen and switch over to Chief Inspector Hudson who's still fuming, of course. "Sir, let me explain—"

"Where are you, Chen? What the hell is going on?"

"Governor Raniero sent his security clones after us. To kill us, sir."

"You and your partner?"

Better if he doesn't know who else is here. "Right. We managed to subdue them and confiscate their weapons—"

"You're saying Governor Raniero issued a kill order. With lethal ordnance."

"Correct."

"And the clones are still in your vicinity?"

You could say that. "Dunn knocked them out, but their armor is shocking them awake now."

"That's not all it will do," Hudson mutters. "You have to get away from them, Chen. As fast as you can. Put as much distance as possible between you."

Tough to do on a moving train. "We should be able to soon—"

"You're not hearing me, Chen. If you don't get far enough away from them right now, you'll be caught in the blast radius when their explosives detonate."

30

What the hell? "What explosives?"

"Their armored suits. Part of the upgraded system. If a kill order is issued, and the clone has lost its weapon...an explosive charge in its chestplate will activate so that it can fulfill its mission."

"Whose bright idea was this?"

Hudson pauses. "You have one minute until detonation."

Ten clones are waking up in that passenger car. If what Hudson's saying is true, we're about to have ten bombs go off shortly after arriving at the terminal, destroying the train as well as the tunnel to Dome 1. Cutting off Dome 6 in the process.

"There has to be a way to deactivate them." I stare at Erik who stares back at me.

"We give 'em their guns back?" he suggests.

"Who is that with you?" Hudson demands. Of course he heard Erik.

"Would that work, sir? Returning their weapons?"

He doesn't answer immediately. "You would be putting yourself at risk. Better to terminate them. A shot to the head will do it. The explosive sequence should then automatically deactivate."

I look at Dunn, but all I see is my own stricken expression mirrored in his black faceplate. "Kill them all…"

Just like Mirela Edwards did in my exo, mowing down that line of clones as if they were inanimate targets on a firing range, blown away by a merciless minigun.

There has to be another way.

"Governor Raniero can rescind the kill order. That would do it, right? Halt the detonation?"

"Chen—" Hudson begins.

"Dome 6 Terminal," the control car's computer announces in a welcoming synthetic voice as the train exits the tunnel and slows to a stop, natural blue-tinted light flooding the compartment.

"You're on a train," Hudson says. He's astute like that.

I end the call, stuffing the old phone into a pocket, and hold up one hand to block the glare. Squinting, I'm able to make out the flashing red and amber lights of an emergency ground vehicle parked outside, along with half a dozen LawKeepers standing ready. Not a single security clone in sight.

Relief washes over me. Governor Hahn is on our side.

But the feeling is short-lived.

"Everybody out." I give Dunn a gentle shove in the right direction as Erik hits the release, and the side door slides open.

But Dunn doesn't exit. Nobody does.

"In case you weren't listening, those clones back there are about to explode."

"Yes, Investigator Chen." Dunn nods solemnly. "But you should not be the one to end them. Allow me."

He unloads Mirela's unconscious body onto Erik's

shoulder and Tanaka onto Drasko's. The two men give me a nod and step off the train.

"Drop your weapons!" the LawKeepers shout, leveling their shockers.

Erik and Drasko do so carefully, Drasko with obvious reluctance. Once they've set their guns on the ground, medics waste no time escorting them straight to the ambulance.

"I will join you shortly." With that, Dunn passes through the sliding door to the empty passenger car, guns gripped down at his sides.

"Let him go." Daiyna places a strong hand on my shoulder, halting me as I move to follow.

"This doesn't concern you." I glare at her.

"He wants to spare you pain." Daiyna's voice is quiet, her eyes filled with compassion. "He knows it will haunt you. Killing them. But it's something he won't feel. Because he's not human."

My eyes sting, and I scowl. "You don't know him at all."

"Maybe not." She lets go of me and heads toward the exit. "But I know people."

Dunn is a person. Not a thing. She realizes that.

Which is why I do what I do next.

I draw my shocker and shoot my partner in the back. Without his armor, he's instantly immobilized and collapses in the aisle. Grunting with the effort, I drag his unconscious body into the lead car and out the side door.

"A little help?"

Daiyna and one of the LawKeepers rush over. I leave Dunn in their capable hands.

"Sera, what are you doing?" Daiyna looks genuinely worried.

"What I have to."

I climb back aboard and run down the aisle through the empty passenger car, a projectile weapon in each hand. I'm halfway to the door on the opposite end when it caves inward, smashed open by the security clones in their glowing armored suits. Not only do they carry hidden explosives, they pack a real punch as far as destructive capabilities. Glad Dunn never qualified for an upgrade.

I raise both guns out in front of me, fingers on the triggers, and prepare to fire.

"Stand down, Investigator Chen." Their voices drone in unison as the ten of them advance. Not creepy at all. "By order of Governor Raniero—"

"The Governor's attempted coup has failed." I hold my ground. "The kill order is no longer in effect." Figure it can't hurt to lie. "Now halt, right where you are. If you proceed, I will end you."

"Explosive charges activated," they announce simultaneously. "Detonation in thirty seconds."

"You would destroy yourselves? To follow an order that's been rescinded?"

"Mission success dictates self-destruction at this juncture."

"Your mission won't be a success. You'll kill me, sure, but I don't have the damning evidence against Governor Raniero. Erik Paine does. And he's safely outside, protected by law enforcement personnel." I shake my head as they continue toward me. I've got the first two helmets in my sights. My aim doesn't waver. "You think you're serving the Governor. Helping him. But you're not. Doing this—blowing yourselves up—will destroy this train and this tunnel. Dome 6 citizens, the most vulnerable in all the

Domes, will suffer without regular shipments of supplies and medicine." I pause, hoping that will sink in. "You'll be hurting more people than you're helping."

No response.

"You're not robots!" I shout at them. "You don't have to do this!"

They don't stop.

"Don't make me shoot you!"

"We will be recycled," they reply evenly as one, resigned to their fate.

They might be. But that doesn't mean I am.

Flood the Link with the truth, I think at Erik. *Do it now.*

Not the proper way to go about it, but with only twenty seconds to go before I'm splattered across the wreckage this train will soon become, I'm not really worried about evidence protocols at the moment.

Done, Erik replies. *Full dispersal to news forums, law enforcement, government offices, you name it. The raw footage is out there, dumped straight from my lenses. I would've liked a chance to edit it first and make it pretty, but...*

No time.

Daiyna said Erik loved me. But I don't have time for love. I don't have time for anything right now.

Take care of yourself, Erik. And look out for Dunn. He won't be happy about this.

I cut the telepathic link.

Ten seconds.

The clones advance. Unhurried. Unworried. I should have more than enough rounds to take them all out. But I don't pull the trigger. I can't.

I killed a man once before. And it just about killed *me*.

The truth—everything Agent Baatar and I said to each other in that maintenance tunnel, everything Erik has witnessed over the past hour—is now on the Linkstream, accessible to everyone. Citizens will see for themselves what Governor Raniero has been up to. Including the kill order meant to hide it all.

Five seconds.

The first security clone is only a couple meters away from me when it stops. The others halt behind it. Guess they figure time's about to run out.

I lower both sidearms. Then I toss them onto the floor. No blaze of glory. Not for me. Just a big blaze for all of us in the next second or two.

Time to see for myself if the hereafter Daiyna and Luther believe in is actually there. I have my doubts. But I guess there's only one way to know for sure.

I clench my fists and brace myself for the explosion that will erase everything I've ever known.

But it never comes.

The neon-blue vertical line on each clone's faceplate flickers, and they seem to snap out of a shared trance, turning to regard their surroundings as if for the first time.

"Investigator Chen," says the one in front, facing me. "How may we be of service?"

I blink. "You can deactivate your explosive charges."

It glances over its shoulder at the clones behind it. "We do not appear to be carrying explosives at the moment, only the shockers in our concealed holsters."

Time has already run out. If their explosives were going to detonate, they would have by now. Which means the kill order must have been rescinded without their knowledge. And that begs the question: Were they ever aware of it to begin with? Or did the directive turn them into mindless zombies while it was active?

"We have been ordered to assist you in the apprehension of Agent Naran Baatar," the clone adds, "who has been acting against the Governor's wishes."

So that's the spin Raniero will put on it. Easy to pin everything on a dead man.

"Please collect the bodies of Agent Baatar and your two deceased comrades. Then meet me outside." I watch them with a wary eye.

"Of course." The lead clone nods as three at the rear of the procession turn to do as I asked. The other seven wait for me to lead the way off the train.

I do so, walking backwards. Not one of them stoops to retrieve the guns I dropped.

The antique phone in my pocket warbles. A strange, annoying sound. Hudson's grumpy face scowls at me from the rectangular screen as I retrieve it.

"You're alive." He almost sounds relieved.

"So are they." I hold up the phone to show him the security clones following me. "None the wiser. Guess that has something to do with their conditioning?"

"I wouldn't know." He sniffs. "You've made some powerful enemies today, Chen. That footage from Erik Paine has put him in danger as well. And Drasko will no longer be able to serve in his undercover role, which will leave certain criminal elements in the Domes unstable." He pauses. "But you have Commander Bishop's gratitude. She wanted me to relay that to you, and she said her father will be in touch.

He's a little busy right now giving a public address of his own, live from Hawthorne Tower."

I step off the train and head toward the ambulance. Mirela and Tanaka's body are inside on gurneys, and Daiyna, Erik and Drasko—uncuffed—are standing nearby. Dunn is sitting on the curb next to them with his helmeted head bowed, cradled in a metal hand. He's fighting one of those shocker-induced headaches you get after coming to.

"Will Raniero and the no-confidence gang be kicked out of office?" I ask.

Hudson exhales. "I seriously doubt it. Bishop is announcing his plan to initiate the first democratic election in the history of the Domes. He is actually going to leave it up to the citizenry—instead of the Governors—whether they want him to continue on as Chancellor. The man is clearly not the revenge-seeking type."

"How about you, sir?"

His scowl deepens. "Me?"

"I was out of line today. More than once. I figure you've got a demotion for me in mind."

He curses quietly under his breath and looks away. "Even if I did, it wouldn't matter. Raniero was wrong in how he went about things, but he was right about you." Hudson fixes me with a cold look. "You're the Bishops' favorite. You've gotten away with too much because of it." He raises his bearded chin. "But your exo-suit has been demolished, and that is a good first step toward putting you in your place."

Had a feeling that would happen. I try not to look too disappointed. "Any chance I can keep Wink and Blink?"

"Your drones." He's never been much of a fan where their

nicknames are concerned. "One is currently undergoing repairs. The other was retrieved from the top floor of the Edwards Estates. I see no reason why you should not be allowed to continue using them. But their armed upgrades will be completely dismantled."

I'll take what I can get. Looking forward to seeing Wɪnk in its shiny new chassis.

"We will see what else is in store for you, Chen. Changes are coming. Trust me on that. As your commanding officer, I plan to be far less accommodating going forward. You may consider your years of preferential treatment officially over. Hudson out."

That could've gone worse, I suppose. At least I still have a job. Wasn't expecting an attagirl. The jury's still out on whether Hudson, like Raniero, wants the Bishops gone—and me right along with them.

I toss Daiyna the phone as I approach, and she catches it one-handed, eyeing the security clones lined up behind me. "Friendlies or hostiles?"

"They might've gotten some new orders." Erik grins. "Governor Raniero decided to change his tune, once the truth got out."

"Thanks to you."

"Just doing my part, Investigator Chen." He gives me a lame attempt at a salute.

"You okay?" I rest my hand on Dunn's shoulder.

"You shot me." He doesn't look up. The headache must be a rager.

"Figured you could use the sleep."

"I was not out for very long."

"Noticed." I nod to the medics as they shut the rear doors

on the ambulance. Like Drasko, both of them show signs of being Plague survivors—long, wrinkled scars along the sides of their necks. "My partner and I will be joining you."

The driver nods back. "Looks like we'll have a police escort to the MedCenter."

He glances at the stone-faced LawKeepers standing by their groundcars, not seeming to know what to do with themselves at the moment. Guess they were ordered to confiscate our weapons and then make sure we get to where we're going. Every one of them bears the same scars as the medics, as well as a prosthetic limb or two. A couple of them sport glowing mechanical eyes.

Dome 6. Home to Eurasia's designated misfits. The *sicks*—citizens who never fully recovered from the Plague long ago. Chancellor Bishop has made it clear that they are free to live and work wherever they like, but the Dome Governors have been far from welcoming, making the process of transferring residence long and arduous with multiple hoops to jump through. Most have opted to stay put, despite the basic living conditions, in order to be around people who understand what they've been through. You don't get stared at so much for being different when everybody in your Dome is special in some way.

According to Prometheus, Solomon Wong was responsible for unleashing the Plague on the Domes way back when. Quite an allegation, with nothing to back it up, as far as I can tell. And it's not like I can interrogate the source. Official story: while the original Domes-dwellers were still ironing out all the kinks in our self-sustaining biospheres, contaminated air recyclers were the culprit. Not a real satisfactory answer for any citizen with half a brain.

Probably another reason why we were brainwashed for so long to *never look back.*

"How did you know the Governor's security clones would not kill you?" Dunn looks up at me.

"I didn't."

"So you risked your life."

"You were prepared to do the same," I remind him. "Before I shot you."

"I am a clone. I am replaceable."

"That's where you're wrong." I hold out my hand to him, but he doesn't take it. Not right away. "There's nobody else on this planet like you, Dunn."

"Or you either, Investigator Chen." He clasps my hand, cold metal against flesh, and I haul him to his feet. Or he makes me think that I'm helping him up. "I do not know what I would do without you."

I frown at that—and at his sudden proximity. There isn't a whole lot of room between us.

He loves you, you know, Daiyna said before. I thought she meant Erik.

I glance at her, and she smiles back. A little one. A start. The woman is an enigma, but I like her. Weird how we haven't known each other very long, but I can see aspects of myself in her. I wonder if she sees the same in me.

"Don't you worry, partner." I pat Dunn's chest. "I'm not going anywhere anytime soon. How can I leave you all?" I gesture at Erik, Drasko, and Daiyna. "We've got a great team here. And there's plenty of work to be done."

Like figuring out a treatment for Tanaka's mutations. Won't help him any, but if we can keep what happened to him from happening to anybody else, I'll consider that a win.

I have a feeling my dad is up to the task.

With Mirela in custody, it shouldn't be a difficult matter to locate and return most of the artifacts to her mother. Except for those that were used to pay off certain authorities regarding the relocation of Drasko's family. Another relocation may be in the works, this time to a secret, secure site. Because now that it's common knowledge he was an undercover operative, there will be those among his former underworld associates—particularly the underlings he bossed around—who'll be interested in seeking revenge on him and the ones he loves.

Dunn turns to regard each of our friends with his expressionless faceplate. One of these days, I'll get him to take off that stupid helmet and keep it off for more than a minute or two.

"We do indeed make a good team, Investigator Chen. I wonder if this is what having a family feels like."

A funny thing to say, but it won't go in my report. As far as I'm concerned, Dunn is completely himself and becoming more so every day. Nothing to worry about there. He's learning who he is, and I have the privilege to learn right alongside him. He's not just a clone, conditioned to serve loyally. He's a man, as human as anyone else.

I look up at him and smile. "Let's get to work."

About the Author

Milo James Fowler is the cross-genre author of more than thirty books: space adventures, post-apocalyptic survival stories, mysteries, and westerns. A native San Diegan, he now makes his home in West Michigan with his wife and all four seasons. Some readers seem to enjoy the unique brand of science fiction, fantasy, horror, and humor found in his ever-growing body of work. *Soli Deo gloria.*

www.milojamesfowler.com

Printed in Great Britain
by Amazon

62973598R00201